# Howling Blooms

## THE ROSE DUET, BOOK 2

## KRYSTAL KAE

DARK ORCHID PRESS

Cover Design: Martin Endeavors, LLC
Editor: Rebecca Joy Editing

Paperback ISBN: 979-8-9895730-6-6

# Before You Read

This book contains mature themes, including a history of violence, bullying, and child abuse (of a main character and side characters), both verbal and physical.

Detailed sexual relations including but not limited to period sex.

Cheating (in the past, not a main character) and a contentious divorce and fight for child custody.

Discussion of body image, past pregnancies, infertility, and reproductive health, including pregnancy after infertility (main character).

Depictions of death and murder, including that of family members. Death of a parent, grief, brief mentions of cancer.

Hang in there, we're almost to that happily ever after.

# 1

# Aim for the Moon

## *Seth*

Clara is trying with all her might to hold back her emotions and put on a brave face. Julie and Emmett are currently being picked up by Joe and Chassidy, and while that might cause my mate trouble any other time, it's especially weighing heavier on her now, on Christmas Eve.

She's bundled up in her puffy coat, feet planted on the powder-fresh snow that has lightly covered her driveway. She wanted to be able to wave goodbye to her kids as they take off, even if she can't make them out through the heavily tinted windows of Joe's truck. They alternate weeks in their joint custody, and the same goes for holidays as well.

The days have grown shorter. It's almost night out even though we're in the early hours of the evening. A few neighbors nearby have lights up and around their houses. Several around town even have those inflatables; they seem to be pretty popular around here. One thing is for sure, though—Alton takes Christmas decorating a lot more seriously than Halloween. I would say the decorations have doubled for this occasion.

Clara sniffles, and I turn her toward me by the shoulders. She tries to avoid my gaze, head tipping low, but not quick enough for me to miss her glassy eyes, rosy nose and cheeks.

"Come on, let's get you inside." I place a hand on her lower back and usher her in and away from the cold. I take her jacket once inside; the rush of the furnace air hits me like a wall and I'm already shedding my hoodie while she begins rubbing at her arms to warm up.

She looks adorable, wearing a thin long-sleeve tee that has about a million and a half Christmas bulbs of red and green strung across in countless rows. Somehow, she found studded earrings that match it perfectly. For the first time ever, her lips are a dark shade that complements her festive spirit. I've never seen her wear anything so bold, and the thought of those lips wrapped around me makes my cock twitch in my pants.

I clear my throat, as if it will help deter the thoughts that are making themselves known. My mind can go from zero to sixty in a millisecond, from appreciating how cute Clara is one moment, to wanting to fuck her senseless the next.

"What would you like to do now? Movie? Sing carols? Roast chestnuts out back? I could make a fire." As much as I know it pains her to be away from her children on such a major holiday, it is still the first Christmas of mine with her. The first of many. I want to make it as happy and enjoyable as it can be, even in their absence. I'm excited that I'm becoming more prominent in Clara's and her kids' lives. I was ecstatic when I was invited to help decorate their tree in the living room, and yet completely confused about the song that they all seemed to know by heart about wanting a hippopotamus. It's a tune I was not familiar with.

I'm weaving into their lives seamlessly. It feels natural even, dare I say it. I'm really fucking happy. If only I can pull Clara from her sorrows to join in on it with me.

When she doesn't even crack a smile or offer me a response, I move in closer. Grabbing her arms, I place them around my waist and wrap her into a gentle hug.

"Clara," I exhale as I let my fingers brush through her hair. "What can I do?"

I swear the heat in here intensifies her sweet vanilla aroma. I take in another deep inhale as I let my eyes close. She will never know how fucking intoxicating she is. More than once, the thoughts of what I might smell like to her if she were a werewolf have plagued me. I wish she could experience what I do every time we're together.

"I'm just glad that you're here." Her hold on me tightens, and it reminds me of how alone she felt before I came along. She's admitted it more than once, and it further solidifies the need we have for one another.

We stay there for a while, in the quiet of the kitchen, even after the furnace kicks off. I wait for her to be the first one to break our embrace, knowing that she needs it. When she finally does, I look deep into her eyes as I take her hand in mine and lead her toward the living room.

The Christmas tree is a foot taller than me but it was still easy enough to put the star on top. I was bestowed that honor, and I think Clara was just happy she didn't have to bring out the step stool for it. The multicolored lights around the tree are the only source of light in the room and we come to a stop before it.

I skirt around the side, my hand diving into the thick branches that Clara tried so hard to fluff out to make them appear fuller. It worked to my advantage, though, for the gift I hid inside.

Pulling out a small box that's wrapped pretty poorly by hers truly, I place it in her hand. It's too big to be a ring box, but still fits in her palm. Clara looks at me quizzically before studying it again.

"How long has that been in there?" she asks, completely caught off guard.

I shrug. "A while."

A small gleam returns to her dark brown eyes and I can feel her spirits rise ever so slightly. "Are you sure you want me to open it tonight?"

I nod in encouragement, eagerly awaiting her reaction to something I ordered some time ago. It's a bit embarrassing how quickly I did. I don't think I'll be confessing that information anytime soon. Not unless she asks.

Carefully, she turns it over and begins to unwrap it. When she uncovers the black box inside, she notes the manufacturer and shoots me another look of confusion, searching my eyes before I nod for her to keep going.

My anticipation is getting the better of me and I lift the lid for her, revealing what's inside. Her free hand floats to her chest as she sucks in a breath.

Nestled against the starry black fabric is a silver bracelet to match the necklace she has with the moon phases of her children's birthdays. But this one...this one is significant in more ways than one.

"Waxing crescent?" Clara asks, and I take the bracelet from the box as she holds out her wrist. "I think this is my birthday moon."

Am I about to blow her mind or what?

"And mine," I offer. Her eyes snap up to me with disbelief as her bottom lip falls away from the thinner top one. "Also, it just so happens to be the moon from our first night together."

She's gaping at me as I secure it on her wrist and position the moon just right so we can both see it.

"I've heard that this moon is capable of renewing energy. A rebuilding phase, if you will." I tuck her hair behind her ear as her eyes become glassy again. I don't know why I press on when I see her get emotional, but I do. "Everything happens for a reason and dammit, Clara, every pain and heartache I've endured has been worth it because it led me on a shitty roller coaster of a ride which eventually led me to you. It took some time, but I'm here now. By your side is the only place I want to be. I want to build a life here with you, Julie, and Emmett."

A tear slips free from her eye and when I lean down to kiss it away, her arms grasp the back of my neck and pull me down to meet her lips. The bracelet's box falls to the floor as I scoop her ass high enough that I know she's struggling on her tiptoes for some sort of balance. Her kisses are hard, moving against mine with so much strength that I assume she's conveying her feelings by action instead of words, and my chest swells in the best goddamn way.

As if I could deepen the kiss anymore, I go for it, devouring her and taking her breath away until she's fighting me for air. Only then do I set her back down on the ground. Her breasts are moving as she breathes and I try not to get hung up on how beautiful she is even while fully clothed. My cock is rock-hard as I divert my gaze back up to hers, as if that would help my plight.

The lights on the tree illuminate the side of her face in an array of color. Whether it's pitch-black, the brightest day, or anything in between, she is my fucking everything.

Her hands find the bottom of my shirt, fingertips grazing my skin as she begins to lift the material up and over. I let her take the lead but help when she can't reach high enough to remove it from me completely. She doesn't waste time as she begins to undo my belt and the top of my jeans. There's a subtle shake in her hands as she does it, as if she's nervous about the act that we've indulged in time and time again.

As if my Rose could possibly do anything wrong.

I step out of my bottoms as she pulls them away and when she goes to stand again, her eyes pause on my length. "What do you want, Clara?"

Her lips roll, that devastating color catching my attention as I look down upon her. She blinks up at me with hungry eyes before she reaches out and strokes me. The muscles in my abdomen tense, and my shoulders cave slightly to her touch. Clara grins as she moves her hand agonizingly slow, coming up to stand as she continues the movements. Her thumb swipes across the precum already leaking at the tip and she smears it over the head.

When she releases her hold on me, my back straightens. I want to take her hand and place it back on me, or haul her off to the bedroom so I can wrap myself so tightly in her that she has nothing left to do but scream as I fill her.

Clara leans to the side and grabs a blanket from the couch, one that she cuddles with frequently when home, and lays it down flat on the cushion before instructing me to sit. I do as I'm told without delay.

If I thought she was hesitant to touch me, it was nothing compared to the quake in her now as she shimmies out of her jeans, underwear and all. That beautiful nest of hair at the apex of her thighs has my mouth watering for her and my cock begging to enter. When she lifts her shirt off, my eyes zero in on her breasts, full and plump. She's still shy around me, attempting to cover her stomach awkwardly as she lowers to the ground once more, parting my legs further while looking at me with another roll of her lips before her head drops down.

The moment her mouth descends on me, I'm lost. A groan slips past my throat as my body sags at the welcome feeling. One hand grips the base of my cock while the other latches onto my thigh.

I think she enjoys playing with me, teasing and licking one moment, taking me by surprise and deep throating me the next. I'm at her fucking mercy. That is, until she reaches for my hand and places it on the back of her head.

When I gather her short hair in a messy hold, she pauses for a moment and gazes up at me through hooded eyes. She comes off with a pop, and I hold back the urge to drive her right back down, fast and hard.

You know what? Fuck it.

I force her down on my dick with my hand while my hips surge upward. The feel of her throat fighting to close on the head is enough to make me lightheaded as I remove her for a brief reprieve before repeating the actions.

Clara knows to tap my hand if it gets to be too rough or too much, and plants her hands closer to my upper thighs. Her short, staggered moans slip through while I take control and bring myself to the edge before yanking her off.

She's struggling for breath as I lean forward and capture her mouth with mine. I haul her up from the floor, up and onto my lap where my cock awaits for the main event. Clara sways a bit, her body still trying to catch up, and my God she looks like I've ravaged her when we've barely begun.

Lipstick is smeared, a breast is trying to work its way out of her bra, and the way her body moves tells me that she's still trying to gain her equilibrium back. But I'm too impatient.

Centering her above my shaft, I bring her down onto it. Her eyes squeeze shut as she calls out, a look of pure pleasure sweeping across her face as she settles onto me. That right there, if I could freeze that face of hers—it's the stuff dreams are made of.

"Seth," she mewls as her head lolls back.

I use her incapacitation to my advantage and reach around her, unclasping her bra. She's high on the feeling of me inside of her and barely notices as I drag the straps down her arms. She doesn't even try to fight me as I remove it, grazing her new bracelet in the process.

She's fucking perfect and she's all mine. It was too soon to give her a ring, but damn I can't wait to claim her in that way too.

"Use me, Clara." I urge her to move before I have to do it for her. My thumb finds her clit and it starts circling. She's so wet for me that there's enough lubrication for my finger to slide effortlessly around, and she's moaning my name once more as she balances herself on my shoulders.

With my other hand I scoop up a breast, pinching her peak until she whines from the pressure. I don't have enough hands to do everything I want at the same time, but I guess we have plenty of that.

Time.

The glow of the tree behind her as she moves is so visually pleasing that I almost forget what we're in the middle of until my spine starts to stiffen. My finger works harder, faster, trying to bring her to the precipice that I'm so dangerously close to.

Clara falls forward as she climaxes, screaming out my name as if it's the only word she knows. It's enough to tip me over the edge as she claws at the back of my head, nails scraping the shorter hair there.

For a moment I'm floating, lost at sea while buried deep inside of Clara. I can't even think straight as I finish emptying into her, grasping at her ass and chest as if I'm clinging to life itself.

Before too long, I'm smoothing her hair back and out of her face, coaxing her to sit up and meet me. I want nothing more than to cuddle up beside her on the couch and just stare mindlessly between her and the tree. Possibly figure out how we can make this right here a yearly tradition.

Perhaps we need to get a tree for our bedroom too.

When Clara finally leans back, she becomes modest. She's trying to cross her arms over her chest but I pull her hands away, keeping them in my hold. She's avoiding eye contact, and I begin lowering my chin so I can try to force her to look at me.

"What's wrong?" I question her, unsure of why she's acting like this.

She lets out a puff of frustration before she rolls her eyes.

"You're going to think it's stupid," she begins to confess, still not giving me enough information.

"Go on," I press, waiting impatiently.

Her lips roll again in tandem with her eyes and she shakes her head. "I bought you freaking underwear for Christmas."

# 2

# A Call Would Have Been Nice

## *Clara*

I'm a giggling mess as Seth steps out from the bathroom wearing his new pair of boxers that I bought for him. I know he likes computer stuff, games and things that I know very little, if anything, about.

What on earth do you get for a man who lives a life so different from your own?

The boxers are made with his "package" in mind. Front and center, it looks like it's a wrapped gift, complete with a bow. It was meant to be funny, but now I just feel ridiculous since he put so much thought into the bracelet he gave me. But as he stands there with a cocky grin on his face, striking poses in his newest article of clothing, I can't help but laugh.

"I like it, it's quite festive." He plants his hands on his hips as he stares at me. "And comfortable."

It wasn't hard to figure out the size he needed, since half of the time his clothes are tossed onto my floor. I've picked them up on more than one occasion and it was too easy to steal a glance at the tag or lining.

I drag my gaze away from his crotch, shaking my head. "You're just saying that."

"Absolutely not. After all, I would love nothing more than for you to unwrap me later." He winks and my heart flutters as my cheeks heat.

Smells from the kitchen are wafting into my bedroom and my stomach growls. I might have put on a spread of sorts for Julie and Emmett before they left, but I didn't eat much myself. This is my first Christmas without them here, without them in this house they've grown up in. Thank God Seth is here; I can't imagine the state of mind I would be in right now if he weren't.

"I should probably get started on the potatoes." I scoot off of the bed as Seth crosses his arms.

"Already?"

"Yes, already." I stand and make my way over to my dresser to start pulling out the essentials for the day. It might be Christmas, but I have an urge to wear all black to match the mood that wants to surface. I struggle with that for a moment, before settling on some comfy black pants to match my underwear and bra. I make my way to the closet to find something that might bring a little bit of brightness to my day.

"Larson isn't supposed to be here until eleven, we've got time," Seth says as he follows me.

"But my mashed potatoes take a bit to prep and perfect. It's not an exact science, it's more of a go with the flow until I get it right."

I keep my back turned to him while I remove my nightshirt, baring my upper half to him while I put on my bra. Seth is quick to come up from behind and he takes the fasteners from me, securing it himself before planting a kiss on my shoulder.

"Maybe I wanted to run around in my present for a while," he states, and I can't help but smile as he kisses the same spot again.

Turning my head to look back, I grin before nabbing my shirt and walking away. "Nobody is saying that you can't."

— )●( —

Seth really does walk around my house in nothing but his underwear for the next two hours. It's fucking distracting but at the same time, such a turn-on. He leans in too close here, brushes a hand across my ass there. A damn tease, that's what he is.

My holiday playlist is filtering in from the living room as we make our coffees and I get to work peeling, boiling, and beating the potatoes in the mixer. I might only be feeding three people today but I also like to have leftovers. My mashed potatoes heat up really well in the microwave too, so I always have that to look forward to.

Today, we're having them topped with chicken and noodles, with the only other wolf that lives in Alton. Larson, who proved himself as an ally of sorts last month, has worked himself into the picture and into our lives. When I found out that he had no plans for today and nobody to spend it with, it seemed like a no-brainer to invite him over.

I charged him with bringing some dinner rolls and that man's rugged face lit up like I'd just told him he won the lottery. Considering I still don't know him that well, I'm hoping to change that today. Seth has talked with him on more than one occasion, and after the ordeal with Seth's family visit, I feel like I owe him as well. He had no reason to protect me, could have turned me away after my plea for help, but he didn't.

"Here." I take a swipe at the mashed contents in my mixer and hold out my finger for Seth. "Have a taste."

Golden eyes study me for a moment, his crossed arms over his chest dropping before he makes his way over. His mouth opens and mine parts slightly as he sinks my finger into his mouth and way further down than what's necessary to taste my offering. He looks positively sinful, muscles on full display, light hair bright against the kitchen lights.

Looking away, I clear my throat, squeezing my thighs as I try to focus on literally anything else. The effects this man has on me, the hold that he's capable of, should be downright illegal. Yet, I wouldn't have it any other way.

Opening a cupboard, I pull out a covering for the food as Seth steps in closer. So close that his partially restrained erection is pressing into my ass and my breath catches as he draws my hair away from my neck.

"What are you doing?" I'm failing to keep my voice level as I put the lid on. "We have company coming soon."

A low hum leaves his throat and I let it ooze over my skin as I feel it through his chest at my back. "*We* do."

Lips find my neck and I can't help but relax my head back onto him.

"I love it when you refer to us like that. Like we're already a package deal."

"Aren't we, though?" I counter, letting a hand drift up to run through the hair along his jawline. His hips drive forward, pinning me against the cabinets at my front and eliciting a sharp gasp from me.

"Damn right we are." He grinds into me again and I grip the edge of the counter. My eyes dart to the clock on the stove and I'm already trying to determine how much time we might have to screw and clean up before our guest arrives. I'm having trouble thinking about anything else right now.

My phone chimes with a notification but it's the furthest thing from my mind as I press myself back onto him. He groans, grabbing my breasts and squeezing. If I wasn't pinned here, I would like to squeeze a few parts of him as well, but I'm at a disadvantage.

"How do you want me?" I arch my back so I can try to look up at him, signaling that I'm ready for whatever the hell he would like to do to me. We now have thirty-seven minutes and while it might be a tight squeeze if Larson shows up early, I am more than willing to take that chance. I know Seth will clean up faster than me anyway, and can greet our guest if I need a few more minutes.

A jingling of keys freezes both of us in our heated state, and I shoot a look of bewilderment at the door before exchanging worried looks with Seth.

"Go, go!" I shoo him out, completely taken aback and frazzled, unsure who on earth would be trying to get into my house.

Just before Seth makes it to the edge of the kitchen, my heart leaps into my throat as the back door opens. Low and behold, an uninvited and unexpected guest comes into view.

My mother.

Dear God, and my father.

"Merry Christmas!" they chime in unison, but their faces falter as they undoubtedly catch a glimpse of Seth exiting the picture, his muscled frame not making it out in time.

I'm full of pure shock, stunned into silence as I stand there with my mouth gaping. It doesn't escape me that my parents could have walked in on Seth and me fully engaged in intercourse and while I'm mortified by that, I'm confused as hell as to why they're here in the first place.

"Guess this is why you were pushing us to come for New Year's," my mother mutters, but it's loud enough to make it to my ears.

"You're letting all the cold air in, Joyce." My dad is shooing her to go inside with a stack of two casserole dishes in his hands. They proceed to enter, kicking their boots to knock off any snow they might have traipsed through to make it around the garage and into the breezeway.

My face feels like it's been in a sauna as I meet them at the door, taking the containers from my dad as they begin to take off their scarves, coats, and so on.

"I...um..." I set dishes on the counter while I fumble with something to say. I don't want to come right out and say that I'm ungrateful for the visit, especially knowing that it's a five-hour drive for them to make it here. But their surprise drop-in is rubbing me the wrong way.

Seth was ready to rub a few things.

Holy shit. The realization hits me like a brick wall that this is really happening. That Seth is going to be meeting my parents today, and I feel so ill prepared. Even worse, Larson is coming over today too. While I'd hoped the three of us would be able to talk freely about anything and everything under the sun—even werewolf-related topics—now my day is taking a drastic turn.

"You didn't call." The words tumble from my mouth before I can halt them, and I shoot a nervous glance toward where Seth exited.

My mother finds a hook for her coat, clearly noting Seth's hanging there too, before returning her attention to me. "Forgive us for wanting the element of surprise. We thought today was going to be hard for you. Your father and I didn't want you to be alone and decided at the last minute to make the trip. Even brought you some green-bean casserole and cheesy potatoes to try and cheer you up."

I nod slowly, eyes still trying to adjust to a state other than stunned. "That...was very thoughtful."

I can't bring myself to look at my dad. For some reason, having a ninety-five percent naked man in my kitchen just seconds ago makes me feel like I've been reduced to a teenager in front of him.

"Sorry, folks." Seth comes strolling in now fully clothed, appearing unbothered by the situation we'd just found ourselves in. If he has any nerves about meeting my parents, he's not showing it as he flashes them a friendly smile. "I'm Seth. You must be Joyce and Charles."

Sticking out his hand, he shakes both of theirs before making his way over to me. I try to remember when or if I've ever told him the names of my parents. Typically, I refer to them as Mom and Dad or Grandma and Grandpa, but he doesn't skip a beat or hesitate.

"Nice to meet you," they both say, but I note my mom's gaze giving him the once-over before he turns to face them again.

"I apologize for the state you caught me in. I won't make you suffer a lousy lie of an explanation."

Oh, so we're coming right out of the gate and addressing it? I shoot Seth a look to *shut up* but my dad ends up chuckling. "There was a time I was comfortable roaming about the house in nothing but my boxers too but"—he pats both hands on his protruding belly—"times change I guess. Enjoy it while you can."

Dad barks out another laugh as my mom shakes her head in slight embarrassment. Her hair is a tad lighter than normal, bordering my hair color at this point. "Oh, lighten up, Joyce."

"We didn't know we would be interrupting"—my mom's hand swirls in a few circular motions before she finishes her sentence—"something."

"You weren't," I stammer, trying to forget about it already. "Seth and a friend of ours, Larson, are getting together today for a meal. We were all going to be alone so..."

"The more the merrier, right?" Seth is so relaxed and I envy him for that. "Clara made chicken and noodles with mashed potatoes. Larson is bringing rolls. With what you've brought here, I think we should all have more than enough to eat."

Seth nudges me with an elbow and my head starts nodding, a bit too exaggerated. "Right, we should. Yes."

"If I thought we were going to impose, we wouldn't have—"

"No, you're not," I cut my mother off. "I'm sorry, I should have told you." I could have. Many times I call my mother on the way to or from work just to have someone to talk to on the drive. We catch up, or I just listen to her ramble on about whatever show she's hooked on that I inevitably take it upon myself to watch depending on how much she raves about it. But this? I didn't even tell her that there's somebody else in my life.

I told my kids, but not my parents. Now isn't the time to try and figure out why I didn't; that will be something to sort out later when I don't have two sets of eyes studying me and my...friend.

"Let me kick on the oven and I can get those dishes thrown in." I turn, plucking away at the buttons on the stove to the temperature needed for their casseroles.

If Seth being in my life wasn't official before today, it sure as hell is going to be now. I want to believe that's what I want. I mean, I already introduced him to Julie and Emmett for crying out loud. Why am I so intimidated by introducing Seth to my parents? Why am I panicking over this?

Probably because there has been more than one occasion to confess, and I left both my mom and dad in the dark about the newest addition to my life. Seth and I have been hot and heavy from the start. A fast burn and a raging fire if there ever was one.

Seth is already striking up a conversation with them as I turn back around, and I argue with myself for a moment about how I want to spin this.

Before I can talk myself out of it, I let my arm wrap around Seth's waist and step up to his side. I need to ground myself, remind this head of mine that I want this and I want *him*. I can't hide it anymore. No. I don't want to hide *us* anymore.

It's time.

# 3

# Meet the Parents, Check

## *Seth*

Some might be nervous to meet the parents of the one they love, but me? Nah. It doesn't bother me at all.

The one thing that *does* annoy me however, is how they were going to let themselves inside to an unsuspecting Clara and probably scare the living shit out of her in doing so. Sometimes she gets spooked even when she knows I'm coming over, so I don't appreciate her parents doing this, even if their hearts might be in the right place.

I meet Larson in the driveway and inform him of our additional guests. He's a bit skittish about their presence, but with how much I owe this man, I attempt to smooth it over with promises of food and beer. Better beer than what he purchases, might I add.

Clara and Joyce are already making their way through their second bottle of wine by the time we all sit to eat at the dinner table. Music floats in from the living room while we eat, but the conversation is flowing so well it often drowns out the tunes playing. With the beginning pleasantries aside, we begin diving into topics that I knew were coming, and I try to be as forthcoming with information as I can be, with mine and Larson's secrets aside.

"What on earth brought you to Alton? If I had my way, I would be camped out on a beach in the Carolinas." Joyce picks up her glass, giving it a slight swirl before she takes a drink. Her daughter is just the opposite, taking a few straight pulls of hers. Her eyes bulge slightly before she shovels a spoonful of potatoes into her mouth at her mother's question.

"That's the beauty of my remote position. I can live anywhere I want. Growing up in Colorado, I always wanted to see places and travel. This job has given me that, but I found that there comes a time when it becomes tiring. I wanted somewhere that was a little quieter than what I was used to. A place to finally put down some roots and make myself a home."

"And what do your parents think about that? Your family?"

"Joyce." Clara's dad clears his throat. "This isn't twenty-one questions."

Clara's leg is bouncing beneath the table and I brush my calf up against hers to stop it. She shoots me a worried look, but it's quick enough that I don't think any of our guests take notice. It's a bit cute how nervous she is.

"It's fine, really." I understand that her mother might be concerned about the partially naked man she saw leaving the kitchen upon her arrival. I'm sure that after what her daughter has been through already, she just wants to make sure that Clara isn't being taken advantage of. "Unfortunately, my family and I are not in a good place. I'll spare you the sad details of my past, though. I'm only interested in moving forward."

I steal a look at my Rose but make it brief. I want Joyce and Charles to know that I am serious about their daughter, even if I'm not flooding them with information on my background.

"Sorry to hear that," Charles cuts in before nabbing a roll from the center of the table. He dips his head down, giving me a good view of the bald spot he's starting to acquire.

"It is what it is." I shrug before plunging my fork into a green bean.

"You don't have any contact with them?" I notice how Joyce's hair is a bit longer than Clara's. Their facial features are similar too. It's like a little glimpse into what the woman at my side might look like in the future if she keeps smiling, those crinkles around the eyes the sign of life and laughter.

"Mom," Clara quietly scolds this time, putting her fork down as if she's lost her appetite.

"Nothing good ever comes from our encounters. They want things that I can't give them. I want apologies that they're unwilling to make or acknowledge." I'm trying to sound nonchalant, brushing things under the rug. But it still doesn't seem to be enough to skirt around the suspicions churning in Joyce's mind. So I dig a little deeper.

"Clara's been the support system I've never had." I offer a polite smile before turning my attention toward the opposite end of the table and our quietest attendee. "Larson here has become a good friend as well. Roots finally seem possible when you don't feel so alone."

"Didn't take ya for the sentimental type." Larson lets out a gruff laugh and the intensity of our table talk takes a light turn.

"What can I say?" My smile spreads naturally as I realize the truth in my words, and widens even further when I look back at Clara. "The impact some have on your life can be life-changing."

While my chest might be swelling with the emotion that Clara invokes in me, I can't help but notice Joyce's rigid posture and pursed lips. Her husband is more relaxed, taking everything in, and from what I can tell he's convinced by everything I have to say.

And here I thought meeting Clara's parents would be no problem. I might have met my match with Joyce.

To my astonishment, Larson hasn't stepped out for a single cigarette since he's been here. Perhaps the beer and the cold are keeping him from doing so, but whatever the case, I'm relieved. The last thing I want is his cigarette butts around our house. We don't need that over here, especially with two young and impressionable kids around.

"Draw four." Charles snickers mischievously as he lays down his card and thwarts Larson's chance at getting closer to an "Uno." The two of them have hit it off far better than I'd anticipated.

"Another beer, anyone?" I offer to the guys as Larson starts retrieving the cards he now has to take on.

"Think I'm gonna need it." He shakes his head. Charles isn't taking it easy on him or his wife. I remind myself never to sit next to him during card games. Either he has cards stashed on him or he's just super competitive. I have to admit, he plays a mean game with this card deck.

I excuse myself and head out to the garage where I've been stocking up on beer. I don't drink much to begin with, it's more of an occasional thing, but I like throwing some back with others and having a good time with company.

The frigid outside air hits me as soon as I exit the kitchen and enter the breezeway. Might have been stupid coming out here in a T-shirt, but whatever. Guess I needed the rush.

My upper half is leaning down into the fridge when I catch a whiff of Joyce. I pretend not to notice as I nab three beers and stand, shutting the door before I finally make eye contact with her.

At least she was smart enough to grab her jacket. There's not much for insulation and no air or heat in this garage. Just add that to the list of things I'd like to fix up.

"Mind if I have one?"

Didn't take her for a beer drinker, but I school my features so she doesn't think I'm a dick.

"Of course." I open the fridge back up and take out another. There isn't much in this fridge but beer. Clara mostly uses the freezer part, so it didn't bother her that I began filling it below and putting it to use.

"You're pretty comfortable around here." Joyce states her fact clear as day as her breath visibly leaves her mouth. I'm not sure if I should be taking offense to it or not. Her face is void of expression, making it even more difficult to discern. "I hope you're not taking advantage of my daughter."

Yikes. So we're going there.

I can understand where she's coming from. How this might look, considering she knew nothing about me prior to today. My past might come off as sketchy, and her introduction to me was not at all what I'd wanted her first impression of me to be. Not wanting to come off as defensive, I try to keep my cool. Even as goosebumps start snaking up my bare forearms.

"Clara's a great woman," I begin, careful not to seem too rushed in my response. "A wonderful mom and friend. She deserves nothing but the best."

"And that's you?" Her expression turns a bit dark, and for a second, I'm taken aback by it. This is awfully brazen of her, cornering me out here in the poorly lit and heat-lacking garage.

"I want to be worthy of her. Of her children. We're both trying to heal our pasts while finding a way to move forward."

That catches her attention, and I know I've got her right where I want her. I may not have wanted to divulge this information at the dinner table, but I sure as hell am going to now. Especially if there's a glimmer of hope that it might get Joyce to back off a bit and see that I'm not trying to take advantage of her one and only daughter.

Clara has a younger brother who's in the military and stationed overseas. She's told me that the family is lucky if they get to see him once every year or two, so I understand why Joyce would be so quick to come to the defense of her child. As a mother should.

Damn, that stings.

"My father abused me in a way that no parent should. I wasn't shown unconditional love from the two people who raised me. The two that should have mattered most in my life. Throw that in with how they reacted when they found out that their one and only son could never father any children of his own, they made their bed." The words are leaving me faster than I can funnel them through my head. "But Clara..."

I pause, trying to figure out how in the hell I can convince this woman before me that I mean no harm to her daughter. That I would literally lay down my life for my mate.

"Clara is the reason I stopped running. She's strong, determined, and honestly, the best damn thing to happen to me in quite some time." I finally feel like the chasing of my Rose has come to a standstill, and we're finally at a point where we're moving forward together. Clara isn't trying to push me away anymore.

Leaving my spot near the fridge, I close some of the distance between us. Joyce's exterior has cracked, perhaps from the onslaught of information I just spewed. I hold out a beer bottle for her, waiting for her to take it. As a peace offering, preferably.

"I hope you'll give me a chance to prove to you that I want nothing but the best for Clara, Julie, and Emmett."

She's hesitant, careful not to break our eye contact as she extends a hand to accept the beer. "Clara's had a rough go of things. I only want to protect her, protect my grandchildren. She doesn't deserve to have her heart broken again."

Not on my watch. It'll never be broken on my account.

"I have no intentions of hurting her or anyone living under her roof." Ours, really. But whatever.

Her brown head nods slowly, and when she finally tears her fierce motherly gaze away, only then do I exhale in relief. When I go to take another breath, that vanilla scent is wafting through the open door toward us.

"Everything okay out here?" Clara finds us, hands hidden at her sides with her arms crossed. She takes a look at what her mom is holding and her brows rise. "Mom, you don't like beer."

*Sneaky, Joyce.*

She offers a slight shrug and shuffles out of the doorway her daughter just crossed through, placing a gentle hand on her shoulder before exiting. Clara eyes me, both concern and worry swirling around those eyes that look even darker out here.

"I am so sorry. It's all my fault. She knows nothing and I mean *absolutely* nothing about you. I'm so—"

I'm wrapping her into an awkward, one-armed hug since I'm grasping three beers in my other hand. "Clara, try not to stress. Everything will work itself out."

She's fighting off showing that the cold out here is getting to her, trying to stifle her chattering teeth and the shakes her body wants to make. The thought of warming her up in our bedroom is appealing, but I have to hold out on doing that just a little bit longer.

"Please don't kill me," she mutters as she looks up and into my eyes.

I shake my head. As if that could ever be a scenario. It's absurd, really. A poor choice of words too.

"They brought their overnight bag. They're planning on staying the night, and since you are Larson's and Dad's beer supplier for the day and foreseeable evening, they probably shouldn't drive."

"It's fine, Clara." Shivers rack her body and I'm soon guiding her back toward the house.

"What the hell was she trying to pester you about out here?"

I place a hand on the back of her neck before she can enter the house. The window on the door is covered, providing us with a few more seconds of secrecy before going back in.

"Just gave her a little more information on my background."

Clara opens her mouth to speak but I capture it with my own. It's cold, but my tongue darts inside to where her warmth awaits. Her body is quick to cave into my touch, and I only wish that I could erase all of her fears and troubles with a simple act such as this. It could never be that easy, but dammit, I would try.

# 4

# Duck My Hall

## *Clara*

Who knew that Larson's laugh could be so loud? That his accent would become so thick and drawn out as he keeps tossing back beers like it's nobody's business. My dad is right there beside him, joking about something involving an old car. I literally can't keep up with how they jump from subject to subject, but it's left my mother, Seth, and me to clean up after today and tidy up the kitchen.

We grazed on food well into the evening, and now we're pushing past ten p.m. My social battery is running low, and the stress of my parents meeting Seth has taken its toll on me when I had zero time to prepare him or myself for it all.

Whatever was said in the garage seemed to help the nagging path my mother was on. She was quiet for a bit after returning, but another glass of wine later, she was loosening up. Any questions asked from there on out weren't as prying or intrusive. They were light, inquisitive even, asking about work, Colorado weather, and dare I say it, pot. Because apparently in her mind, everyone there smokes it.

Her words, not mine. I couldn't believe she'd *actually* said that.

Seth took each question she threw out at him with a calmness and grace that only made my heart flutter faster and my cheeks grow redder. Perhaps the alcohol was a bit to blame, though. I hate how wine always makes my face hot. I switched out of my long sleeves some time ago and am now wearing a dark green shirt that's cut a little low. I also traded my wine for water when my head started to feel funny, threatening me with the chance of a headache.

When the day began, I had no idea just how drastic of a turn today would take. Now I'm leaning on the kitchen island, watching both sets of adults converse—forgetting that I am one for a few seconds—and enjoying the scene before me. It had been a while since I hosted anything, and this? This has been an unexpected treat.

Mom is talking to Seth about her recipe for apple salad that he's never had the pleasure of tasting. I pout a little, wishing she could have brought that along today too. But that dish requires a bit more time and work on her part. It also doesn't help that my dad always eats the marshmallows and she has to run him out of the kitchen just so she can save them.

My mind drifts in another direction, examining Seth as he casually leans an arm on the kitchen counter, his wolf tattoo peeking out from beneath his sleeve. It's not hard to imagine Seth with his clothes off, underwear and all. From my line of sight I would be denied the view of his lower half, but what a treat it would be. One last gift before this holiday is done. My body is humming, like electricity is running through it and sending signals down into my core. Images of our bodies together, writhing and climbing toward the precipice—I've lost count of how many times we've strived for that high at the end of it all.

"Everything alright?" Seth asks when he catches me staring, no doubt a weird look plastered on my face. I feel warm, fuzzy, and I just want to... Well, I just want to fuck him.

I snap up straight as my mother's gaze turns to mine. I then cross my ankles and squeeze my thighs as if that will help with the throbbing that's going on between my legs right now.

"Good. I'm good. Just...tired." I offer a polite nod but I do it so fast that I have to blink away the dizziness it brings on. How on earth can my mother suck down the wine and still be standing tall? Talking like she's unaffected? It isn't fair. Just how high is her tolerance?

"Maybe we should get going, then." Seth glances back at Larson whose eyes are barely open a crack as he rambles about something I can't understand. Have his words gotten worse within the last few minutes? "I can take Larson home. Is it alright if we come back for his truck tomorrow?"

I resist frowning. Seth is leaving me, but I want to believe that he'll return without my parents' knowledge. "Yep, that'll work."

Seth leaves us and walks the short distance to the dining table, breaking up the camaraderie. Seeing Larson so at ease makes me even happier that we invited him over in the first place. He could have spent all day alone, like any other day in his cabin. But instead, he's been surrounded with company and laughter. Maybe he'll be a new regular at family gatherings. By the way my dad's face falls at the mention of him leaving, I think that might be inevitable.

Before long, Seth is offering farewells and escorting Larson out of the house. It takes a good half an hour before they actually make it out of the door. Midwest goodbyes take a while, and were it not late December, I'm sure it would have carried on outside as well.

I'm left alone with my parents for the first time today. I wish that fact would sober me up really quick, but my head is swimming a little as I find both sets of eyes looking my way.

"I'm sorry," I blurt when the silence starts growing arms like a six-legged monster. Although, why six? "I'm sorry I didn't tell you guys sooner."

"Seems like a nice fellow," my dad offers, rubbing a hand over his belly. He looks like he's about to pass out, and I'm not sure if he's going to be able to ascend the stairs to the spare bedroom. It would definitely thwart my plans of sneaking Seth back into the house tonight.

"He is," I agree before looking at my mom again. "He's a really great guy."

"Sounds like he's had a bit of a rough life." She leans on her forearms, playing with that little bit of white wine left in the bottom of her glass. It's hardly even a sip at this point, maybe a few drops.

"He has," I admit, not fully knowing what all Seth has told her thus far. "His family and ex-fiancée really did a number on him."

"Ex-fiancée?" my mom counters, almost gobsmacked.

My eyes widen, afraid that I've just spilled too much. I gulp, trying to rein in my panic at disclosing something so personal.

*Dammit, Clara. Why?*

"Just how serious were they?" My mother is already getting worked up over this news, and when I glance at my dad, he's completely oblivious and on the verge of his head kicking back and into a slumber at the dining table.

"It was a while ago," I say.

"And how long is a while? Is there a chance that the two of them will get back together?"

"No, no!" I shout a bit too loud, causing my mother to register slight shock at my outburst. I take a breath, trying to level out my voice. "No, she is out of the picture."

"You're sure?" she pushes, and I want to snap.

"Yes, I'm sure. She broke off their engagement because he couldn't have any children." I smack my own mouth when I go to cover it, hating that my loose lips won't stop talking.

My words hang in the air, looming dangerously close, and I want to take them back. That wasn't my news to tell.

"What a bitch," my dad grumbles as if he's a part of the conversation, then goes back to dozing off, mouth gaping open. My mom and I exchange a glance before we start laughing. It's enough for him to jolt awake again and we're soon leaving him at the table and taking our conversation to the living room.

We sit on the couch, about a cushion away from one another. We're still close, but it's enough space to look at each other without being on top of one another. I no sooner get comfy when my phone starts ringing. I draw it out of my back pocket and my face lights up as I see Julie and Emmett on the other side of it, ready for a video call. It's enough to make me want to cry tears of joy.

Scooting closer to my mom, I swipe to answer. I don't care if the excitement is for my mom, me, or the both of us together. Hearing my kids squeal "Merry Christmas" has my eyes watering. Julie had texted earlier, wishing me the very same line with a cute meme she found from one of the shows we watch together. I had thought that would be the most I heard from her. But the fact that the both of them are carving out some time to call me means the world.

I pass the phone to Mom who goes on to explain that they will be back for New Year's. Both kids are a bit bummed that they're missing her and Grandpa today, but she promises to bring a batch of banana bread when she returns. However, I guess that isn't good enough, because the kids want to make it with her, so they're already making plans for when she returns. The thought of everyone being together again and the house smelling like that mouthwatering bread is a vision I am looking forward to.

The call lasts for about twenty minutes before my phone starts to alert us that it's dying. The dreaded question of whether my dad is going to make it upstairs or not is made clear when he all but crawls along the wall to make it in here, and falls onto the couch. My mother apologizes profusely as she covers him with a blanket. His graying hair doesn't seem so obvious now from this point of view. It's a show of his age that my mother, on the other hand, keeps trying to hide in her own hair by dyeing it like clockwork every four to six weeks.

I make sure my mom is situated upstairs before making my way to my bedroom, flipping off lights here and there as I check to make sure all of the doors are locked. I quickly take my leave, tiptoeing through room after room, sneaking around like a kid trying not to alert anyone of their presence.

The angry red battery on my phone is glaring at me as I type out a message to Seth, giving him the all clear.

> *Dad's passed out on the couch. Let me know when you get here.*

Quickly, I place my phone on its charger and right as I do, his return message pops into view.

> *Already here. Go to your bathroom window.*

I'm stunned for a moment, trying to figure out how that's helpful. There's a tub in front of the referenced window, and I can only imagine that his head would be high enough to look in through the frame.

Making a dash to the bathroom, I raise the blinds and about jump out of my skin as I find Seth's face there, beaming at me as if in silent victory that I'd been caught off guard. I unlock the latches and draw the window up. I'm hit with the freezing night air as I realize my screen is missing. Just how long has he been waiting back here?

He makes crawling in my window look so easy, and I'm mad that I'm denied the sight of his muscles as he hoists himself up and through it. His legs stick straight out as he uses the tub as leverage to pull himself in, then promptly flips around and closes the window. Stepping out of the tub, he leaves his wet shoes behind in it.

I can feel the cold radiating off of him. His nose is red but his eyes are alive with an intensity that has me hauling myself at him.

My heated and inebriated blood is racing for him, and we undress each other in a frenzied state. I want to crack some holiday joke, using a play on words to make it dirty, but my mind is going a mile a minute as he whips me around to face the mirror above my sink.

Erection pressing into me, he's groping my chest as his lips leave mine and trail down my jawline and toward my neck. He groans into me as he squeezes my nipples and I whimper, pressing my ass back into him. I'm trying to imagine how he's going to have to squat to enter me; his height could be problematic in this position.

This is the furthest side of the house, and there's nothing but a storage room above us, but I'm starting to wonder if I'll be quiet enough. I've had a close call with Emmett, but if my parents were to hear a peep from me, there would be no denying what's going on in here.

I gaze into the mirror, seeing our combined lust on full display. My hand is in his hair and the bracelet he gave me last night slides around my wrist, the silver catching my attention briefly. It's enough to draw Seth's notice too.

He stops, bringing my hand down and holding it at the center of my chest. I'm captivated by this small token, knowing the meaning behind it and how the damn stars—or perhaps moons in this case—aligned in bringing us together. My heart balloons, soaring on everything Seth makes me feel. I know that right now I'm fucking horny beyond repair, but there's more. So much more rising to the surface that if I don't say it now, I might explode.

Yet somehow, not even the wine is making me brave enough to say what I really want to say.

"What is it?" Seth turns me around, barely giving me enough room to do so before closing in on me again. His cock, a hard protrusion that's almost debilitating, digs into my soft flesh. Tipping my chin up, he searches my face, waiting for me to answer him.

"I..." I'm panicking. Afraid of speaking the truth when Seth has poured so much into this relationship between us and I feel like my words might never compare. "You know I care for you, right?"

I'm stricken with instant regret, hating that I'm unable to pluck the one phrase out of my brain and spit it out.

"You"—he searches my eyes, bouncing carefully between them as if searching for something—"care for me."

My voice leaves me high and dry, stranded on some unknown island that has no apparent escape and I'm all on my own. All I do is nod slowly.

Seth studies me for a moment, and just when he opens his mouth to speak, he snaps it shut. He's been grazing my arms over and over, but now he stops abruptly and brushes all of the items next to the sink toward the back of the counter. Things are jostling, items are falling over, and it causes a tiny ruckus that feels too loud for the space we're in. Just when I'm about to scold him, he lifts me by my waist and sets me on the now clear top.

I let out a hiss as the cold counter registers on my ass. I'm barely half on it, but Seth is already nuzzling himself in between my legs, worsening the throbbing below. His cock, ready and waiting at my entrance. As much as I want to help him enter, I'm afraid to move for fear that I might fall from the counter. He hasn't dropped me yet, but there's a first time for everything.

"Clara," he growls as he places a hand at the base of my skull. It pulls at some of my hair as he leans in, breath so close that I can feel it fan across my face. "Tell me, how much do you care for me?"

The urge to swallow is strong, but my throat is refusing to cooperate and my thoughts are skidding around, barely allowing me the chance to string a coherent sentence together.

"I...I mean..." I glance down between us, wanting to end this conversation and get to the part where we don't have to speak, but I have the feeling he's not going to let up. "A lot."

"Clara Rose," he warns, an edge to his tone as a hand starts exploring down my thigh and skimming across the top of my pubic hair. I know he's not exploring further south on purpose. His avoidance of touching me right where I want it, where I want *him*, is maddening.

My grip on his biceps tightens as I struggle internally with where to go from here. He's holding out, backing me into a corner of sorts, all because I brought this up in the freaking first place.

Who the fuck says "I care about you"? How else did I expect Seth to react to that? He's poured out his heart and soul to me time after time, confessing how much he wants me, a life with me and the kids and everything that comes with it. And I can't say the one thing that would show him that I'm capable of reciprocating his feelings?

I don't fucking deserve him.

My breath catches on a weird hiccup type of sound before I can utter anything. "I don't know how to do this."

His fierce demeanor fades. Fraction by fraction, it morphs into one of confusion. The grip on my neck falters, and he releases me. My neck feels wobbly now without his steady touch.

"I...thought we were working through this. Talking things through when you want, giving you space when you need it."

"No, no, no." I'm shaking my head. "It's not your wolf stuff. I mean, yes I'm still working through things but...God dammit, Seth, I love you and I'm scared that I love you because the last time I loved someone, it broke me." My hand snaps over my mouth to keep me from yapping more. My wide eyes study him as he stands there a moment, almost completely unaffected by my blabbering until a grin sweeps across his face.

"Was that so hard to admit?" One corner of his mouth tips up a little further than the other and next thing I know, his fingers are diving into my center without any kind of warning.

Mouth falling open, my back arches as much as my position will allow.

"Will those words come easier while I fuck you like I love you?" The way his fingers twist and turn has my breath kicking up a notch. He proceeds to pose the head of his cock at my entrance and I'm already panting, the want and need that I have for him boiling to the top and trying to spill over. "Guess we'll have to find out."

Unhurriedly, he pushes himself inside, looking down between us. It feels so intimate, so barbaric to watch him disappear inside me, that my head is spinning. I'm shocked by how much I can see over my stomach. It's erotic as hell.

Once he's fully positioned inside, he takes me by the back of the head again, forcing me to look at him. I feel so vulnerable around him and right now, embarrassingly so.

Seth moves at a gentle pace, rocking his hips back and forth. I want him to move faster, to take charge and take over. But there's something so raw here, so enticingly delicious that I can't help but go along with the ride he's put me on.

It feels fucking amazing.

I'm warm all over, my body responding to each give and take, and I clench around him each time he rocks into me. Our combined breathing is so loud, filling my ears with our exchange. My feet struggle to stay up around his waist as I cling to him.

Gold eyes hold my focus, and as much as I want to let my head fall back so I can bask in his fullness, I know he's waiting. But instead of giving him what he wants, I somehow find it within me to tease him. "I hope you love me every time you fuck me."

His gaze turns fierce again, igniting my blood that's already aflame, and his grip on me tightens as his hips still.

Then, I drive it all the way home. "I love you, Seth."

Who knew that his dick slipping into me would make me capable of finally speaking those words? Somehow, he must have known that it would.

Our lips meet and when they do, it's so hard of an attack, it's almost bruising. His thrusts pick up speed, breaking our lips apart, and when sounds start to tear from my throat, he's quick to bring his mouth down on mine again. It's as if he can swallow my desperate pleas and need for release.

Higher and higher we go, rising to the top, and when we reach it, I swear I see stars.

# 5
# What-ifs

## *Clara*

Christmas might be officially over, but Seth and I are lying in bed, cozied up to one another. Neither of us has been able to tell the other goodnight, so our conversation veers this way and that. It's past two in the morning and the house is deathly quiet except for the occasional furnace kicking on and off. You wouldn't even know that my parents were around at all. My dad is a champion when it comes to snoring, so that's saying something. Perhaps the beer he drank is giving him and all of us a peaceful night's rest.

Still kind of awkward, having them here right now. Although, I can't deny how great it made me feel that they were willing to make the trip down so I wouldn't be alone for Christmas. The thought had never crossed my mind to make the trip up there, but then again, I'd been pretty preoccupied with this hunk of a man beside me.

"Tell me." Seth sways me from my inner thoughts as he inhales. "What were you like when you were pregnant?"

I blink a few times, wondering where his train of thought is headed, and there's no filtering the words that tumble out of me. "Fat and miserable."

My humor falls on deaf ears as I feel him stiffen before scolding, "Clara."

I roll my eyes before I let out a sigh. I don't want to gloss over how terrible I felt and tone it down until it's a lie. Pregnancy wasn't kind to me in more ways than one.

"Each pregnancy was rough," I begin, traveling down memory lane. "The morning sickness lasted well into my second trimester each time. With Julie, I ended up in the hospital for dehydration. With Emmett, the doctor put me on some nausea medication but it made me sleep a lot. I felt like a zombie at times, dragging through each day waiting to be put out of my misery. It wasn't until I started feeling kicks that I finally began to feel hope."

"That helped?"

I nod against his side before continuing. "Pretty sure I felt Julie for the first time while I was showering. I must have stood there for about half an hour afterward, arguing with myself that I had really felt something. With Emmett, I was in the car and sipping on a vanilla shake. Perhaps he was just excited for something that wasn't crackers.

"It's hard to believe that they were ever small enough to fit in my belly. That I could hold them in my arms." My thoughts come to a screeching halt and I wince at my words. While I might think back fondly to my kids and their starts with the negatives aside, it's something Seth has never been able to experience for himself.

I sit up, bringing the sheet up with me to cover my breasts. My eyes have adjusted enough to see him clearly. The white covering outside brightens the room more than normal. Every crease and divot in his fine form is a sight, but it's not enough to sway my thoughts away from how this might be difficult for him.

"I'm sorry if this is...if this makes you uncomfortable." I swallow hard, eyes flitting away from his golden ones that remain expressionless.

Seth sits up, the blankets pooling around his waist as he brings me back to face him with a tender touch on my chin. "I asked, Clara. There's nothing you should be apologizing for."

His thumb gently brushes against my bottom lip and my eyes close on reflex. My thoughts scramble for a moment, thinking about how he'll never get to experience all that comes along on the road to parenthood. All of the firsts, the excitement and accompanying frights that make you feel like you're in way over your head. My heart aches for him. To never have the opportunity to feel a kick or be present for the birth of a child of his own. How Seth was robbed of this pains me in the worst way. My eyes begin to burn just thinking about it all.

"Hey," he soothes, as if he can sense the turmoil inside my head. "I've made my peace about these things long ago. Being a dad might look different for me now than how I had originally planned, sure, but it's out of my hands."

"So you still want that? To become a dad?" I swear my heart skips as I turn my gaze back. There's a softness to his face, a look of pure warmth that has me wanting to mold back into his side where we were just moments ago. He knows that I can't have any more children. It isn't exactly first date talking material, but we went there.

"A father figure of sorts for Julie and Emmett, yes. Whatever they need. Whatever *you* need."

Tears free-fall without any signs of slowing. Even though my tubes are tied and each pregnancy riddled me with troubles, I would literally give this man anything. I hate that he was treated so poorly by the woman who claimed to love him and the parents that raised him. That the one thing that he had absolutely no control over, tore up his life and any future he might have been planning for.

What am I even saying? Would I really entertain the idea of having another child with Seth? I know he couldn't conceive one of our own doing, but surrogacy? Adoption? What are the chances of a tubal ligation reversal being successful? Would I really be willing to start over from square one with him?

Holy hell, we just met a few months ago and I'm already spiraling down trails and paths to possible futures with him. Now, adding another child to the mix?

It's too soon. Too early to be thinking about such things with him when we're still sneaking around most of the time. So why am I wanting this for him, for us?

"Would that be enough?" I ask shyly. "Would the three of us be enough for you?"

To know his truth on this is at the forefront of my mind as I gaze into his bright eyes. When I exhale, I fail to take in another breath, fearing that his silence is going to provide me with an answer that might hurt.

"Clara—" He cups the side of my face. "The three of you is more than I could have ever hoped for. Dreamed for, even. Had I known this future with you, Julie, and Emmett was even a possibility, I would have chased after it much sooner."

Damn him and his words.

Fresh tears spill as he closes the gap between us and takes my mouth. His lips press hard as he draws me in impossibly close. I can't control the tears that fall. I still don't understand this mate bond or his dedication to us. His willingness to jump at any opportunity to swing in for a rescue or lend a listening ear. Seth is too good to be true. I still struggle to believe that I'm even worthy of this. Worthy of *him*.

Our kisses became more drawn out and relaxed as he takes me back down to the bed with him. I let a hand play with his chest hair as he massages the back of my scalp with his fingers. It begins a calming effect that's threatening to bring sleep in on its golden chariot, taking me away to a rest that I know I need.

But this damn mind of mine won't shut up.

"Can I ask you something?" my voice pipes up, but I can't find it in myself to open my eyes.

"Anything." He doesn't skip a beat. I can't help but wonder if he's even tired at all.

My fingers pause in the midst of their touching and I try to focus on how I want to phrase my question. "Hypothetically speaking..." I work over a swallow as I try to push the words out. "Had you moved forward with your ex, married her, and met me several years later, would we still have this bond thing?"

The movement on my scalp stops. My eyes reopen from the sleepy trance he was putting me in. When he takes too long to answer, anxiety creeps in and I can't hold back my next question.

"Did you have a mate bond with her?" While I assumed that he hadn't, I guess I'd never really asked before. Seth made it seem like I was the one and only, but there's still so much that I don't know. I'm taking tiny and hesitant steps toward learning about the werewolf side of him, but this is something that I never really clarified. Just because he claimed that I was his once in a lifetime, that doesn't necessarily mean that it hadn't happened twice to him.

"No, not with Penelope."

My brows shoot up at an alarming speed. This is the first time he's even mentioned a name for his ex-fiancée, and I'm already trying to piece together what kind of woman he used to have on his arm, the one who he once imagined a life with.

"I would have left her for you."

It takes a few seconds for that statement to sink in and next thing I know, I'm rising from the bed again with a jolt, not even bothering with covering myself up this go-around. It's actually the furthest thing from my mind.

"As in, *I* would be the other woman?" Words come out in a heated rush as I'm wide awake once more.

Wow, how the tables have turned with that realization. If the mate thing applied to Joe and Chassidy, I think I would still want to murder the woman.

And him.

"The *only* woman," Seth clarifies as he sits up again. He draws his knees up, the sheet now falling away, and I struggle to keep my focus on his face and not his distracting male anatomy that always seems erect and at the ready. Does it hurt being hard all the damn time?

"You would break up your marriage for someone you don't even know? All because of my smell?" I scoff, and as Seth tries to reach forward I smack his hand away with the back of mine. He told me that my scent had drawn him to me his first day in Alton. The sugary sweet smell of vanilla, like a fresh baked batch of cookies. I had thought it absurd and laughed it off, but now? Knowing that he would have thrown away his relationship with this Penelope woman for me after a sniff?

Absolutely ridiculous.

"Something would have broken us up. If not for my failure to get her knocked up, I'm sure something else would have driven her away. Even so, had we been together when I found you, sure, she might have been pissed, but she would have eventually come to an understanding."

"Bullshit!" I spit back, my temper rising. "I'll never forgive Joe and Chassidy for what they did to me. What they did to Julie and Emmett."

"I didn't say forgive." Seth's voice deepens, and I swear it settles into my bones with its heaviness. "We have two different situations going on here. Joe knew what he was doing when he was sneaking and fucking around with Chassidy. I wouldn't hide you away and blindside someone with a divorce before moving out."

Seth lurches forward and before I can register a gasp of surprise, he has me pinned down to the bed and his hips are settling between my legs. "You are mine just as much as I am yours. There is no separation between the two of us, not anymore."

His hand dives down between us, quickly plunging into my center. I know I might have cleaned up from our earlier encounter in the bathroom, but there are still remnants of him that give enough slickness for him to move about. A moan escapes my mouth and when I open my eyes again, I can see his intent. As if it wasn't already obvious with what his hand is doing.

His fingers leave, and just as swiftly, his cock enters me. The back of my forearm rises to my mouth as I squirm and hold back the cry that wants to leave my throat. My hairline beads with sweat in an instant, my body acclimating to his sudden reentrance that you'd think I'd be used to by now, but I'm not. I'll never understand why every time he enters me, it feels like the first time. Yet I crave it every single time.

"Clara Rose," he groans, and I swear he's vibrating my entire body as he speaks. "Look at me."

It takes a beat, but I lower my arm. I swear to everything that is holy that his eyes are on fire, taking on a new life as they burn into me and he withdraws his hips just to take me again. He holds my chin still, forcing my gaze to him as his mouth parts.

I love it when I can see pleasure radiating through his face. I want him to feel good and come undone. And inside of me. Every last drop he can give. I can't explain the need behind it each time, but I want it desperately. Is our little chat tonight giving way to some sort of dormant breeding kink?

When his hips surge forward again, I can't contain the throaty cry that leaves my lips, and both of my hands snap over my mouth.

A devilish grin crosses his face as he cups one of my breasts, scooping it up as best as he can. "Are you going to be quiet or do we need to take this somewhere else?"

I throw him a quizzical look, not knowing where else we could possibly go that would grant us—specifically me—the freedom to be as loud as I need to be without waking my parents.

Seth withdraws and I pout, hating how empty I feel. He gathers a blanket from the foot of the bed and pulls me up by my arm until I'm scooching off of the bed and onto my feet. He wraps me up and scoops me into his arms as I flail momentarily. Things are moving too fast for me to comprehend as he does nothing to cover his frame and escorts me from my room. I hide against his chest, fearful that any slight creak of the floors might awaken someone.

My dad is snoring surprisingly lightly on the couch as we pass the living room and make our way into the kitchen. The steady hum of the refrigerator fills my ears and only then do I peek out to see that Seth plans on exiting the house. I brace for the cold as he steps out and the night air nips at my exposed feet and face. I nuzzle into him further. When the door shuts behind us with a gentle close, I let out a rush of words.

"What do you think you're doing?"

I haven't the slightest idea where in our exit Seth picked up the garage key, but he opens the door and quickly whisks me inside before shutting it. My teeth are chattering already, nipples hardening at the drastic change in temperature.

Although it's dark in here, I swear I can make out my breath as he crosses over to my lonely van and its sliding door. With it being parked in the garage, I never bother locking it. The inside lights illuminate as he sets me down and I tug in my blanket closer.

The concrete beneath my feet sends an unforgiving surge of cold up to my ankles and I shiver, gawking at the naked man before me.

"You're joking, right?" I gape at him as he opens my door and presses the button to move my seat forward. I'm barely offered a smirk before he returns to the seat behind mine and folds it down like he's mastered it by doing so a million times already. He doesn't even pause to figure out the sequence to stash the seat, and the next thing I know, it's disappearing into its little compartment below.

"Seth, it's too cold out here." My words run together as I squeeze my covering tighter, as if I can find some sort of missing heat somewhere.

"I think you underestimate my ability to warm you up." His naked frame ducks into my van and he snatches my only visible hand and tugs me in. He presses the button to close the door as I let out a giggle at how ridiculous this is.

We're hiding from my parents, and in my own house. Actually, outside of my damn house. Sneaking away in the hopes that we don't get caught.

Seth's hot breath hits me on my neck before he's sucking and kissing. Only when I let my guard down does he begin to draw the blanket down and coax me into his hold. I let my hands wander across his facial hair, enjoying how it feels as they move around to his head.

It's cramped in here, and the plastic beneath my knees is unforgiving, but I keep going. I'm so caught up in the moment, so head over heels for this man, that I'm now getting ready to let him screw me in my vehicle. I'm not sure if I'll ever look in the rearview mirror again without imagining this.

Every touch isn't enough. Every caress isn't close enough, and every kiss isn't as deep as I need it to be.

I'm straddling him as he buries his head between my breasts, and when I sink down onto his shaft, I let out a sharp cry. An unfiltered and embarrassingly loud noise that has Seth humming in appreciation on my skin.

The temperature around us grows, as if a small heater has kicked on, and I roll my hips against him, reveling in the groan he releases as he picks up a breast and begins to tease my nipple. The graze of his teeth has my head shooting back as my grip on his shoulders tightens.

"Seth," I moan in appreciation, suddenly thankful for his quick thinking on getting us out here where we can be free to fuck as loud as we want. Better yet, as loud as I need to be.

I was never this vocal, this noisy with sex, before he came into my life. Now, I can't imagine it any other way.

Maybe he really was made for me.

"Seth," I breathe, taking his head in my hands as I try to pull him away from his attack on my chest. He lazily releases my hard point and gazes up at me through lashes that look incredibly dark in the dim lighting.

"Yes, beautiful?" He searches my face, trying to discern what has caused this disruption. His name for me has my thoughts derailing and there's no filtering what comes from my mouth.

"I don't know what our future holds, but I want you in it." My grip on his face tightens as a shiver rakes through me. "No, I *need* you in my life."

He stares at me for a moment. My words hang in the air as if they're out on a clothesline waiting to dry in a summer breeze.

"I love you," I utter again, but this time it comes out so much easier that I can't suppress the grin of pure happiness that takes hold of me. "I love you, Seth."

I swear his cock twitches inside of me as he places a hand on my waist and the other cradles my face. His palm is warm and I turn into it, letting my eyes close briefly to savor his touch before flicking my eyes back.

"You have me, Clara." He moves and his hand makes a beeline for my clit, and the moment that first swirl makes it to my brain, I want to melt. "I meant it when I said you would never go a day without knowing how much I love you."

The circling motions have my lower jaw dropping away, and I lean in to where our lips barely graze one another. "Not a single day?"

I can feel him smile against me as I rise up and lower again. He swallows my next moan and his tongue darts out to taste my mouth before he finally responds. "Not a single fucking day."

# 6

# Ultimatum

## *Seth*

Clara is beaming. It might be winter, but she has a glow to her that's mesmerizing. I can't help but stare at her, aware that she's all mine but still blown away by this change. By what her family together is capable of doing to her and her spirits.

Julie and Emmett are home and their grandparents arrived before lunch. They baked a bunch of stuff shortly after their arrival and it was all too much amongst our six bodies to eat for New Year's Eve.

The only banana bread I'd ever had was filled with nuts, and while Joyce's lacks that ingredient, I found that I actually like this recipe better. I think what did the trick was Clara swiping across a warm slice with a dollop of butter. It sank into the bread almost instantly and my mouth was weeping before my teeth even bit into it.

Charles met me with a swift pat on the back at my arrival and a little joke about me being fully clothed this time. I laughed it off, wanting to make fun of the situation myself, but stopped when I noted just how close Emmett was. I didn't want to chance anything there. Charles also asked about Larson, who we'd invited again, but he said he was going out of town for something. I tried to press him, letting him know he was welcome, but he waved it off and offered his apologies as well as a special hello message of sorts for his newfound buddy.

I know that Joyce and Charles will always be left in the dark about Larson's and my other forms, the other lives we lead and how we found out about one another. But that's the way it has to be. And as long as everyone gets along? I don't see any reason we all can't be friends.

But this... This must be what it's like to put down roots. Finding someone to share my life with, kids that I want to get to know and help them grow and flourish. Hell, I've already joked to Clara about her parents being my in-laws, and she just laughed it off as she walked a load of laundry back into her room. She didn't deny it, though, which only further fueled my desire to start planning something I've been dreaming of. I just have to get Julie and Emmett fully on board. Winning them over will help tip things in my favor, to the point that my Rose won't be able to say no for any reason.

I sit on the couch, watching Clara, the kids, and Joyce try to battle it out in a game that has them shouting and hollering at the television screen. Emmett was adamant not to wear the wrist strap, but after a close call with his sister, he secured it to himself to prevent any other possible accidents.

Clara is so full of life, so happy and present in the moment. I swear she hasn't stopped smiling all day. She's so damn beautiful I want to reach out and touch her but I refrain most of the time when considering our audience. But I'm pretty sure that if I pulled that plump ass into my lap and kissed her, I would taste her enthusiastic joy.

"Beer in the garage?"

I blink and turn my attention toward my soon-to-be father-in-law. Charles might think I'm grinning about his query, but my mind is elsewhere.

"Yes!" Julie shouts over the minigame she won, and she does a quick bouncy spin that seems to be her go-to victory dance.

"I'll get some more." Clara tears my attention away easily and I throw her a quizzical look. "I'm kind of hot. I could use the cooldown. You can fill in for me."

She removes the strap from her wrist and I stand to take it from her.

"You sure?" I ask, fully prepared to go and grab some more drinks so she can stay. I'm beginning to think that she likes playing hostess. At least, when it comes to the family that means the most to her.

"Yeah, of course." Her hand lingers on mine for a moment, as if she's considering something. Something flashes in her eyes, perhaps a heat that not even the outdoor temperatures can bring to a simmer. She clears her throat before taking a step back and giving orders to the other players. "Don't take it easy on him!"

Clara takes her leave and I suppress the urge to follow after her. It isn't until Emmett elbows me that I'm reminded of the game that's about to start. They don't even give me the chance to get familiar with this new minigame or which controls to use. I don't have the slightest idea what the object is, but at the sound of a whistle, my thumbs go at it to try and figure it out for myself.

"Go right, go right!" Emmett orders, and I quickly find my bearings. My heart rate is climbing as the character Clara picked out wobbles on the edge of a narrow path. The dress she's wearing makes it harder to decipher just how much room I have for error and I overestimate, sending the little character off the ledge; it takes a moment for her to respawn.

Julie lets out another holler and points to the rest of us as she beats the clock and earns herself another point in her favor. She's definitely got the competitive streak in her and it's souring Emmett's mood. The look on his young face says it all as he gives his glasses a frustrated shove up his nose.

Joyce takes each defeat in stride but I have to admit, she's a good team player. I don't think she's won a single round of anything yet, but it doesn't stop her from playing again and again, keeping up with her grandchildren even if she doesn't entirely know what's going on.

It's not until four games later that Emmett finally secures a win of his own and I swear when he jumps, he reaches my height. I hold up my hand and he high-fives me. His eyes light up with excitement as he shrugs off his sweater and gives it a toss onto the couch.

Julie rolls her eyes, reminding me of her mother who still hasn't returned yet. I pass off my controller to a rather puzzled-looking Charles and excuse myself to go and find her. My long strides carry me through the empty kitchen, and I'm soon picking up the pace as I exit the house and enter the garage. The door is left ajar and my heart stammers for a moment, fearing that something is wrong. With the temperatures in the teens, Clara wouldn't need this long to cool off and grab drinks.

The relief that floods through me when I find her slumped against the fridge is brief, like a flash of lightning. I barely register how I make it over to her, kneeling and placing my hands on the sides of her calves as I try to ascertain what's wrong.

"Clara," I urge her to speak and the seconds drag on, making time pass impossibly slow. Her head is on her forearms, hair burying her face. Her phone is on the ground beside her but only illuminating the time and the date. "Clara, what's wrong?"

She sniffles, barely raising her head enough for me to make out her dark eyes. I expected them to be puffy and swollen from tears, but there's nothing. There's an emptiness there, cracking my chest open even though I have no idea what's going on.

"I can't help you if you don't talk to me. What's going on?" I press, hoping that she'll see that I'm right here. Ready and waiting to accommodate her needs or whatever she requires of me right now. It's such a drastic change that I can't help but mentally scratch my head, trying to figure out what in the hell happened in the minutes we've been apart.

Her stillness is eerie. The silence is almost more than I can bear, until Clara finally finds it in herself to move her arm. Without looking, she picks up her phone and uses her fingerprint to unlock it before handing it to me. I know my brows are pinching as the screen lights up and I see a message thread with Joe.

*Keep that stranger away from my kids or I'm taking full custody.*

I read the message over and over as if miraculously, I'll read something new. Red dots my vision. Anger begins to unfurl deep in my belly as the phone darkens and the screen turns off.

The motherfucker has the nerve, the *audacity* to send something like this on New Year's Eve, knowing full well that Clara has company alongside her time with the kids. I know I'm no secret now, having slowly been integrating into this household, but this is a new low.

At some point I stand, leaving Clara alone and on the floor. The fact that Joe is forcing her to choose between her kids and me, a position he has no right to put her in, has a troublesome wrath sparking. My body is beginning to vibrate and I bite down hard on my molars.

Now is not the time to fucking shift. That wouldn't do anyone here any good. But the thought of slashing Joe's tires to a point beyond repair would be a start. Breaking into his house and causing irreparable damage that would take weeks, or better yet months, to fix—that would be another idea. Too fucking bad he lives in such a quiet neighborhood. The chickenshit would probably run with his tail between his legs if I were to meet him in a dark alley.

I know damn well that I can't kill the bastard, but I can make his life a living hell. But retaliating would only come back on us, on Clara. Anything that happens from this point moving forward would undoubtedly point back in our direction.

I'm furious. Fucking mad and—

There's a click of a door and I look down at Clara, who's shriveling up and shutting down. She might be oblivious to her mother who's about to enter, her ears not hearing at the same level as mine. There isn't enough time to wipe the scowl from my face and when Joyce enters the garage, it catches her off guard.

Her hand rises to her chest as if in a state of shock, before she sees her daughter on the ground before me. She's careful for a moment, taking in the scene before her face morphs into something protective.

"What's going on out here?"

There's been a mask in place ever since Clara stepped foot back inside her home. It pains me to see her act like this, trying to brush her internal struggle to the side for the sake of her family and their limited time spent together.

Clara has let her guard down so many times with me, let me see some of her worst thoughts and fears, but this? This side of her is a damaging punch to my gut. I can barely focus on anything else but how this one text interrupted her life and turned her whole day and evening upside down.

I feel powerless. Each scenario I try to concoct, every possible avenue I could try to explore and solution I want to attempt, isn't good enough.

From digging into Joe's finances not long ago, I don't think he would have the means to take Clara back to court, but maybe I'm wrong. Perhaps his parents are backing him? They don't necessarily seem rich by any means, but their home down in Missouri had to have cost them a pretty penny when they purchased it back in the eighties. And Chassidy? How in the hell is she even making any money? OnlyFans?

I shudder at the thought of men jerking off to her whiny ass on camera.

Time stands still, yet keeps ticking toward midnight, picking on my nerves with each passing second.

We've gathered around the television, the feed brought up from the countdown in New York City and its infamous ball drop.

Julie is the brightest-looking one out of the bunch, holding her sparkling white grape juice in a fluted glass in one hand while she's texting someone with the other. Emmett's glass is filled with pop, and I swear he's been downing cans of it just to keep up with his grandpa. Who, by the way, hasn't drunk me under the table and has actually taken a step back from his efforts to do so like he did on Christmas.

I pretend not to notice as Joyce leans in toward her daughter for a hug and whispers that everything is going to be okay before taking a step back to be by her husband. Only then does Clara look over her shoulder, and I witness her flex her hand as if I'm to come and join her at her side.

Although I might not be swooping her down into a dip for a New Year's kiss at midnight, I'll take this. She isn't shutting me out, and instead is looking for me to be with her. I try not to overdo it with my need to touch her and be with her constantly, but this I can do.

She attempts to smile up at me, but it doesn't make it to her eyes. I recognize that look in her. She's trying with all her might to keep things stitched up tight, when really, she needs a release. Be it with her words, crying, or a heated spew of profanities geared toward her ex and the trouble he's causing and disruption he's brought about.

It's not the night I wanted for her. It's not the way I wanted to ring in our first New Year's together and with everyone she loves.

I wish I could speak freely with Clara. I want nothing more than to offer her words that would help ease her worries, even if for just a little while longer. I hate that Joe has stripped her of the good time that she was having and tainted what could have been a wonderful memory.

Leaning down to her ear, I keep my voice low. As much as I want my lips to brush her ear, I resist. I would do about anything to bring back the vibrant and cheerful woman who was bouncing around the house earlier, flashing her perfect smile for everyone to see.

"He doesn't get to determine your happiness," I start. Her hand tightens on mine and my thumb begins steady strokes. "We're going to get through this. Together."

# 7

# He Took Notes

## *Clara*

Joe is most likely already lawyered up and ready to take action. I'm not going to let him get the upper hand if I have anything to do with it.

Seth has been my rock since Joe sent that text, but at the same time, it feels like he's handling me with kid gloves. But even so, we have devised a plan. One that my mother is even getting on board with, offering to help financially if I need it. I know it isn't the right time—and it might not ever be—to tell her about the weight Seth lifted off of my shoulders by paying off my mortgage and then some. With that one perplexing act of his, the money that was going toward my mortgage is now going into savings. For once, it's building and accumulating interest right alongside the excess Seth gave me and won't take back.

Using a lawyer from outside of my surrounding towns seemed like the best fit. Someone who wouldn't know a single thing about me, my history with Joe, nothing. I wanted to start from scratch and with a person who no Serring had ever met. I hate being put in this position, the literal corner that Joe is backing me into, but I feel that it has to be done.

I want to show Joe that I'm serious. That I have the backing to take him on and the support system behind me to do it. I'm not going to let him win. Over my dead body.

An unsolicited shiver runs through my body as I mull that last line over.

Cranking up the heat in the van, I continue on my route to work. I took the morning off to place a few calls to potential lawyers that Seth, my mom, and I hope might be a good fit for the situation.

I shift in my seat uncomfortably. There's a deep ache signaling that my period is going to worsen my attempts at turning my mood around, and I take a deep breath before I reach a hand over and into my purse. I'm sifting through it, trying to find the bottle of pain reliever I usually have on hand, but I'm coming up empty. I don't even recall taking it out of there.

Dammit.

I want to beat my head on the steering wheel, but since I'm going seventy down the highway, it probably isn't the safest choice to make. I glance at the clock, trying to determine if I'll have time to make a quick stop somewhere. When I eventually take the exit into Pembrook, I know it's not likely that I can make it work.

Guess I'll just have to suffer through it. That heating pad is going to feel like heaven tonight.

Pulling into a parking space, I brace myself for the cold. Luckily, a few people are gone on vacation with the passing holidays, so I don't have to park in the farthest spots from the building. I get out and scurry up to the building as fast as I can without looking like a penguin trying to outrun some predator. A lousy chuckle escapes me as I picture what I must look like, all bundled up with my coat, hat, and scarf. Hugging myself as if I can prolong the heat from the van.

I kick my shoes off to free myself of any snow that might have accumulated in my trek across the parking lot before stepping in. It's almost too hot in here after being outside. I set my purse on the ground and begin taking off my layers and placing them on my set of designated hooks. There's a whole row of them in the hallway for everyone but the dentists. They have their own offices so they don't have to use these.

Making my way in, I offer a few hellos before settling in beside Melissa, who's playing with a pen in her hand. It makes a ticking type of sound as she wiggles it back and forth and I swear she's going to send it flying if she doesn't stop soon. I feel her eyes on me before I turn to face her.

My brows rise as I take in her perfectly curled hair and a new sweater that I haven't seen her in. The blue only makes her eyes look brighter.

"Everything alright?" She looks at me expectantly. But I'm tired of talking about lawyers and custody and the unnecessary havoc it could have on the kids. It's all mentally and physically draining.

I bury my head in my hands, elbows on my knees as I let out a sigh. There isn't anyone in the waiting room so we might have a few moments to ourselves. Melissa has been getting little crumbs of information for some time now, but this new revelation with Joe? This is a whole new cookie that's crumbling.

"Joe's going to try and go for full custody." I peep through my hands to find blue eyes bulging and her mouth agape. "That's why I took the morning off. I was trying to get a head start on finding a lawyer."

"You're joking!" Sylvie's voice cuts in from behind me and I jump at her sudden appearance. Her cartoon scrubs have a stark white background and I can't say I recognize any of the characters on them.

I let out an agitated sigh. My body folds over again as my cramps deepen and I'm already regretting that I let anything spill in the first place.

"Holy shiiiiiiit." Melissa draws out her last word in a strained whisper. There are a few more things I would like to add to that, but when I look up again, I have the suspicion that her statement wasn't directed at me or my recently announced plight.

"Damn," Trisha breathes on an exhale as another hygienist comes into the picture behind her. Their jaws drop as they take in something behind me and when I swivel my chair, my heart stops and forgets how to do its one job.

Seth is strolling in through the waiting room and up to the front desk. He's dressed in light blue jeans and I can barely make out a dark green henley beneath his black jacket that I told him more than once isn't warm enough for Iowa winters. As if being devastatingly handsome isn't enough, he's carrying a vase of white roses that are thankfully about half the size of the ones he ordered last time.

He remembered. White roses.

I might have given him a little crap over how heavy the last bouquet was, and seeing that he'd paid attention to that perks up my attitude. Even if our encounter is now on full display for my coworkers to witness.

"Delivery for Ms. Clara." Seth flashes his teeth and I swear I've lost all coherent thought.

"I'll take that for you." Trisha sneaks up from behind and takes it from him, placing it on the lower counter and skimming over the top of it as if searching for something. I'm quick to give it a once-over, seeing for myself that there is no card this time. Thank goodness, considering how nosy the other women are around here.

"A-anything else for you?" I manage to find my voice, unsure of how long he's going to let his unexpected delivery draw out.

"Yes, actually. I have an appointment." He smirks, keeping his eyes locked on mine while his words register. I haven't even had the chance to boot up my computer yet and I'm rolling over toward Melissa and giving her a little shove.

Sure enough. Seth Woods is marked on the calendar as a new patient for a cleaning. When did he sneak this one by me?

"Looks like we have all of your information and you filled out your forms online, Mr. Woods." I clear my throat when a thickness tries to gather. "Please, take a seat and they'll call you back shortly."

Seth taps the counter and his gaze doesn't leave mine until he turns away with a small thanks. A playful grin splays across his face as he pivots.

"Who the hell hired him for delivery?"

"Does he deliver anything else?"

"What gives, Clara? Who are these from?"

Trisha, Melissa, and Sylvie are all scanning the flowers, and I barely have any room to push my chair back enough to stand. Seth has his legs stretched out and crossed at the ankles, a smug look on his face as he settles. He's getting way too much entertainment out of this, and I have to admit, it's pretty funny even if the spotlight is pointed in my direction.

It's also giving me the chance to come right out with the truth or keep it hidden a while longer. I weigh my options briefly, considering the women around me won't let up on their badgering. They're still pestering me with questions from the last round of flowers. I know my cheeks are blushing; the heat in them tells me so.

My smile feels forced at first before it spreads naturally, crossing my face for the first time in days, and it feels like it's been too long. If the muscles were capable of creaking, showing how weak they've become, I would need oil like the Tin Man to loosen me up.

Seth's right. Joe doesn't get to dictate my happiness. He doesn't control me, and I'll be damned if he's going to make me choose between my children and the man in my life who makes me really, truly happy. What Seth and I have, while I still can't wrap my head around it most days, is remarkable. I didn't think I would ever be lucky enough to have what we have. And the way he treats me? I want to believe that our relationship will be a good example for Julie and Emmett to see.

Well, putting our sneaking around aside. They don't need to know about that.

Heart rate kicking up a notch, I widen my stance and face the three girls head-on. Collectively, they go silent and wait with bated breath. It's the quietest they've been since I showed up today.

Instead of giving them any kind of explanation, my lips twist to the side and I skirt around the group and through the side door that leads into the waiting room. There's a smirk on Seth's face again, as if he knows what I'm finally going to do.

Releasing a breath, I hold out my hand and he takes it as he stands. Eyes cast down, I approach the window and prepare myself for the rest of the afternoon I'm going to have with my coworkers, because there's no turning back now.

They're gawking at me. Full-on jaws dropped and eyes wide when I straighten myself out.

"Seth, these are some of my coworkers." I direct his attention with my free hand as I go down the line of them. "Sylvie, Melissa, and Trisha. Ladies—" I turn my head back toward the man of the hour. "This is my boyfriend, Seth."

There are a few beats of silence as I look into his eyes, and I swear his genuine smile at hearing me say that out loud somehow speaks volumes. It's as if we've both been waiting to hear it become official in this way, and he has been so incredibly patient for it to happen. In his own way, that is.

"He is not," Sylvie states, while Trisha has her hands cupped in front of her chest in excitement.

"This is so exciting! Hi!" Melissa squeaks as she bounces up and down a bit, her curls moving ever so slightly.

"Nice to meet you all." Seth offers a small nod in their direction and squeezes my hand.

"Thank you for the flowers." I beam up at him, but his face cracks for a moment. It throws me off-balance. "What is it?"

He leads me away from the window but says a few parting words to our spectators. "I'm just going to borrow her for a moment."

They all nod a bit too enthusiastically, and I can make out the slight murmur of one of them wanting "borrowed" as well. I'm pretty sure it's from happily married Trisha, but I know Seth has people of all ages drooling over him, so I'm not entirely surprised.

"Is everything alright?" I ask again, growing uncomfortable.

"Yes, and no." His voice drops and he uses his backside to shield me from the view of others. It helps, knowing that I'm not on full display for them. "I'm not sure if I'll be able to make it to Julie's game later."

"Oh?" My heart sinks a little. Julie mentioned in passing that she's cheering at a basketball game tonight, and when Seth showed interest, she invited him. The offer came from her directly and without any pressure. I didn't even detect any mixed feelings from her regarding it.

Seth and I had weighed the idea of him going, and while I was hesitant since Joe would be there, Seth made sure I knew that he would support any decision I made in the matter.

"Is it work?" I ask.

He sighs through his nostrils. "I'm afraid that I don't have much information to go off of right now, but Larson has asked that I go with him somewhere. He kind of pulled the 'you owe me' card."

I mull that information over, even though it isn't much. Seth and I both owe Larson a lot for protecting me after Seth's family came into the picture, intent on killing me and taking him back to Colorado. Things have been silent ever since. No more calls, no more unexpected visits, nothing.

"Does it have anything to do with your family?"

He shakes his head no, and just when he opens his mouth to speak again, the door behind me opens. A cold draft rushes at us and in reflex, I remove my hand from his hold and hug myself from the sudden intrusion and reminder of how chilly it is outside.

"You've got your phone?"

Seth gives me that knowing look, telling me that he does. He's even got another one solely for work.

"Just be safe, please." I have no idea of Larson's intent on this little trip of his, but I can't help but worry. It's in my nature at this point in my life. Even if I think I have things figured out, there's always a part of me that's nagging to remind me of what could go wrong if things don't go right.

"Don't suppose I can give you a kiss before I go?"

My heart races as I peek around him to see the group of three has turned into four, and only one of them is checking in the man at the counter. As much as I would love to throw my arms around Seth and kiss him hello, goodbye, and thanks for the flowers, I already have a bunch of Curious Carols ready with an absurd amount of questions, and I have no idea how I'm going to fend them off.

Thank goodness there are about five others off work today, maybe even six.

"Seth." His name is called by another hygienist, and I lean up on my tiptoes for a quick kiss. The warmth is brief and the contact isn't enough to satisfy what I really want, but it'll have to do.

When Seth turns to go, I snatch a hand out and seize his. Smile quickly fading, he looks at me, perplexed.

I step in closer, keeping my voice as quiet as I can so no other soul can hear. "Careful not to bite. They don't usually work with canines."

I release him, and we part ways. His expression is pure shock until it dissipates into lighthearted amusement. In turn, I suppress the need to giggle as I scurry away.

Perhaps I should tease him more often.

# 8

# New Game, New Rules

## *Seth*

I didn't want to be cooped up in Larson's truck. I was afraid I might come out smelling like an ashtray and if there's a chance I'll be making an appearance at Julie's school tonight, that isn't the first impression I want anyone there to have of me. Therefore, I insisted we take my vehicle for this strange outing.

We've been on the road for about an hour and Larson is still remaining tight-lipped as to what this is all about. It's eating away at my nerves, not knowing what I'm getting myself into, and it's dampened any chance of an easygoing conversation.

Larson gives a direction here or there, mumbles a memory or two on occasion, but other than that, it's been an awkward little road trip.

There's tension in his frame as he sits still, only the occasional glance out of his window. For the most part, it's eyes forward and lips sealed. He's got a flannel coat on and a ball cap. Boots that have probably spent more time outdoors than I did in my entire childhood, given their visible wear and tear. Maybe I could get him a gift card or something for new shoes, since I won't be getting to replace his front porch until the springtime.

"Slow down. Yer turn is comin' up on yer right," he gruffs out.

I put my signal on even though I'm pretty sure we haven't passed anyone since we turned onto this gravel road a few miles back. I have the feeling that this winding path could be treacherous without four-wheel drive. The thin layer of snow is packed down enough to show that there has been travel, but it's minimal.

There's a narrow opening in the tree line with a fresh set of trails from tires already passing through. I turn in and cast a quick glance down at my phone in the cupholder closest to me. I have zero reception here. That's just great.

"What have you gotten me into, Larson?" We're out in the middle of nowhere and his silence on the matter is getting the best of me. Why is he dragging me out here and what the hell is so important that it had to be today?

He lets out a grunt and slaps his hands on his upper legs. "Guess I should be the one to tell ya, since I called in Edgar to begin with."

The road is barely wide enough for my truck to travel through, and there are low-hanging branches that I fear are going to scratch up my paint job. I'm not normally one to freak out about something so cosmetic, but I've grown rather attached to this truck. I've had it for four years already and know every feature like the back of my hand.

Plus it's paid off. That's a major plus.

There's a clearing up ahead, a small one, but enough to show three other vehicles and a small log cabin. There's heat coming out of a chimney that needs some serious work. The whole place is a bit run-down and I can't help but wonder if anyone really lives here in its current state.

Outside, a group of four men and one woman come out and around the house. They must have heard our impending arrival, the quiet of the surrounding winter doing nothing to stifle our presence.

"Better catch me up to speed quickly," I mutter as I pull up behind a little sedan that looks like it's been sitting out here with the elements for some time. You can't tell me that thing will turn over anymore. I could probably give it a good kick and it would cave in on itself.

There's a scent. No, scratch that. Multiple scents begin to flood into the cabin of my vehicle, and I glare at the dipshit beside me. "I don't want any part of a pack, Larson, you know that."

"It's not that. Not exactly." He's pushing his hands away from him as if it's almost absurd that I assumed that. Why the fuck else would he be bringing me out here to meet other werewolves?

"You said you weren't a part of a pack. That you and Edgar help when it's needed. So what the fuck is this?" I'm almost ready to slam the truck in reverse and speed back out of here.

I don't want to answer to anyone. I don't want the pressures and expectations of being in a pack. I was raised in a strict one and I fucking hated it. I didn't want anything to do with the hierarchy and rules that come along with it.

"Just give 'em a listen, Seth." Larson puffs out an exaggerated sigh. "I knew ya wouldn't come along if I told ya the truth. But these people? They're *good* people." He straightens his jacket before tugging on the door handle. "Just give 'em a chance."

He hops out, taking the stale scent of cigarettes with him. I hadn't realized how accustomed I'd become to it in our drive out here. The door shuts, and I'm left with two choices. Leave, or find out what they want.

I feel like I should know better. That they have some type of angle in all of this and I want no part of it. I'm angry that Larson lied to me about being a part of a pack when this sure as hell looks like one. The smallest one I've ever seen, but still.

My eyes scan across each individual in various states of dress. Edgar is among them, wearing one of those aviator hats that looks too big on him. I haven't seen him since he took my cousin Adam away. I know better than to ask Larson what happened to him. The less I know of his demise, the better.

Glancing down at my phone one more time, I note that I still have no service. I get the urge to punch something, but there's nothing within grasp and I'm on full display. Strangers staring at me and watching, waiting.

Well fuck me with something hard and sand-papery.

I cut the engine but leave my keys in the ignition as I exit. Shoving my hands in my pockets, I leisurely make my way to the front of my vehicle and lean my back up against it. The warmth from it is quickly evaporating with the temperature out here. The trees might be able to provide some relief from the biting wind, but not all of it. There's a hint of food in the air, something meaty if I had to guess. I'm not proud of the way my stomach betrays me by wanting to stay and find out what's cooking.

"Seth Ries," a man on my right calls, and he's already on my shit list for using my birth-given last name.

"It's Woods now," I bite out, eyes narrowing at the man who is the bulkiest out of the rest. He's giving wannabe alpha vibes. "Seth Woods. And you are?"

I'm unaware of how much they know or how, but what they've managed to dig up so far is already putting me in a worse mood. My fists are balling in my pockets.

Larson, aware of my reluctance to participate in whatever the hell this is, steps in to act as a buffer. "I know what yer thinkin' and we're not a pack, Seth."

My vision turns to slits, believing that this is the exact opposite. What I don't expect is for the rest of the people around us to start laughing. Like they've found something funny. For the first time since arriving, my body slackens ever so slightly, and I adjust my position. "Then what the hell is it then?"

"Christ's sake." The young woman steps forward, a bit perturbed. She's bundled up the most. A wide scarf around her neck and a beanie on her head, a puffy knee-length coat and thick boots lined with fur. "We're all outcasts, so to speak. None of us belong to any pack."

"And you are?" I don't skip a beat.

"I go by Katrina now." She begins to traipse forward and sticks her hand out for me. Her eyes are a bright blue and her skin is almost as white as the snowy atmosphere around her. She's covered up so much, I can't even make out what her hair color is. Eyebrows are hidden too.

I'm hesitant, but I shake her hand. She has a firm grip. Strong, and she wants me to feel it.

"A group of outcast werewolves that don't belong to any pack but have formed a secret pack of their own?" I give her an annoyed look.

"No one is in charge, even if they think they are." Katrina looks over her shoulder at the big one. "That brute is Leo. Wouldn't marry the woman they deemed acceptable, since he went twenty-five years without finding his mate. When he failed to comply, his so-called pack killed his mother. The only blood relative he had left."

I try to remain emotionless as I cast a glance his way. His stony exterior gives nothing away, just a dead set stare at the ground a few feet ahead of him. I assume he's the one closest to my age here.

"This over here"—she hooks a thumb over her opposite side—"is Chet. He outsmarted his alpha with his head instead of strength." The lanky fellow scratches uncomfortably at the back of his neck. "Nobody wanted him to lead. Refused to accept him and called him weak when he spared the life of the old alpha. Barely escaped the pack when they all turned on him.

"Javi next to him ended up finding his mate, but the problem was, she was already married to someone else within her pack. Someone who claimed they had a mate bond with her even though she denied it." My eyes fall on the dark complexion of the man next to Chet. He's the shortest of them all, but looks like he could use a few more leg days to keep up with the bulging biceps in his jacket. "They ran off together soon after."

"But their mate bond..." I finally speak, confused as to why Javi's pack wouldn't honor something so sacred. Or hers, for that matter. But I guess we aren't so different when it comes down to it. My own family was willing to kill Clara simply because I'd taken the life of my cousin, Carter.

Katrina snorts an unflattering laugh. "You'd think that would matter, right? Well how about when I found my mate who just happened to be human? They tried to kill him all because he wasn't like us. Didn't matter that he could be. That he could change if he wanted to. They didn't even give us a choice."

I'm stunned. So much so that my feet feel cemented to the ground and I fail to breathe.

Did Clara and I ever stand a chance to be accepted with a bond between human and werewolf? I know that our situation is rare, but I'm gutted to find out Katrina's news. Not even given the chance to see if her mate would want to be turned—nothing.

"She's missing the part where she killed about half of her pack so she could get out," Edgar cuts in, and Katrina glowers in his direction.

She then settles herself and shrugs in nonchalance, but I bear witness to her taking a moment to reel in the anger growing in her frame, taking in a deep inhale and closing her eyes.

Edgar steps in closer, looking around at our small group before crossing his arms. "Look, we all have our pasts. Wrongdoings that pushed us too far. So far, that we couldn't take it anymore."

I have half a mind to ask Edgar where he fits into all of this. Larson had been reticent about him too, merely stating that our encounter in November wouldn't be the last I saw of him. Guess he was right about that.

"Larson here tells us you're a good guy with a troubled history of your own. We may not be a pack, not like the ones we grew up in, but we're friends. We keep each other updated on any pack business we might come across, news that might need to be shared. We look after each other and come when someone needs help. We live our lives the way we see fit, not by some outdated and blasphemous rules deemed necessary by packs that want to rule with an iron fist."

I want to spout off something a bit sarcastic, but refrain. These people have no reason to confide these things in me. Edgar stood to gain nothing, no benefit from helping me and Larson not so long ago. And hearing about how these various packs have turned on their own is maddening, appalling, and downright disgusting.

"A lot of packs have attempted to get me to join them over the years. Some of those encounters didn't turn out well," I say coolly.

"So we've heard," Katrina states, and one of my brows shoots up. "We might have accumulated some friends in other territories over the years."

"We've also heard that you change more than most." Javi finally speaks, with a slight accent. "You don't just change on the full moon."

I study each of those around me, confused by why this would be any of their business. Even before Clara, I would change whenever I needed to vent or even just take a run. I've always known that my choice in the matter is unusual. Why go through the painful shift more than one has to?

When my eyes land on Larson, it's like I can see the wheels in his mind, backpedaling.

"Is there a problem with that in this 'not a pack' pack?" I give each one of them a hard look, waiting for someone to say that there is. While I might sympathize with them to a certain degree, it's just that. I can't afford for it to be anything more. Letting my guard down so early after meeting them is not the tone I want to set.

"You willingly do that to yourself?" Javi pushes, and I can't make out why he's so intent on finding out this piece of information.

"You're either stupid or smart," the big lug on my right chortles. Leo, I think it was. "Time will tell which, I suppose."

"So what, you all just really wanted to meet me or something?" Should I be honored to be among their circle, or jumping in my truck and leaving? I can't decide. While I don't feel threatened by any of them, I've been on my own for so long that perhaps I don't know what it means anymore to be a part of something. Even if it isn't a "pack" in the way I used to use the term. Not the kind I used to be a part of.

Edgar sighs, scratching beneath his hat and behind his ear. "I told them of your troubles with your old pack. What they tried to do in taking your mate."

My jaw clenches as I'm reminded of that day. Fearing for Clara's life one minute, to ripping my cousin's neck out the next in the hopes of finding her in time before something unimaginable happened. Both Carter and Bradley met their end that day, and by my hands. I didn't like taking lives, but they forced my hand. Both of them.

"What he's trying to say," Katrina cuts in, "is we support you. We know you have no reason to trust us, but Larson trusts you and that's enough for the rest of us. Yes, we might be curious, but we understand the need to live your own life and by your own rules."

"And as long as you don't draw unnecessary attention, there won't be any problems." Leo puffs out. I swear he's trying to make his chest look bigger. It doesn't work, though. He looks...off-balance, to put it nicely.

"Look out for one another, help when needed, and don't change anymore than I have to. Sounds like rules."

"We've survived this long living the lives we want. This...this helps us do that." I swear Katrina's eyes have saddened. I don't detect anything but sincerity coming from her, and I can't help but wonder about her and her human mate now. Out of everyone, she's the one I want to talk to. I've never met another wolf who has found a human mate and I want to pick her brain about it.

But we're not there yet. I'm holding my cards close, almost like they're a second skin.

While I don't appreciate the fact that what I've spoken in confidence to Larson might have been disclosed to these people around me, I choose to bite down on that disappointment for the moment. Someday, I might be grateful that I'm not alone with my painful past that's been bleeding into the present day, but for right now? I believe I need time to think about this.

I've been running so long, and now that I'm finally rooting myself in Alton, I guess there are worse things than having a few allies. But it will take time and some trust-building before I can truly call them such.

# 9

# Penny for Your Thoughts

## *Clara*

By the time my workday is done, I'm already exhausted. I've only worked half a day and it wasn't even that busy. But the buzz of Seth's arrival and his introduction, the flowers, and the news of our being a couple sent the whole building into a tizzy. Even Dr. Neiman got in on it, congratulating me, complimenting the floral arrangement and saying that Seth had done a good job. He's surrounded by a staff of mostly women, so being able to acknowledge and create small talk on subjects such as this seems effortless for him.

On the drive home, I call my mom and let her know about the progress I made this morning. Since she found out about Seth in a less than ideal kind of way, I make it a point to call her more regularly again. Our chats had fallen by the wayside since I met him, and I know I can only blame myself. But now that she's in the know, it makes it easier to talk to her.

She reminds me to put on a brave face tonight should Seth and Joe be in attendance together. Their meetings have been brief so far, and Seth wouldn't even shake his hand when they first met. But now? Now I'll be showing Joe that Seth is still in the picture and isn't leaving. That even though the message and ultimatum he sent me were met with no response, Seth being at the game tonight, should he come, will be my answer.

I'm wound up tight. So undeniably freaked out that I'm at odds with myself over whether I really want Seth to show up or not. But Julie took a chance on inviting him to see her cheer, and I don't want his absence to possibly upset her. I can't seem to get it out of her if she really wants him there or if she was just inviting him out of kindness. I want to believe it's a good thing, especially since I wasn't met with any resistance to Seth coming over for Thanksgiving, an early Christmas, and New Year's. The occasional dinners, even.

Pulling into the garage, I leave the door open and rush inside. I have a little bit of time to change out of my work clothes, grab a quick snack, and head back out to the school. I'm halfway through dragging a cheer shirt onto my upper half when the doorbell rings.

My phone is in the kitchen, denying me the chance to see who it is. Seth has a key, unbeknownst to my kids. While I don't suspect it's him since I haven't heard a peep in a few hours, I'm still rushing to the door in the hopes that it is. That he made it in time to accompany me to the school and can talk my nerves down for me.

What I don't expect is a woman I don't recognize, in a navy peacoat and matching hat with a furry ball on top of it. Her face is contoured to show off her cheekbones and structure as she grins at me.

"Clara?" she questions with a smooth voice.

I cast her a questioning look, already dreading the amount of cold air I'm letting into the house by holding the door open. "Depends on who's asking."

Her smile deepens and she drops her gaze for a moment before her hazel eyes snap back up to mine. Blonde waves cascade down her front, almost like she belongs in some department-store catalog. Like the porch light is her spotlight or something. I don't think she has a bad angle for any camera.

"Is Seth here?" She looks over my shoulder and into the house as if searching for him, and something about how she does that rubs me the wrong way. I start inching the door closed, growing increasingly uncomfortable with this stranger popping by.

Her hand is fast to stop the door, palm flat against it in a flash. "I know he's not here. It's not a scent I could easily forget."

"Who are you and what do you want?" My voice comes out more stern than I expect it to, but I try not to let her in on that.

"You and Seth have caused quite the stir back home." She releases the door and curls her fingers as she looks at her nails like she's contemplating something. I swallow hard, fearing that she's like Seth. A wolf at my doorstep.

And here I opened my home without a single care as to who it might be. As if I didn't have a freaking cousin of Seth's snooping around not two months ago.

"My kids are expecting me," I start, but there's a small quiver in my voice this time around. "If there isn't anything else—"

"I'm staying at The Terrace in Pembrook before I head back tomorrow." She finally releases the door and crosses her arms beneath her chest. It's like her coat has been tailored to fit her. "Told the family I'm on a girls trip with friends I don't actually have."

Her humor has no effect on me. The urge to try and shut the door in her face is strong, but knowing that I failed at that once already, I fear that trying it again might be pushing my luck.

"I expect you and Seth around, shall we say...eight? It's a lengthy drive back home."

There's only one word swirling around in my head. I can't seem to think of anything else. I'm confused as hell. "Why?"

She sighs heavily, as if it should be obvious. But her lack of answers so far is only making my agitation grow.

"Who in the hell are you?" I straighten myself, evening out my feet. She takes notice, eyeing me up and down at a leisurely pace, and the look pisses me off more.

"Penny." She flashes a grin that almost looks sinister with the darkness behind her.

Holy shit.

Penelope, Penny. It's too much of a coincidence. It *has* to be her.

"Oh, so you've heard of me." She lets out a faint laugh as if she's pleased with that knowledge.

"Nothing good," I shoot back, and her face falters. A crack in that pretty facade that can change to something dangerous in a nanosecond.

"Look—" She recovers as she takes a step forward. It takes everything I have not to cower in front of her. There are only a few inches of difference between our heights, but it's her demeanor that makes me want to shrink and hide. I might know what she is, but I have no idea what she's capable of besides being a bitch who would up and leave her fiancé for something he literally had no control over. Throw away their relationship over the first bump in the road. "I'm the one doing you two a favor. Meet me at eight."

Penelope turns and begins to take her leave, and I'm too stunned to even think straight.

Favor?

What favor could she possibly have to offer us? It doesn't make any sense!

Her slender frame disappears out of view, heading back toward the garage, and only then do I shut the door and lock it in a rush.

First, the mysterious trip Seth is on with Larson. This surprise visit from an ex-fiancée, and now the basketball game where I will inevitably have to remain cool as a cucumber about everything, putting on a brave face while the past and present men in my life are under the same roof.

What in the hell has this day become?

I'm seated beside Emily, Mags' mom, trying my best to keep up with small talk here and there. Mags is on the cheer team with Julie and we're here to support the two of them without paying much attention to the game. Emily is one out of a few parents that I can actually stand to be around. She doesn't fret about looks and doesn't go all out to pretend she's the perfect mom. She also stood by me and helped smack-talk Joe after news broke out about his mistress.

We always talk about meeting up outside of school events, but never seem to be able to make that happen. I guess I'm just grateful that I don't have to sit alone at these things. I know I'm here for my kid, but it's nice not to feel isolated even in a packed gymnasium.

The screeches of shoes make my nose scrunch as the high schoolers move about the shiny gym floor. I glance at my phone to see if there's anything from Seth and to my surprise, I find that I missed a message somehow.

*Headed in now.*

While my heart wants to leap with joy that he made it, it takes a back seat. My eyes shoot across the sea of faces, down toward the front where I see Joe, Chassidy, and Emmett sitting. Joe is completely engrossed in the game while Chassidy is flipping through something on her phone that I can't make out. Emmett is playing some game with a buddy of his next to him. I can't recall his name for the life of me, and make it a point to ask next time Emmett is home.

I don't want to come off as overbearing, but I try to keep up with who my kids associate with. They aren't the most talkative bunch sometimes with their day-to-day lives, so I try to at least know who they hang out with.

Our home team scores and the crowd around me cheers. I'm a bit late, but offer a few claps as my eyes begin to flit between both points of entry on the right side of the gym. My attention is swayed when the cheerleaders begin one of their usual chants. Pom-poms with the school's colors are hitting each beat as they cheer for their team. I think I know all of their chants by heart, and I can't help but mouth them as I watch Julie.

Her hair is pulled up into a tight ponytail and she has glitter highlighting her face. She never raises her voice to anyone but her brother normally, so I still find it a bit comical that she likes to yell out loud to the masses.

I want to stand and clap when they finish—as I always want to—but resist. Nobody cheers for them like they do for the basketball team. The same goes for the little pep band stationed on a balcony to my left.

Something catches Julie's eyes and she breaks away from her line of formation with the other girls and heads to the nearest doorway.

Guess she found Seth before I could. I can't hear her, understandably, but she's enthusiastic as she greets him and then points at the incline in my direction. She offers me a quick wave of her hand and I wave back, and I know the moment Seth sees me because of the way his face lights up.

I hate to be the bearer of bad news for him tonight. I couldn't even bring myself to text him about Penelope. Something like this seems like it needs to be discussed in person. And thank God, I think our whole encounter was caught on camera. I really should thank him again for installing them.

Seth makes his way up, taking the incline easily in strides. It takes me double the footsteps on these risers. I ask Emily to scooch over a bit and I don't think anyone could miss the surprise followed by curiosity spreading over her features when she makes the connection. Seth flashes a grin as he sits and I notice that he came in without a coat.

This man.

"Hi, I'm Emily." She's eager about introducing herself and sticks out her hand. Seth takes it and gives it a brief shake as he sits beside me, brushing up against my leg.

"Emily, this is my boyfriend, Seth. This is Mags' mom."

"Ah yes, I've heard about her. Which one is she?" Seth looks over at the cheerleaders while Emily points in her direction. Mags is easy to spot, practically the shortest one and in the front row with brown hair and a plethora of freckles on her face. She hates them, but I hope her opinion of them changes someday. I think they're beautiful.

"You're holding out on me, Clara." Emily does a quick waggle of her eyebrows and I can't help but roll my eyes as Seth lets a hand rest on my knee to keep me from bouncing it. "Keeping him all to yourself."

I know she's teasing, but if only she knew the severity of it all. I just wish things would calm down and settle already. Especially with the surprise visit this evening. I hate to surmise that things are going to get worse before they get better, but that's how things are looking right about now.

Something happens on the court, enough to draw a few boos and hollers of displeasure, but I can't find it in me to care. It's like I'm in that Chinese restaurant again. Or the store where Seth and I found our new bedding. Hell, it happens every time he's out in public.

The attention he draws, the focus he pulls from others, is unsettling. I don't even understand why it's bothering me so much right now. Is it that I'm in such close proximity to them all? That I know teachers, kids, and parents are all casting glances our way and some lean in to their neighbors to whisper remarks?

Looking down at Seth's hand on my knee, I want to cover it with my own but I can't move. It's like I'm glued to my seat and my limbs are being weighed down by some unseen force.

The idea dawns on me that it might not even be someone present that's bothering me. Just the blonde beauty who showed up at my damn house. Penelope might have had her body covered in winter gear, but I know she's pretty and fit and at one time, was loved by Seth. They wanted and had planned on a life together. Coming into direct contact with someone who by looks is the exact opposite of me is sending me spiraling.

Was that the motivation for this visit? I feel stupid for not thinking about it on the drive over to the school. Seth's family couldn't take him by force. Lives were taken because of it. So is this how they're going to try and go about it? Luring him back like this? I feel like someone knocked the wind out of me and added to the aches and pains of my unrelenting cramps.

A frustrated exhale leaves me as I think back to how I failed to find the damn pill bottle at the house so I could try and get some relief.

"Everything alright?" Seth leans in, close enough that I can smell that he's been outdoors among pine trees or something. He smells kind of...earthy?

"Not really," I release on a low breath, not meeting his eyes and fixing my concentration on the cheer team once more as they start a new chant. Seth squeezes my knee and I swear, it's like I can feel both of our composures slipping.

While I want to be focused on Julie, I feel as if I'm seeing but not comprehending anything happening. I want to find out about Seth's day with Larson and why the secrecy, but I'm so fixated on his ex and everything else that I can't get my head on straight.

I don't know why I do it, but next thing I know my vision lands on Joe and we lock eyes. He sits there shaking his head in disapproval, making sure I see it before he turns to face forward. And I didn't think I could feel any lower than I already was.

I want nothing more than for this day to end. To wrap up in my bedding and curl up into a ball and sleep. It might be the only chance for an escape.

# 10

# She Comes First

## *Seth*

The drive back to Clara's house takes too long. It reminds me of how often I apparently like to speed, considering she's been steady on her cruise control the whole drive back. I'm probably riding too close to her rear end, but it still doesn't feel close enough to her. Not until I'm physically touching her will I be satisfied.

I can't fight the smirk as I reflect on my devious reason for being a little later to the game than I'd planned. But when I saw Joe's truck, I couldn't hold back. Knowing that both Julie and Emmett aren't going back to their dad's place tonight, but instead staying at friends' houses, I might have casually tripped and punctured one of his tires with a screw. I set it up so that when he backs out of his parking space, he'll have no choice but to unknowingly drive it in further. It's a bit childish, sure, but I'm not going to lie and say that it didn't make me feel a little bit better.

The corner he's pushing Clara into isn't acceptable. Like he has room to threaten and criticize my mate. He isn't setting a good example for anyone around him, and I fail to see how the kids living with him full time would be beneficial to either child.

My thoughts then sway to the earlier encounter I had with the strays who've banded together. Our visit was brief, and that's how they like to keep it. They don't meet on any set schedule and they don't hang out and go to bars or shit. I'm still at odds with myself over the whole situation, and Larson still wouldn't talk much on the whole drive home. It finally resulted in me turning on the radio in the hopes that time would pass faster.

I did find out that Leo's mate had stayed home with their adopted children but sent two crock pots full of pot roast, baby carrots, and potatoes to feed everyone today. It was just as delicious as it'd smelled from outside of the cabin.

My Rose pops out of her car the moment she parks it. The action is so quick, I half wonder if she's even had a chance to turn off the vehicle. But the cut of her exhaust pipe tells me that she did. Her arms are crossed and she has this perturbed look on her face that has me leaping from my truck and ready to dive into whatever is bothering her.

Did Joe say something? Did he *do* something else before I arrived at the school? Fuck, I know four tires might have been overkill and would definitely be seen as intentional but maybe I should have done it.

Then it hits me.

It completely stalls me in my pursuit to get closer to Clara and my head swivels around as if I can find the one responsible for that faint smell. My past just can't keep quiet and refuses to stay away.

It can't be.

"She's not here." Clara spins on her foot and heads out of the garage, barely giving me enough clearance before hitting the button for the large door. "At least, she shouldn't be."

Does she know? Did she meet her?

I'm hot on her heels, so close that her vanilla scent is filling me completely and screwing with my senses as I look both ways through the breezeway to ensure that no one is about to come up on us.

"Penelope wants us to meet her at The Terrace tomorrow at eight." Her statement, as she kicks off her shoes and hauls her purse onto the kitchen counter, throws me for a loop.

"What happened?" I'm brushing past her and checking the house even though I can't make out much of a scent in here. Clara's is too powerful, too intoxicating throughout, and there is no undercurrent of anything else.

Whipping out my phone, I pull up the camera feed.

"How many wolves from your past are going to show up out of the blue at my doorstep? For Christ's sake, what if the kids had been home?" She's not quite shouting at me, but she's angered and understandably so.

My mom had a plan to get me to come back and rejoin the pack. To marry Penelope and raise her children as if that might persuade me to leave Alton behind. I won't pretend to know why my ex's husband wasn't going to be in the picture much longer; I hadn't cared enough to even ask.

"Did she say what she wanted?" I urge her to continue, placing myself at her side as she braces herself on the island. Her yellow and black cheer shirt is one that I haven't seen before, and I've been through her closet more times than I can count. She's pissed, and it's directed right at me as she speaks.

"A favor. For us." She lets out an odd grunt. It's strange and forced coming from her. She's out of sorts, her head slowly turning side to side as she leans forward, pressing the counter into her lower stomach. It looks uncomfortable. "Can you believe that? What the fuck kind of favor would your ex-fiancée have to offer?"

"I can assure you, I have no idea," I clarify, careful to tread lightly around her. Damn, are the deaths of three not enough to get my family to take a hike? "But I intend to find out."

"No!" Clara erupts from behind me just as my hand reaches the doorknob. I go still, trying to let the air between us settle before I turn to meet her.

When I do, there's color rising to her face. Her lips are pressed thin and her heartbeat is picking up the pace, but with a steady and strong beat. She looks fierce, even.

I'm ashamed to say that it's a huge fucking turn-on, and I divert my gaze, trying to think of something else.

"What do you want me to do, Clara?" I put the proverbial ball in her court to see which way she wants to take this. If she tells me to stay, I will do so. If she wants me to call in the cavalry—that she has no knowledge about yet—and enlist the band of outcasts I'm now in touch with to put a stop to things, I will.

I wish I could get a first-class seat to witness what she's thinking about. If she's arguing with herself or merely trying to dwindle my question down to a singular response. Clara doesn't have that many wants and needs, but right now? Right now I need to know how I can help her.

"I want you to stay," she states, then takes a beat before turning and heading toward the cabinet where she keeps a mini grocery store's stock of products for numerous ailments. Bottles come crashing out and she starts to mutter curses as she rummages through it in search of something. Just as I come up behind her, she finds what she's looking for and pops off the cap to dispense two pills into her hand.

"Is something wrong?" I observe as she leaves the mess and proceeds to go to the fridge and pull out a reusable water bottle to wash them down.

"What's *not* wrong?" She shakes her head as she returns the drink and turns again to face me. "My ex is using you as an excuse to take my kids. You're off on some secret mission with Larson to God knows where. Your ex-fiancée is showing up at my house. My cramps are threatening to take me to the ground, and I just want cookie dough and blankets and sleep. I just want to fucking sleep and for trouble to stop finding me. Is that so much to ask?"

Clara throws her hands up, her frustration melting away the fire that was once in her eyes, giving way to everything that's weighing heavily on her. I don't even think, just move, closing in around her in a gentle embrace. She's rigid at first, but a few long seconds in, she's drawing her arms up and around my waist.

"I'm sorry," she mutters against me, and I'm quick to shush her.

"None of that. I always want you to speak your mind and let me in. I can't help if I'm in the dark." Her breathing starts to slow and I rest my chin on top of her head as I let my hand draw circles on her shoulder. She begins to relax into me, heart slowing, and the tension in her body begins to leave.

"First things first," I start, making sure I have her undivided attention before I continue. Clara looks up with those beautiful, sad brown eyes and I lose my train of thought for a second before I speak. "Orgasms can help with cramps."

She rolls her eyes and tries to release me, but I don't loosen my hold and she's forced to stay. "Do I even want to know how you know that? Better yet, don't answer that."

I chuckle lightly. "How about you go take a shower. Try to relax. Hm?"

She sighs. "I haven't even heard about your day yet."

"We have time. Let's just focus on you right now." I offer her a light smile and kiss the top of her head, then reluctantly release her.

Shoulders caving forward a bit, she takes her leave and heads out of the kitchen.

I stand silent and still for a few minutes. I want to chase after her and at the same time, give her a little space. She's obviously stressed and a lot of it is because of me. Actually, a large chunk of what she just spouted out is my fault in one way or another.

I'm confused as fuck about Penelope coming here and approaching Clara. She could've easily found me and yet she picked my mate as a target. While I hated offing my cousins, especially Carter, knowing he had a family of his own, the thought of doing the same to Penelope if she becomes a threat is unsettling. There's a chance that her children would become orphans, and I don't wish that on anyone.

But surely she's smart enough to know what she's risking by coming here, right?

The shower kicks on and my thoughts take another turn. I'm sauntering off toward the bedroom and the house falls into darkness as I turn off the under-cabinet lighting in the kitchen. Pulling clothes off as I go, I strip down to my underwear and deposit my clothes in the hamper in the bedroom.

I lean back onto the bed, sprawling myself out as I listen to the waterfall from the shower. The door is open a crack, and I can hear little splashes here and there from her doing her hair and wringing it out. My cock is hardening while I imagine her loofa roaming across her slick body, the suds from the soap coating her skin and filling the air with a luscious scent that has no right to smell so perfect it's almost sinful.

Something starts buzzing and my head perks up at the sound, as if I can see through walls and into that room. My dick twitches, recognizing the sound, and I groan to myself.

I'm well aware that I pretty much put it in her head to have an orgasm, but the thought of her doing it herself when I'm right here is messing with my capability of giving her space.

I want to give that to her. I want to be her relief from the cramps she's suffering from. Perhaps I didn't make myself clear enough.

Moving as quietly as I can manage, I prowl like a predator stalking its prey. Removing my last remaining article of clothing, I open the door and then return it to its original state. The exhaust fan might be on, but there's still heat swirling around in here from the temperature of the water. She's always been a fan of hot showers.

Clara lets out a small whine of pleasure and I let my eyes close. I play with the idea of listening to her get herself off, but I know I'm weak and I won't be able to do that. Not when I want to be responsible for the moans and breathy pants that come from her throat. I want her so enraptured that she forgets about any ailments her body and mind might have.

I stroke my cock as I step closer. My hand is lingering on the shower door handle, desperate to see the state she's in and ready to take over.

"Oh," she whines, and I suppress the urge to groan. I can tell she's trying to be quiet. To not alert me that she has taken matters into her own hands.

With the full moon tomorrow night, I won't be able to be here. At least, not inside the house anyway. I'd better make tonight count and take care of her while I still can.

I slide the glass door open, revealing my curvaceous Clara slumped against the wall with her back facing me. One hand is bracing herself against the wall at her front while the other must be holding the toy against her clit. She's completely unaware that I'm here, so lost in thought as her hips move to meet the vibrations of whatever toy she's chosen.

It's not until the door closes that she jumps, heart rate skyrocketing as she turns to face me, eyes wide, frantic, and...fearful?

She backs into a corner, fumbling with the dark toy to turn it off, and attempts to try and cover herself. Her skin looks so beautiful in here, even as she tries to hide. Her creamy color is a bright contrast to the ocean-blue tiles that surround her and stretch toward the ceiling.

"Wh...what are you doing?" She pants as if she's embarrassed, but I can't tell why. It's been a challenge, but Clara has slowly been growing more comfortable around me, especially in her naked form. Maybe not in the light of day, but at night, she's been more daring in showing herself.

The water is almost scalding as I step into the stream of it, closing in. "You didn't think I meant for you to take care of this orgasm on your own, did you?"

She stares at me, bottom lip falling as if in shock before she snaps it closed and diverts her gaze. "If I wasn't clear out there with my little meltdown, I'm on my period."

I study her, recognizing that her voice has dropped and it's letting me in on why I was met with such conflicting emotions upon my entrance.

"Is that supposed to steer me away?" I ask as tenderly as I can even though my cock is throbbing unfavorably.

Clara blinks, as if she's struggling to get the words in her head out of her mouth. "That...that doesn't bother you?"

There's no hesitation as I shake my head in denial.

"It doesn't gross you out?" she pushes, and I shake my head again, stepping away from the stream as I close in. Her breath catches, freezing as she stares up at me.

"Does it bother you?" I breathe next to her ear as I tip her head up. "That I want you even now? That I want to make you feel better in any way I can?"

My hand drifts down between us and I remove the toy from her grasp. She's used it before, so it doesn't take me long to find the little button that brings it to life. The vibrations soon mingle with the sound of the falling water and I return it to her clit to attempt to get her to calm down. It's like she's crawled back into her shell and I need to coax her out of it.

I've seen enough shit in my life, washed remnants of lives lost from my own body, that a little blood from her doesn't disturb me in the slightest. While she might be hurting, she's not injured or washing someone else's blood away.

"Turn around, Clara," I tell her, and place her hand over the toy so she can keep the pressure on her clit.

"But—"

"Clara." Repeating her name, I urge her to continue. If she's truly troubled by this, I know she'll tell me to stop. If she does, I'll leave her to finish things on her own. A part of me knows she won't, though. I don't quite understand her apprehension in this, but she's not pushing me away so I stay the course.

I nudge her shoulder, and she flashes me a concerned look before turning. I use my foot to lightly knock at her ankles, signaling for her to spread her legs. My hands are roaming her body, savoring every touch as if I haven't memorized every inch of her plump and mouthwatering figure already.

My cock, as if it has a mind of its own, nestles itself between her thighs, and the ease with which it does so has my eyes rolling back in my head. I'm ready to bury myself balls deep as I listen to Clara struggle against the toy that has a hold on her.

"Seth," she says as if she's in pain. I lower myself, trying to line up to take her. "I'm close."

Her voice soars on a high note as I slide into her.

Fuck.

She's tight. Wound up like she's been tied up and bound and...shit. If that image doesn't ignite something dark and wild inside of me.

Clara is already spasming around me, squeezing me as if she's fucking strangling my dick, and my head kicks back as I hold on to her hips to steady her. Her voice is amplified by the shower walls and hitting me from all angles, consuming me with her release.

The buzzing shuts off and the toy drops to the ground and bounces once before coming to a stop. I give Clara a moment to come back to me, to find her bearings before I move. But damn, she's giving my cock a workout through her orgasm and my balls are tightening. Pretty sure if we used that little toy again, her movements alone would bring me to the brink.

Both of her hands are flat against the wall now, and I draw my hips back and push forward. She's tense, shaking before me, and I run my hands up and down her sides to soothe her.

My legs stretch with each mellow thrust; my thighs move and hands accommodate her in any way I can. I follow her cues, adjusting here and caressing there. Clara probably has no idea just how her body sings for me and begs for my touch. There's no hurry or rush, not tonight.

I savor each and every whimper and whine that leaves her lips. I only wish there was a mirror in front of her face so I could fully appreciate her pleasure. But there's something about hearing and feeling, taking away the sense of sight, that has my spine stiffening, alerting me to the build within me.

My hand drifts over her stomach and down until I reach her clit. She moans at the first swirl, the little sensitized bud bringing her further up the hill that I want her on.

I can't determine if I'm sweating or if the heat from the shower is simply coating me, but I'm drenched. Deliriously drunk on the connection between us and the need to feel her come on me again.

The thought occurs that Clara had better feel good after this. I don't want to make a liar out of myself if she still suffers from her cramps in the aftermath of this, or worse—that her plight might be aggravated by sex.

Grunting as if the sound might stave off my climax, I lean down and toward her ear. "Come for me, beautiful. Give me one more."

She shudders at my words, shoulders shaking and body quivering as if my breath just let out a rush of cold air all over her.

Fingers circling faster, I grit my teeth as if it might help me hold off just a little bit longer. I pull at her ass, as if it might give me a little more room to dive in deeper, and it must do the trick.

It sets her off, her scream of ecstasy filling the air and setting off an explosion of my own to meet it. I'm rendered useless, temporarily paralyzed while she rides out her orgasm on my cock and my vision threatens to blacken.

It's almost too much. The constrictions are so tight in her channel that I have no other choice but to pull out. I hate to do it, but I have to. I have nothing left to give, nothing left to pump into her and yet her body still demands more.

My head falls into the crook of her neck as I struggle to bring my fucking soul back into my body.

# 11

# Friend or Foe?

## *Clara*

I'm tense and on edge. No, scratch that. I'm freaking the fuck out over this meeting with Seth's gorgeous ex-fiancée.

We're on the outskirts of Pembrook and approaching The Terrace. The hotel is the perfect place for people just passing by or those who might want to hide away from the hustle and bustle of the town. It's close enough to enjoy all that Pembrook has to offer, but far enough out to remain quiet and quaint.

The large five-story building isn't anything fancy by any means. No historic value or special meaning behind it, like some you might find in the heart of the town. Its brown and beige hues almost make it look dirty in comparison with the snow that's surrounding it.

I shift in my seat as I note the time on Seth's truck. He gives my knee a reassuring squeeze and I muster up a lousy and forced smile before returning my gaze out my window.

My thoughts take me back to last night and I let my eyes drift closed. How Seth handled me in the shower, from the sex to the washing of my hair and so on. How he carried me to bed and brought me cookie dough from the fridge to snack on.

The fact that he wasn't deterred by my period, that it didn't bother him in the slightest, was an odd occurrence that I hadn't expected. Joe had been so turned off by my menstrual cycle. And the one time we tried doing it during that phase, let's just say, it didn't go well. I hadn't even realized the scar it had left on me and my mentality about period sex.

"There's nothing dirty about it," Seth confessed to me in bed. "It's natural what your body goes through. Why would I punish you for that?"

When I think about that darkness mixing with the water at our feet, I can't help but cringe. I'm still embarrassed, even if Seth showed zero signs of it bothering him. Something that once was so private is now of no worry or care to this new man in my life. It's going to take time to get used to.

Be it the sex, the pills I took, or the combination of the two, I can't deny that I felt better afterward. My body might have wanted to turn to jelly, but my cramps eased significantly.

The cookie dough and cuddles didn't hurt either.

"Hey." Seth pulls me away from my thoughts and I come tumbling back into the present. He parks the truck and takes my hand in his, giving it a squeeze. "Remember to try and stay calm."

An unflattering snort of a response comes out and it's so quick there's nothing I can do to stifle it. "Right."

"Penelope could have pulled something last night and she didn't. She's chosen a public place like this so a repeat of November doesn't seem likely, but we can't be entirely sure."

"Is it going to be weird?" I drop my gaze to the floorboard. "Seeing her again?" Seth observed the video with her more than once. The short conversation we had and her leaving just as fast as she'd arrived, like she was on a mission from the start. Seeing her in person has already messed with my head. We couldn't be more different in the way we hold ourselves, the confidence or lack thereof with which we speak, and obviously, our appearances.

She's probably a Pinterest-rocking picture-perfect mom.

"Clara." Seth pulls me out of my self-doubt and inner turmoil with the turn of my chin. "The life we're creating together is the only thing that matters to me now. Protecting it. Keeping it safe. I won't let her jeopardize that."

I swallow hard. His gold eyes are bright with the early morning sun, even behind my sunglasses. He hasn't been his normal and playful self this morning, but I'm sure that seeing the ex who dumped you over a decade ago might ruin your mood to begin with. Especially when she shows up unannounced after your mother had plans to bring you two together again when your cousins failed to haul you back home.

Wow. That's really fucked up when you look at it that way.

"I love you," I breathe out quickly, as if I need to solidify that fact one last time before this visit. I'm scared that even though Seth claims that he's mine and vice versa, there might be something to spark between him and the woman he once loved. Has he really, truly moved on? Is that door permanently closed? Bolted and welded shut to never reopen again?

"I love *you*, Clara." He kisses the back of my hand before grabbing my gloves from the cupholder I stashed them in. "No matter what, stay by my side. You don't leave or go anywhere without me. Not even the bathroom."

I raise a brow. "Do you really think they'd try to kidnap me again or something?"

It sounds absurd the moment I say it. Of course they would. They were going to kill me. One of his cousins was stalking my house in an attempt to find me, and if it hadn't been for the new cameras Seth had installed, they might have been successful. I would have unknowingly served myself up on a silver platter for the taking.

I shove down the thoughts of how dangerous this is. How I'm risking so much to be with this man who makes my heart skip on the regular and other times, beat faster. The only person who truly sees me when I'm down in the dumps and doesn't turn a blind eye when my overwhelming emotions get the best of me.

You'd think that his werewolf business would be enough to scare me the hell off. Something has to be wrong with me in the head.

"Stuck on you like glue," I blurt, offering a strained smile.

Seth just grins. "If that's what it takes."

We exit his truck and the cold hits me hard. Seth takes my hand and leads me to the front doors and we enter. They slide open automatically to reveal a lobby with people passing by toward an area on my right where the smells of a continental breakfast are flooding the air. Coffee is the most prominent aroma, but it's the undertones of bacon that beg for my attention. There are the sounds of utensils clanking and a few children squabbling, but it all fades away when we come to a halt.

Up ahead and on the left is Penelope. She's leaned up against a wall in a hallway with signage that directs to conference rooms. She's expressionless, just standing there in a long-sleeve tee and vest. Jeans are tucked into her boots and her arms are crossed, hair in perfect waves again but without the hat she was wearing yesterday. She's even more slender than I imagined.

Penelope pivots and takes off down the hall, and we follow after her at a distance. My grip tightens on Seth's as we travel away from the growing ruckus in the breakfast area. No one stops us. Nobody even bats an eye at our passing. There are two people at the front desk, but they're fully engrossed in whatever business is going on with the patrons at their counters.

We approach a door that she disappeared through, and Seth enters first, placing me behind him for a moment. She's already waiting for us on the opposite side of a table that's large enough to fit a dozen people. There's a giant whiteboard on the far wall and a small stand with a coffee maker but other than that, it's pretty plain.

Seth closes the door with a kick of his foot, never letting his eyes leave the woman who has lured us back here without having uttered a single word.

"What do you want, Penelope?" His voice drips with disdain and the seriousness of it has me holding my breath.

Guess we're getting right down to it then. It doesn't escape me that I'm confined to a room with two werewolves. Should I be alarmed by that fact? Maybe, but I'm not. Seth has only lost control once, and that was after getting off of the phone with his mother. Hopefully this encounter goes nothing like that.

"You look good, Seth."

I can feel my lips tighten as she looks him over. Jealousy sparks, sending my mind on a road that it really shouldn't go down right now.

Seth loved her enough to marry her.

I can't help but wonder how long they'd been together. The future they'd imagined and how far they would've gotten if Seth had been able to have children. Then I remember how shallow and heartless she was to throw him away for something like that. For not being able to have children of his own.

"You'd better have a good reason for being here." Seth is solid as stone beside me. I can't even make out if he's breathing or not. His mood, however, is one that doesn't come out much.

I didn't think he would meet her again after all this time and hug it out, but this distance he's keeping—I like it.

"Why haven't you marked her yet?" Penelope takes a step and places her hands on the chair before her, gripping it. She's holding his gaze as if I'm not even here. It doesn't stop me from turning my head back and forth between the two of them.

What was it Seth said? Bite to mark, scratch to turn? I've gained bits and pieces of knowledge about his werewolf side as I grow more comfortable to ask.

To become a werewolf, you have to be scratched on the night of a full moon, but severe enough to be life-threatening. To mark a mate, you have to be bitten. I remember it sounding a bit backward, and I have a hard time comprehending that anything sharp that comes from a werewolf and forms a mark of any sort wouldn't be detrimental.

Were I a wolf myself, we would've marked each other already, according to Seth. I guess once you find your mate, you solidify that with a bite as soon as you can. Seth sheepishly admitted that that was a major part of the reason he showed up at my house after our first date. He didn't know how to walk away from me, let alone how to act around me. He had to claim me in any way he thought he could, without hurting me or scaring me off. He wasn't wrong, though. I much prefer his dick instead of a fucking bite mark. If he had bitten me right off the bat, pretty sure I would have died of a heart attack.

"It's none of your concern," he gruffs out, heated.

Penelope shakes her head. "It *is* my concern when your fucking mother is still trying to set us up!"

Woah, what? Does she not want that either? I'm so confused.

"Alice has it in her head that you're not serious. You haven't claimed your mate and it's because she's a human. She's not good enough for you." I swear I can feel heat radiating off of Seth as she adds, "Her words, I swear."

Penelope looks pissed. There's no smirk on her face, nothing giving any indication that she's two-timing us, but then again, I only met this woman yesterday. I know nothing about her.

"You mean to tell me that you have nothing to do with this scheme to get me to marry you, rejoin the pack, and raise your children?" Seth says belligerently.

"Ha!" Penelope responds with a choked laugh. "Hell no! Sorry, but I hate your parents. The last thing I want right now is them as in-laws." She pulls out the rolling chair she's been grasping and sits down, propping her feet up on the table.

"Then what's this trouble that your husband got into? I thought he was out of the picture?" Seth's anger hasn't faltered; he's still fuming and I feel like he's moments away from hauling a chair across the room. I don't know if there's anything I can do to bring him back down, but I squeeze his hand anyway.

His head snaps in my direction, catching me off guard. Golden circles blaze into mine for a moment before they soften. I understand that he's being protective. That this entire encounter is trying him and most likely fraying his nerves. But we might have a bumpy road ahead of us before things get resolved.

"Warren has an infatuation with underage girls. He's being dealt with while I'm away." Her face becomes cold. A sneer lifts her features, and I know I'm doing nothing to hide the shock and disgust on my face at hearing her acknowledge something so damning out loud. "He's lucky I didn't kill him in his sleep, but we've been living apart for months."

Are all werewolves this bloodthirsty? Then again, I can't imagine if I'd found out something like that about Joe. It was bad enough that he left me for Chassidy to begin with. But not knowing the extent of this infatuation with younger women during our marriage is disturbing. Was there anyone else before Chassidy?

"So what, you'll raise your kids on your own? The pack is *okay* with you doing that?" Seth sounds accusatory, but some of the venom in his voice is backing off. He lets go of my hand for a moment, shrugs out of his light jacket and throws it onto the table before scooping my hand up again. I use that time to rid myself of my gloves. I barely get them shoved into my coat pockets before he takes hold of me again.

Penelope lets out an annoyed, short laugh. "Definitely not. But I've practically been raising my kids on my own already. I don't need him. He was a shitty dad and an even shittier husband."

I recognize how she's already referring to him in the past tense, and it rubs me the wrong way. Did this Warren really mean so little to her? To their children? Geez, is he already dead as we're speaking about this?

Witnessing this confrontation is already taxing. Initially, I thought she was here for Seth. To try and convince him to come back with her. But she's not doing that. There are no guilt trips or reminiscing of their past together. I can't detect any desire for her to go along with the plan Alice cooked up.

"Would that be enough?" I find my voice enough to speak up, and only then do I garner Penelope's attention. I face her head-on, leaning onto the table with my free hand. "Would marking me get Alice to back off?"

I feel Seth's gaze on me, but I hold Penelope's. She's intimidating, but I try to hold steady. I'm tired of pretending that I'm not here when she brought up this whole marking business to begin with.

"I can't say for certain." She's the first to break eye contact and I feel like I can breathe a little deeper. "Alice is playing her own game, but she's using that as a bargaining chip since Mike is dying. She's desperate to keep her pull within the pack. Seth, if your dad dies and you're nowhere around, she's fucked.

"Alice needs to know that Clara is more than just a plaything. Screwing around and filling her up isn't going to be enough to tell her that you're committed." Penelope's hardened stare slides to Seth. "You know that."

It's like there's something hanging in the air between them. Something that I'm missing, and my eyes flit to each of them. I don't want to sound like I'm completely in the dark when I'm still learning about this other side of Seth, but I thought we were in agreement that this marking thing wouldn't have to happen. Or I guess, it was more my call that I didn't want to be bitten, scratched, or anything while he was in his wolf form. I have kids to worry about.

"How is Alice going to know? Is she sending others to stalk and check up on us?" I hate to ask, but I can't help myself. It's not like she's been back to my work and visiting under false pretenses. I would know.

The room falls silent and no one speaks. It picks on my nerves one at a time and I don't know how much longer I can take it.

"Well?" I push, looking between the two of them.

"It's you," Seth states. I swear he's shooting daggers at Penelope as his chin tips down. "The job has fallen on you now."

Penelope tilts her head, not doing anything to argue with Seth and his accusation. "They tried to get me to come first, thinking you would drop everything and come back. Lord forbid I wanted to stay home because my eldest was in the middle of football season. That's when Carter got drafted to come up here."

Seth shakes his head, as if in disbelief. "Like either of you could have convinced me."

"I think Carter rather enjoyed getting to skip out on his fatherly duties. He was sneaking around with Tammy—news flash, not his wife—behind the scenes. He was stupid enough for one of my kids to catch him." She scoffs before continuing, "He was so lazy, I'm shocked he even wanted anything to do with bringing you back."

I feel like we're veering off topic from the thing that seems to be the holdup in all of this. I don't care about this cheating cousin of Seth's, just how we can keep his family off of our backs. Once and for all.

"If Seth marks me, will your word be enough for them to believe it or will they send someone else?"

Penelope cocks a brow at me before a smirk crosses her perfectly shaped lips. "You're catching on quick." She leans forward, elbows on the table, and balances her chin atop her knuckles. I catch that there's no ring on her finger. I guess she really was ready to cut ties with her husband after all. "With news of a marking, I'm sure someone will follow up for confirmation."

Seth grunts beside me. "Clara—"

"Stop." I hold up my hand in his direction. "They've wanted to kill me before. What's to keep them from doing so? From coming after my kids?"

Penelope pauses for a moment, dropping her gaze. "I heard you had children of your own." There's a flash of movement from her in Seth's direction, and I can't tell if it's pity for Seth or maybe she's still holding it against him that he can't produce children of his own.

So help me, if she utters one fucking word about that, werewolf or not, I will haul myself across the room and attempt to strangle the bitch for hurting him. Well, as long as she doesn't try to wolf out on me.

Damn. Do I hate her more than Chassidy, or are they on a level playing field at this point?

"I've never heard anyone talk about going after them. Now that's not to say they haven't considered it, but just from the information I've come to know myself, I don't think they would lay a hand on them."

As much as I want to be comforted by Penelope and her questionable honesty, I'm not. I have no reason to trust her and her words do nothing to dampen my concerns. I knew that being with Seth would have its challenges, but this? The chance of putting Julie and Emmett in danger is growing to new and distressing heights.

It's bad enough that Joe wants to take them from me, but what if these wolves try to use my kids as some sort of bargaining chip or something? They could use them to get to me, to get to Seth.

Oh my god. Are my kids better off with Joe than me? What the hell have I let myself get into?

My palms are growing sweaty. In fact, it feels like the heat has kicked on and I'm suffocating. I can't take in enough air and my chest hurts. This head of mine is acting like it's too heavy for my body and I can't seem to keep it upright.

"Clara." Seth is at my side, trying to steady me.

"What…" I shake my head as my eyes start to burn. "What in the hell is wrong with you people?"

I look at Penelope not with hate, but disappointment and confusion. Her hands fall away and she sits up straight. I don't know if I expect her to retaliate or what, but she just sits there with a blank expression.

Seth is trying to move his hand in calming circles at my back, and my head hangs down. Clenching my eyes, I try to think about all the good that has come since Seth came into my life, but right now? All I can seem to think about is the negatives.

Finding out about werewolves, for starters. That they are very much real. Seth is one and guess what? There are a lot more. I've been stalked, hunted, and I've been a damn target. Hell, I've witnessed a fucking murder!

"It's no wonder Seth wants nothing to do with this so-called family," I mutter. My voice doesn't even sound like me, and it feels distant. I just drop it lower, almost a whisper as it's geared toward Seth. "They're never going to stop, are they?"

If this is what it feels like to be backed into a corner, I want nothing to do with it. But what choice do I have? While I don't want to lose Seth, I fear that not even giving him up would satisfy his family. Honest to God, I don't know what it's going to take to get them to leave me, leave *us*, alone. Even if Seth were out of the picture, they would probably still come after me to hurt him.

Penelope's chair rolls as she stands. We're barely into the morning and I'm already exhausted. Mentally, physically, and any other way I could possibly be wiped out.

I guess it was pretty dumb of me to believe that I could have it all. A life with Seth, my kids in the picture. A second chance at a stupid happily ever after. I thought it was within reach and that I could have that for myself. No, it wasn't perfect. Definitely not how I might have imagined it, but it was a future I hoped to expand on and explore.

"I know I might not be believed," Penelope starts, and it's the softest I've heard her tone since meeting her. "But I'll tell them that you've marked her. I can't guarantee anything, but it's a start."

Seth pauses his ministrations on my back. "You'd do that?" The question causes a lull in the conversation before he speaks up again. "You would be risking too much. Lying about something like that."

"Yeah, well, I guess I owe you."

The fog in my head lifts enough that I can look at her again. Is this her olive branch? Some weird way to apologize for screwing him over all those years ago? Unless there's something else that I'm missing. I don't know enough about their history.

"She won't have to lie if it's the truth." I look up at Seth who for once looks completely dumbfounded, and he does absolutely nothing to cover it up.

"Look, I won't pretend to know everything there is about these stupid pack rules, but from one mother to another, I would never, *never* dream about putting your life or the lives of your kids in jeopardy. Not even after how you treated Seth." I inhale deeply for what feels like the first time in too long. "They're killing your husband for God's sake. What's to stop them from doing it to you when you do something they don't like?"

Penelope's jaw slackens, eyes wide before recovering but not fast enough to go unnoticed. It's like she's never thought about the tables turning on her, and it reads across her face.

*Take that dose of reality and think about it on your travels back home, Penny.*

"I'm ready to go now," I say in Seth's direction, gathering enough energy to move. I take one last look at Penelope, hoping that this visit is the last time I ever see her.

It's because of her and her cruelty all those years ago that Seth is in my life now. And as much as this unknown future with him scares the shit out of me, I'll give her that miniscule bit of credit for helping shift him in my direction. It might have taken some time, but he's here now and I need to do whatever I can in this fragile and human body of mine to keep him here.

I can't bring myself to look at her again, but I grab my coat and offer a small farewell. "Thanks for the favor. You'd better get back home before the full moon tonight."

# 12

# Treading Lightly

## *Seth*

Today has been weird as shit. Coming in contact with my ex-fiancée and having her in the same room as my mate is a terrible mindfuck.

I hadn't known what to expect when I came face-to-face with Penny after all these years, if any residual feelings might resurface, but they didn't. In fact, I was just as pissed at her in that conference room as I was while watching the video of her and Clara talking on replay last night.

It's strange to me that Penelope seems to have no care that her husband is being executed while she's away. That she harbors no feelings of sadness or guilt for losing the man that she jumped to and married after she'd shoved me out of the picture without looking back. It also makes me wonder just how deep of a grave Warren dug for himself.

I hope that whoever is killing him makes him suffer first before it's lights out.

After leaving the hotel, Clara and I made a stop at a local coffee shop for breakfast, but ended up taking it back to Alton instead of dining in. I made a quick visit to my place to gather some work stuff and clothes before we headed back to Clara's home.

I tried more than once to talk to her about the little meeting this morning, but she just kept giving me the cold shoulder.

Clara's now napping on the couch, and has been for the last few hours while I tried to work in my temporary setup in the office. She kept the blinds and curtains closed in the living room, curling up with her blanket and her back turned so she could bury her face. She wouldn't talk to me about Penelope, marking her, or anything discussed in that conference room this morning. Just nibbled at her breakfast, drank her coffee, and lay down.

I don't know if she's just trying to digest and wait for the right moment to talk things through, but I'm trying desperately not to push her too hard. If that panic attack she had was any indication of how overwhelmed she was, I don't want to drive her into another one.

I'm sure her period is giving her a hard time too, considering it's vastly different from her cycle last month. Throw my shit on top of that, and maybe I deserve the silent treatment.

I'm trying to concentrate on work, and this new project we're getting ready to kick off is a monumental task. It's like I'm stuck on one tab when there are a few dozen open, waiting for me to get back to them. My boss usually frowns when I work on the weekends, but with the unexpected time I took off yesterday due to that meeting out in the middle of nowhere, I'm now falling behind.

Speaking of...

Quietly, I move out of the office, and as I detect Clara's faint, slow and steady breathing, I make my way out through the kitchen and back door. It's super bright out today. One of those "looks can be deceiving" days where the sun is out but it's still bitingly cold. I know Clara keeps harping on me to get a thicker coat, and in the back of my mind, I know I should. I think I'm just enjoying being stubborn about it right now. It's a little cute how worked up she gets about it.

I dial Larson, and he picks up just before I think I'm going to head to voicemail.

"Hello?"

I can imagine he looks just as baffled as he sounds. I don't necessarily call him that much.

"How exactly does this network work? Am I supposed to let you all know that there's been another wolf in the area? One from my old pack even?"

There's a long pause and for a moment, I'm wondering if I've made a mistake. I thought we were supposed to keep each other up to speed on this kind of shit.

"That's exactly what yer supposed to do. What in the hell's goin' on now?"

I fill him in as best as I can, keeping my voice low. I stare off into the naked trees, knowing that I'll be staying out here tonight like it's my equivalent of a doghouse. The very one that Clara refers to on occasion. If she doesn't talk to me soon, it's sure going to feel like it.

"Hate to say it," Larson begins, and I visualize him pulling a cigarette out from between his lips before he continues, "but it is kinda strange that ya haven't marked her yet."

"But she's a human. She's still trying to come to terms with what I am. It's her choice."

"I understand that, but by *not* marking her, yer putting her in danger. If she bears yer mark, any wolf that crosses her will know she's spoken for."

Reflecting on the encounter with the other wolves yesterday and the briefs on their own troubles in their lives, I shake my head. Not even me marking her is good enough for some packs. I'd always thought the mate bond was so sacred. The one thing that couldn't be messed with. Until yesterday, that is.

"What about Katrina and Javi? Their mate bonds didn't seem to hold any importance to their packs. Am I foolish to believe that mine with Clara might be anything different?"

Larson sighs, and his reluctance to answer is growing tiresome. I swear if he's finishing his cigarette before responding, I'll drive myself over there and pry it from his fingers so we can finish this damn conversation.

"Seth—" Another pause. "I think ya know by now that each pack operates differently. What rules are upheld to one, may be but a weak guideline to others. In most cases, it seems the mark is enough. But I can't promise ya everything will turn out alright if ya do or if ya don't."

Well, this phone call has been a lot of help.

"Clara's a smart woman. Talk to 'er. In the meantime, I'll give the crew an update."

"Crew?" Is that seriously what we're calling our little band of misfit werewolves?

"Crew. Group. Casual acquaintances...es." He barks out a cough that makes me cringe. It doesn't sound good, and it makes me wonder if it's just from his smoking habits or if he's coming down with something.

The door opens behind me and I spin around to find Clara, wrapped in her blanket and squinting her eyes as she steps out. I end the call with a quick-cut "Thanks, bye," and stow it in my pocket.

"Clara, it's freezing out here." I'm rushing forward to try and usher her inside but she barely moves.

"I'm well aware. Henceforth, the blanket."

Who says "henceforth" anymore?

I raise a brow as I run my hands up and down her arms to try and create some warmth. I'm not amused by her defiance, and the irony doesn't escape me of how I'm somehow beginning to sound like her.

"Do we need to build you some sort of shelter out in the woods or something? Give you blankets to keep warm tonight? I don't think they make any doghouses big enough for you. We'd probably have to make one ourselves. And by that, I mean you. I wouldn't trust anything that I try to hammer together."

I'm having trouble deciphering if she's being sarcastic or not. Maybe a bit of both? Clara's giving me mixed signals. Her heart is beating quickly, but her face is sullen.

"I would recommend a power drill, not a hammer. And my fur is surprisingly warm, even in the climate around here."

She shoots me a look of disbelief. "It's supposed to be in the single digits tonight. Cold, Seth. It's going to be really cold."

"I'm well aware." I fish my phone back out of my pocket and unlock it, heading straight for the little weather icon on my phone. "See, I have this app that tells me the highs, lows, and the precipitation. It also—"

Clara slugs me in the arm with a fistful of blanket, and only then does her face falter, revealing a small smirk. A playful chip in the poker face she's been wearing.

I wrap her in my arms, a shiver racking through her body as she lays her head on my chest. The cold air is making her nose run and she sniffles, burying her face into the blanket and against my chest.

"Are you ready to talk about this morning?" I ask gently, trying to gauge how my question affects her.

She shakes her head in denial, and my spirits sink a bit. We're going to have to. I need to know why she wants my ex to believe that she's going to be marked. Why she wants Penelope to not have to risk anything by lying about it. This is a major decision for her if she's seriously considering it.

"We do need to talk about it." My hold on her tightens as she shivers again. I can feel her mouth fighting to move, teeth begging to chatter away.

"We will." Her voice is barely audible, tucked away beneath the blanket. "Just not right now."

# 13
# Decisions That Bite

## *Clara*

I'm sick to my stomach. The swirling nerves and doubts clouding my head are almost enough to send me to the bathroom.

Seth opted for an early dinner, but I didn't want anything. I can tell he's holding back. I know he wants to talk about our meeting with Penelope, but I can't. I can't deal with his ex or her failure to show any remorse, knowing that her husband was probably being killed if he hadn't been already. Sure, he deserves to be punished if he was doing God knows what to underage girls—castration is the first thing that comes to mind—but I don't know nor do I care to know the extent of his sins.

One thing is for sure, though. I made my mind up this morning and while I feel crazy, it seems like the only thing that makes sense. The kids aren't here and I'm not sure if I'll have another opportunity to make this happen. I still have the majority of tomorrow to deal with the aftermath of the choice I've already made.

My blanket has become a part of my attire today. I've carried it around myself practically everywhere. Now here I stand at the back door with Seth, in his embrace once more as he draws a hand up and down my spine.

I'm sure he's well aware that I'm holding something back, but he's not doing anything to push for me to open up. The space he's giving me is a bit unusual. He has his own ways of getting me to talk when he wants to.

Maybe my hormones are to blame for my attitude. We'll just go with that for right now. My period has been almost nonexistent today and I can only assume it's due to the stress that I'm under right now. I'm probably going to pay for it later.

Daylight is fading outside and I'm met with the fact that I'll be on my own tonight. I know Seth won't be far, but I don't particularly like knowing that my bed will be empty on his side.

Stupid full moon.

I can't help but wonder if this will get any easier over time. Saying goodbye and seeing him off. It feels silly fretting over one night apart, but I guess it just goes to show how attached I've become. We don't have to be screwing around or talking for me to enjoy his presence. We can just chill out and binge-watch a show or movie while cuddling together on the couch and I'm happily content. For crying out loud, I'd thought "Netflix and chill" literally meant just that. You can guess my surprise when Seth disclosed its hidden meaning, and I was both appalled and impressed that something that sounds so easygoing means something the total opposite.

The ease and comfort I have around him is unmatched. I keep coming back for more and I can never seem to get enough. Is this what love is supposed to feel like? Having a companion, friend, and lover that you actually look forward to being with no matter the circumstances?

"Promise me you'll eat something?" Seth's chest hums as he questions me.

"I'll try," I mutter. I know it's not the answer he wants, but I don't want to lie to him either. I'm not hungry, and the thought of forcing food down right now is low on my priority list. "Are you sure I can't get you a blanket or something? I have some older ones stashed upstairs."

He chuckles effortlessly. "If it will make you feel better, sure."

I break away and, at a leisurely pace, head up to the spare bedroom and fetch a checkered blanket that I know for a fact hasn't been used in ages. It's a bit worn, but still thick. I think it was a Christmas gift from my in-laws one year, and I don't much care for the pattern on it so it was shoved up here some time ago. What I can recall is the kids using it for a fort downstairs. Dragging dining chairs in by the couch to make the tent bigger for them to stash numerous toys and stuffed animals into their little makeshift playhouse.

When I return, Seth wraps an arm around me as he tips my chin up. He searches my eyes for a moment before taking my mouth with his. The kiss is slow, pressing against me slightly as if he's hesitant to seize anymore than that. His tongue doesn't even try to dart in and yet it feels like my body is trying to heat up for the first time today.

His hold on me tightens, our need for one another blossoming like a flower trying to burst through a layer of snow. It shouldn't be blooming, and yet it's fighting to come through and make its own path to rise to the surface.

Releasing the blanket, I cup his face and kiss him harder. I take charge, letting my tongue dive in and taste him. We moan together as he backs me up against the door but keeps my head from hitting the hard surface behind. His beard feels so soft beneath my touch, but it still tickles my palm unless I apply enough pressure.

Our kisses turn rough. There's nothing polite or gentle about the growing desire between us, and we're grinding and pulling at each other like there's another way we can get closer but it's never enough. Not until he enters me and fills me up completely.

Holy fuck. Is this what Penelope meant?

Seth groans; it's not one of pleasure but something else entirely. He draws back, leaving me panting. My mouth goes dry as I look up into his golden hues that burn brighter than ever before.

His teeth are elongating and his body jerks so unnaturally it looks involuntary. Sharp, jagged movements are contorting his body this way and that. My hands cup over my mouth as I watch the man I love and the faces he makes as he tries to mask the pain he's undoubtedly feeling right now.

By his own admittance, each change to this form and back is nothing short of agonizing. When something snaps and his back arches, I can't help the tears that fall at witnessing it firsthand.

It's too hard to watch. Too hard to see him go through this, and I choke back a sob. This is so much worse than when I saw him change back into a human last November.

So. Much. Worse.

A leg twists harshly, bumping into a dining room chair, and I leap over to open the back door. He grunts as he hunches forward and takes notice. The freezing air pricks at my skin as it rolls in like a wave.

I watch as Seth moves, his shirt tearing, dragging himself away while he lets out a wretched and pain-filled whine that borders on animalistic. The fabric of his clothing is no match for the bulging muscles that pulsate to their own rhythm. He stalks out of the doorway, somehow already threatening to make the width of it bigger in the process.

I can see his breath as he takes his leave. Harsh pants of air escape him as I stand behind and watch him leap over the porch railing and dart for the trees. There's a stagger to his departure, and my heart aches. I grieve for the man that has no choice but to go through with this.

The knowledge that he'll have to endure these transitions until the day he dies is almost too much. There's no stopping it once the change begins. There is no menopause-type light at the end of the tunnel to look forward to one day.

Even after his image disappears from my line of sight, I can't keep the tears from falling. I swear they might freeze to my face, but not even that deters me from mourning what Seth has to go through each month. What he can willingly force upon himself each time he changes forms when there isn't even a full moon.

I'm not sure how long I stand there. I don't know if I'm waiting to see him return, to hear something, or what.

But I swear a piece of my heart just ran out and into the woods with him.

I hope he doesn't kill me.

Well, I know he wouldn't intentionally do so in a life-ending kind of way. I'm talking about the decision I've made for him to mark me. I don't take it lightly, but yet, I feel like this is one thing that I have the power to change, and perhaps tip the tables in our favor even if it's ever so slightly. My only hope is that it gets his damn mother to back off.

Mrs. Alice Ries won't take Seth's word as an answer. Perhaps marking me will let her know that he's serious. And having her prized Penelope deliver the news of what's soon to be true, could potentially help our case.

Penelope doesn't owe us anything. That I am well aware of. She has no reason to help, and yet she was willing to lie for us. I won't pretend to know why. Lord knows I hate her for her past decisions and actions, but for now, she might prove herself beneficial. It also doesn't hurt to know that she didn't have any plans to take Seth back with this scheme his mother cooked up. I guess neither of us have the time of day for Alice and her games.

Look at that, Penelope and I have something in common.

By now, my snow boots are laced up and I've had to double up on socks. I've slipped into some leggings and put my jeans over the top to help brace myself against the night air. I have a long-sleeve shirt and hoodie on, and it takes a small force to close my coat over the lumpiness beneath.

There's a knitted hat that I've placed on my head before pulling my hood up, and I drag on my gloves. I'm pretty sure I look like a blackened marshmallow with my getup, but I don't exactly want to be sticking out like a sore thumb in the leafless trees either.

When I turn off the dining room light, only a slight glow from under the kitchen cabinets filters in. Outside, it's more luminous than most nights. The white on the ground and the full moon see to it that I won't be swallowed up in darkness. This could be a downright stupid decision, but I don't take a flashlight with me. It doesn't look like I'll need one.

I feel ridiculous as I grab the blanket Seth left behind and step outside. I'm a mumbling mess as I talk to myself, reminding my decision-making that the sooner we get this marking business over with, the sooner we can put it behind us and move on. It's not like he's officially moving in or marrying me. Nobody besides Seth, wolves, and myself will even know about this bite.

But where *is* he even going to bite me? I guess we never discussed that detail. I'm bundled up from head to toe, my face the only part of me naked to the cold. Seth can't exactly talk right now either, and up until now, I thought that might be a good thing.

What on earth am I thinking?

No. Seth has already gone through that horrible change and shouldn't have to do it again until the next full moon. This has to be tonight, and we have to do this now. No more waiting, wondering, or stalling.

Time and time again, Seth has confessed his love for me and shown me that he's not going anywhere. This? This is something I can do to show him how serious I am in return.

When I can no longer see my house, I come to a stop. The air entering and leaving my nose almost stings, and I know it's already turning red from the temperature. The brisk weather is already trying to eat through the materials on my legs, but my upper half and feet are remaining warm and cozy for the time being.

I quiet, looking around as if somehow my eyes will magically land on the werewolf I've come out here to find. The night is so still that I can only hear myself breathing and the ground crunching as I shift my weight from foot to foot.

The trees around me look dead beyond repair. It's crazy how they can look so dull and haggard when they'll spring back in a few month's time. Lush, full of life and so much green.

"Seth?" I call out, trying to keep my voice level. "I know you're out here but I need to see you."

Nothing responds. No snap of a branch here, no footsteps there. The lack of sound around me makes me more uncomfortable. Did something come up that Seth would've had to run off? Or worse, what if Penelope never left or there are more wolves around?

Dammit. I really should have thought this through.

My mind races back toward the thunderous night when I ran out here to find Seth and was met with his and Larson's nightmarish forms. And here I believed I'd thought everything through, but not this. I was really, really wrong.

Left foot taking a step back, I try one more time before I change course and return home. "Seth, please. If you're out here, show yourself." I then decide to fib a little, hoping to convey how serious I am that he needs to make himself known. "Don't make me wait out here all night. I'm dressed for it."

Only then do I bring the blanket currently resting around my shoulders and shake it out. As if to show that I am prepared to try and get as comfortable as possible in my staying.

There's a crunch up ahead and I still, trying to zero in on its precise location. Another crunch, and something shifts into view.

I hold my breath as I wait, willing my eyes to cooperate and focus. There's movement, that I know, but it's just far enough that I can't make out any kind of figure or shape.

Crunch, crunch, crunch.

Golden hair catches in the moonlight just up ahead, and only then do I finally relax. Seth's coloring is just like the top of his head, and the sight makes my heart beat a little faster.

Talk about rolling the dice and taking a chance on my fate. I really need to stop making rash decisions.

On all fours, Seth doesn't look as intimidating. Even with his long snout, he's not as menacing as Larson was on his hind legs and standing tall.

"Hey," I greet him as he nears, suddenly growing nervous. I didn't really think through what I want to say, but now here we are and the night isn't going to get any warmer. So I come right out and say it. "You need to mark me, Seth."

His steps come to a complete halt. He's about ten feet away if I had to guess, all muscle, fur, and...well, a werewolf. There's a gruff sound coming from his throat, and he doesn't look at me while he shakes his head in defiance.

I'm almost offended.

"I've made up my mind and I'm not going to pretend I'm Penelope's number one fan, but let's not discredit and make a liar out of her. She's got a family of her own." I hate bringing her up, but I need to if I'm going to state my case.

"And don't get me started on your mother," I begin again, and he grunts. "If there's even the smallest chance to show her that you're serious, that *we're* serious, then we have to try."

Seth takes a step back and I try to take one forward. So far, this isn't going how I imagined it. His reluctance to do something that I know he wants is eating away at me. He could have hidden this whole marking thing from me to begin with, but he didn't.

"Look, Seth, I'm not going to pretend that I'm good with proclamations of love because you know I'm terrible with words but..." My eyes close as I sniffle. I'm not sure if a ski mask would even help my face right now. I pull off a glove and stick my hand out. I have no idea if it's good enough or if he can even bite me there, but I'm trying. "I love you, Seth. If anything has come from our relationship these past few months, you should know that. I'm doing this because I want to. I want to do this for us and for any fucking werewolf that dares come across us. To show them that I belong to someone."

I step forward once more, and he finally brings those golden pools up to meet mine. They're so breathtaking that I lose my focus before continuing. I scramble for a moment, trying to remember what I was hoping to accomplish.

"That I belong to you."

Silence stretches before a whirl of warm air leaves him. While on all fours, he almost comes up to my shoulders.

Using his nose, he pushes his head into my hand and nudges at my sleeve as if it will do something. But I'm so jam-packed right now, nothing budges. I swear his wet nose is going to leave icy marks on me.

I search his eyes as he nuzzles into me again, but the forcefulness of it is increasing.

"My...arm?" I ask.

There's a small nod, and while he might not be able to speak to me, he's doing enough to help me limp along until I understand.

I unzip my jacket and stuff my free glove in my pocket. I'm shrugging an arm out through the sleeve of my non-dominant side and I hiss as my bare skin meets the cold. My heart is beating rapidly as I hold my arm out to him.

Using my other hand, I try to do the equivalent of cupping the side of his face. He's too large for my hand, but it doesn't stop me from running it up along the backside of his pointed ear.

I feel like I should be scared. Like this is some sort of dream that's going to spin and turn into a terrible nightmare. Yet, I can't help but feel at peace around him. To think there was a time not so long ago that I was so overcome with fear over his supernatural being status. Drowning in my own tortuous thoughts and conclusions about his secret that I had uncovered.

There's barely any time to register, I'm so lost in thought, that I just catch the tail end of Seth opening his jaws and clamping down on my forearm.

I cry out from his teeth as the pain registers. I know he draws blood because I can feel the cold licking at the liquid coming from it. Eyes burning and head pounding, I feel like I'm starting to spin.

Seth releases my arm and I'm met with the hard-to-miss result of my decision. Gnarly marks coat my arm. Thick punctures are producing large amounts of my life force, running off my arm and onto the ground.

I feel dizzy, cold, and like I'm having an out-of-body experience. The countless trees around me are dancing in a taunting and menacing manner.

Next thing I know, I'm falling into darkness. Only the brush of something wet registers, swiping across my arm. Then it's nothing but warmth.

# 14

# You Have Me

## *Clara*

It's too hot in here. Like the thermostat has been cranked up to ninety degrees and I'm sweating it out.

I'm not sure when I passed out on the couch. The little orange glow from the television brand name penetrates the darkness.

Am I in a straitjacket or something?

Tossing and turning, I almost lose my balance and send myself off of the couch and to the floor. Luckily, I catch myself with an arm that's already free, but the moment it makes impact with the ground, pain radiates up through it and I thrust myself back up and onto the couch.

Eyes blinking rapidly, I bring my arm up so I can take a better look.

What the hell? It looks like I've been freaking mauled!

Sitting up straight, I haul off every piece of clothing until I'm in my undergarments. I'm careful of my arm as I make my way toward the hall bathroom, but my bare feet slip in something wet on the floor. I want to be grossed out about the unknown substance, but I press on.

The flip of the light switch temporarily blinds me and I think I mutter about every curse word known to mankind before I can finally open my eyes and see the destruction before me.

It's jolting. Memories of Seth clamping down on my arm bring in a whole slew of emotions that I'm not capable of keeping up with. I'm panicked as I run water over my wound and try to lightly scrub at some of the dried blood around the marks. The fucking bite that I was practically begging for.

I'd better not turn into a fucking werewolf or so help me I will go off on him.

I'm too stunned to cry, trying to figure out what kind of freaking aftercare I need to administer after getting bitten. My little tube of Neosporin seems like a joke, and none of the bandages in the first drawer are a match for something of this caliber. I fling open the cabinet under the sink and tear things out in the hopes of finding something else.

There's a bit of relief as I locate square pads of gauze and a roll of medical tape that seems a bit discolored by age. But I don't exactly have the time to be picky. I place the white pieces on my arm with shaky hands as I kneel down. I wrap and wrap and wrap until I'm almost out of what little was left of the roll, using my teeth to tear it off.

I slump back onto my ass and against the bathroom wall as I look at my crappy and ill-made wound dressing. I don't even know what to say, let alone think as I replay the scene of Seth biting me. It's on repeat, a never-ending loop of me asking and him chomping.

Leaving my mess behind, I make a quick turn into my bedroom and grab the lighter of my two robes from the back of the door. I'm still too warm for my fuzzy one, and that thought alone sends worry through me. My temperature better not be any kind of indicator of an infection. Could Seth's bite cause something like that?

There are no clocks in my bedroom and my phone isn't on the charger. I huff in frustration. I'm racking my brain trying to figure out how I got back to the house, but I can't remember anything past the bite. I'm padding back out through the hallway and into the living room when I step in something wet again.

"What the…"

Awkwardly walking on my heel, I step over to the wall and flip on the light. I see pools of water leading from the dining room and into the living room. There's a bit of debris and dirt mixed into it, and I note a scratch on the floor that you have to look at just right to spot.

I follow the puddles into the living room where I awoke on the couch. I'm beyond grateful that I didn't get blood all over it, but I'm still going to have some cleaning up to do. On the other hand, my clothes might be past their saving point.

My stomach grumbles and I feel it through the thin fabric of my attire. I'm hungry and I have trouble recalling when I last ate. Seth told me to do so before leaving, and I didn't listen.

It's starting to make sense now.

I could have passed out from the bite, sure. From a mixture of shock and lack of food in my system. It's blurry, but I remember how disoriented I was in the woods before awakening here. It seems a little out of reach, but I half wonder if Seth somehow managed to deposit me on the couch. I know he can walk in his wolf form on two legs as well as four. I just have trouble thinking about him handling me and walking through the door at the same time.

I swivel around, trying to find the mark in the flooring. Lowering, I let my finger drift out and drag across the marking.

Maybe it isn't so far-fetched.

Jogging into the kitchen, I finally locate my phone. There are a few notifications from the back door camera and I click on the first one. The time stamp isn't long after I left to find Seth. I study the darkness, trying to decipher what made the camera go off, until I see Seth's prominent form emerging from the tree line.

Sure enough, he's carrying my limp body. It's strange to admit how small I look in his hold. Seth's head swivels back and forth; I assume it's to make sure he's in the clear to approach the back porch. Luckily, living on a dead-end street gives me only one neighbor to worry about on my side of the road. It's not until I see him reach for the handle that I move on to the next video to find Seth leaving. He leaps off of the deck and lands on the ground on all fours, quickly disappearing with a speed that makes the video end in less than ten seconds.

I'll be damned.

The sound of a latch stirs me, and my head perks up. I glance at my phone to see the time; the rising sun is a faint color escaping through the window coverings in the living room.

I spent the night snacking, cleaning, and trying to sort out my thoughts. I felt at odds, and that's putting it lightly. I should be relieved that this bite thing is over with and we can move on, but I am far from it.

What if it didn't work? What if it doesn't help the position we're in and Seth's mother still tries to come after us? And how in the heck am I going to explain away this bite mark that is surely going to leave permanent scarring? I might have until March or April to try and come up with some sort of explanation before I start putting my winter clothes away.

As soon as I whip around and out of the living room, I find Seth standing on the opposite end of the dining table.

There's a wild look in his eyes as his chest rises and falls in heaves as if he's been running, exerting energy that has his blood racing and the hair atop his head all askew. The blanket I took to him last night drops to the floor, the sound an indicator that it might be both damp and frozen.

"Clara," he breathes, and I'm moving before he can even finish my name. I throw my arms up around him and he catches me, not stumbling from my attack on him. He nestles his head into my neck and breathes deep, a low grumble sounding in his chest. I back away for a second.

Seth should be freezing, yet his body is warm and slick with sweat. It makes most of his chest hair stick down but there are a few curls springing up again as it dries. He smells like winter and earth.

He pulls my arms down and away, examining my bandaged arm. I'm a bit embarrassed by my lack of first aid knowledge and wound dressing, and when I try to tug my arm out of his grasp, he only tightens his hold.

I took something for the pain a few hours ago, and as Seth begins to unwind the gauze I can't help but fear how he might react when he sees his mark on me. Will he be excited that it's complete, or devastated by how terrible it looks? It's a fifty-fifty shot, and his expression is giving nothing away as he gently pulls off the remnants; I keep my focus on him as my covered skin finally gets a chance to relax after being wrapped too tightly.

He grips my arm harder and his mood darkens, sending a course of electricity through me. I follow his line of sight and my jaw drops. Where once there was a definitive bite mark, awful holes that punctured my skin, there is now nothing but light white divots in my arm. The size, severity, just about everything I was freaking out over last night, feels like an atrocious yet distant memory.

"How..." I'm completely dumbfounded. Struck by the drastic change in my partially self-inflicted injury. I flex my hand and twist at the wrist but I can't detect any ounce of discomfort. That's gone, as well as any possibility of the fever I once suspected.

I yelp as Seth picks me up by the back of my thigh and waist, setting me on the dining table. "Now, where were we?"

He tips my chin up, and I look into his eyes and search between the two of them. I'm failing at forming any coherent thought when his erection becomes prominent as he parts my legs with his hips.

My brain is too lazy to catch up, reflecting on the state we were in before he began to shift last night. Seth had me pinned up against the back door, and he seems eager to go back to that. It's almost too easy to forget that I want answers. And I have a *lot* of questions.

"But Seth, we…" His hand dives between us and tears away my underwear as if it's nothing, jerking my hips in the process. Luckily it was an older pair that had seen better days, but I'm left gawking at him as an amused grin crosses his face. "We need to talk."

My voice sounds weak as I finish my thought and when he plunges a finger inside of me, I know all possible conversation is flying out the door he just walked through.

"The only thing I'm interested in is finishing what we started." His thumb crosses my clit with a stroke while he positions himself between my knees. "Open up for me, Clara."

My brows pinch as my body responds to his touch. I lean back onto my hands, the air in my lungs growing heavier as I welcome him in.

"Let me show you how much I love you." He lets another finger join in, and I'm coating his fingers already.

"I know, Seth." I pant as I take in the sight of him before me. He's perfectly lined up to take me and while I know we have things to discuss, they keep getting pushed further away. "Never a day without knowing it."

"Hm..." He hums his appreciation as he works me over with his hand. I want to hold on to something to give me purchase, but I'm met with solid wood at my touch. "Were you scared?"

When I fail to answer, his hand stills.

"Of...of what?"

"In the woods." He leans in closer. "Were you scared?"

I shake my head in denial. "Not of you. I was scared of what I might find if you weren't out there."

It took some time to get to that point, sure. While I am still learning bits and pieces about Seth, his past, and his werewolf form, I can't deny that I'm growing more and more comfortable around every aspect of him. I have trouble separating myself from him, wanting him around all the time. He has been my rock in more ways than one. A fucking godsend when I felt at my lowest.

Seth removes his hand and before I can protest, his hips move forward and he's gliding into me. My head tips back as he lets out a groan of appreciation.

I should be tired, exhausted even from the night's events and my lack of sleep, but Seth has a special way of garnering my attention and keeping me awake. I'm grateful to have the house to ourselves and the freedom to literally be fucked on my dining table without the need for hiding or fearing any interruptions. Soundproofing the basement seems like more of a necessity now, since Seth is becoming a prominent figure in my future. He mentioned doing that, and the prospect of turning it into our own little playroom is exhilarating.

Seth withdraws for a moment. I have something to say on the tip of my tongue, but when he rams back into me, I lose whatever it is altogether. The table moves with him, the legs audibly scraping against the floor.

Locking one hand around the underside of my knee, he brings my head closer with the other. I look at him through my lashes and hooded eyes, too blissed out to think straight as his movements slow. The rolls of his hips keep me fully engaged with what he's doing down there and while I might not be able to move much, I place my hands on his sides.

Sex has easily become an addiction with this man. Not only do I crave his presence, but his touch, his voice, and his ability to *see* me and choose to stay.

"I want all of you, Clara Rose." His words send a chill through me as he speaks against my lips, lightly brushing them without planting a kiss.

I try to lean forward to chase after him, but he pulls back just enough that I'm unable to. I'm left winded, but I still offer a meek response. "You have me."

He grins, his grip tightening on my neck as he pulls my leg further to the side and rolls his hips again.

"Fuck," I whine when he drives in deeper. My body wants to fold forward and at the same time I want to arch my back away. The only thing I do know is that I don't want him to stop. Not now, not ever.

"Claiming every inch of you will never be enough." He's teasing my lips again but in total control, pulling back with both his mouth and hips until I form a pout. "But it's a start."

"Wasn't biting me enough?" I joke lightly, but he looks positively feral. It's devastatingly beautiful, the way Seth can look like he's going to tear me to shreds yet devour me with a single expression. The severity of his hard features is enough to make a full-grown woman pass out.

Maybe I'll even pass out again.

I try to swallow but nothing happens. My grip on him tightens. He's going to ruin me. I can feel the power of his intentions circling around us like an unseen mystical force.

"Lie down, Clara," he orders, and a shiver rakes my spine. He releases my neck, and I follow his direction as he parts my robe. The table is an unforgiving surface, hard on my back. He pushes my knees up and outward and the wicked grin he wears has my hands rising above my head in search of the edge of the table. I barely latch onto the edge of it and he plows into me, making the table move again.

Seth's calculated in his movements, drawing me to him with every push and pull. I'm climbing too quickly for him not to be using my clit to drive me to the brink. Garbled cries come out each time he re-enters, and my eyes are screwed so tight that I can't even manage to look at anything.

I can only focus on my white-knuckle grasp on the table, our mixed chorus of voices, and the promise of an orgasm that will shatter me.

# 15

# It's a Marathon, Not a Race

## *Seth*

She's on the verge and I can taste it. Clara is so close to begging me to stop, but I don't know if I have it in me to quit should she ask. No, she would probably have to demand it.

I've been fucking her on and off all day and she's exhausted. Seeing the remnants of my mark on her has made me a wild, untamable beast and I can't get enough of her. It's like something in my DNA changed with that bite and I can never taste enough, feel enough, *fuck* enough.

I want all of her pleasure and satisfaction. To hear the cries and screams tear from her throat when she comes undone. There's barely enough time for her pulse to calm before I'm gearing up for another round.

I'm not even sure of the last time I saw her brown eyes looking back at me.

Clara knows she can tap out, and yet she lets me indulge in her over and over again. I've never experienced a high such as this before but it's burning so fervently and showing no signs of stopping. To be honest, I'm surprised she's let me take her as many times as I have. I didn't even know I had it in me to go so many rounds. I should have a sore and limp dick by now.

Is this what it truly feels like to mark your mate? No wonder I have so many damn cousins, aunts, and uncles. I would undoubtedly knock Clara up every year if that were an option. I know Clara is done having children, and my ability to give her any is sitting at a steady "fat chance in hell," but what I wouldn't give to see her belly swollen with my child.

"I...can't..." Clara whimpers, and I'm brought back into the present. Her back is to my chest, sweat gathering between us as I hold up her leg and drive my cock slowly back in. My muscles are aching from exertion but somehow I keep going.

Her walls surrounding me clench tight as if she can hold me off, and I kiss her shoulder. "Just give me one more, Clara."

I've put the both of us through the wringer today. From the table, to the kitchen, the hallway, and now our bed. Clara and I might both be feeling the aftereffects for days.

And I don't want it any other way.

I can't imagine how my balls have anything left in them, but I'm so close. I'm careful as I handle my mate. There's a cry of protest, but I can now detect in that sweet, tired voice of hers that she's close. Her body is going to let her have one more orgasm before she crashes and only then will I try to pry myself away. Even the thought of that pains me, but I press on in the hopes that I might finally be sated.

There's a thought about how I might have ravaged her body to the point that she might not let me touch her for the foreseeable future, but I push it away as her body spasms without much notice. The grip she has on me sends me spiraling with her, and my hold on her has to be bruising but I physically can't bring myself to loosen up.

I'm muttering sweet curses as Clara's cracked voice turns to a minor sob. I come back down to earth, lowering her leg as she shakes like she's been out in the winter weather. Her hair is partially covering her face and I sweep it away, kissing her temple shortly after.

I might need to apologize and beg for forgiveness, but I'm rendered silent right now. I withdraw and she tries to jerk away from me but I hold her in close. I know she doesn't have enough energy to fight me off of her, and she stiffens before she finally caves and relaxes.

I pepper her with kisses until she calms down, her bare skin cooling and heart rate declining into her resting pace. It's not until she's knocked out that I finally draw up the covers and peel away from her.

Right now, I don't trust myself. I can't seem to control my urges around her and I need to separate before I fucking damage her. I slip from the bed and stalk off toward the bathroom in search of a rag to try and clean up the mess I made of her. I let the water run warm before running two washcloths under it, squeezing out the excess before returning.

Clara hasn't moved an inch. I dive under the covers and clean her as best as I can. Out cold, she doesn't even take notice. I know how she likes to clean up after sex, and I haven't given her much of a reprieve to do so since I started screwing her like a madman.

This is going to come back to bite me in the ass.

Giving the rags a toss into the hamper, I grab a pair of boxers and slip them on before heading out of the room. I close the door softly and amble out to find my phone.

I'm buzzing. I know I should be tired after being awake all night, but I'm not dragging in the slightest. I make a beeline for the fridge to find my jar of pickles and open it, plucking a long slice out as I scour the fridge for some protein. My ravenous state from the bedroom has led me here and I need to find something to take my mind off of Clara.

I inhale deeply, the scent of vinegar barely enough to stifle the smell of sex and my mate on me. The scent of her is a treat, and I don't have any plans to wash her off of me anytime soon. My eyes roll back as I reflect on how my beautiful Rose was sprawled out a few hours ago on the countertop, crying out for more of my tongue lashings, and I'm already growing hard again.

Fuck. What is wrong with me?

Shoving the rest of the pickle into my mouth, I find some leftover lasagna and set it on the counter beneath the overhead microwave. My phone screen flashes and I mosey over to nab it. Perhaps food isn't a big enough distraction.

Never mind, scratch that.

A phone number that could never be erased from my memory now has my undivided attention. It doesn't even need a name. She hasn't been a contact in my phone for a long, long time.

Not knowing what in the hell Penelope could possibly want now, I click on the message.

> *Just for the record, I'm sorry. I'm too chicken-shit to say so in person.*

I stare at the words on my screen until it goes black, conflicted over how I should feel about this. These words should heal old wounds or provide me a sense of peace maybe? Closure? But they do none of that. While it doesn't do much for me now personally, I can't help but feel a bit proud about how she must have changed over the years to get to this point.

Penelope was too stubborn to ever admit she was wrong. She would fight tooth and nail to prove why she was right and wouldn't back down. No, our relationship was never perfect, but when we were together she was the only future I could seem to imagine. This, though? This feels like a mighty big step for someone I used to know.

Unlocking my phone again, I note that the message was sent a few hours ago. I think about how and if I should reply. I'm still thrown by her visit to begin with. First of all, that she came alone, and second, that she wanted nothing to do with the scheme my mother concocted. But to be fair, Penelope never was a fan of hers or my dad's to begin with.

My thumb swipes out a quick message and I send it without a second guess.

> *Just for the record, you won't be lying when you say that I've marked Clara. Protect your family. Thank you for trying to protect mine.*

Short, to the point, and hopefully the last I'll hear from her.

The rest of the day goes by too slowly. I keep checking on Clara periodically, her steady breathing and failure to change positions proving that she's still out.

I end up working in the office to get my mind on something else, and it helps for a little while, that is until I notice the time. I begin scrubbing down countertops and turning on the wax warmer in the living room before taking off for the bedroom to find a new set of clothes. My stash over here has grown over time, and I'm to the point where my clothes are split somewhat in half between my rental and here. I have half a mind to wake Clara but refrain, knowing that her body undoubtedly needs the rest after what I put her through today.

And last night.

Think I'll be lucky if she doesn't try to kick me out.

It's early evening when I see Joe's truck through the window and I make my way out of the house, taking the breezeway around the garage to meet him in the driveway. I carefully study his tires and while his truck is dirtied up from the elements and driving in them, there's no denying that there is a new tire in place of the one I tampered with. It smells new.

Did I do so much damage that he had to get a new one instead of patching up the old? Those tires weren't cheap.

"Hey, Seth!" Julie's face lights up for a moment when she lays eyes on me but falters when she realizes that her dad is getting out of the truck. She's all bundled up, just like her mother when she's outside.

"Where's Clara?" Joe puffs out his chest out like a damn gorilla. He looks ridiculous. His coat looks like he just bought it and ripped off the tag.

"She's not feeling well and sleeping it off," I answer, careful not to let my disdain for him show in my voice.

Emmett hops out of the back of the truck, letting himself out when Joe doesn't open the door for him behind his seat. He offers me the same enthusiastic greeting, but the roar of the diesel engine almost drowns out his voice.

They both mumble goodbyes to Joe but neither of them give any hugs. No displays of affection or any inkling that they're going to miss him. It feels like they're doing it more out of habit than anything. I know sometimes Emmett gives Clara the cold shoulder when leaving, but what he's doing to his dad somehow seems worse. The way he skates around his father is kind of unusual.

"Just try not to be too loud," I tell the kids as they begin to head toward the house, but before I can depart too, Joe clears his throat.

I've had a few encounters with him. Never shook his hand, even when we first met, and after what he's been putting Clara through, I don't have the time of day for his shit. I pivot to meet him. Joe's already crossed his arms and has raised his head a few inches as if he's trying to appear like he's looking down at me.

Funny, considering he's about Clara's height. He's not rail thin, nor does he have much bulk to him, but it's almost laughable how easy it would be to take him on. It wouldn't be a fair fight.

"Thought I had made it clear to Clara that—"

"I'm going to stop you right there." I place my hands on my hips as I try to roll back the anger that wants to spread and take over. Joe looks like he's fuming, and that's all the ammunition I need. "The bullying Clara around? That stops now."

He scoffs before he lets out a full belly laugh. "I don't know who you think you are, but this? This isn't going to work." He gestures at me as if somehow, I'm the problem and I've offended *him*.

"What, Joe?" I spit out his name like I've tasted something foul. "Afraid that Clara might actually be better off without you? That with Clara and me, Julie and Emmett could have a more suitable and stable relationship to look up to? Lord knows the example you've set with Chassidy is a damning one."

His face reddens and I can tell his fists are balling from how his arms go firm. His coat is looking kind of tight now.

I take a step forward. "Threatening Clara? That's enough. And if you stick to your word and try to go for full custody, just know that she has unlimited means to beat your ass into the ground so that all you'll have left is supervised visits if you're lucky."

He snorts as if he doesn't believe me, and I cut him off just as he tries to open his mouth to speak again.

"You think just because you have a job with a big, fat paycheck that you can have it all, but you'll drown yourself in more debt just trying to win. My cousin is a damn good lawyer and knows all the ins, outs, do's, and don'ts of custody battles. You'll wish you'd never even tried to go against Clara and me."

Joe doesn't need to know that Bradley is dead and technically his skill set was nowhere near up to par on familial matters, but that's beside the point. And no one needs to know the not-so-legal ways I've amassed the information I have on him to begin with, but I could let Joe in on it a little bit. Let's just add some fuel to the fire.

"So tell me, Joe. Do you have the means to keep up your mortgage, truck, and credit card bills while you fight a losing battle? It doesn't take an idiot to figure out that you're behind on your property taxes. What else are you behind on?"

I swear if his face turns any redder, he might burst from the pressure. His name-brand coat might as well pop a few buttons to let out some of the steam that's emitting from him.

"If that's all—" I take a step backwards, flashing a grin just to piss him off even more. "Thanks for bringing the kids home."

I'm halfway around the garage when I finally hear the truck door slam and though it's barely detectable, he's shouting profanities in his cab. I smirk, knowing that I've done enough digging into his finances to decipher the pile of debt he's accumulated. The man's been making a lot of bad decisions.

Guess he's the one that has to choose now. Either keep Chassidy and their high-living lifestyle they have together, or his kids. Will he be able to make the same choice he tried to hang over Clara's head?

Let's not forget how the lawyer Clara picked doesn't think that Joe has any ammunition or cause to go after sole custody. She suspected he's just bluffing to try and get what he wants.

The house is already smelling like baked apple pie when I walk in, but I can still detect the undertone of sex. I glance down at myself, debating if it's just me I sense, but brush it off as Emmett comes barreling down the stairs.

"Do you want to play Four Figures?" His eyes are alive with hope, excitement thrumming through him, and as tempting as it is to take him up on his offer, I have to remind myself of how Clara might approach this.

"That depends," I start, trying not to sound too authoritative. "Is all of your schoolwork done and ready for tomorrow?"

Julie prattles about something from across the room just as Emmett's eye twitches. That, and his slight pause in answering me, tells me all I need to know. His shoulders sag, informing me that he is well aware he's been caught.

"Homework first." I give him a small pat on the shoulder as he crosses in front of me and sidles up to a barstool at the island where he tossed his backpack. "Then I will take you up on your offer."

Emmett buries his head in his folded arms and groans just as Julie lets out a sound of annoyance.

Guess nobody is in a good mood.

I make my way into the dining room to see Julie emptying out all of the contents of her bag and rummaging through it all. She makes the same sound again, but louder.

"What's wrong?" I come to stand on the opposite side of the table and examine her school belongings that are taking up the spot where I fucked Clara. Working down a swallow, I decide to sit down in a chair to hide the erection that tries to surface.

This isn't awkward at all.

"I think I left my calculator at Dad's." She throws her hands up as if this is the worst thing that's happened to her. "No, I *know* I left it there. I tried working on this last night but Dad just *had* to take us to the movies."

"Hey, I liked that movie!" Emmett shouts, and I try to shush them but it does nothing.

"Yeah, of course you did. *You* wanted to see it. *I* didn't." She's articulating her words profusely and it's more than evident that she's telling the truth. "I haven't had any time to work on this stuff and it's due first period."

"Okay." I'm scrambling to see how I can fix this. "Math, right? I like math. What are you doing?"

Julie's gaze pins me to my spot. Like there's no way that she believes I'll be able to help her and she's going to send me packing. She holds up her book, the red and white cover proving her right.

Algebra II.

Shit. Is this girl some sort of genius at school or something? Taking early college classes? I struggle to believe that an eighth grader is taking this class. It was nowhere on my radar back when I was in school.

I'm not proud to show defeat here, but there's no pretending otherwise. Pretty sure I scored a D in pre-algebra and considered that a victory. It was still passing. "Um...okay. I don't like math that much."

"Ugh!" She plops down in the chair nearest to her and buries her head just like Emmett did moments ago.

This is going so well.

There's a creak of a floorboard and I can tell that Clara is up and moving around. I'm fighting with the urge to go to her while trying to come up with a solution to the prominent problem at hand. "I can...go to the store."

Julie shakes her head as she sits up. "We can't afford another one. It's too expensive, and we ordered this one online anyway."

Of course she has to have some fancy gadget for this class. I might be computer smart, but this? This is a whole other level of mindfuckery that I never thought I would have to entertain. Shouldn't she be doing geometry or something else?

I resist the urge to speak on this with anything but contempt, but I try my damndest. "Would your dad be able to grab it?"

Crossing her arms, Julie's gaze drops as she speaks. "No. He's taking Chassidy to some stupid event at work. Getting all dressed up and everything."

Of course he is.

I'm scrambling, trying to figure out how to solve this. "Do you...have a house key? I could run you into town to get it?"

Her head snaps up. "Really?"

"Of course." Who am I to put a stop to a teenager actually wanting to get their homework done? "I'll just wait out in the truck while you run in and grab it."

Jule's eyes become hopeful and she's shoving things back into her backpack as I stand. Emmett has been watching us the entire time, not bothering with getting started on his own work.

Guess Joe has been taking the "fun parent" shtick a little too seriously. These kids aren't getting their homework done until the last minute and it's all falling onto Clara's shoulders and eating into what little time she has with them before they return to school tomorrow.

"Emmett," I start, and his head pops up. "Think you can get your homework done before we get back? Hopefully we're gone for about half an hour."

He pushes his glasses up his nose and leans back as he clasps his fingers together and stretches. "Yep. Done."

"Don't rush through it." I snag my jacket and I have one arm in before Clara exits the bedroom. She's wearing a long-sleeve shirt and pajama bottoms that are too long. They hide over half of her feet with their length. Her hair is piled into a small messy bun, and there's a warmth to her face as she crosses her arms over her chest. I clear my throat as I make eye contact with her. "Are you feeling any better?"

My question has both kids turning toward their mother, and she offers a sheepish grin before it fades away. "I think so."

"Are you okay? Seth said you weren't feeling good." Julie zips up her jacket but remains at a distance. "You're not contagious are you?"

Clara's eyes flick to mine before darting back to her daughter's. I can't help the smirk that takes over and I have to look away, biting my tongue. I know I'm the cause of her sleeping the day away, but I regret nothing. At least not yet. We'll see if she tries to kick me out of our bed tonight or not.

Clara's voice is quiet as she replies, "No, I don't think so."

"Seth's going to run me to Dad's so I can get my calculator. Do we need to pick anything up for you at the store?"

For some reason, when Julie asks that, my chest warms. It speaks to how her mother has raised her. She's concerned and offers to help in any way she can, even if she's unsure of how.

"No, sweetie. I'll be alright, thank you." Clara leans against the wall beside her. "Do you guys want to pick something up for dinner? Or do you want me to get started on something here?"

Julie jumps right in. "Can we just do something simple like...pizza rolls or something?"

"Yeah! Can we, Mom?" Emmett chimes in. Who would've thought these kids would get so excited over pizza rolls?

"Sure. I'll give you guys a head start before I pop them in the oven." She crosses the rest of the way into the kitchen and does a small circle of a rub on Emmett's back before she brings her brown eyes back to mine. "Are you alright with that for dinner?"

I shrug. It's really no big deal to me what we eat tonight. "If that's the general consensus, I'm all in."

"You really don't mind running Julie back into town?" Clara looks nervous, and I'm not sure why, if she's worried about Julie, Joe, or perhaps both. Maybe it's something totally unrelated, but I can't be sure when we can't speak openly and freely at the moment. Maybe I'm totally off base and it's me she's worried about.

"It's not a problem. You just rest," I tell her.

Clara raises a brow, and her eldest and I head out the door.

16

# Building and Burning Bridges

## *Seth*

We make it about five miles away from Alton before Julie finally breaks the silence. The radio has been playing low; today's hits can barely be heard over the force of the heat leaving the vents in my truck.

"Can I ask you something?"

I look over to see her staring out her window, into the darkened and lifeless forest. My curiosity is instantly piqued, even if I'm a bit leery about it. "Of course, shoot."

Julie's knee bounces a few times and I have to suppress the grin that crosses my face. She takes after her mother so much it's almost mind-boggling, but sweet at the same time. But knowing how much Penelope hated to be compared to her mother during our relationship, I know to keep my mouth shut and avoid stating such things.

"You really like my mom, don't you?"

I try to guard my reaction. Is she trying to pull the equivalent of *what are your intentions* or is she simply interested in the fast-growing connection between her mother and me? She's only ever known Clara to be with Joe in her lifespan.

"I do," I start, but I'm having difficulty trying to figure out if I should have an explanation for her. "Does...that bother you?"

"No, no." She shakes her head as if she's panicking and trying to backtrack.

Instantly, I'm afraid that my presence has become too much. That I've overstayed the welcome extended to me for Thanksgiving and everything that it's led to after. Am I over too much? Am I too overbearing to be around?

"I just..." She pauses.

I wait, trying to keep my body relaxed and not let Julie see how anxious I am to hear her out on whatever she's willing to openly admit out loud. I've never had any reason to believe she wasn't comfortable around me, not since we first met and she darted up the stairs and away because she and her friends had been eyeing me on morning jogs while they rode the bus to school. She's been pleasant, easy to talk to, and even invited me to watch her cheer. What the hell am I missing?

"Mom just seems happier when you're around."

While her statement might excite me a little, I can't help but detect an ounce of sadness in the tone of her voice. Does she fear that I might try to take her mother's time away from her? Julie and Emmett mean the world to Clara. She has to know that, right?

"I don't think I've seen your mom any happier than she was on New Year's Eve." I reflect fondly upon that, remembering how high up in the clouds she was. Clara's vibrancy could have rivaled the sun. I might have snapped a few photos on the sidelines when no one was looking.

"Until Dad had to go and ruin it." Julie's voice turns sour. It's enough to make my head swivel in her direction. She's no longer looking out the window as we take the exit to Pembrook. Instead, her hands are folded in her lap as she stares down at them.

"You know?" I ask gently, trying not to provide too much information and hoping she'll dive into what she's aware of. I don't want to assume anything at this point.

"I mean…" Her eyes widen and I tear my gaze away and onto the road. "Why does Dad get to make the demands? Emmett and I didn't get a say in whether or not we met Chassidy, or where we get to live. We don't get to have an opinion on anything. Why—"

Julie comes to an abrupt halt as I stop at a sign. There are no cars around and it gives me the opportunity to really look at her.

She's panicking, I realize, and I'm at a complete loss for words. Joe is still her father; he'll always have that parental claim on the kids. And as much as I despise the guy, I have to be extremely cautious and mindful of what I say regarding him.

"I'm so sorry. I don't know why I…I…" She shakes her head, hands trembling. "I shouldn't have said anything."

Pulling off to the side of the road, I put my hazards on. I can't think straight, drive, and navigate this conversation at the same time. It's too overwhelming to juggle all of these things while keeping her safe.

"Hey." I take my hands off of the steering wheel and place them on my thighs. "I won't pretend to be some know-it-all. I don't have all of the answers and I know you have no reason to confide in me, but just know that I want nothing but the best for your mother, you, and Emmett. What you want to talk about, we'll talk about. If you want to keep your lips sealed, then so be it. If you need to vent, vent. I won't judge you."

She considers my onslaught of words, taking her time to process them and really think them over. I know this young lady beside me is a smart one—this freaking math class she's in is one heck of a start. But seeing how she interacts amongst friends, family, and the stranger I know I still am, I can tell she's someone that's going to have a promising future.

"My dad *really* doesn't like you." She balls her hands into fists, her face almost in regret at what she's telling me. Anyone who's got eyes and ears could deduce that.

"I won't pretend I'm his biggest fan either," I concur while eyeing the line of view my headlights create in the darkness up ahead. "But I promise to play nice if that's what you all need."

A small, nervous laugh makes its way out of her throat. "I'm sure you didn't sign up for all of this family drama when you met my mom. Sorry you've been dragged into all of this."

If Julie only knew the shitshow I've introduced her mother to, including my family that won't back the fuck off. While I don't anticipate Julie ever knowing the full truth about me, I figure it doesn't hurt to come forward about a little bit of my past as well.

"I would be lying if I said I came from a perfect background. No family is perfect. There is drama to be found if you go looking for it, and sometimes you don't have to look very hard."

She scoffs at that. "Emmett wishes for things to go back to normal. I don't even know what that is anymore."

I take a beat to let that settle. Emmett is probably young enough to not know the extent of how serious things are. How his father had an affair and has practically rubbed Chassidy in Clara's face ever since. The lengths Joe is willing to go to make her life a living hell. Maybe someday he'll see it and stop hoping for something that isn't going to happen.

"The only way to go is forward. If you keep focusing on the past, it'll only hold you back, keep you from living up to your potential and the happiness that can be found if you just give it a chance." I never felt fulfilled until Clara came into my life. Never gave a future much thought after my dismal past and the scars it had left me with. I was so closed off to any more possibilities that I lived my life day to day instead of trying to plan for something I could never see myself having.

A home. Love. Family. Someone to share every facet of my life with no matter how dark or radiant it might be on any given day.

"Promise me you won't hurt my mom?" Julie catches me totally off guard with that one, the question coming out of left field.

There's no way she's ever going to understand just how important my mate bond with her mother is. No way to convey how I have killed and I would die for her. I wouldn't even think twice.

"Julie, I know we're still getting to know each other, but your mom..." I search for the words that won't make me sound like a pathetic and hopeless romantic who has no sense of reality. "Your mom is exactly the type of person I've been searching for. Her kindness, her devotion to her family, she's what I've been missing in my life. As long as she'll have me, I'm not going anywhere. I could never hurt her."

It's Julie's turn to mull over my words and when something clicks, she adjusts her position and crosses her arms as she holds her head high. "And what about her awesome kids?"

My head tips back on a laugh. "I'm just trying to go with the flow with you two and try to help out as I think your mom might. But to be honest, you guys have me scrambling tonight. What thirteen-year-old is in Algebra II?"

This time, Julie giggles. As I turn off my hazards, she goes into detail about how she's in a class of primarily juniors. How she surpassed her peers years ago and has been steadily progressing ever since. She seems to have a love-hate type of relationship with math, and while it might be "pull her hair out" difficult at times, it's incredibly satisfying when she finally cracks a problem.

We're cruising through the streets of Pembrook as she jumps from talking about school subjects to after-school activities. I make a point to tell her how well she did cheering at Friday night's game and she invites me to the next one this coming Thursday. This car ride is the longest conversation we've had, and it's so refreshing to get to know her in this way without any distractions. I'm fully immersed in Julie's world and she can't help but smile through each response and topic. Sometimes I can barely get a word in before she jumps into another matter.

Until we arrive at Joe's house.

"He's not supposed to be home." Julie's glee comes to a screeching halt and her demeanor changes drastically. She's not at all excited to see Joe's truck and Chassidy's little yellow car in the driveway. I pull up to the curb and park. "I'll try to make this quick."

I wave it off like it's no big deal. "You're fine, don't worry about it."

The uneasy look on Julie's face has my body going rigid. She no sooner closes her door than my fingers are tapping on my leg in a nervous manner. I keep checking my phone in case Clara might message, but there's nothing. Time moves slowly while I wait for Julie to exit the house.

The neighborhood is quiet. Some porch lights are on, others are dark. The house on my left has failed to close their blinds and there's some action-packed movie playing with explosives. I don't recognize it, but drag my attention back toward Joe's two-story abode that he paid way too much for considering what the houses around him are valued at.

When five minutes pass, the suspicion that there must be more going on than finding a damn calculator peaks. I don't even bother turning my truck off before hopping out. I know in my gut something is wrong, and I'll be damned if anything is going to go south on my watch. I'm barely halfway up Joe's driveway when I hear him yelling at the top of his lungs like a blood vessel is going to pop.

"—be damned if I'm going to let you anywhere near that man!"

"What did he ever do to you?" Julie shrieks as I come barging in through the front door. I don't care about knocking or using a fucking doorbell, and as I make out the situation before me, I still.

Julie is cowering on the carpeted steps that lead upstairs to where I assume her room is. She's clutching her calculator to her chest, tears streaming down her face while Joe's figure towers over her. Face red and heated, it's no wonder his daughter is afraid of him right now.

Chassidy is off to the side in their large living room, curled up on the couch as if she's watching some reality television show but dressed in an evening gown that has her breasts pushed up unnaturally high. They look like little water balloons compared to Clara's. She startles when she finally takes notice of me and Joe's abrupt silence.

"Did you touch her?" I all but spit out as I approach him. The look on his face deepens, pure hatred and disgust mixing together in a deadly concoction.

"Touch her? *My* daughter? You've got some fucking nerve! You're trespassing!" Spit flies from his mouth and while I would love nothing more than to haul off and punch him, I know I can't. There's too much at stake here.

"Julie, go out to the truck." I try to remain calm, but my composure is slipping.

Joe takes a firm stance in front of her, blocking her only way out. I'm sure he thinks he's in a pissing contest because of our words earlier, but he doesn't stand a fucking chance.

"She's not going anywhere with you!" he rages.

Julie cowers behind him, a small yelp escaping her throat at his outburst as she covers her ears. The effect this man has on the women in his life is startling. And yet, Chassidy is still sitting idly by, watching and doing absolutely nothing to diffuse the situation. Is this a normal occurrence around here? Has she witnessed Joe and this temper before to be completely unfazed by this?

"Well she's certainly not staying here," I say.

"And what are you going to do about it? You think you can come in here and—"

"Look at her!" I shout back when he steps into my zone. "Look at what you're doing to your daughter! Is this any way a father should treat their child?"

"What would you know about having kids?" he retorts as spittle hits me in the face.

"I know enough not to do what you're doing to Julie right now. You can be pissed off at me all you want, but you have no right to treat her like this." It's a risky move, that much I know, but I sidestep around him.

"Let's go, Julie." She barely sets her sights on me before she screams as a fist hits my face.

I hate to admit it, but Joe can pack quite the punch. Pain registers but I push through it and flex my jaw. I didn't think it would be so easy for him to take such a small piece of bait, but I guess it goes to show just how much he hates me. I can take it, but I hate that Julie has to play witness to this side of her father.

I put on a little bit of an act, feigning hurt as I return my attention to Julie who stares at me with a horrified look on her face. It reminds me of the one Clara wore when she found out my secret in the woods. Right before she took off running away from me.

"Go to the truck, please," I urge. She blinks once before pushing to her feet and vaulting toward the door and out of sight. She's a blur as she goes, and I stand to face my attacker. "If you know what's good for you, you'll give Clara full custody."

Joe sneers as his face morphs as if I've said something funny. "You're out of your goddamn mind."

"Maybe I am," I state as I turn my back on him and take a few steps in the direction of the door. Cold air is rushing in but it does little to calm the heat my body is producing. What I wouldn't give to return the favor and land a blow on him. Actually, I think I would run out of fingers thinking about the things I'd like to do to him.

Remnants of my past creep up and along my spine until they invade my mind. My father and grandfather, their harsh words and fists that sometimes held items that literally scarred me for life. Repressed memories of bruises, bloodied wounds, and broken bones.

Thank God I never had any siblings and I was the only one to take the blunt force of their "affections."

I swivel, a dark grin on my face. "Have fun at your event tonight."

# 17

# Whatever It Takes

## *Clara*

Julie comes rushing into the house as soon as I close the refrigerator door, face puffy and contorted to the point that fear seeps into my veins at a rapid pace. I struggle to keep my footing as her arms wrap around me. Seth isn't far behind, closing the door as I let loose a shiver from the temperature Julie wears on her coat.

There's something off about him. His jaw is set, face tight and eyes wide. He's...angry.

"What's got into you?" Emmett speaks with garbled words around a mouthful of pizza rolls.

"Emmett, can you take your food upstairs?" Seth's tone is so serious that not even I want to trifle with it.

"I'm not allowed to take food upstairs," he argues, but I manage to loosen Julie's hold on me as I crane my neck over my shoulder.

"Just don't make a mess and make sure to bring your stuff back down," I order, and he raises a brow. I can't believe he's going to try and argue with me about this, especially right now. I've caught him sneaking things up there and reprimanded him for trash and evidence left behind. But right now? I'm giving him a free pass. "Just go, please."

Emmett waits, testing my limits, and I know my eyes are narrowing to the point that I'm giving him "the look." I know he's curious and wants in on whatever is about to go down in this kitchen, but I'm already on edge over what is going to be discussed. If I can shield him from these shitty matters a little bit longer, I will.

"Fine," he groans as he retrieves his drink, plate, and the bottle of ranch. He takes his sweet time crossing the kitchen and I know he's dragging out his exit as long as he possibly can.

"Please close the door," Seth calls up the stairs, and when I hear Emmett's door shut, Seth returns his gaze to mine. Only then does Julie finally release me.

"Will someone please tell me what in the heck is going on?" I can't decide who to focus on and my eyes dart between the two of them.

"Dad hit Seth!" Julie shrieks on a whispered yell that sounds painful, and my jaw drops. I'm stunned into silence, barely comprehending what she just said as Seth moves closer. Joe is an asshole, sure. But he was never one to resort to physical violence.

"Just for the record, I'm fine." Seth's delivery is calm, but there's a darkness in his eyes that betrays his voice. There's some redness along his cheek just above his facial hair and I snap a hand over my mouth.

"Dad's lost it, Mom. He completely freaked out over Seth bringing me over. Please don't make me go back there. I *can't* go back there." Julie chokes back another sob before throwing her arms around me again. This time it's around my neck instead of my middle.

I don't know what to do, let alone say. This isn't the first time Julie has voiced her opinion on wanting to live and stay here, but this shake in her voice and urgency of her words has my knees threatening to give. I don't know how to give her what she wants without a custody battle that I dread with every fiber of my being. I know it's going to get ugly. But maybe it's already begun.

"Seth," I say while searching his face. "What... How...?"

His hands are shoved into his jacket pockets and he doesn't flinch as he begins, "Julie was taking a while to grab her calculator. I decided to check it out and I overheard Joe yelling and rushed inside."

"He wouldn't stop." Julie shakes as she steps back and wipes at her eyes with both hands. "Dad wouldn't listen, he wouldn't stop!"

"Okay, okay." I take her hands, ignoring the wetness from her tears. "And then what happened?"

"Joe wasn't going to let her leave with me," Seth begins again. "He was blocking Julie, trapped her in the stairwell. When I tried to help, he hit me."

It's on the tip of my tongue to ask if Seth hit him back, but I forgo it for now. I've seen Seth kill his cousin for crying out loud. Would he really hold off on my cheating ex-husband, especially if it's concerning my daughter?

"Getting Julie out of there was my only priority." The heaviness of his words sets in deep. "Then I wanted to talk to you about filing a police report."

I stall for a moment. "Do we really need to get the police involved?"

I bite my lip as Julie squeezes my hands again. My gut is telling me that we do, but at the same time, last November Seth took lives of his own. Do we need police involved in any form in our lives?

I have half a mind to tell Julie to go upstairs so we can hash this out, but she's not getting any younger. While I might have to filter what I say and how I truly feel, a part of me wants to include her in this.

Is that wrong of me? Wanting to protect her yet yearning to give her a say when she's told me time and time again that her father won't give her that? A voice in the matter.

"What do you want to do, Julie?" I face her and keep my face guarded as best as I can. Her bottom lip trembles as she contemplates. Sniffling, she swipes at her eyes with one hand before finally nodding.

"I don't want to go back there. If this—" She hiccups as she tries to compose herself enough to speak. "If this is the only way, we need to do it. But what about Chassidy?"

"What about her?" I ask, hating how in the dark I am.

"She was there." Julie looks over her shoulder at Seth. "Sh-she saw it all and she did nothing. Just sat there, staring while Dad yelled and screamed at me. While Dad hit Seth. She's probably going to come to his defense on the whole trespassing bit."

Shit.

It occurs to me that things might have already been said in the car between Julie and Seth on the way back home.

So it's Julie and Seth's word over Joe and Chassidy's. Great. Would a police report even do us any good at this point, or would it be to Seth's detriment? Sure would be nice if I personally knew a police officer to ask some hypothetical questions in my time of need.

"My only regret is not storming in sooner." Seth crosses his arms, feet still planted firmly. "I never gave entering that house a second thought. If Joe wants to go after me for that and trespassing, I'll go after him for assault."

Eyes falling to the mark on Seth's face, I pause. I've seen Seth struggle with bouts of anger, but not in this context. I know Joe isn't the only one to ever land a punch on him, but I still have trouble believing he wouldn't react. "You didn't hit him back?"

"No." His answer is quick, voice stern, but I can tell there's something not so deep down inside of him that wanted to do more. I mean, *I* want him to beat Joe's ass for wreaking havoc on our daughter, scaring her and bringing her to the point of tears. It hurts that Joe has gone this far. He's gone past a boundary that he can't come back from. I never knew he could be capable of this.

"I…" My eyes fall from Seth and drop to the floor. Neither of them have removed their coats or shoes, blowing in with news that made my stomach turn. I may have snatched a few pizza rolls while I waited for them to return, but my hunger has now completely vanished once again. I look to Julie, who's right at my height since I'm in my bare feet, and the hand still holding her tenses. "Julie, how about you grab some food. Let me make a call and we'll go from there."

I can't find it within myself to offer any kind of half-ass smile, but I pad out of the kitchen and nab my phone from the counter as I go. My mood is taking a nosedive as I try to take deep breaths but even that doesn't help.

I'm pissed off to high heaven.

Closing my bedroom door, I round the corner and move through the bathroom until I can shut myself in the closet. It's too damn cold to go outside and this is the only room where I can try to have a conversation without ears listening in. That is, unless I start shouting.

I dial Joe as I sit down on my padded bench and wait. After the second ring it goes to voicemail and I hang up before calling again. The attempt to ignore me only pushes me further into madness. He'll have to turn off his damn phone before I give up. I don't know what I expect to get out of Joe and this conversation, but here I am, trying to talk to him anyway.

"What?" His voice cuts through the phone and catches me off guard when he finally picks up. I've dialed at least half a dozen times already.

"Want to tell me why my daughter is a ball of tears? What the hell, Joe?"

The line is met with some background noise and I glance at the phone as if it will help me decipher where the heck the sounds are coming from or where he's at. So help me, if he ends this call without any kind of explanation, I will give Seth my blessing to do whatever the fuck he wants to. If it means going to the police station? So be it.

"Joe." I spew his name with rage, standing from my bench as if it will help me match my rising anger before I shriek, "How could you?"

He can threaten me all he wants. He's already taken away the life we had and carelessly thrown away our vows, but this? Resorting to violence and yelling at our daughter who did nothing but hitch a ride with Seth over a freaking calculator that she needed? The nerve!

The background grows quiet. I glance at the phone, seeing that it's still connected by the increasing numbers on the length of the call time.

"This is what you wanted, isn't it?"

I'm taken aback, searching aimlessly around the closet and unable to focus on anything as I wait.

"Me, backed into a corner?" he continues.

"Like you haven't done the same to me," I spit back. "How many times have you threatened to take the kids away? And don't get me started on the stupid ultimatum you gave me. This stops now, Joe. Tonight was the last fucking straw. I'm not taking your shit anymore."

"Seth had no right coming into my home—"

"What about Julie?" I shout back. "What about your daughter who wants nothing to do with you now? She never wants to step foot in your house ever again. Aren't you going to ask how she's doing in the aftermath of your shit?

"You *hit* him! You hit Seth in front of her, what is wrong with you?"

I want to go flying off the handle on tangents and curses but I hold off. I never could have imagined that things would boil down to this, but there is no way in hell I'm letting either kid go back to him when I now know what he's capable of.

"You really think you can handle the kids on your own? Or, I'm sorry, with *Seth*?" Joe sounds like he's choking on his name this go-around. Good, I hope he does.

"I can and I will," I state bluntly. Joe doesn't have to know the weight that Seth lifted off of me by paying off my mortgage even if I'm still struggling to accept it some days. "The sooner you come to terms and accept the fact that they're better off with me, the faster we can resolve this. You'll be hearing from my lawyer."

I end the call before he can get another word in. I'm standing there fuming, wondering how we got here. I am done feeling trapped and pushed around when Julie, Emmett, and I are the ones who were wronged from the start. I'm done taking his shit and it's time to move on.

Deep down in my heart and the blood pumping through it, I know the kids are better off with me. Julie is ready, that much is obvious, but Emmett might not be so willing to accept the reality I want to reach. One where Joe's presence becomes less and less.

Joe feels toxic. To the point that I swear I can taste the acidity from him miles away. The urge to rinse my mouth out with some water from the sink edges into my mind and when I turn, I'm met with my tall and golden statue of a man leaning against the doorframe. Normally, the quiet approach might give me a scare, but I think I'm too high on rage to be bothered by it.

We study each other for a moment, almost sizing each other up. I haven't had the chance to talk to him, and I mean *really* talk to him since I passed out and slept the rest of the day away. I want to curl up into his embrace and check him over for any harm besides that blow to his face, but I'm almost afraid to touch him.

And earlier, every time he touched me, he ended up inside of me and screwed me until I couldn't take it anymore and let sleep win over. Has Seth biting me awoken some sort of sexual awakening in him that makes him seek my body and release over and over again? My body is growing warm just thinking about how many orgasms we've achieved, combined even.

"I, um…" I clear my throat, dropping my gaze as I try to approach in the hopes to move past him but he blocks me with his figure. "I need to check on Julie."

My body stills as he lifts an arm and uses his thumb and forefinger to latch onto my chin and tip it up. "She's grabbed some food and has already cracked open her book at the table."

Working to swallow, I try to pull my chin away but his grip only tightens, and I search his eyes that are fixated on my lips. "Emmett."

He grins. "I let him have my share of pizza rolls and he is happily gaming it up in his room."

Dammit.

"I… We…" We're too close. My body should want nothing to do with him after the day we've had. How my center can still rev itself up when it should be battered, bruised, and exhausted is beyond my level of comprehension. The soreness is strangely mild considering his wicked touches, tongue lashings, and hip thrusting. How can my body have anything left to give at this point? "Seth—"

My breath catches as his head dips down and his lips brush against mine. "I'm proud of you, Clara."

I stare at him in wonder before it turns to confusion. What on earth does he have to be proud of? I haven't done anything.

A low rumble of a chuckle vibrates his chest and I wish I could feel it against me. "For making that call. Fighting for your children."

I back up, crossing my arms. "I'm sure I just pissed him off even more."

"All the better reason to report him for assault." Seth eyes me with a stern look. "Use this to your advantage, Clara."

Suspicion unfurls in my head as I study him. This feels too convenient. Money problems aside, I've never known Joe to back down from a fight. But the thought of him having a mark of assault on his record, the manager of a popular events center that brings in all sorts of traffic and people from all walks of life, would definitely be problematic for him and this custody battle we're on the cusp of.

"Is there something you're not telling me?" I pry. He sighs, and I know my assumption is right.

"We had a few words when he dropped the kids off earlier. Might have ticked him off."

Well that can't be all of it and I gesture for him to continue. Why would Joe go off on Seth over a few words?

Seth rolls his neck before shoving his hands into his pockets. He doesn't break eye contact. Instead, his stare is almost...aggressive. I know it's not toward me, but I can't help the shiver it wants to send down my back.

"I told him that his threats need to stop. That you have my full support and I have a cousin who is a superb lawyer in these types of custody cases."

I can't help but wonder if there's any camera feed of this encounter between him and Joe and if I might be able to bear witness to what unfolded while I was passed out. I'm sure this only fueled Joe and his anger. It probably pushed him over the edge when he saw Seth again tonight.

"Which cousin?" I ask.

Only now does Seth flick his eyes away. "Bradley."

Brain coming to a screeching halt, I can't help but gawk at him. I drop my voice to a hushed whisper. "Bradley? As in your *dead* cousin, Bradley?"

The very one whose throat I saw Seth rip out in the woods? That can't be.

"Joe doesn't need to know that."

I scoff, placing my hands on the sides of my head as if I can keep it from spinning. This is bad. Isn't this bad? Why would Seth say something like that?

"Clara, if you don't want me to go through with this and file a police report then I won't. But in all honesty, I think we need to try and take this route. I knew Joe was hot-headed but I didn't think it would take so little to make him act out." Seth steps forward and I drop my hands. "I fully believe we need to use this to our advantage, but if you tell me to drop it, I will."

Seth's cheek has now reddened. I know he can heal ailments such as this fairly quickly, so time is probably of the essence. Never in my wildest dreams did I think Joe would be capable of something like this and if Seth set him off, what else will? Julie is already begging not to go back and I'll be damned if I am going to force her.

Deep down I know that we have to move forward with this. What's stopping Joe from growing violent with the kids? Is he showing this side to Chassidy or anyone else? What on earth did Seth uncover today? He might have instigated it, but Joe was the one to act on it.

"Do it." I work to swallow while I'm fighting with the urge to talk myself out of it. Was this a one-time thing with Joe or is this just who he is now? "File the report."

Seth steps forward and places a kiss on the top of my head. "I'll call you when I'm done."

# 18

# Bet on It

## *Clara*

Seth offered small texts here and there while he was at the police station, and the kids have already gone off to bed by the time he arrives back. Kicking off his shoes on the rug by the door, he follows behind me until we find ourselves in the bedroom.

I've been at war with myself ever since he left. Arguing that this is for the best to get my kids back and under my roof while also chalking it up to a momentary lapse in Joe's sanity. I don't want to believe that he would be capable of hurting either of our children and raising a fist to Seth. But him bringing Julie to the point of tears and denying her the chance to leave his house has left an atrocious feeling in my gut.

Then there was the camera footage from earlier today while I was sacked out. Sure enough, my ex-husband and current leading man of my life had words. Unfortunately, even with the volume all the way up on my phone, I couldn't make out the entire conversation. But I swear Joe's face turned so red he probably could have melted ice. He was a freestanding furnace in my driveway.

"They wouldn't mind speaking to Julie tomorrow." He studies me as he delivers the news, and I don't know why I'm surprised by it. Why wouldn't they want to talk to her? Julie was there and played witness to the whole altercation. "I told them my only priority was her safety and talking to her mother before making any decisions on the report. I bought her a little time. They're expecting her after school but only if you consent."

Seth produces a card from his pocket and hands it to me. I can't seem to control the shake in my hand when I take it, looking over the name and emblem of the force. I just nod.

"That is, if Julie still wants to at that point. I told them that you would most likely bring her if she follows through with it."

"Okay," I mutter as I turn my back and go to set it on my dresser. When I turn back around, I see that the mark on his face has darkened and my heart sinks. It hurts, knowing that Joe did that to him.

I am well aware that Seth has been through far worse, though. From the abuse his family doled out, to the battle with his first cousin's arrival, and the fiasco last November that resulted in a severe shoulder injury for him. A punch to the face presents itself like the lesser of those. Even if Joe was provoked, he had no right to lay a hand on him or raise his voice to Julie. Terrify her, even.

"Seth, I'm so sorry." I tear my eyes away from him as I bury my face in my hands. I hate seeing him like this. And the fact that he was injured because of someone I know somehow feels even more awful—like I was the cause of it.

He moves fast, taking me in his arms as his chin rests on top of my head. "Clara, you have nothing to be sorry for. I took a chance on his anger, ready to accept anything he might dish out."

"I didn't know he was capable of that."

"But now we do," he breathes, and our embrace deepens.

We stand there for a while, existing in the quietness of my home. I grow warm beneath him and let my eyes close. His presence soothes my warring thoughts and allows my mind to go blank for a little while.

I focus on our breathing, how he bends to form around me, and how short I feel.

I breathe in, recognizing that he smells off. I assume it's from sitting in a police station, but there's still a hint of something that I can't place. My head begins to move and he lifts his, granting me a chance to look at him.

"I should make you sleep at your place tonight." I quirk a brow and his puzzlement is almost enough to make me laugh. "After what you put me through today," I clarify. "Did biting me awaken some sexual demon in you or something?"

"Did you not enjoy it?" A sinful grin crosses his face and he lightens his hold on me. "I know I certainly did."

I push off of him and go to sit on the bed, crossing my legs when I bring them up. I've never known—let alone heard of—any kind of man that could go for that many rounds. I'd never in my life had so many orgasms that close together. What in the hell did that bite do to him?

Heat is creeping up into my cheeks as he draws nearer, removing his shirt. I'm scooting back on the bed to try and put distance between us but it does nothing to deter him. The thigh-clenching wickedness that he exudes in his facial features, the prowl of his body, is almost enough to break me.

"Seth, don't," I warn as I get closer to the headboard. It sounds weak, but I push on. "I'm pretty sure I'm going to be leaking you for days. Give me a break, would you?"

While my period has seemed to go on hiatus, I'm still wearing a freaking pad right now because of him and how full he pumped me. Taking a quick shower to wash my lower half felt like a joke.

A low groan comes from his chest as he drops his head for a moment before meeting my gaze again. It has by body tightening and my heart thudding around wildly.

"I was going for weeks."

For a moment, I'm too stunned to speak. I can't deny how freaking hot it is for Seth to admit something like that, but at the same time...

"Gross." I scrunch my nose as I grab my pillow. I use both hands and hit him on his side with it. I know it will do little to drive him away, but I leap up from the bed only to be pulled back down and onto the mattress. As if he knows I'm going to shriek at the abrupt move, he covers my mouth while he pins me down.

I stare, wide-eyed, as my heart runs as fast as a hamster in its wheel. I'm panting as if I've attempted to sprint around the block, and my clothes are already sticking to me with my increased body heat.

Seth looks down upon me with sultry appreciation as he bites his bottom lip. I've never seen him do that before and my female anatomy is trying to tell my brain to get on track and let him take me again. I shouldn't be able to even walk or string thoughts together after he screwed me so many times. How can my body possibly want more?

I move my head back and forth until he releases my mouth, and I don't skip a beat. "Remember that doghouse I teased you about a while back?"

He tilts his head to the side, the gleam in his demeanor cracking ever so slightly. I see the recognition and I continue as he pulls his hand away to rest by my shoulder.

"It's that little house that you never stay at anymore." I'm struggling to keep my voice at an even level.

"My home is here, with you." He runs a hand up and along my side, exposing my skin, making me squirm beneath him. It's hard to not want to grind myself against his leg between my own. The pounding down there is growing more uncomfortable now. "By your side." He curves his hand over the swell of my breast. "And when that's not enough, inside of you."

This man is impossible.

He is going to ruin me. If I let him go any further, I'm not sure how I'm going to be able to function. Sure, I might be turned on, but how much is he expecting my body to take?

Looking at him straight on, I deliver the words that I hope might be my only saving grace tonight. "If you don't keep that dick of yours in your pants, I'm kicking you out."

Unblinking, I wait for him to answer. For his face or body language to change, anything. But he just stares at me as if I've said nothing. Not even a laugh at my attempt to be serious, and there's no argument on the subject.

"How about a bet or something?" I sigh, growing more and more apprehensive in his silence.

Seth raises a brow but other than that, he remains still above me. It's obvious his curiosity is there, though.

I know it's a risky move, but in all honesty, that's part of the thrill of it. "If you can go twenty-four hours without touching me, I'll give you something that you want."

He studies me, as if he's thinking long and hard, and yet he won't move from his position above me. "You're not serious."

"I am," I butt in, and his face morphs into an expression of shock. "Seth, you've fucked me into next week all within the span of a single day."

Finally he leans back on his haunches and scratches the back of his head. I swear his eyes are bulging to the point that it looks like it might hurt. "But...I just marked you."

Leaning up onto my forearms, I shoot him a questioning glance. "And that means you can't take a chill pill for a little while? Seriously, how are you even functioning after today?"

It's like I'm bearing witness to a train wreck inside of his head. He looks absolutely beside himself and unable to hold eye contact. He searches the bed at my side as if he's trying to figure out how he's going to survive after cutting out the intimacy part of our relationship. Which, let's be honest, is a huge freaking chunk.

"All I know is that I can't seem to get enough of you. I need to touch you, to *feel* you, to be whole."

My heart jumps at the sentiment, but while the feeling might be mutual, I can't keep letting him screw me until I pass out. "Okay, how about touch is okay, but...no sex for a week?"

"Fuck," Seth mutters as he twists and falls to the bed, landing on his back. "Are you trying to punish me?"

I can't help but gawk, trying to figure out why this feels like the end of the world to him. And here I thought a small adjustment such as that, allowing some sort of physical touch instead of none at all, would be better.

"Come on, don't look at it that way." I turn toward him and prop my head up on my hand. "Tell me, there has to be something that you want. Something I can give you that will make this a little bit better. What would be a good motivator?"

Seth stares at the ceiling, still clothed on his lower half but just as magnificent as ever. His golden hair catches the light from the lamp on the nightstand. His chest rises and falls as something must cross his mind. His eyes slide over to mine and I eye him curiously.

"And...?" I prompt, thinking that something has finally struck him.

"If we go a week without sex, anything?"

I sense trouble on the horizon. Perhaps I should set some guidelines, but I don't want to look like a liar now that he's peeling himself off of the ceiling. My reply comes out hesitantly. "As long as it's nothing too crazy."

Seth doesn't skip a beat, rising to a seated position. "Marry me."

I stare up at him, second-guessing whether or not I even heard those words come out of his mouth. This man did *not* just ask to marry me in bed after taking sex off of the table for a week.

Laughter bubbles up through my throat as I rise to sit in front of him. "Very funny, Seth."

"I'm not joking." He reaches for my hand and takes it in both of his. Mine feels so small trapped within his touch. He curves my hand that used to wear a ring and I follow his gaze down. "I want to marry you, Clara."

A whole slew of images and thoughts come rushing into my mind. Questions that I've wondered about here and there if the idea of marriage ever came up between us. Now here it is, front and center.

"Seth—" I take a shallow breath, trying to scramble my thoughts together. "That's a big ask. We haven't even talked about marriage. There's...there are things we would have to discuss."

"Like?" he prompts, as if he's ready to dive into this topic right now.

*Careful what you ask for next time, Clara.*

"For starters, I'm getting ready to head into a custody battle. And...and then there's the kids. We're still new, Seth. Our relationship has barely been out and in the open for...well, I don't know how long. Then there's the whole name thing. Do I want a different last name from my kids? I might really fucking hate Joe, but how would it make Julie and Emmett feel? And would you even want me to take your last name? Is it weird if I do since you aren't using your birth name? How did you even settle on Woods as a last name to begin with? I don't even—"

Seth captures my mouth with a kiss, pressing hard enough to stall my thoughts that are spewing out of my mouth faster than running water. I'm the first to break away, taking in a giant gulp of air before removing my hand from his and wiping sweaty palms on my pajama bottoms.

"Clara, I'm not asking to marry you when the week is up, but I'd be lying to you if I said marriage has never crossed my mind. I think about it probably more than I'd like to admit. I didn't mean to upset you."

The thought occurs that the tables have turned. Just minutes ago he was freaking out over having to keep his member in his pants, and now here I am, overwhelmed by the possibility of marrying this man who I just let bite me last night.

Sure, I have thought about marriage within this head of mine, but it feels like a fantasy. I'm still coming to terms with Seth in my life, what he is, and the relationship that we're falling into and still forming. I guess I shouldn't be surprised by his candor. For the most part, he's always been open and honest with his intentions for me, for us.

The idea of Seth putting a ring on my finger and taking vows scares and excites the hell out of me. But the last time a man did that, I thought it would be for forever and boy, was I wrong. I know it's unfair to compare Seth to Joe. This man before me has already treated me a million times better than Joe ever did. He's come to my defense in more ways than I can count, and his affection is one of the many things I love about him.

"I'm sorry but, can we put marriage on the back burner for now?" Shyly, I look up at him. There isn't a hint of disappointment in his warm eyes, just...love. Adoration perhaps? He nods his head in agreement and only then do I finally let loose some air that I'd been holding for too long to the point that my head starts to feel a little funny. "Dare I ask if you have anything else in mind?"

Seth considers this for a moment, much calmer this time. "A trip."

Okay, this doesn't seem like a terrible alternative. "What kind of trip?"

"One that allows us to leave Iowa for a bit."

He's stated time and time again that he's here to stay, but when he phrases it like that I feel the need to joke. "Trying to leave already?"

Seth laughs. There's a small quirk to his lips as he scratches the side of his face. "Let's just leave it at that for now. But on another note, what are you going to choose should I fail at this weeklong bet?"

My hands go to my knees as I sit up and ponder that. I was so ready to give him something, I hadn't even given any thought to what I might want in return. Seth went from marriage to a trip, and lightning fast at that. What on earth could I want that he hasn't given me already?

A safe space. A listening and attentive ear. Someone to hold me when I cry and stand by my side no matter what I'm going through. Without my permission or knowledge, he put an end to my financial burden of a house payment, but I can't deny the room it's given me to breathe, having that lifted off of my shoulders.

Seth is a gift, just by being himself and coming into my life.

"If you get to be vague, then so do I." My mind is racing and what I arrive at is something I've given thought to a few times. I'm not sure how Seth would take it if I brought it up. For all I know, he could shut me down entirely, so I decide to keep my cards close. "A night of my choosing. When winter is over."

"A night?" Seth chuckles in amusement. "Beautiful, in case you haven't noticed, we have each other every night."

"Then let that add to the mystery of what I want to experience." I beam, pretending that what I'm thinking might not be a terrible task to begin with, but who's to say he's going to be able to abstain for a week anyway to find out?

"Deal?" I stick out my hand before either of us can ask any further questions.

Seth raises his and grasps my hand, pulling me toward him and eliciting a sharp yelp of surprise. "Deal." The gleam in his eyes tells me he's getting way too much enjoyment out of this little game. "Now, what are the rules?"

# 19

# Stay Strong

## *Seth*

I'm not sure how the days and nights can move so fast yet at the same time, drag on for an eternity and a half. Stupid me just *had* to ask about ground rules for this bet of Clara's. I swear my cock has been rock-hard ever since. She swats at me if my pelvic region even gets too close to her.

Hand holding, light kisses, and slight cuddling is okay. But heaven forbid I try to spoon her in bed. It's like she knows my resolve is slipping after just three nights. We're barely halfway through and I think I could chop down a tree with my hard-on.

Clara took Julie to the police station on Monday and surprisingly, we haven't heard a peep from Joe since Clara ended the call with him on Sunday night.

Together, we've been compiling the documentation the lawyer requested, and I've been helping her scan what documents she has along with a police report so the lawyer has it by the time we meet next week.

She's been so strong in the midst of all of this. Ever attentive to her children while simultaneously juggling my horny ass and the trouble brewing and bubbling over between her and her ex-husband.

Brain misfiring, I get hung up on that word. *Husband.*

I completely zone out from my computer monitors, hand hovering over my mouse as I reflect on a flustered and panicked Clara at the mere mention of marriage. Sometimes, I fail to remember that she's not a wolf. That our mate bond is one thing to me and something else entirely for her.

I inserted myself into her life without ever looking back. Fucked her when I couldn't mark her and marked her when she practically begged for it even if part of it was because she was trying to protect her family.

But why is marriage met with such heightened emotions? I'm fairly confident that her word vomit would have kept going until she ran out of air. Is the idea of a ring on her finger too much for her right now?

"Earth to Seth?" Dante's voice brings me out of my thoughts. Thank God this isn't a video call so he couldn't see me spacing out.

"Sorry, what?"

"Are we ready for the next phase or not?" He sounds a bit perturbed, as am I, trying to adjust myself in my chair. The fabric of my shorts is too constricting on my shaft that has gone neglected. I haven't beat myself off yet, wanting the first person to touch it to be Clara.

Or perhaps I'll make her watch as I bring myself to the brink. Watch her squirm as I stroke—

"Seth!"

I clear my throat. "Yeah, yeah sorry. We're good to go."

"Dude, what's with you? You alright?" Concern is thick on his voice now, and it wars with the images of a naked Clara occupying my mind. I pinch the bridge of my nose before turning my attention to the screen on my right.

"I uh..." I clear my throat again. "I think I'm going to try and bring Clara to San Diego."

There's a long pause. I half expect his wife to butt into the conversation as she has a knack for doing. I never know when she's close by or listening in.

"Waaaaait..." He draws out the word and I inhale deeply. In that single word alone, he's getting way too much enjoyment out of this already. "We're going to meet *the* Clara? The woman who's pinned you down?"

*I wish she'd pin me down.*

"There's a lot going on around here, and even though I'm going for work, I might skip out on a few sessions at the conference so I can spend some time with her. Get her to unwind and relax a bit."

"What about her kids? They coming too? You know there's a lot of drunks and uppity-ups at these things."

Little does Dante know, I'm already ahead of that little dilemma. Clara's dad is more than happy to come down for the week to watch them. He's even hoping for a chance to sling back a few beers with Larson while in town. I assured him that his favorite brand will be stored in the fridge in the garage. Joyce, on the other hand, won't be able to take the time off of work, otherwise she would come in a heartbeat.

Once I explained to them how hard this has been on Clara and that I want to give her some breathing room, they caved almost immediately, wanting to help out. I am growing more and more fond of the two that raised my Rose. Now if only I could meet her brother.

"They'll be taken care of by their grandpa, and I've already put a bug in one of Clara's coworker's ears about it." That Melissa is one who loves to chat. I gave her my number in case there's any trouble with Clara getting that time off after talking to their boss, but I haven't heard anything of the sort yet. I think Melissa is enjoying being in on this little secret a bit too much. My little dental cleaning was a successful visit all around.

"That's awesome. Susan's been asking about her. I think we'd both like to meet her if you two could spare some time for us and a lunch or dinner or something."

Fully prepared for this, I let out a chuckle. "Yeah, I think we could make that work."

The conversation between us begins to morph from personal, back into what we're actually getting paid to do. We stay on the phone for another twenty minutes, highlighting what we need to hash out in our next phase and any lingering questions that might need sorted out before we bring this project up again at our next team meeting. We're ahead of schedule at this point, so I'd like to think that my dear old boss will be pleased with that. I know that the equivalent of a pat on the back will probably be met with more work and more projects, but you can never say I don't have anything to do when it comes to my work.

Glancing at a new notification on my phone, I tense. I hadn't anticipated Penelope ever needing to contact me again, but her message contains a few words that instantly make the world stop, even if only briefly.

*Mike's dead.*

My dad has finally met his end. I can't move, unable to tear my gaze away from my phone as it goes dark. There's nothing more than a little message icon, the date, weather, and time now showing in the wake of that news.

I knew it was coming and yet this blow came out of nowhere. I'm not sad. Hell, I'm not even feeling any regret, so why do I feel...numb?

That man shouldn't have been able to wear the dad title. I won't pretend Father's Day was ever met with his favorite foods or thoughtful cards, love from a doting son. Those days had none of that. There was nothing to celebrate.

Our last call wasn't anything to stir any emotions besides hate. How could he expect me to forget the past and his hand in how I was raised?

"I'm sorry," "I won't do it again," and "Please, stop" were all phrases I learned at an early age. It wasn't until I finally changed, put on more muscle than him, and learned how to fight back that he finally withdrew his efforts to stifle me.

Was that his version of tough love? It certainly wasn't anything a *father* should be capable of.

I think that's why I got so pissed at Joe over his interaction with Julie. There was nobody to help me. Nobody to save me. Not my mom, my grandparents or uncles. I'd be damned if I ever let something like that happen to Julie and Emmett. Not on my watch.

Drawing up my generic "out of office" for work, I shove away from my desk and stand. Should I be angry? Sad? Relieved that one of the abusers of my past was finally taken out of this world and I didn't have to do it myself?

Head racing, I take a few steps but can't find any more footing to leave my office. The trips down memory lane stall me as I stare at the exit of this room. I have trouble recalling a time I was actually *happy* to have Mike Ries as a father. A single moment when I wanted his presence or to hear his voice. How disturbing is it that I can think of none?

Not even as a young boy did I ever want to be anything like my dad or my grandfather. They were the spitting image of each other, and their actions made them more twin-like than father and son.

Thank fucking God I didn't turn out like them.

But that still doesn't explain the gnawing grip this news has on me and why I can't force myself out of here, to move. Why is his death holding such a heavy weight over me from states and hundreds of miles away?

Shouldn't I feel...free?

# 20

# Some Scars Never Heal

## *Clara*

Seth has been quiet today. I sent him a text letting him know the kids and I made it home safe and sound but he's been unresponsive. There's no indication that he's even seen my message, so I send another after dinner to let him know it's still alright to come over after the kids go to bed.

I know that our little wager we have going between us has been a little touch and go, pun intended, but I don't think that's the root cause of this.

Perhaps I'm looking too far into a problem that simply isn't there. Maybe Seth is just caught up with work and is just in the zone.

Another thought rises to the surface, one that has my stomach in a ball of knots just thinking it.

The last time he went radio silent, his own family had taken him hostage and held him at his house. A cousin had begun to hunt me down with the determination to end me. A chill runs down my spine.

Eyeing my only child within view, Julie, who has her head buried in homework at the table, I begin to make my rounds to make sure all of the doors are locked. The front porch light is already flipped on and once I'm done, I sit down on the couch on the opposite end from where Emmett is sitting.

"Is Seth coming over tonight?" he inquires before I can even settle. Emmett is watching some Youtuber do some stupid stunt that would most likely get the cops called if it were any other person doing it.

"Um...think he might be busy with work. Probably not tonight." I press the button on the side of my phone as if a message from him will magically appear, but there's still nothing.

"Could we have taco pizza with him tomorrow? He's never had it."

I raise a brow at him, but he's not doing me the service of eye contact, his attention only partially involved in the conversation. "How do you know that?"

Emmett shrugs, but the move looks minimal beneath his blue hoodie.

"You don't even eat the pizza. You just pick off the chips," I retort. It's one of my pet peeves. If you want the chips on the pizza, you need to *eat* the pizza that they're on. Emmett doesn't even realize what he's missing out on.

"You know he just wants pepperoni." Julie raises her voice slightly, joining in on the conversation. "With a side of crunched up chips."

"Shut up!" Emmett finally drags his interest away from the television and it's like he can shoot daggers through the wall that hinders his view of his sister. Only when he sees me scowling does he backtrack.

"Sorry," he mumbles to me before growing a bit red in the face.

I swear, it's like they forget I'm even here sometimes.

"I know Julie's got cheer tomorrow night, what if we shoot for Friday? Pizza and a movie night in?" I say loud enough for the both of them to hear me clearly.

"Yes," Emmett hisses in victory.

"Yep." Julie comes strolling in and plops down on the couch beside me before leaning her head on my shoulder. I tilt mine on top of hers and we sit there, watching a grown-ass man do shit that has me mentally scratching my head with his absurdity.

It's not until I send a worried text that I finally get a response from Seth, telling me that he'll be over in about five minutes. When he arrives, he all but blows in through the front door and heads straight for my room.

Guess I should call it *our* room at this point in the game. Seth is quickly diminishing the number of nights I sleep alone and honestly, I don't think I can ever go back to life without him, nor do I want to.

"Is everything okay with work?" I question as I shut the bedroom door quietly. I turn to find Seth in the middle of the room, still facing away. It's normal for us not to speak until we're in here, fearful of voices traveling up the stairs. At least here I can chalk some noises up to the television.

Well, it's debatable for some of those noises.

His avoidance has me treading lightly in his direction and when I'm about a foot away, he swivels so fast that I jump. Startled, I search his eyes but he keeps them fixed off and to the side of me. I grow nervous. It's more than an inkling telling me that something is wrong, and his silence before me is suspicious enough.

"Seth..." I start, but don't know how to follow through.

"My dad's dead."

It takes a second for his words to click. I'm so focused on the narrowing of his eyes and his rigid form that I almost don't comprehend it.

I struggle with what to feel, with what to say, perplexed if I should be consoling him and providing any comfort or praising the demise of the man who caused Seth so much pain. The problem is, I can't decipher what avenue to take with his stone-cold exterior.

I'm a mix of emotions myself, and I don't want to be. I'm furious about how a man I never knew treated his one and only son, yet I mourn for a man losing his father.

Carefully, I reach for his hand. The surface is cold yet the blood pumping through his veins beneath my touch is warming it quickly. It's like he's been outside for some time.

Seth finally blinks, then shakes his head before lifting his chin up as if he's looking at the ceiling now. That jawline of his looks more pointed than the view I'm accustomed to.

"Is there anything I can do?" I give his hand a gentle squeeze. His reluctance to speak up is pulling at my heartstrings. We knew that his dad had cancer and the possibility of a year left to live. I guess time wasn't on his side after all.

Is he torn up about the news of his father's passing? How did he even find out? It doesn't seem that far-fetched that his mother would have called, even though Seth has stated more than once that he's done with the family, the pack, and everything and anything related to the life he once had.

"He doesn't deserve my grieving." Seth finally breaks the silence, but I'm not afforded a view of his face. "He doesn't..."

His free hand darts up to his face and pinches his nose before he finally lowers his face into view. He takes in a sharp inhale as his body starts to shake. I can't make out if it's anger or something else. Could he be upset enough to bring about the change that will turn him from man to werewolf?

"Seth, just breathe." I try not to get panicked by the possibility swarming around in my head. I'm not sure Seth can be quiet enough to get through the shift without disturbing the kids upstairs.

"I don't understand." His arms swoop around me as he bends and holds me beneath him. I wrap my arms around him in return, trying to hold on tight and provide him what little comfort I can.

Seth sniffles, and I swear I can feel my heart breaking. I place a hand on his head as I hold him close, and when I feel something wet on my shoulder, my eyes start to burn in response.

I know Seth has had a hard life. A past that he wants to forget and move on from and a family that shunned him. A so-called family that wanted nothing to do with him for over a decade before rolling back into the picture again. Beneath his shirt, literal scars from a dad and grandpa who beat him. Who fucking *whipped* him.

As much as I loathe seeing Seth's reaction to his dad dying, I can't help the roiling anger that takes hold of me. I know I had a slim to none chance of ever confronting the bastard and his disastrous and barbaric treatment of his son, but I sure as hell will form a compelling speech in my head about the piece of shit that he was.

Not until Seth pulls away do I relent. Dwelling on Seth's past and the pain caused there will do us no good right here and right now. His eyes are glassy, cheeks wet from streams of tears that track down into his facial hair, and I know that if I look on my shoulder I'll find a puddle there.

Seth has been my rock since he came into my life. It's time for me to return the favor, in any shape or form that he needs.

"Is there anything I can do?" I lift his hand between us and encompass it with both of my own.

Everyone deals with death differently. If he needs to let everything out and cry and mourn, so be it. If Seth needs to expel hatred with actions and words, then let's run out and into the forest where there are no witnesses and several trees to take it out on. All I need is for him to let me in.

His golden hues have turned gloomy. A face that is capable of holding such light is now painstakingly tugging at every fiber of my being. How does one cope with the news of the death of a parent when they were the complete opposite of close and being on good terms?

"I can't be alone with my thoughts any longer." He works on a swallow. The bob in his throat is more pronounced than usual. "I just need to be with you."

I rest my head on our hands for a moment before kissing his knuckles. "I'll always be here for you. You'll never even have to ask."

# 21

# Hasty or Calculated?

## *Clara*

Seth fell asleep on my lap sometime after midnight and I wiggled down into the bed next to him shortly after. He hadn't wanted to talk and I wasn't going to force anything from him, especially if he wasn't ready. It already sounded like he was struggling with this news and the only thing I could think to do was to turn on the TV after he arrived and let us watch mindlessly to fill the silence. I turned on a reality show that I haven't seen the most recent season of, but even with the new twists being introduced, it wasn't enough to keep my brain occupied.

I can't help but wonder when Seth found out, and how long he went between then and coming over. I hate that I wasn't there for him when he found out. Even with Seth's admittance of how much he despises his family and the way they treated him, I don't fault him grieving or question why he is.

While watching strangers before me, I reflected on each time I can remember someone passing. My great aunt. My grandpas on both sides and my one grandma on my paternal side. The cousin I barely knew who was in a terrible accident out in Michigan. Each time I had different reactions and responses. Grieving times varied from days, to weeks, to months. Sometimes it depended on the bond, the connection we'd once shared. For others, like my cousin, the horror of a young life taken too soon by a freak accident clung to me in an almost unnatural way.

Then there's my great uncle who I veered away from in a store because of how out there he was. The guilt still eats away at me to this day, remembering how that could have been my final interaction with him. I can't even recall the last time we had a conversation together.

I know my experiences with death pale in comparison to what Seth is going through. I can't imagine being in his shoes.

At some point in the night, Seth curled up along my backside as he normally does, forming around me with an arm around my stomach. I used to flinch every time he did it, but the more times he sees me naked and explores my body, the more I'm letting my guard down.

Carefully, I reach for my phone. Seth's even-paced breathing hasn't changed since I awoke, and while it's a bit strange to have stirred before him, I turn slightly to try and keep the glow from my phone shielded away from him.

It's almost time for my first alarm to go off, but I go in and toggle them all off so he can sleep uninterrupted a little bit longer. Then, I go to the internet and search for his father.

For a moment, I wonder if it's too soon. If Seth was notified immediately after his father's passing, perhaps the obituary won't be available yet, but to my surprise, I get a hit fairly quickly. Uploaded last night to a rather peculiar-looking funeral home's website.

*Michael Alan Ries, 60, of Torenbrook, Colorado, lost his battle with cancer...*

I read each word, silently mouthing them as I learn about Seth's father. He married Alice Young and I don't know why, but I'm surprised that they mention their "one and only son" who was their pride and joy. I'm sure my eye roll is loud enough to wake Seth, but his steady breathing allows me to keep going. Mike started a local hardware store that branched out into surrounding areas, and there are mentions of his hobbies—hunting, fishing, and hiking. Quite the outdoorsman. I wonder if his wolf nature was responsible for that or if he *actually* enjoyed those activities.

The family listed within the article takes up over half of the piece, and Seth's name is in there along with the surviving family members, even noting that he lives in Iowa. My nose crinkles, hating how they're involving Seth so much when he's had nothing to do with them in a long time.

When I get to the end, I note that the funeral service is planned for the day after tomorrow.

*Shitty timing,* I think to myself. But at least neither of us have to be alone as we try to navigate our trials and push forward. I'm gearing up for a possibly ugly custody battle and Seth's dad just so happens to pass away quicker than we anticipated.

Seth's nose nuzzles into my neck as he inhales. I quickly hit the side button on my phone and stow it beneath my pillow, turning my body in his hold to face him. He has yet to open his eyes, but his features are relaxed as I bring a hand up to rest on his side.

"Morning," I exhale, trying to keep my voice light.

Returning my greeting, he adds, "What's got you all worked up?"

Brows pinching, I can't help but wonder what he's talking about. "I...don't know what you mean."

Seth inhales through his nose this time as he readjusts himself on his pillow before finally opening his eyes slightly. He looks dreamy. Not that he doesn't any other time, but there's something so serene about the image of him before me. Rousing from sleep is another look he wears well. "Your heart rate." His gravelly morning voice is a sultry sound that I love to hear even if he's in the midst of almost catching me and my detective work. "It spiked and you're still trying to come down from it."

"Oh." I laugh nervously. "You just startled me. I was just browsing on my phone. I'm sorry if I woke you." I give his side a gentle squeeze, nothing but firm muscle beneath my touch. There's such a stark difference between my flabby parts and his taut frame.

Silence falls as Seth's gaze drops to my lips. I wait patiently, wanting him to make the first move. But at the same time, I feel like we're seconds away from when the news of his father's passing comes rushing back and restarts his silent torment all over again.

Bet or not, if Seth needs to find some kind of comfort in the form of intimacy, then so be it. If I need to call off from work today to be with him, I will. Whatever he needs from me, I will do everything in my power to accommodate.

"Clara—"

"Yes?" I cut him off a bit too abruptly and my lips roll in on themselves sheepishly.

The hold he has on me lowers toward my hip, and he takes a handful of my rear before returning his focus to me. "I need to go to Colorado."

I'm a bit stunned for a moment. There's panic on my part, then understanding, then an insurmountable amount of confusion. I won't fault him for wanting or needing to go. What I won't be able to ignore is how much it scares me for him to do so.

"Do I need to go with you?"

My offer is shot down immediately, his mood turning dark. "Absolutely not."

While my heart might be in the right place in asking, I fear what he might encounter by going. With a grieving family, how will these members react to seeing Seth after so much time had passed? How will they react when two out of three of his cousins died by his hands just months ago?

"But…" My bottom lip trembles as I try to convey my worries. "What if you don't come back? You…you're responsible for killing your own family members. What if they retaliate? What if you don't come home?"

That last word spins around in my mind on repeat and tightens my throat. This is Seth's home now. By his own admittance and now mine. Whether it's the state of Iowa, his physical address across the bridge, or right here, this is where he belongs.

"As long as you're here waiting for me, I'll always come back to you."

"But…" My eyes are starting to burn again, thinking that he's not taking this seriously. "Do you have to go alone? What about Larson? Could he go with you?"

Seth turns pensive, as if the wheels inside his head hadn't thought about that alternative. "I'll pay him a visit today."

I'd almost expected him to meet me with some kind of stubbornness, but perhaps he's seeing an ally as a possible necessity. If it means Seth might have a better chance at staying safe, it helps suppress my rising distress.

Knowing that the funeral is so close but not wanting to show my awareness of it, I tread lightly. "How soon will you need to go? And for how long?"

"It's a lengthy drive, but maybe two, three days tops."

I swallow hard, hating that he'll be away for that long. Especially not knowing what kind of greeting he'll be met with.

Just yesterday, Seth was kind of unavailable, shutting me out whether he'd meant to or not. My mind took me back to November when I thought the worst might have happened. "We need scheduled check-ins or something. I don't mean to be overbearing or sound overprotective, but after everything we've been through so far, we need to have a plan."

There's nothing I can do to stop the shake in my voice. I suspect that's what causes Seth to pull at my hips, bringing me impossibly close until I can feel his breath on my forehead as he kisses me. His bare leg draws up and over mine, locking me in place, and I'm now flush against him. I don't even try to push him away, not even with his ever persistent erection pushing against me.

"I need to do this, Clara."

"I know." My voice breaks as my eyes begin to leak. There's not a chance I would ask him not to, no matter how selfishly I might want him to stay. "I just want you safe."

It's on the tip of my tongue to joke about the talk on marriage that I royally screwed up when he'd mentioned it just days ago, but I refrain. I don't think this is the time or the place to bring that up. Not when the man's father literally just died and Seth is going through an unpredictable ride of emotions.

Mike Ries might have been a son of a bitch who hurt his child in ways I could never understand, but he was still that—a father. Even if Seth sought a life without him in the picture.

"Whatever schedule you see fit for check-ins, I will abide by it until I am back here and by your side."

I nod, even if it's minimal with our close proximity.

His hips roll into mine and it catches me off guard. My breath hitches as Seth takes me by the mouth and my hands frame around his face, savoring him. Body responding, I rock into him. Our bodies' demands are evident. The urgency and feverish state has us pulling at each other as if there's a chance that we can mold ourselves into one.

My core is throbbing with the desire for us to secure ourselves together. I play with the waistband of his boxers, curling the tips of my fingers in as I trail across beneath it. I'm almost ready to dive beneath before Seth seizes me by the wrist, groaning in regret.

I use the break to say, "I really don't care about the bet right now."

The grip he has on me, both physically and mentally, is intoxicating. The possibility of Seth being gone for three days is almost unbearable. It feels silly of me to think so, but I can't deny it. Not with who's involved and what's at stake here.

His voice pitches lower as he mutters my name. It brings about a chill as I look into his eyes. I'm ready to submit to him; he doesn't even have to ask. If this is how I have to send him off on his way to Colorado, I can think of worse ways to go about it.

Seth plants a hard kiss on me, one that makes me struggle for the last remnants of air within my lungs, and then he releases me. His entire hold on me, gone. Rolling off the bed in one swift move, he goes to stand and begins to dress while I'm still struggling against lightheadedness.

I sit up, questioning his sudden rush. He must sense it, because there's a small upturn at the corner of his mouth. "I'm taking you on that trip."

Shoulders deflating, I cross my arms in a pout. "Screw. The. Bet."

The corner of his mouth pulls at the rest and he's full-on grinning at me now. He drags on his sweatshirt before he kneels back on the bed on all fours. There's something gleaming in his eyes, even though the room is still poorly lit. "You started this, Clara. I fully intend to see it through. And win."

My jaw drops, realizing that he's doing the exact same thing I did to him before this bet started. Seth had been hot, bothered, and ready to go for whatever round we were on, and I shut him down. Took sex off the table because after he marked and ravaged me, I couldn't even manage a conversation with him otherwise. It was like he'd popped a bottle of Viagra and the Energizer Bunny was a dear friend of his.

Hand wrapping around the back of my neck, he brings me close but this time his kisses are slow and relaxed. I pull at his shirt to entice him to stay, but he resists, laughing as he stands.

The turnaround in Seth's mood from when he arrived last night to this morning is remarkable. It's confounding how he could go from down in the dumps and grasping to understand his feelings to this mischievous and playful side. Was there some sort of epiphany he had in the night to cause the sudden change?

Regardless, it seems as if his head is fixed right and on his shoulders again. I move on the bed, lifting my oversized nightshirt a bit so I can move better. I hug him around his middle, press the side of my face against his chest, and speak words that are getting easier to say out loud with each passing day. "I love you."

There's no hesitation when he folds his arms around me, curving his stature as he settles into the hold we have on one another before returning the sentiment.

From the sound filling my ears, I swear my heart beats in time with his. I just hope he knows what he's doing with this trip.

# 22

# Happy Travels

## *Seth*

The early morning talk with Larson doesn't exactly go according to plan but it isn't a waste of time either. He poses a good point, though. Clara shouldn't remain here without any sort of protection. If both Larson and I were out of the picture, it wouldn't be a smart move. Within an hour, I have a volunteer to accompany me to Colorado. It's not who I expected, but I'm not going to turn down the plus-one either.

Only after hammering out the details, packing a light bag, and driving over an hour to an airport, do I finally come face-to-face with her again.

Katrina. The blue-eyed werewolf who just so happened to have found her mate in a human, like myself, is waiting for me as I make my way toward the TSA checkpoint. She has a backpack and small suitcase on rollers in tow. It's her eyes that I notice first, and now that she's without all of her winter gear that bundled her up, I can see her bleach-blonde hair. It's darker at the roots and I'm not sure if that's a style choice or she just needs a touch-up. I can recall my mother dyeing her hair any time her roots began to show; it was a constant battle for her.

It was Katrina's idea to fly instead of drive. To create a paper trail should anything go south, from the plane tickets, to the rental car and the hotel. She was quick to throw my mother and cousins under the bus, saying that their stalking and tactics were "stupid and flawed." I didn't think to ask why, but took her up on her course of action. She's the one doing me a solid anyway.

Knowing that she single-handedly finished off members of her pack in her escape, I have to give her credit. She might be small compared to me, but I have no idea just what she's capable of. Katrina stows her cellphone in her back pocket as I approach.

"Nice of you to come." She raises a brow as if she'd been waiting for me for some time. Her attitude is unexpected.

"Sorry?" I pose the single word like a question, not knowing why she's in a mood when *she's* the one who volunteered in the first place. Larson's phone was loud enough, I heard her clear as day.

Katrina rolls her eyes before her head shakes. "God, chill. I live like fifteen minutes away from here."

She spins on the ball of her feet and heads toward the escalators that lead upstairs. I follow after her, under the assumption that she knows where she's going.

This airport is smaller than most that I've visited. Its beige and white interior is warm and inviting. There are posters and murals from colleges and sights around Iowa. Even that pitchfork guy and his wife in front of that white house. Clara said it's from a small town—smaller than Alton if you can believe that—and it isn't that far away. Nowhere in our conversation did she tell me why the house is considered gothic. The little white house looks nothing of the sort if you ask me.

Katrina and I carry through the security line without saying another word to each other, going through the motions of emptying our pockets of anything the officers deem problematic. Neither of us are chosen for the pat down, and we walk away without a fuss as we collect our belongings and continue to our gate. Luckily, there aren't too many people flying out to Denver this afternoon, and as another plus, it beats spending over ten hours in the car with someone I've only met once.

I shoot Clara a quick text, letting her know that I've arrived at my gate and that I'll message her as soon as the plane lands. I screenshot my flight info so she has it in case she wants to keep tabs on it. She's quick to reply, as if she was already on her phone when my message came through.

My Rose wasn't exactly thrilled when I told her my company is another woman on my drive up here. It took some persuading and a few promises to get her on board, but she eventually saw my side of it. I can understand where she's coming from, though, especially since Joe took advantage of her and fucked up their lives when his dick landed in someone else. But that won't be the case here.

I promised to call her tonight when I'm settled into the hotel and again when I awake tomorrow. We agreed that I'll send her updates every two hours after that point. And, should anything go south and someone needs to be alerted, I told her that if I send the message -*Red*- then she needs to contact Larson immediately.

Katrina plops down on a chair and gives me the side-eye as I do the same beside her. My shoulders rise in confusion before I blurt out, "What?"

"No business talk until we're in the rental car." She puts little pink buds in her ears and begins thumbing through her phone.

So that's what we're calling it. *Business.*

I don't want to be alone in my thoughts, replaying possible scenarios and outcomes until I drive myself crazy. But as much as I would have loved to have my mate by my side to calm my unsettling thoughts, I know it's too big of a risk.

Leaving my bag in my seat, I take off to find a snack, and possibly a book.

The flight is uneventful and smooth. I sit in an exit row for the extra leg room and only one other guy takes the aisle seat while I take the window. The book I chose was the last one in its spot, with gold swords and bloodied roses on the cover. I nabbed it from the title alone, and came across an enemies-to-lovers storyline that actually kept my racing mind at bay while on the flight. I've never considered myself a reading guy, especially when it comes to romance novels, but this one has a grip on me for some damned reason. I have to admit, for vampires, it is kind of entertaining.

After we land, I stuff it into my bag and give Clara another text before the seat belt sign goes off. It always annoys the hell out of me that practically everyone jumps up at the same time, gathering their luggage and waiting in the aisle as if they could get off any faster.

Example A, my closest neighbor in dress pants and suit jacket. He has his shoulder bag on and is tapping his foot with his arms crossed and a heavy frown on his face as if exiting the plane is the worst thing to happen to him today.

A child begins to whine and I can't help turning over my shoulder to look. There's a young mother, her hair pulled back into a messy ponytail, who's trying to wrangle the young boy who is trying to flee from her hold on him. To be honest, I'd forgotten there were any kids on the plane. Either he slept for the duration of the flight or was thoroughly entertained through it all. Until now, that is.

The woman is trying to quiet him, face and neck growing red with embarrassment as her eyes flit to the strangers around her. I can't imagine her even being out of high school yet by her youthful appearance. The boy is still in diapers or pull-ups, judging by the lining I can see poking out over the elastic band of his pants.

Mr. Suit in the aisle looks back at the boy in disgust and I'm moving before I can even think it through, kneeling on the seats and turning in their direction.

"Hey, little guy," I say gently, and eyes that match his mother's blink at me in curiosity, his plight momentarily forgotten as he pauses within her hold. "What's your name?"

There's a smudge of orange dust on the corner of his lips as he blinks up at me. "Bennie."

The grin that sweeps across my face comes naturally. This little toddler is a cute one and not at all frightened of me. Sometimes kids get intimidated by my facial hair for some reason. "Did you like the plane ride, Bennie?"

With that, he nods his head enthusiastically, straight brown hair shaking with him. "Yeah! Clouds are huge!" He stretches his arms out real wide with the raising of his voice, earning a few chuckles from some of the other passengers, some of whom were just glaring at him in disapproval earlier.

All except for the stick-in-the-mud suit guy whose clean-shaven jawline has turned tense.

Bennie's mother gathers a few things from their seats and shoves them into a large diaper bag that honestly, I have no idea how it fit underneath the seat in front of her.

"They are," I agree with him. "You know, you were so good on this flight, I didn't even know you were behind me. You must have been really good for your mom."

It's easy to see that the mother is exhausted and running on fumes. I only hope that this is her final destination and she doesn't have to worry about hopping on another plane just to do this all over again.

The guy in the suit is quick to take off, rumbling a low curse of some sort, and I let the row beside me go before I step into the aisle. I offer to help the mother, taking the large bag as she follows behind. It's not until we've exited the jet bridge and are out of the line of traffic do I stop.

"Thank you, sir." She hauls the bag over her shoulder. It's stuffed to the brim and looks like it's trying to counteract the weight of her son on her other side now that she's picked him up.

I shrug. "It's no problem. Is Denver your final stop?"

"Yes," she sighs. "Thank goodness. My grandparents live here and flew us out to see them. It's been a loooooong day already."

Definitely explains why she looks so tired, stressed, and little Bennie is ready to expend so much energy. From the look on his face, he recognizes where he is. He's buzzing with excitement.

"Grammy?" He's all hopeful, balling up his fists close to his chin.

"Yes, Grammy is picking us up."

The squeal that leaves him has me chuckling, until I catch sight of my traveling companion on the phone. She shoots me a glance as she turns away. Are we still supposed to pretend we don't know each other or something?

"Well, Bennie is going to be an expert traveler in no time if he keeps this up." I go to take a step away, but offer a few parting words. "Glad you made it to Denver alright. Be good for Mommy, Bennie, alright?"

He nods his head so hard that the mother has to regain her grip on both him and the bag on her shoulder before I take my leave. She thanks me again and I take off, headed in the direction I know will lead me to the car rentals.

Katrina tails me at a distance. She remains on the phone while I wait for someone to get us some wheels, and it's not until I head out the door that she hangs up. She utters a swift thanks before throwing her bags in the trunk and getting in the passenger side.

I'm attempting to manually adjust my seat when Katrina finally talks. "Hotel?"

I cock my head in her direction, narrowing my eyes. "Where else would we go?"

Hotel today. Funeral home tomorrow. Then we leave on the next flight we can nab out of here. That's the plan I want to stick to. If I can be in and out of Colorado within twenty-four hours, that would be even better. I'm not going to the visitation or funeral. I have no intention of being bombarded with family members. I know I wouldn't exactly be met with open arms and warm greetings.

Katrina crosses one leg over the other and lays her hands in her lap as she waits for me to make sure mirrors and everything are lined up to my liking. "Didn't know if anything had changed since this morning."

"This isn't going to be some happy reunion. The sooner we can leave and return home, the better."

"Agreed," she snips, before turning her gaze out of her window.

Putting the small sedan in drive, I head out. The car is already starting to warm up as I weave in and out of traffic as if I've been driving around here my entire life. I might not have darkened Colorado's borders since I left, but knowing how to get around comes back to me in full force as I begin to navigate where we need to go.

Once traffic lightens up a bit, I loosen my grip on the steering wheel to a more relaxed stance. Katrina doesn't seem like one for small talk, but the silence in the car is starting to eat at my nerves. It's not like I was expecting us to get all buddy-buddy on this trip, but I'm having trouble figuring out why she was the one to volunteer for this with what little information had been given.

If the tables had been reversed, I would have demanded more answers before agreeing to come. Katrina is already aware of my past pack, the terms in which I left, and the deaths of my cousins last fall, so why was she ready to jump in on this trip when there's a funeral involved? Is this non-pack of theirs really that close-knit that they look after one another in this manner?

"May I ask you something?" I tread lightly as I flip on my signal so I can get around a truck that's going way too slow for the highway.

There's a pause before she finally breaks out of her outward stare, but only brings her gaze forward. I don't know if she's just stubborn or testing my limits here. I decide I don't care and move on.

"Why did you volunteer? You don't even know me."

Katrina's eyes narrow into slits, and it's not because of the snow reflecting brightly around us.

I'm not going to deliver a damn monologue, but I'm going to get her to talk one way or another. We've still got a bit of a drive before we get to the hotel we've booked in the next town over from where I grew up.

"You guys know about my old pack. Their desire to try and kill my mate and take me back here. This visit could turn ugly if I'm not careful. Why risk it when you have a mate of your own back home?"

"And five kids," she offers, giving me the first glimpse into a life I know nothing about. But the way she answers has me second-guessing even bringing her along in the first place.

If my family were to try and pull some stupid shit while I'm here, I can't risk it. I can't put her life in jeopardy. Not with a family at home.

I make a last-second decision and hard turn onto an exit ramp. She curses and braces herself as the sound of a horn goes off from behind. "What the fuck?"

"You're on the next flight back home." I shake my head in disbelief. No way in hell am I going to be responsible for five kids losing their mother and her mate losing the love of his life.

"What is *wrong* with you?" Her blue eyes turn violent as I peel into a gas station parking lot and come to a stop.

I wasn't planning on picking a fight with Katrina, especially so early in our little outing to Colorado, but you know what? Plans change.

"You do realize that this pack lost three of their own trying to get me to come back here? They were willing to kill my mate—"

"Who do you think killed that son of a bitch, Adam? Huh?" Her words hang in the air, as if I can see them forming around her head. I study her, both puzzled and alarmed by this piece of information. I told Larson I didn't care what happened to him, and he only assured me that he would be taken care of.

"You..." Not only did she kill members of her own pack to get out, now she's an assassin of some sort? What, Larson and Edgar brought her in to finish Adam off?

"Me." She meets me with gritted teeth. "Believe me, I know what I signed up for. Don't treat me with kid gloves just because I'm a mother. I can take care of my goddamn self."

Katrina might be half my size, but knowing her body count could very well be up there right along with mine, I have to respect her for that. I guess I was lucky enough to leave my pack without a scene. At least, there wasn't one to my knowledge. And it took my dad nearing death for them to try and bring me back. But Katrina? Finding her mate and killing anyone who stood in the way of her having that?

It makes me think that this woman beside me might be the perfect traveling companion after all.

Maybe I do need her by my side should we find ourselves in battle. She has something to fight for too.

"Then let's make sure you make it home safe and sound, as soon as possible."

I break eye contact, settling back into my seat as I shift the car into reverse. I can feel her heated stare on me as I make my way back onto the road that will lead me toward the highway.

This compact car might not be big enough for the two of us hot-headed wolves.

"Now how about we score some food before I go feral?" she muses unenthusiastically.

I can't help the bark of laughter that leaves me, easing the tension between us ever so slightly. "Feral? You can't be serious."

She shrugs as she leans back in her seat, examining her nails as she nonchalantly states, "Fuck around and find out."

I won't deny that witnessing Katrina do such a thing could prove quite the sight. But for no reason do I want to find myself a target in her eyes. And I'm sure not going to let food be the cause of it.

# 23

# A Final Goodbye

## *Seth*

I didn't sleep worth a shit.

The hotel bed was too empty without Clara's body next to mine. The smell of her lingers in my memory and nothing more. I should have packed a shirt of hers to remember her by, but even I can admit that's a bit overboard.

My call with her last night was shaky. Clara was careful in each statement or wording she chose, hesitant and uncertain every time she spoke. We stayed on the phone for too long, to the point where Clara's breathing grew heavy and I could imagine her lips parting as she teetered between sleep and consciousness.

I know the irony of all of this trip. Swearing off my family, leaving them in the past and wanting nothing to do with them. Killing them off when they wouldn't bug off and take a hike. Now, here I am in Colorado to see my father who finally succumbed to his disease. I'm coming back to the place and its people that I swore I would have nothing to do with ever again.

I'm still unable to figure out the "why" in it all. This unexplainable need to see him one last time. Will seeing his dead, cold, and lifeless body put my mind at ease? Will it help put an end to the torment he caused when I lived under his roof? I fucking spit on my grandpa's grave when no one was looking, grateful that he could no longer cause me any misery. So why am I running back here before a funeral that I have no intention of being a part of?

There's a family burial site that my dad will be laid to rest in. Only close members of the pack will be present for the graveside service even if all are welcome to attend the visitation and funeral. I have no intention of setting foot back on the pack's territory. That would be a suicide mission. The funeral home? Now that is as neutral of a space as one could have. A place for even those outside of the pack to mourn or pay their respects.

After sending Clara a text, I find Katrina already waiting for me in the lobby. The place is buzzing with activity. The area that houses the complimentary breakfast is chaotic and I note the presence of countless young guys who might be traveling for basketball or something. I don't envy the chaperones who are trying to get a handle on their shenanigans as one raises their voice in some kind of roaring order to quiet them.

"Finally," Katrina mutters as I close in, and she slips her shades down over her eyes as she takes her leave, heading toward the sliding doors. She has a disposable coffee cup in hand and while I wouldn't mind grabbing some to go for myself, I decide it's probably best to avoid the show in the dining area.

"Didn't sleep well?" I ask curiously. I sure didn't.

She scoffs as she takes a swig of her drink. "You'd think I would have, not having a kid or two trying to climb into my bed, but no. Apparently I can't sleep with or without them."

"Do they have nightmares?" The winter weather rushes us as the last set of doors open and we make a hard right to travel down the row of cars to find ours. I'm then reminded that my truck is back in Iowa and we're stuck in a damn rental. At least I didn't have to put the miles on my own vehicle.

"Nightmares. Weird sounds. Thunderstorms. The cat gets the zoomies and wakes them up so they can't get back to sleep." She sighs. "There's always something."

I can't help but grin, pondering if Julie and Emmett did that in their younger years. Sadly, I only ever went to my parents' room one time after having a nightmare of my own, and it was the last time I ever darkened their bedroom doorway. Some people just shouldn't be parents. A shiver runs through me at that memory. My mother might never have raised a hand to me, but my father did enough for the both of them.

That unsettling imagery lingers for a moment as we reach the car, and just as I touch the handle, I stop as something registers. "Wait, you have a cat?"

Katrina rolls her eyes before she shoots me an annoyed look. It's freezing in the small space we confine ourselves to, and only then do I realize that my key has a remote start. It was stupid of me to not think of starting our ride up sooner. Then again, my head isn't exactly screwed on straight and hasn't been since finding out about my father's passing.

"We do. And no, we don't get along. We steer clear of each other."

Felines don't care for us wolves and usually flip out around us, hissing and hightailing it out of there to get away from us. I haven't met one yet that likes me.

"What's the plan?" She crosses her arms and I can't help but feel guilty for how long it's taking the engine to warm up.

Shifting my mind to a state of focus, I grip the steering wheel just a little tighter. The cold leather creaks from the squeeze. "The funeral home should be opening now and we have several hours until any family arrives for the open visitation. I went to school with one of the mortician's sons and I'm hopeful that with a few words, I can buy some time."

"And where do you want me while you're"—she gestures oddly in my direction—"doing your thing?"

"There's a foyer you should be able to wait in but you shouldn't have to get comfortable. I don't plan on being there long."

Shortly, I'm turning onto the main drag that will lead us out of the current town we're in and take us directly into Bluewater Springs. The only town my younger self ever knew before leaving and creating a life of my own.

Memory lane begins to unfold and my thoughts take a turn as more and more negatives rise to the surface. I struggle to find times that I was happy. Places that instilled any sort of peace or reprieve.

I remember finding the courage and strength to mold and shape my body in a gym full of peers that once picked on and laughed at me. Once I proved that I could bench-press twice as much as they could, they started to look at me differently.

Only then did Penelope come along. I know she was far from perfect, but the relationship I had with her in the beginning was a small light in a dark cave. When she took an interest in me, only then did so-called *friends* begin to surface.

One of which is now standing outside the funeral home's back entrance and smoking a cigarette. While people thought he was weird in school, they also liked that they could ask him anything and everything related to death. He was teased for it, sure. But to this day I can still recall the faces of those whose curiosity was piqued when he spoke of such topics. From someone dropping dead, to their transportation and the embalming process, and so on. Hell, I was one of them.

"Do you know how many exits there are?" Katrina pulls me from my thoughts, interrupting our silent ride that is now coming to an end.

"Two for guests. The main entrance out front and a side entrance that has a ramp for wheelchair accessibility." I purposefully turn the car to approach the back entrance so Katrina can see the garage door where they bring the bodies in. It's only a few yards away from the door where my fellow graduate stands.

"That there is Mitch. His dad owns the place. At least, last I knew he did." I park the car in front of him as he puts out his cigarette and the little plume of smoke evaporates. "He knows about our kind but I don't know where his loyalty lies. It's been too long. These exits are for anyone who is employed here."

"Got it." She unbuckles and we exit the vehicle. Katrina moves swiftly, shutting her door before I'm fully standing. She's definitely a quick one.

"Surprised to see you here," Mitch calls out in a raspy voice. I hate to admit that I'm a bit saddened that he's never kicked his smoking habit. If he's been doing it since high school without stopping, no wonder his tone is a wreck. He's wearing a black ball cap and a dark overcoat. He looks so much like his dad it's insane to me. Although, with the lines on his face, he looks like he's added on about ten years.

Casting a look around, I find the neighboring houses are quiet. In the distance, a train can barely be heard in its passing, but other than that everything is still. I only hope that coming so early will be to my benefit.

The funeral home hasn't changed much. The old, two-story brick building still has the charm from its era. The white windows, though—those look new, their pristine frames in a bright white. There are remnants of vines that have died and I can imagine how green they could be as they climb through the summer.

The upstairs used to house Mitch's grandparents. But since they passed, no one else decided to move in up there. He used to joke about the place being haunted by them to get a reaction out of classmates. Even tried to make a quick buck out of doing ghost tours until his dad busted him. Quite the entrepreneurial spirit if you ask me.

"Good to see you too, Mitch." I stow the key fob in my pocket and round the car. Katrina meets me on the other side, zeroing in on him, her face almost set in a scowl. I'm starting to wonder if there's anyone that she *does* like.

"I'm assuming you're not here to sign the guest book." Mitch crosses his arms. He's bulked up a bit since high school, his once lanky frame almost forgotten.

I merely shake my head, unsure of how to steer this conversation, but decide to test the waters to see if I can get a better read on him. "Don't suppose I can convince you to cremate the bastard?"

Katrina's head snaps in my direction, taking in a sharp inhale of breath. I could be playing with fire here. Mitch could owe something to my family and alert them of my presence. Or maybe, just maybe, he might take mercy on me and help an old friend. I don't know how much has changed around here and this could become a very dangerous game. I have to keep my time here short, for both Katrina's sake and mine.

Mitch barks out a choke of laughter, but it's not enough to ease the building tension inside of me. "Sure you're not going to throw a lighter in his casket? I might have good insurance on this place, but I don't want to test that out."

He snickers before turning his back on us to open the screen door, waving us to follow him. Katrina uses her eyes to tell me to go next and as much as I want to protest, I trudge ahead.

The hallway is lined with a dark brown carpet and stark white walls. Not only have the windows outside been updated, but the smooth surface of the walls surrounding us as we make our way through the back ways of the funeral home are showing even more changes from what I remember. I remember Mitch's dad getting after me for flicking off a piece of plaster once upon a time.

"Piece of work, your dad." Mitch leads us to a door at the end of the hall that leads us into the main chapel-esque room that holds the funeral services. Smells are hitting me left and right, some familiar and others faint. But there's one in particular that has me on edge. There's no mistaking it, and it puts me further out on a ledge I was already ready to dangle from.

"Has she been here recently?" I clear my throat. "My mom."

"Alice was in late last night. Had to tell her multiple times to leave and she threw quite the fit. Not sure if she was expecting to stay the night or what. She's been a handful ever since she and Mike started planning his funeral. It's even worse now that he's gone."

There is a small part of me, no matter how minuscule and buried deep it is, that mourns for one's loss of a mate. No matter the piece of shit that he was, I've heard you're never the same after losing the one person you're meant to spend your life with. Some would rather throw themselves into the grave after the passing of their loved ones, spiraling into a dark depression that threatens to consume them.

My stomach does a weird flop at the mere thought of losing Clara. I faced that fear one time already, when I thought my cousin was going to kill her. But even then, I didn't have time to dwell on it. I had to act, and fast. Now isn't the time to dive into that either, not if there's a chance my mother could show up again and cause more problems.

"I'll start spraying your traveled path, but I can't make any promises. Just try to keep your wandering around to a minimum." I shouldn't be surprised that Mitch knows enough about our scents and how well our senses work. While I appreciate the small act, I know time is of the essence.

He skirts past us and toward the cleaning closet as I take a deep breath and walk into the chapel.

There are two sets of rows with an aisle in the center. While the layout is the same, the space has completely transformed. Solid oak pews shine elegantly beneath the overhead lights, and to my left, stands and shelves hold about two dozen plants and floral arrangements already surrounding the sleek black casket. The fabric overlay spills out, showing just how close I am to seeing who is tucked away inside.

"I'll just...wait out here." Katrina's soft voice barely reaches my ears. She closes the double doors until there's nothing more than a small gap, giving me a little bit of privacy.

Everything goes eerily still. I stare at the casket, frozen in place. I can't breathe, can't think a single thought as I stand there unmoving.

What do I want out of this? What did I expect to find? The sarcastic thought of punching a dead guy comes to mind, but only then do I shake my head at how ridiculous it sounds.

I want to move, but my body isn't cooperating with what my brain is telling it to do.

One foot. Just move one in front of the other. That's all I have to do.

*Get your shit together, Seth.*

A heated breath shoots through my nostrils and I start moving. The shell of a man before me halts me once more as I come to a standstill.

I thought I might be angry beyond relief when I finally see him in person again. I wasn't prepared for the onslaught of mixed emotions clogging up my throat as I take in the frail man before me. His hair is even thinner than the photo I found online, hairline receding even worse up close. Death clings heavy to him, and lines around his face and hollowed eyes show the stress and turmoil his body must have gone through. How long had he been wasting away to become this tiny...this small? He should be taking up more space in the casket.

It's almost hard to believe that he was ever capable of the damage he once inflicted.

I blink away as I recall the strike of a whip across my back. A reminder of the past that may never take its hooks out of me. I swear the marks on my back are swelling with heat from the remembrance of each lash. Each hit, punch, and scrape. My body could never heal properly because I hadn't gone through my first shift yet.

I cringe as I recall each argument, every mutter, curse and shout that left his lips. How spittle would fly when he got himself worked up because *I* was the problem.

Fucking piece of shit.

This is how I want to remember him. Dead. No longer capable of causing harm or barking orders. He was never a father to me in the way he should have been. He was an abuser that never had to face his actions. I should have been ripped from my home at a young age, and he should have gone to jail.

But no. Who would believe that an upstanding citizen such as Mike Ries, who owned several hardware stores and went to church, flashing his mask of a smile for all others to see outside of our home, would be capable of destruction against his own flesh and blood?

The worst part? His brothers and sisters knew of his temper. The pack did nothing to stop him from beating me and fuck, my Uncle Scott lived next door to us for some time and did absolutely nothing.

One time I was met with a sympathetic look from him, but he never spoke a word about it. You can't tell me he didn't hear what was going on next door. The screams, the cries, the begging and pleading for it to stop only to be silenced with threats of more.

"You'd better be in a fucking inferno," I all but spit. Anger breathes life into me as I stare down at him. "Thank fuck you never had any other children to screw up."

Relief floods through me at that thought. Thankfully, that will be my burden alone to bear.

More words want to come out, but a voice flies through the air and directly to my ears, making unease spread like a wildfire.

"Seth?"

# 24

# What Else Could Happen?

## *Clara*

Waiting for each text update from Seth is like staring at a pot of water and waiting for it to boil. I know I shouldn't watch it, but I can't help it. If I was still a nail biter like I was in my youth, I'm pretty sure I would have bitten them down to the point where I would make myself bleed. I don't know how to not worry about him.

Julie, the smart girl that she is, could tell that something was off with me this morning as I scrambled about the house picking up or organizing things that probably didn't need to be done right at that precise moment. She asked me on more than one occasion if I was alright, and I put on the best face I could muster. Not even my short and quick call with Seth could calm me down.

I don't feel like it's my place to tell the kids about the passing of Seth's father. Especially given their history. While I don't expect him to go into full detail about their past, a death is still a death.

How long will his absence go unnoticed? It's a very real possibility that he won't make it back for taco pizza tomorrow night, and there is probably zero chance he'll make it back to see Julie cheer again tonight.

Emmett, on the other hand, is growing more and more irritated each day he goes without seeing or hearing from his father. I take Joe's silence as an omission of guilt, but Emmett? He went from thinking that he'd done something wrong, to placing the blame onto me. It almost sickens me to not point the finger at his father. To say that *he* is the reason I'm not letting the children have contact with him. But I keep my mouth shut even as Julie grows uncomfortable each time Joe is brought up.

It is still technically my week with the kids, though. Trouble could really start to brew once Sunday night hits and the kids are supposed to go to Joe's place for his week.

Julie informed me that she has spoken with her brother about that night, what their dad did, and Emmett just shrugged it off. What's even worse is the thought of how Emmett might react when he finds out that I am going after sole custody of both him and Julie. No more splitting time amongst two houses and two parents. No more back and forth. Stability. My confidence is growing that I can provide that for them.

With Seth by my side, I feel I could conquer just about anything, even if I'm shaking in my damn boots to get there.

I just need him to come home safe.

"Who's that?" Melissa rolls her chair over and bumps into mine, jarring me from my thoughts; I quickly exit out of the internet browser I had pulled up.

"It's no one," I mutter as I lean back in my chair, trying to act casual. But Melissa has known me for too long now. Worked by my side for years to know when something isn't right, which, I'm not proud to admit, is too often as of late.

"What gives, Clara? Are you sure you're okay?" She leans her elbows onto her knees as she tries to gain my attention. "Did Joe do something else?"

"No, no." I wave my hand. "He's been like, radio silent, which is strange, but it's not him."

"New man problems? Just tell me where he lives," she jokes, and only then does my face break, even if it's minimal.

"It's not Seth. Not exactly. It's just…" I look around us, trying to check for listening ears and prying eyes, but all the hygienists seem to be occupied and there's only one person in the waiting room. I stand long enough to close the window divider and sit back down. "Please don't breathe a word of this to anyone. It's really not my news to tell, but I can't help how conflicted I feel about it all."

"Of course." She nods almost too excitedly. "Pregnant?"

"What?" My eyes snap open. "No!" I all but whisper-shout. "No, you know that I had my tubes tied."

Melissa shrugs, her curls barely moving with her shoulders. "It happens, Clara. Happened to my cousin."

Oh yes, I'm well aware. She was all too happy to tell me about her relative's surprise pregnancy when Seth strolled into the office not so long ago. She even teased about how my tubes were probably trying to straighten themselves out in preparation for him putting a baby in me. Little does she know that even that wouldn't be enough. For whatever reason, Seth can't have children of his own. And that is nobody else's business. Even if I ponder and dream about a life where that would be possible with him, it's just that, a fantasy.

"It's not that, and if you ever breathe a word about this or act funny around Seth regarding it, I'll kill you."

The glimmer of humor in her eyes fades as her expression becomes serious. "Damn, Clara. Now you have me worried."

I give a brief and watered-down version of the death of Seth's father and the sneaky bitch of a mother who came here, snooping around. I don't elaborate on the abuse Seth endured, only enough to lead to my confusion as to why he had to go visit the corpse of a man he hates, no, *loathes*. Nope, that still doesn't sound like a strong enough word.

Melissa doesn't need to know about Seth being sterile, the werewolf side of him, his ex-fiancée showing up and... Dear God, what in the hell kind of box office flop has my life become?

"Damn." Melissa sits back in her chair, wide-eyed and speechless. I know Seth isn't perfect and never claimed to be, but this information on the man who is a hot topic of a lot of gossip around here has stunned her. Wasn't what I was going for, I just needed a shoulder. Someone not on the inside to vent to. This definitely isn't something that I would go to Larson about either. And my mom? Absolutely not, this is too much drama to talk to her about.

"That bitch did give me weird vibes. The way she kept looking at you. She was so strange."

Seth's mother Alice is certainly that. Delusional even for thinking that Seth would up and leave, to marry Penelope and help raise her children. But coming to my place of employment? That was crossing a big line. If only Melissa knew that the woman tried to have me killed too.

"Do you know if Seth's ever...talked to someone about all of this? Like a therapist?"

I pause on that for a moment. I can't recall a single conversation regarding it. Someone who went through that kind of abuse and trauma as a kid and into their teen years, surely he's done something, right? He's been moving city to city since leaving Colorado all those years ago. Has there ever been someone he could confide in?

"Honestly? I don't know. If he has, he's never said." What are the chances we can find one that's a werewolf so Seth can speak freely and get all of these burdens off his chest? It doesn't seem entirely impossible, but how can you ever truly know who to trust with information like his?

"Look, he obviously has strong feelings about the bastard. So much so that he chose to go back."

It's my turn to shrug now. "Maybe Seth just wanted to make sure that said 'bastard' really is dead and can't hurt him anymore."

That realization is a heavy one, something that I hadn't even thought of before now. I was just so confused as to why he would want to go back in the first place when he said he never would again. But this? Will this be some sort of closure for him so he can move on? Knowing Seth, I don't think he's going back to offer any forgiveness. No, there was way too much hatred and pain for him to do something like that.

Seth also wants privacy, opting not to go to the actual funeral. He doesn't want to cause trouble or have an audience of any kind. He wants to go unnoticed. A family reunion of any kind is definitely the last thing on his agenda.

"Hey." Melissa reaches forward and sets her palm on my knee. "I'm not a shrink, but everyone has their demons. Seth's just so happens to be a shitty biological father. And a weird as fuck mom."

Wow, I've never heard Melissa cuss this much.

"But he's got you, Clara. Someone who cares about him, even with this baggage. Choosing him even though you've got your own shit to deal with. Choosing him when the only other two people in his life that *should* have mattered, failed at their one job as parents."

The front door opens and when I swivel to see who's approaching the window, my heart rate skyrockets. I can feel it in my chest, my neck, my fingertips.

Most of the officers that come here are not in uniform, coming in on their days off or such. This guy looks to be here on business, walking up to the counter with a purpose and I can hear the brushing of his arms against his black coat.

Melissa stands and opens the window, offering a polite greeting as if we hadn't just been diving into sensitive topics just seconds ago. "Can I help you, officer?"

He clears his throat. The thick mustache above his upper lip has a small strip of gray on his right side. "I'm looking for a Mrs. Clara Serring."

Any saliva I had in my mouth evaporates as I meet his eyes. "I'm Ms. Serring," I clarify as I take a wobbly step to stand. My chair creaks at the sudden movement. Or maybe that was my knees. I'm not entirely sure.

The officer takes his hat off, showing off hair that is peppered more than that mustache of his. His face softens as he lowers his gaze and takes in a small breath.

The growing silence eats away at me. Right now, I fear for the worst. That something has already happened to Seth within our short two-hour check-in time frame and I swear if this man gives me such news, I'll lose it.

I'll break. Shatter so hard that I don't think I'll ever be able to superglue the pieces back together. No, they wouldn't even fit anymore.

The next words out of him have my stomach bottoming out.

"I'm afraid there's been an accident."

# 25

# Pushing My Limits

## *Clara*

I'm walking as fast as my legs and feet will carry me.

The stark, bright lights of the hospital as I move through the corridor to the waiting room I was directed to are almost blinding. My thighs rub together as I walk along with the shuffle of my coat as I begin to rip it off.

Does anyone even like hospitals? The looks, the smell, the constant reminder of death looming around, and I almost forget that I gave birth to two children here. Why does a place of life and death bring on so much uncertainty and dread?

I'm texting out another message to Seth, telling him to call me as soon as he can. I can't pretend to know what's going on at this exact moment for him, but I need him. I need to hear his voice. His reassurance that everything is going to be okay. That he will soon be on his way home and back to me.

So help me, if Joe fucking goes out like this? Leaving all of these decisions to me? I'd never forgive him. We've been divorced long enough for him to change his emergency contacts.

I come skidding to a stop at the small waiting room of about a dozen chairs. They look hard and uncomfortable with their navy blue flat cushions. The weather channel is playing on a television that's mounted up in the far corner of the room, and a small table beneath it has a self-service coffee station.

There's not another soul in here. At least not living.

Hauling my purse and coat into the first chair I come to, I go to sit down but pop right back up again. My heart hasn't stopped racing since that officer stepped up to the counter at my work.

"Joseph Serring was involved in an automobile accident this morning. He's en route to the hospital as we speak."

The man's words have been playing on repeat ever since. The officer was even kind enough to offer me a ride, but I waved him off. I probably shouldn't have driven here on my own, though. The tunnel vision and my distracted driving was most likely putting myself and others at risk on the short drive here.

In fact, whenever someone else is speaking, it sounds distant. Like something is plugging my ears, muffling words that take too long for me to register.

*Chassidy,* I think.

I need to call her. As much as I will hate to be confined to a room with her, she is the one that needs to be here. She should know that Joe was in an accident and while the details I know are extremely limited, I can at least acknowledge the fact that she should be present no matter the outcome.

With shaky hands, I scroll through to her number and call. With each ring I grow more and more impatient, trying to figure out what in the hell to say to her.

*Hey, the married guy you slept with was in a terrible accident. You should come to Pembrook Hospital and wait it out with the mother of his children.*

But when I go to voicemail, my brain misfires. Her nasally voice fills my ears and just when I'm bracing myself to leave a message, I receive the annoying message of her box being full.

I mutter a curse as I hang up and try calling again, but this time it cuts to the voicemail message after a single ring.

Is the bitch intentionally ignoring me?

I type out a quick message, urging her to call or come to the hospital immediately and then I'm dialing the only other person who I hope can talk me down off the ledge I'm on.

Probably not the best time to unload on her, but since I can't talk to Seth, I feel like it's my only other option. I'll go crazy if I'm left alone in this room without someone.

Not until my mom picks up does the damn break, and I begin to sob.

Three hours.

Joe has been in surgery for three hours upon his arrival at the hospital, and I've only been given one update regarding his status. Even then, there wasn't much to go on.

Joe has lost a lot of blood, and the severity of his leg injury is pretty bad after wrapping his car around a tree. The nurse giving me the update stated that he's going to have a bit of a road to recovery.

I have given up on Chassidy at this point. I didn't waste much more time on contacting her, especially since I drained about half the battery on my phone while my mom was talking me down out of hysterics.

I might hate Joe for what he did to me and to our family. For the way he treated me in our time together and now apart. But even so, I would never wish him dead. He's caused me a lot of pain and heartache, but the possibility of being the one to deliver grave news to Julie and Emmett? I can't fathom it. God, I'm already dreading just telling them about the accident to begin with. I can't bring myself to drag them out of school, not knowing what the outcome of this will be. What kind of state Joe might be in if he pulls through. If it gets to the point that I need someone to check in on them, I know Larson would, without a doubt.

An elderly couple enters the room that I had been the sole occupant of the entire time I've been here so far. If I had to guess, by their frail frames, white hair, and the joining of their hands, I'd assume they're married. But their forlorn faces have me turning my gaze away.

I type out another text to Seth, biting the tip of my thumb in fear over the lack of communication from him. It's been too long since his last check-in and with my current state of mind, it's too easy to keep stumbling down the rabbit hole of worst-case scenarios.

> Seth, please. I need to know that you're alright.

Heaven forbid, if he sends back his message of "red," I'll lose any ounce of sanity I have left. I've never really been the praying type, but I am ready to pray to whatever entity might listen to me right now.

"Mrs. Serring?"

There's a split second when I think to correct someone yet again for addressing me like that, but when I see a tall man in scrubs with a sense of authority, I'm shooting up to my feet without doing so. "Is he okay? Is the surgery over?"

He nods slightly, but I can tell there's more. But before I can form any more questions, he gestures to his right. "How about we step into a room for some privacy."

I work to swallow, my brain telling me that this is serious. That he might be delivering bad news and doesn't know if I'll cause a scene. Is this what they do when they tell you someone didn't make it? That they did all they could but Joe succumbed to his injuries?

My body is stiff as I follow Dr. Tambren—I note the name that's embroidered on his scrubs. We make a hard left after about ten steps. The room is small with a couple of chairs and an upholstered loveseat that matches the chairs from the other waiting room. So much blue, lights and darks, as if they're trying to calm you. Even the two table lamps in here bring down the mood. Gone is the stark and white hospital setting, into another that feels like it's meant to provide a sense of—

That is one *big* box of tissues.

Turning slowly, I meet the doctor and cross my arms, but I can't find the courage to look him in the eyes. "Just tell me, please."

The doctor clears his throat but remains in the doorway, not bothering to shut it. "I understand that you are his ex-wife. Is there someone else you would like us to contact?"

I shake my head. Thank goodness somebody told him that I'm no longer married to that man. "No, it's fine. He's still the father of my children. Couldn't change that if I wanted to."

Dr. Tambren takes a beat, a long one at that, before continuing. Fuck, I need Seth. The timing of everything colliding in our combined lives couldn't be any worse than this.

"Mr. Serring was driving under the influence of alcohol. He had twice the legal limit in his system."

"Shit," I mutter, clasping a hand over my mouth. Oh no, is that why Chassidy hasn't been answering me? "Was anyone else hurt? Was anyone else involved?" Only now do I finally look at him, his face a bit scruffy as if he hasn't shaved lately. It's the scruff that drove Joe crazy when he had it.

"Thankfully, no. But he did make it out of surgery and he'll probably be in the recovery room for about an hour or so."

"Wait, he's alive?" I gasp with a strangled sound that makes it sound like I'm not getting enough air.

Dr. Tambren nods. "He is. But these next few days are going to be rough. He sustained several fractures to his left arm but the one that caused the most damage is the injury to his femur."

The doctor keeps talking, and I'm hearing but not following. It should make sense, what he's discussing with me, and I catch onto a few words here and there, appreciating the manner in which he seems to be dumbing down the steps and actions they took in order to save his life. You can't tell me he talks like this in those fancy reports I assume he has to put together. Case files or whatever doctors do. I won't pretend to know with my limited knowledge in the dental field. It isn't until he finishes that I catch up and tune back in.

"Had it taken someone longer to find him, he might not have made it. He's one lucky man right now."

I'm not sure when my head started nodding, but when I catch myself, I will my bobble of a head to stop.

"Is there anything I can have the nurses get you? Do you have any questions? I know that was quite a bit of information."

This time, my head goes the opposite way. "No. No, thank you, doctor." My chest aches and my head hurts. I don't understand what I'm supposed to do in this moment. I'm not Joe's wife anymore, but no one else is here. His parents live out of state and until now, I had nothing to tell them.

"I can have someone come get you when he's out of recovery. But feel free to use this room or you can go back to the waiting area. We also have your phone number should you need to leave."

"No, I'll stay," I state out loud. "I'll be here."

Dr. Tambren offers a small nod and shuts the door as he leaves me. I eye the battery on my phone before dialing Seth again. I'm barely holding myself together as I focus on my breathing while I wait for each ring.

One. Two. Three. Four. Then onto a voicemail box that isn't full.

I hang my head in defeat, hating that the one person I need to lean on right now is out of reach.

"Seth—" My voice breaks, and as much as I try to keep it together, I'm failing miserably. I don't know what kind of scene I'm going to walk into when I see Joe and I can't believe I'm going to be doing it alone. "I need you. Please, *please*, please be okay. I need you to be okay. Call me."

# 26

# Will Words Ever Be Enough?

## *Seth*

"What are *you* doing here?"

Careful not to flinch at the menacing words coming from my Uncle George, I pivot to face the alpha of my old pack. I sense Katrina coming into the picture behind me as well.

Down the aisle and standing in the doorway, is the father of my cousins who met their ends in Iowa. I doubt he knows that I'm directly responsible for two of them and not all three. I'm sure that doesn't even matter to him when over half of his children have been annihilated. But to be fair, I did give Carter more than a verbal warning upon his first visit. Little did I know, he was tasked with more watching and stalking afterward.

While my uncle is younger than my father was, he certainly hasn't aged well. His hair has turned wispy, some spots longer than others. The lines on his face make him appear to be grimacing full time, and there are age spots forming along his temples. But even with that being said, the way he carries himself, with that air of superiority, is even more unwelcoming.

As if on cue, my mother comes into view, dressed in a black dress with her hair tied back into a low bun. There are tissues wadded up in her hand as she follows her brother's line of sight down the aisle and toward me. I freeze.

This is exactly what I didn't want to happen. This is why I came early, so I could avoid any interactions. How was I supposed to know that my mother would be here from open to close each day my dad is a resident?

"Seth." She forces my name from her trembling lips, and I can't tell if she's happy, shocked, or angered. Her face just looks stunned, an emotion that I can't say I've seen very often on her.

"You have some nerve showing up here." My uncle begins his descent down the aisle and Katrina steps in closer at my back side. My fists clench and arms tighten, preparing for what I know could turn out to be a very, very unpleasant encounter.

The apple didn't fall far from the tree with Uncle George. He was as mean as my dad and as stubborn as both him and my grandfather. While I can't recall him ever physically laying a hand on any of his sons, there were signs. I saw, hell, even heard enough things to determine that maybe Carter, Bradley, and Adam's upbringing wasn't far off from my own. And yet, they stuck around.

A part of me would like to think that perhaps I did their children a favor. If there was any chance that any of those brothers were wreaking havoc on their own families, maybe I did them a service. I have trouble imagining any of the three were the loving, doting, and kind fathers that are depicted in movies, commercials, or online. Their pictures on social media were merely a highlight reel in most cases. Like they were trying to show the world how happy and perfect their lives were.

That's what it feels like every time I see those kinds of photos. Everyone smiles like everything is okay in the world, in their everyday lives. I did too at one time, putting on a mask and pretending that my home life wasn't a living hell.

My mother grabs onto her brother-in-law's arm, trying to stop him in his pursuit of me as he nears, and I firmly plant my feet on the ground. Great, even she fears what he's going to do to me.

"For God's sake, George. It's his father! Leave him alone!" Her voice strains as she tugs on him but he shakes her off as if she's nothing but a nuisance.

"You're not welcome here!" His voice booms and I hear footsteps from the back hallway, increasing in speed. Before I know it, Mitch is entering just as my uncle sends a flying fist in my direction.

I duck out of the way and take a step back. I swear I can feel heat radiating off of him as I regroup and find my center of gravity before he attempts another hit. I know this man is most likely still mourning the loss of his boys, and now one of his brothers. His emotions are probably sky-high.

There's a distinct click from behind me before Mitch shouts, "That's enough!"

He shoves the rifle into my uncle's face and he holds his hands up in surrender, but his face shows he's pissed beyond belief as his chest rises in aggravation.

"He. Killed. My. Sons!" His spit makes it far enough that it's mere inches away from me.

"And whose bright idea was it to send them? I let Carter off with a warning, it's not my fault he didn't listen," I shoot back at him. "And who gave my mother permission to fucking kill my mate?" I ignore the gun between my uncle and me, stepping forward.

"A life for a life!" Uncle George utters the same words I heard one of my cousins say. An order that my mom gave, sending my cousins in the pursuit of Clara. "As I see it, you and little miss here can tip the tables right again!" He jabs a finger in Katrina's direction and I growl.

"You really don't want to do that." I swear Katrina's voice has dropped an entire octave. She doesn't have a bright or cheery voice to begin with, but this new sound of hers is perilous.

"Who the hell do you think you are? You're not even Seth's mate. You smell..." He leans forward a bit, inhaling. "Different."

"I'm someone you don't want to trifle with."

My uncle laughs. Full-on maniacal laughter that would send chills up any other normal person's spine. "You? You puny little—"

"Tell me." There's an odd calmness to Katrina's voice now, one that has the hair on my arms standing as I look at her. She could probably cut through stone with her blue-eyed stare. "Has the right hand ever turned up?"

Her utterance makes zero sense to me, and the way she cocks her head to the side is chilling. But I swear my uncle's eyes go deep black before he's lunging at her. "You bitch!"

As if Uncle George is nothing but a sack of potatoes, Katrina moves quickly, hurling his thick frame up and over her. He lands with a sickening thud while my mom shrieks.

As he scrambles to pick himself up off of the floor, he knocks over a stand, the assortment of blue and white flowers crashing to the ground as its contents create a mess that wets the floor along with shards of glass.

"I *will* shoot!" Mitch jabs the rifle in his direction as my uncle grunts. He's stumbling, trying to gather his footing. Apparently not bouncing back like he used to. He's not necessarily out of shape, but definitely out of practice when it comes to physical combat.

"Piss off, boy!"

"No!" Mitch jerks closer, as if he's not afraid of the man before him. Even though he knows what we are. I'm sure in his line of work, he's seen a lot. Probably dealt with even more than I can imagine. "Now get out of my funeral home before I put you on my table!"

*Damn. Go, Mitch.*

The respect I have for him right now is totally out of left field, but I can't help the grin that takes over.

"And don't even think about returning for the visitation or the funeral tomorrow. You are officially banned from the premises."

"You can't be serious!" Blood rushes to his face. "That's my brother in there!" He points at the casket.

"You step foot on my property again and I'll call the cops. I have video surveillance of you trying to attack someone." Mitch keeps his gun fixed on my uncle as he points to multiple spots in the room.

Collectively, we all follow to see what he's showing us. Sure enough, strategically placed but hidden well, cameras are tucked away. I have to give Mitch a hand, he's brilliant. Maybe a bit stupid in making an enemy out of my uncle, but impressive all the same.

"I was doing you a favor, Alice. But no more!" Uncle George is right up in my mother's face. She flinches as he continues, "The deal is off."

Uncle George stomps out and down the aisle. I halfway expect a door to be slammed somewhere, but there's nothing. I can't help but wonder if the front door has some sort of self-closing mechanism to prevent him from doing so.

"Oh, Seth!" My mother tries to approach with open arms, her grief returning, and I take a step back.

"Don't," I warn as I hold my hands up to stop her.

Mitch proceeds to make sure that my uncle really left. Katrina eyes me before following after him, probably trying to make sure there's no retaliation of any kind. I give her a small nod, acknowledging her purpose.

I can deal with my mother. Not that I want to, but I will.

"I'm not staying," I start, and my voice is anything but kind. I know that won't work with her. I don't expect her to listen to anything I have to say. I'm sure she'll argue. Glaze over the fact that she ordered the kill on Clara while fleeing back to Colorado.

"But you've come all this way." She has the nerve to sound broken by that. Not once have I ever given her any inclination that I would come back. Staying was never a part of any equation of mine.

"Not to pay any respects. That I can assure you."

Her mood plummets, her grief swallowed up by something sinister. "But he's your father."

"He was no father!" I scream the words so loud that her shoulders rise up toward her ears. "He was an asshole who loved you and nobody else! If anyone should have been sterile, it was him. Thank God his line of the family dies with me."

"You don't mean that." She shakes her head in denial.

"Oh, but I do," I seethe. Rage is settling into my bones and I can sense the vibrations that bring on the change wanting to surface. I can't do that now, not here. The last thing I need is Mitch turning his rifle on me next. "Fathers aren't supposed to beat their children. They don't break skin and bones, terrorize and frighten. And mothers?" A sick laugh leaves my throat. "They aren't supposed to turn a blind eye and pretend they don't see what's happening."

My throat strains on the words I choke out. My eyes begin to water. "Where were you?"

She drops her gaze to the floor, lips sealed tight. Dad is gone, and she's still silent.

"Where were you when your son was crying for help? I know you heard me begging for them to stop." A tear tracks down my cheek, and I swear it evaporates on my heated skin before it can reach my facial hair. "How could you do *nothing*? Absolutely fucking nothing when I needed someone the most? Someone to fight for me. Someone to save me!"

Katrina reenters at the back, her blonde hair swaying as she jogs to me with wide eyes. "We need to go."

"What? What, no!" My mom looks between us, but I'm not about to second-guess it. If Katrina thinks it's time to hit the road, she must have a good reason.

"I overheard him making a call. He's trying to bring in reinforcements. We have to go. Now."

"Look, I appreciate the business you all provide, but this has seriously got to stop." Mitch is still armed as he takes long strides to close the gap between us. "I'm not going to have room for all the bodies if there's a bloodbath, and I'll be damned if I'm going to give that funeral home on the west side of town any chance to take any business away from me because of inadequate space."

I rub a hand over my face, hating how this visit went downhill so fast. I'm not sure how I even have the mental capacity to joke at a time like this. "They still painting the dead like clowns?"

A soft chuckle leaves him as he shakes his head. It does little to lighten the heavy mood in here, but it's enough to give my body a break from being so worked up.

"They've always put on too much makeup. And they don't even have the capability for live streaming services yet. I mean come on, in this day and age?"

This time, a small laugh leaves my throat and it's not even forced. I wish we could have had a little more time to catch up. With him, I wouldn't mind.

Katrina clears her throat and when I look at her, she's trying to direct my attention toward the back hall for our exit.

"Are you going to be alright?" I ask him, genuinely concerned about his safety and well-being. He didn't have to let us in. He didn't have to try and defend someone who he hasn't seen in so long. We were never that close by any means, but I don't want him putting his life in any kind of jeopardy because of me and my surprise visit.

Mitch sighs. "Whether they like me or not, they need me. I'm paid too well for keeping secrets and catering to their needs included with that. You, however..."

I nod, knowing it's time to go. I thank him and turn away, acting like my mother hasn't been here this entire time through this little conversation.

"But...Seth." She has the nerve to try and bring forth her emotion that feels as if she's trying to persuade me to stay, even though there isn't a chance whatsoever. Not when I have to get back to Clara and the kids. Not when I have to get Katrina back to her family.

Perhaps if she'd ever shown me that she cared, that she didn't condone my father's actions, even just the tiniest bit of concern or a sympathetic look, perhaps things would have turned out differently. Maybe I would be by her side right now. Staying with her and being a shoulder for her to lean on as she navigates the struggle and aftermath of losing her mate.

But I can't. There isn't a single part of me that wants to, that cares enough to. She might be hurting, but she ignored the countless years I felt alone. Uncared for. Unloved.

She's made her bed. And now, she has to sleep in it by herself.

Maybe I'm a dick for thinking like that, but I can't move past that. I choose to move forward and with the life I'm building with Clara, Julie, and Emmett. Even Larson and the weird pack of misfit werewolves.

"They're going to kill you, Seth." My mother's voice shakes. "They'll never take you back into the pack now. The deal your father and I made with George, it was for your own good. To keep you safe."

"Since when have you cared about my well-being?" I shoot back. "No. It's too late for that. Let them try."

"Seth." Katrina's tone is a forceful one. We don't have any more time to waste.

"Goodbye, Mom." I barely meet her eyes, and offer Mitch my thanks before taking off and back through the corridor. As I take in my surroundings outside, I note George standing off in the distance. He's on the phone talking to someone, air swirling around his mouth. Katrina and I jump into the car and I'm jerking the gear handle into reverse before I even hear the click of her seat belt.

"Shit," she mutters as I fly out of the parking lot and take off, waiting until the funeral home is out of sight before I tug mine on. The car is already alerting me with annoying dings that I haven't buckled in yet. The tires struggle against some packed snow after a stop sign, but I press on until we're surging forward and before I know it, we're on the outskirts of town.

"We should be able to nab our stuff in time before checkout," I begin, trying to level my breathing from being worked up. "Then airport?"

"Yes," Katrina states, looking over her shoulder at the road behind us. I'm already ahead of her, making sure we're not being followed.

"Care to tell me about this right hand business that pushed my uncle past his breaking point?"

Katrina smirks. It's information I wasn't privy to until today, but it was enough to send Uncle George into a tailspin. I assume it has to do with either Adam or Bradley, knowing that my mother was responsible for taking Carter's body back to Colorado.

"Let's just say Adam got a little handsy with me."

Vague, but okay. "I guess the less I know, the better?"

Katrina turns her head. "Exactly."

Mere minutes is what it takes us to throw our stuff into bags, check out, and head out the doors of our hotel. We stay vigilant in our surroundings and the people within. Before I know it, we're tossing our suitcases into the trunk.

"We have company," Katrina breathes cooly, but I can tell there's an edge to her voice. I pull out my phone and see several texts and calls from Clara, cursing as I nonchalantly try to catch a glance at who Katrina's referring to.

Sure enough, my uncle is waiting outside of a truck with another passenger in there, although I can't make out who it is. We can either wait like sitting ducks, or take a chance on our drive to the airport. I'm confident that I can outdrive them, as long as we don't pass any cops. My mind is racing, thinking about the length of time we'll have to be on the road, but the fact that I've missed so much from Clara has my stomach twisting into knots.

Something's not right.

The need to get back outweighs everything else. If we can just get to the airport, we should be fine. With countless cameras and faces, it will be even harder for them to try and pull anything there. We just have to get away.

But they have our scents. And now that my uncle knows that my accomplice here was involved with the death of one of his sons, I fear that this mess is going to get dragged back to Iowa. Even if we manage to make it back to the Des Moines International Airport, I have this nagging and persistent suspicion that this is far from over. My uncle wants blood. He wants revenge for the lives that were taken, and I would be leading those with that thirst right back to Katrina's and my families.

Fuck.

"They're not going to stop," I begin as soon as the car doors shut. "I can see him bypassing my dad's burial to come after us." I pull out of our parking space and as we take our leave, I find that my uncle is doing nothing to hide the fact that he's going to follow us. "We can't lead them to our homes. We can't risk them coming to Iowa."

Katrina thinks for a moment. And just when I think she's going to argue, she surprises me. "Agreed. So buy us some time."

I shoot her a glare. "What?"

"Just drive!" she orders, and I put my foot on the pedal, taking off.

27

# Bitter Walls

## *Clara*

I ce-cold terror floods my system. Every pore, every vein and blood cell in my body. You'd think I'd be used to it by now since it's a somewhat common occurrence as of late.

I stare down at my phone, scared for both Seth's and Katrina's lives as I see that one word on my screen.

*Red.*

I'd been holding out hope that Seth had lost track of time somehow. That everything was going to be okay. Is there a time difference between here and there? I kept thinking that I had to give him the benefit of the doubt, and where did that get me? I don't even know how I'm still functioning at this point. How much stress can I possibly put my body through today before it's had enough?

Larson. I need to call Larson. I have no idea what I'm even supposed to say as my hands wobble like I've forgotten how to use them. I almost don't even hit the right contact because I can't get a grip on myself.

I stand, pacing the small and private waiting room I've been confined to while I wait on news of Joe leaving the recovery room.

Larson's voice picks up mid-ring. "Clara?"

"He texted," I gush, winded. "Seth texted it. Red. Something's wrong but I don't know what. What happens now?"

I cup a hand over my mouth, hating how useless I feel while stowed away in a hospital waiting for an unconscious Joe and news from Seth who is currently hundreds of miles away.

"Well crap," Larson grumbles before the line goes dead. I gape at my phone, shocked that he hung up on me without anything else to say. I'm about ready to call him back when a long overdue call comes through.

I've already talked to my mother, and made the call to Joe's parents who are going to try and get the first flight to Iowa, but this call feels even worse. But it's also about damn time she called back.

"Chassidy," I cut in as soon as I pick it up.

"What in the hell do you want? Haven't you ever heard of sleep?"

My lips thin, pressing together so hard at the thought of Chassidy literally sleeping through every call and text I tried in my attempts to get ahold of her. Instead of calling her out on it, I bite my tongue. Gathering every ounce of strength I can possibly find—which isn't much—I deliver what little I can before I lose my shit on her.

"Joe's been in an accident. You need to come to the hospital." I then promptly hang up on her. If the ex-wife of the man she's now with was calling repeatedly, wouldn't she wonder why? The kids aren't even staying with them; she had no obligation for them at all this week.

I want to scream. I know it wouldn't do me any good, but I desperately need an outlet. Which, speaking of...

I dial my work, and thankfully Melissa picks up. She must see my name on the caller ID because she's instantly shooting off questions.

"Clara, are you alright? Is Joe alright? What's going on?"

"Honestly, no. I'm not fine. Joe just got out of surgery and I'm waiting until I can see him. But hey, can I ask a favor?"

"Um...yeah. Of course. Anything."

I ask her if she can bring my spare charger that I keep stored in my desk drawer when she goes on lunch, which is only about a half hour away now. I have no idea how long I'm going to be here, and not knowing when or if Seth might be able to call me, I need to be able to rely on this phone for any communication from him or Larson.

I'm still waiting to receive news on Joe when Melissa sends me a text that she's arrived. A small grin crosses my face as I realize she must have ducked out for an early lunch to bring it over, and I open the room's door as I call her and give directions as to where to go.

With my luck today, I would leave just as somebody tried to come and get me to take me to wherever Joe will be transferred to.

Before I know it, Melissa is briskly coming into view, coffee and charger in one hand while she hangs up the phone and stows it in her coat pocket with the other. She picks up the pace, meeting me halfway as she throws her arm around me.

"Damn, is this just 'shit on Clara day' or what?" She squeezes me for a few good seconds before releasing me, handing me both the drink and charger. I throw her a quizzical look.

"So what, I nabbed your favorite hot beverage on the way over. You need it."

I take a quick sip, savoring my favorite holiday drink that will probably be leaving soon. Actually, I'm surprised it hasn't happened yet. Perhaps they're just using their supply until they run out. Normally, it's iced coffee all the way and every day. But this? This delectable and hot sugar cookie latte is the one and only exception.

"Thank you. I feel like I'm being put through the wringer today." That, and then some.

"Well hey, I've got some time to kill. Let me wait with you for a bit. You shouldn't have to do this alone."

"No, I don't want to impose. You're already taking a different lunch hour—"

"Clara." She feigns annoyance. "Shut up, will you? I'm here and I'm staying until the last minute I can afford. Now what do you need?"

Right now? To start the day over again. But even then, that doesn't seem like enough.

Melissa really does wait until the last possible second to head back to work. She's giving herself a very narrow ten-minute window to get back and I know that's pushing it depending on traffic.

She's barely gone two minutes before a nurse knocks before coming in. He's young, probably just out of school or still in it if I had to guess. But there's kindness to his eyes that instantly makes me like him.

That, and he's also the first one to just call me Clara. I hate the formalities of miss and missus. Yes, it can be polite, but I don't care to be called by my married last name. Not anymore.

He escorts me to the elevator and we ride it in silence until we arrive at the third floor. Someone is being pushed in a wheelchair by another nurse in neon green scrubs and another woman is using the railing to my left to help steady herself while her company keeps her IV stand nearby.

"Now, Mr. Serring is heavily sedated. He awoke briefly in recovery and he was trying to pull off his oxygen mask and ask questions. If he does wake up, just press the little red button on his bedside to call for someone."

I nod as we head into room 304, bracing myself for whatever scene might come into view.

"Is there anything I can get you? Anyone you need called?"

I shake my head no.

"Okay. Well, my name is Devon if you need anything. I'm just down the hall and to the left at the nurses' station. If there's anything you need, please let me know."

"Will do. Thank you, Devon."

The steady beeping of monitors picks at my already shot nerves. I can already make out wrappings or wound dressings of some sort on the leg closest to me as I start to enter, but most of him is hindered from view by blankets.

The shades are drawn about three fourths of the way down, dampening the brightness of the room. There's only an overhead light above the bed illuminating a barely recognizable ex-husband of mine. My hand shoots up to cup my mouth.

Banged up doesn't even begin to cover it. Joe has swelled up so much already. Bruises, cuts, and colors mar what can be seen of his skin in a sickening array of injuries. One of his arms is also bandaged up, and I can't seem to recall which bone there was fractured. Is that the one that was broken in two places? Is there anything left of the tree that he hit?

I really should have been paying better attention.

A burp somehow manages to escape me, one that tastes of bile, and I run to the bathroom, scared that my drink is going to come back up. My stomach twists one way and turns another as I lean over the toilet waiting to throw up but it never comes. I struggle to take deep breaths, reminding myself that at least he is alive and the outcome could have been much, much worse.

Thankfully, nothing comes out. I stand, leaning my back up against the cold tiled wall as I try to reel myself back in. I count as I breathe in and out, gathering any wits about me that might still be hanging on in this wild and tumultuous ride I'm on today.

Quietly, I exit and re-enter the room, just in time to almost collide with another unknown nurse in scrubs. We startle each other before we both apologize for the small mishap.

"There's a woman named Chassidy that's um...well..." I can tell this nurse is trying to consider her words before speaking aloud. Her hair is braided down her back with wavy pieces trying to escape. "She's causing a little bit of a scene but she's not family so..."

"She's the current girlfriend. I'm the ex-wife." I sigh heavily. "Apparently Joe never updated his emergency contacts after we split." The thought crosses my mind that I should just leave her out there. I'm ticked off that she apparently slept the morning away and in my opinion, took far too long to get here after hearing about her boyfriend's accident to begin with. But deciding to be the better person, I put my spitefulness aside. If I were in her position and not being allowed back to see Seth, I think I would lose my head on somebody too.

"As much as I don't want to share this room with her, can you guys just let her come up?"

The lady eyes me curiously for a moment before opening her mouth again. "Are you sure? I can tell her no visitors at this time."

Tempting. So, so tempting.

I swallow, then speak through gritted teeth. "It's fine, really."

A pain-stricken groan sounds from behind and the nurse and I exchange looks. We both take off in unison as we witness Joe stirring, rubbing at his face only to complain about that as well. I can't imagine there's a spot on him that doesn't hurt at this point.

"I'll go get the doctor," she states as she scurries out of the room. She's so light on her feet, I barely even hear her exit.

"Fuuuuuuck," Joe wails in a crackling voice as I step up to his side.

"Joe?" I exhale, trying to garner his attention. "Joe? Can you hear me? It's Clara."

More sounds come from his throat, and I'm searching his bed to see if there's a button to administer pain medication or something.

"I know your fucking voice, Clara. I'm not stupid."

"No, but you are fucking stupid for driving while drunk, Joe. What the hell?"

*Don't even start with me, asshole. You're just lucky you didn't hurt somebody else.*

"I hear somebody is waking up." Dr. Tambren from earlier swiftly enters with the most recent nurse that I almost ran smack dab into.

"Joe? Joe!" Chassidy's shrill voice echoes down the hall and I can't help but cringe. She skirts into view, hair perfectly curled and pristine makeup applied. She's a vision of pinks and ripped jeans hugging her figure, boobs pressed up to showcase her little assets. I highly doubt she ever closes her coat. I mean, how can anyone see them if she tries to keep herself warm?

She darts in, clearly making the moment about herself, and she shrieks as she lays her eyes on Joe, who's still whining about his pain.

I'd whine too if I heard that voice coming after me.

I tuck myself in the farthest corner of the room as Chassidy tries to throw herself on Joe in a dramatic scene. Joe lets out a sharp cry and she jumps back, and I can't help but cover my mouth at the carelessness of her actions.

"Careful, please!" the nurse shouts at Chassidy, and she takes a horrified step back. The nurse is quickly putting herself between the two of them, and I swear she's about to go off on the newest arrival.

Chassidy goes quiet for a moment before she hiccups. "I can't. It's too much!" She sprints out of the room and out of sight, and the doctor, nurse, and I all exchange bewildered looks.

Why did I feel the need to include her in all of this? The woman Joe left me for who I can't stand? One look at him and she hightails it out of here. If she thinks anyone is going to chase after her, she couldn't be more wrong.

I glance at my phone and my heart gives a little leap as I see a message icon, but as I unlock my phone, my hope quickly fades.

Larson's message simply states to call him when I can. I look at Joe in the bed, then to the doctor who's trying to ask him some questions but is being met with short and temperamental answers.

"Excuse me, I have to step out for a second." My feet are scurrying out of the room as fast as they can without it looking too desperate. Joe is alive, somewhat alert, and in better hands at the moment so with that problem aside, I call Larson.

As soon as I hear his gruff voice answer, I turn toward the wall and lower my voice. "Larson, have you heard anything? Are they okay? Is Seth—"

"A couple of friends are headed down there. They ran into a bit of trouble, but they're keepin' their wits about 'em."

"What does that even mean? Are they on their way back? Seth hasn't called or texted. Nothing."

"I'm sure he'll reach out when he can."

Larson is too vague, his answers too short, and absolutely nothing so far is helping to quell the rising frustration and sick dread that's clawing up my spine with the unknown. This was supposed to be a quick trip down to Colorado. Say his peace—whatever Seth needed to accomplish—and come home. Now, he's hardly been there twenty-four hours and there's already trouble?

"You've got to give me something to work with here, Larson. I'm at the end of my rope and I don't know how much longer I can hold on until it snaps."

Two nurses pass by, engaged in their own hushed conversation, but I catch their concerned glances as they pass by.

"Is something the matter, Clara?" Larson asks hesitantly.

I glance up at the ceiling. Tiles that are too white, next to bright lights that would probably give me a migraine if I look long enough, stare back at me. Pulling the phone from my ear long enough to check the time, I sigh as I bring the phone back to my ear and put my free palm to my forehead.

Time is running out before I'm going to have to face reality. I'm going to have to inform the kids about Joe's accident. I know Julie and Emmett. They'll be worried and scared which is totally expected. But they will want to see their dad.

I'm still processing what happened and have questions of my own. This bubble that I've been in most of the day is getting ready to burst and I hate that I'm going to have to prep my kids for this. The scene with their father laid up in a hospital bed, all banged up almost to the point of being unrecognizable, is something no child should have to see.

My words come quick, filling Larson in on the details of my day and Joe's accident. There isn't all that much to tell yet, but he's been around long enough to know my ex-husband and the drama surrounding our divorce. I'm comfortable enough telling him for the time being. Larson assures me that he'll look after the house, the kids, and offers any other help I might need while going through this. Before I can even think through his generous offer and thank him, Dr. Tambren is exiting Joe's room. He makes eye contact with me and I mutter a quick apology and promise to call Larson back soon.

There's a wariness to his eyes that has me stowing my phone in my back pocket, giving him my full attention.

"Thank you for everything, Dr. Tambren." He nods, and while I expect he might have something to say, I get the sense that he's holding something back. It pushes me to talk instead, wanting to get his opinion about Julie and Emmett. "Do you think it's alright if I bring our kids in to see him at this point? Should I wait or... I mean, I've never... Nothing like this has ever happened before. I don't know what I should do."

He nods in understanding. "How old are they?"

"Thirteen and nine."

"I think that would be acceptable then, yes. If I were you, I would try to inform them of what they'll be walking into. Give them some idea of the seriousness of his injuries so they're not blindsided."

"Of course," I agree. Seeing their father like this, or any loved one, could be very jarring. "Um...I'm not sure how often I'll be here. You know, ex-wife and all. But I did get in contact with his parents and they're on their way from out of state. I'm assuming you'll be seeing a lot more of them than you will me."

"And the woman who left the room rather...emotional?"

I roll my eyes, a movement that's as common with the mention of her as breathing at this point. "That's Joe's girlfriend. I spent half of the morning just trying to get a hold of her and then she doesn't even last thirty seconds in there. So honestly? I have no idea."

I want to ask that I be removed as Joe's emergency contact but don't just yet. Maybe that's not even possible right now; I have no idea. For the kids' sake, I won't even mention it. I can put on my big girl panties long enough to deal with this, putting their needs before my own, their dad's health before my sanity, so be it. Sure, I still care for Joe. He will always be their father and there isn't a damn thing I could do to change that. Even if he is a stupid fucking asshole for drinking and driving.

Dr. Tambren doesn't mention Chassidy again, just gives me a brief update and tells me how long visiting hours are. The road for Joe's recovery is anything but short and pleasant, which I had suspected from hearing about his injuries and seeing him now. I thank him again, and the staff that works alongside him for all they've done so far, and we part just as the braided-haired nurse leaves.

I can't help but notice pinched lips and her face set in a scowl. I stare at her for a moment before returning to Joe's room, a string of breathy curses leaving his lips as he appears to be taking himself in. But when he catches onto my presence, I stop dead in my tracks.

"What are you even doing here?" he sneers, and I have half a mind to give his bad leg a shove at his level of brainlessness.

"You." My hands clench as I try to bite my tongue. *Ungrateful bastard.* "You haven't changed your emergency contact information."

His words slur a bit, but anyone with hearing could listen and gather the looming anger behind them. I'm sure his pain isn't helping either. "I'm sure you're just loving this."

I scoff at him. "Right. I love how you drank this morning then decided to get behind the wheel drunk and crash into a damn tree!"

Joe shakes his head slowly before ripping the oxygen tube off of his nose in aggravation. "This is what you want, isn't it? This is the ammunition you need to take the kids. Full custody. Just what you wanted."

I gawk at him. The audacity this man has. Not once today have I contemplated plotting or planning on using this against him. And the first things he says to me, the woman who showed up and stayed, are filled with nothing but hatred.

What did I ever see in this man?

"You really think Emmett and Julie would be better off with you?" Joe tries to adjust himself in the bed but cries out in pain as he continues. "With *him*?"

"Seth." I step forward, glaring at him. "His name is Seth." My voice quivers with his unknown status right now. I have no choice but to be strong. I don't have any other options right now. If I don't, I'll crumble to pieces. "The sooner you get it in that thick, idiot head of yours, the better. You don't have to like him, but Julie, Emmett, and I all do. He's not going anywhere."

I take a step forward, his eyes growing large even though one of them seems to be swelling more than I could visibly notice the last time I was in here only minutes ago.

"Now get your shit together, because I'm bringing the kids to see you tonight and your ass is going to be the shining example of why you shouldn't drink and drive. Hope you're proud, Joe."

And with that, I turn on my heel and leave.

I hate to admit it, but Joe is right. This is precisely the ammunition I need. I would be a fool not to take this freak accident and use it to my advantage. Joe is beginning to make poor decisions left and right, leading him on an obviously dangerous path. One that could have taken his life today. One that could be to Julie's and Emmett's detriment.

I know he's being pumped full of drugs and more than likely not thinking straight, but as soon as I leave the hospital, I call my lawyer.

# 28

# Too Much at Stake

## *Seth*

Two vehicles have been following us for the past several hours. I'm fairly certain that there were three, but that blue SUV disappeared over forty minutes ago. The others have kept their distance, but even through the thickest of traffic they prevailed, tailing us as we crossed into Nebraska.

Katrina has been in occasional talks with some of the members of our not-so-pack pack. Edgar, Leo, and Javi are apparently on their way to meet us. Our goal is to finish this before we cross into Iowa. None of us want this fight bleeding into its borders.

The tense silence that has befallen the car ride is maddening at times.

My phone has been on silent since the funeral home this morning, and I've noticed calls and texts from Clara. I knew she's worried, probably sick with it.

It isn't until the traffic thins out and slows due to some detour for road work that I finally pick up my phone. I know it has been too long since an update. That my emergency message for her to contact Larson probably led Clara to believe the worst was happening.

"Here, let me." Katrina snatches my phone after I unlock it and before I can protest, she hits play on my voicemail messages. The speaker comes to life with a frantic and distraught Clara. Her voice sends a chill through me. The leather of the steering wheel creaks as I lurch the vehicle forward, practically riding on the bumper of the truck ahead of me. The speed limit might only be fifty-five in the work zone, but it feels like we're going at a snail's pace.

Another message plays, the crack in her voice clawing at me in the most horrid and gut-wrenching way possible.

Why did I come to Colorado? Why did I put both Katrina's and my life in jeopardy over a father I never wanted to claim as my own?

Sure, I hate Joe with a fierceness that belongs in the pits of hell, but I will always set that aside for Clara. If the douchebag was in a car accident, it affects her and their kids, obviously.

But at least he can't hurt anyone if he's in the hospital. Or at least, so I hope.

I should've been there. I should have been by Clara's side as she went through the waiting and uncertainty.

"We need to get gas soon." Katrina hits the lock button on my phone and slides it back into its cupholder. "Then you should call her. I need to make one as well."

It's on the tip of my tongue to ask her if we will both be calling our mates, but I'm not sure if that's appropriate. Katrina has already been on the phone with the wolves that will be meeting us in about another hour, but I've never once been privy to anything else personal about her. Not since finding out about her children and lone cat yesterday.

"How long have you been with him?" I clear my throat as if that will help relieve the ache of hearing Clara so troubled. I need something to focus on to pass the time until I can hear her voice again. She'll most likely scold me for ditching our two-hour check-ins on my first full day away, but in all honesty, I am trying to keep us safe. Katrina and I both have lives we need to get back to. "Your mate?"

Katrina stares out her window, so quiet that I think she's just going to ignore me altogether. I carry on with some information of my own to help break the ice. "I caught onto Clara's scent while out on a jog. She was arguing with her ex-husband's mistress. I sought her out the very next day."

It's strange how something that happened last September feels like only yesterday while simultaneously feeling like something far in the past. Life before Clara, without her, felt so empty before her vanilla scent wafted into my nostrils and changed everything.

"He was bagging groceries at a local store," Katrina finally begins. It takes a good solid minute before she tears her gaze away and looks down into her lap, hands folded neatly. "I thought I was going mad in there. I could smell it. Smell *him*." She breathes deeply, letting her eyes close briefly as she leans her head back against the headrest.

"How old were you?" I ask.

I started out working at fourteen years old, bagging at my dad's store. While I don't think Katrina and her mate would have been that young, I am curious.

"He was seventeen. I had just turned nineteen and was going to college."

Okay, so not that young then. That's a perfectly acceptable and predictable age to find your mate. It can happen at any point in your life, sure. But most packs want you to protect your line and start having children as soon as you hit adulthood.

Knowing that her pack didn't accept that Katrina had found her mate in a human, my inquisitiveness grows.

"And your family, your pack, was there ever a time that they approved?"

Her hands tighten, signaling that the answer is a hard no.

"I told my parents that night. Drove straight home, not even paying for my food. I just abandoned my cart and left after I saw him. Saw his nametag." A deadly calm comes over her, an eerie quiet settling between us as we finally make our way out of the construction work and I begin to speed up and weave in and out of cars.

"They were disgusted. Telling me that I was too young to know what I was talking about and that I was mistaken." Her tone drops. "Didn't stop me from stalking him that night, waiting for him to get off of work so I could follow him home. Let's just say there was a lot of sneaking around before my parents outed me to the pack. And they were just as unsupportive of the bond I so desperately wanted to make. So much so, they tried to kill him right in front of me."

I can't help it. I'm enraged for her past, not even having been a part of it myself. It then begs the question I've asked myself more than once—if my bond with Clara would've ever been accepted by my own pack. That is, if I had still been a part of it.

"There." Katrina's hand shoots out, pointing at a rather large truck stop that seems to be extremely active. Perfect for us to get out and take care of what few things we can before hopping on the road again until we reach our meeting point with the others. I nab the first gas pump I find and I'm dialing Clara as soon as I exit the vehicle. My legs are weary with their lack of use, and I nod to Katrina as she heads inside the station. I watch as the two vehicles I've had my eyes on go to their own pumps. If luck were on my side, they would have ran out of gas before now.

Dammit.

"Seth? Oh my God, are you okay?"

I stare hard at my Uncle George, his face in a permanent state of a threat that doesn't need any words.

"Seth!"

"Sorry, Clara. I'm here. Things haven't exactly gone according to plan."

"But you're okay? You're okay, right?" Her panic-stricken voice is pulling at me like invisible threads. Like my body knows it's trying to get back to her.

"Look, I don't have long. We're gassing up the vehicle and working our way back." Even with a busy gas station, I can't risk the other wolves hearing me or the fact that others will be meeting up with us. I don't want them calling in extra reinforcements to what they already have. Let them think it's just Katrina and me for a little longer. "Are you alright?"

"Fuck," she mutters, and it's like I can sense her tears slipping, rolling down her cheeks toward puffy lips. "No, I'm not. Not really. I'm barely hanging on here."

I close my eyes as I stick the nozzle into the vehicle, taking a steady breath in as I try to remain calm for her. "I'm sorry I've worried you. I'm sorry that I'm not there for you right now. How are Julie and Emmett taking the news?"

I should ask how Joe is doing, but if he was dead, I'm sure I would have heard about it by now, so I don't bother. He's low on my priority list. My Rose, her kids, and their well-being is at the damn top.

"They're...dealing. I'm taking them to the hospital to see him here shortly." She drops her voice, as if to not let others overhear. "God, Joe's even an asshole after a fucking car accident."

That, I have zero problems believing. The guy is a piece of work.

"When will you be home?"

I wince, trying to think of how to word it so I don't cause anymore worry but I'm coming up blank. I have no idea how long this is going to play out. Knowing my uncle, he'll want blood for the loss of his three sons. The pack will want my head on a spike and most likely Katrina's too for her part in things.

Home. Never thought I had a real one. Until Clara.

"I'm working on it, I promise." I can't give her any false sense of time to hope for. It would only shoot me in the foot if I couldn't live up to it. "I won't stop until I make it home. We're in Nebraska now—"

"That's good, right? You're on your way."

Not entirely, but I can't admit that out loud. "I'm trying, beautiful." The gas clicks off and I remove it, noting how my uncle's vehicle seems to be ready and waiting for me to leave, and Katrina is exiting the convenience store with some snacks and drinks in hand. "Clara, I'll try to have Katrina keep you posted if I can't. I'm going to give her your number. Just hang in there and I'll be home as soon as I possibly can. Be strong."

"Please be careful," she pleads, and I can't shake the grip it has on my heart. I never should've put her through this. I never should have left. Being at her side should have been enough, and now I've put Katrina at risk as well, and on the radar of my old pack.

"I love you, Clara."

"I love you too, Seth."

It pains me to hang up, but I do. I make it a vow to not let that be the last time I hear her voice. That I will do everything in my power to make sure everyone, aside from my old pack, gets home to their loved ones, whoever they might be.

# 29

# Showtime

## *Seth*

Our cellphones lose signal, which is what Javi had informed us would happen upon getting to our location. We've driven about twenty minutes on a dirt road that has minor remnants of snow. Thank goodness, because this vehicle wouldn't be able to handle much more. It's too low to the ground and not capable of any kind of off-roading purposes.

Katrina and I shoot each other a look of understanding before we exit the vehicle, knowing that we have each other's backs. We've even made some plans should the worst-case scenario happen, should one of us not survive the fight we have coming.

Both the jeep and truck that have been tailing us since Colorado come to a sliding halt behind us. There are shouts, curses, and feet hitting the ground as we exit our vehicle and turn to face them, yet we start backing away, gaining distance.

There are thick woods at our backs. No farmers or residents around for at least a mile from this location. We hadn't even crossed any other vehicles on this road since we turned onto it. Hopefully, it stays that way.

Uncle George, his brother Rodney, and a couple of distant cousins hop out. I'm a bit taken aback by a young man who looks like he's barely conquered his shifting abilities. He's too young to be here. He's not ready. Even so, there are five in total so we'll be matched in numbers if I count the kid.

"Murderer!" Uncle George shouts as if he's been holding it in for the entire drive that led us here. It's a strange word that he chooses to use at this moment, knowing that he more than likely encouraged his sons to go to Iowa to retrieve me by whatever means necessary. Given that my mother gave the orders that ultimately led to their demise, one could say she was responsible too.

"No one else needs to lose a life today," I start, but my uncles and one cousin laugh. All except the kid who just stares. A dead stare that gives absolutely nothing away of what he's thinking. His hair is pushed back, but dark pieces are escaping and falling across his forehead.

Uncle George spits some tobacco as they continue toward us. "I think the lives of you two will tip the scales right again."

"How many have to die before you stop? Huh?" I shout even though I know it falls on deaf ears. All of them are bloodthirsty except for the boy. "What will it take for you to understand that you can't win without further damaging your pack?"

Uncle Rodney laughs this time around, a belly laugh that's so deep it would probably raise hairs on humans.

"Don't do this." I give one last-ditch effort. Katrina and I are at the tree line of pines now. Ready to take off and dive in there. The others should be coming in from the east in the hopes that my family won't catch onto their scents until it's too late.

"Oh, we're doing this." Uncle George stops, holding up a closed fist for the others to halt in their pursuit as well. "Then, as a little treat, we'll pay a little visit to that pathetic little thing you marked as your mate."

A roar rips from my throat, bones cracking to the point that I'm rendered blind for a few seconds as I let the change take over. Clothes rip to shreds as I see red. The mention of my mate and their want to take her life has me pushing through it, accepting the beast inside of me that wants to protect. No, *has* to protect.

I've never actively hunted down anyone to kill. Every life I have ever taken has been because I had no other choice. When it came down to my life over theirs, there wasn't any other option for me than to end them. Even if I wanted to grant them mercy and a warning like my late cousin Carter, it came back to bite me in the ass. Some wolves just don't know when to stop.

Katrina and I are supposed to lead them into the forest, away from vehicles and away from the clearing we were instructed to park in.

"Shit, he's changing!"

"Is he fucking mad?"

I can barely make out a small voice which I assume belongs to the boy. "But it's not even a full moon!"

My neck cranes. I catch sight of Katrina and tell her to go. In a split second, she takes off, her footsteps light and disappearing before I start to stand on my haunches. In the time it takes me to change, the people before me that I used to call family could have at least started to call on their werewolf forms, but now they've waited too long and I have the advantage. Why they didn't take a chance to harm me while I was shifting is beyond me.

I look at the line of them, and the youngest one staggers back and to the truck before Uncle Rodney lifts an arm and fires a warning shot into the air. I growl, a sound that reverberates through my body and into the ground I stand on.

Fucking guns.

"What do you think about that, Seth?" Uncle Rod jeers, bumping an elbow against his brother. The looks they exchange remind me of my dad and their father. It's a look that threatens to physically make me sick, reminding me of all of the harm and pain that followed.

It's idiotic of me to think I can outrun a gun. I'm sure his aim is true, considering how much time he used to spend at ranges. I could charge them, risk it all and take out the alpha. From his movements he's long past his prime anyway and I can't understand why no one has challenged him yet. You challenge an alpha, you either win and take the title as your own, or you're dead. There is nothing else.

"Cover me." Uncle George keeps his eyes on me as he speaks to his brother. Rod nods, gun fixed in my direction as the alpha begins to shed his clothes. I lower onto all fours and begin to back away ever so slowly into the trees as his bones begin to break and body begins to twist this way and that. For someone who was so appalled by my shifting, he sure isn't missing the opportunity to try and upstage me.

Let him try.

His heartbeat is all over the place, an unsteady rhythm that's unnerving. A spike and elevation while changing, that's normal. Whatever his heart is doing is not. It affects him, slowing his change and drawing it out longer than it should be. I'm perplexed as to how I could even notice it from my location.

"That's right, run away, you coward!" one of my cousins shouts, but for the life of me, I have no idea what his name even is. He starts removing his clothes and shifting, signaling that they're all most likely prepared for a fight.

Well, except for the young one. I can't stand the thought that he was dragged along into something he didn't ask for, all because his alpha demanded it. His lower lip trembles as his eyes dart nervously around as if he's trying to figure out how he's going to fit into this equation.

The overall consensus is that they want a fight. They are sure going to get one.

George shakes through the rest of his change, scraps of clothing falling onto the dead earth. Thick, graying hair coats him as he lets out a bellowing howl in the late afternoon sun. Once he locks eyes on me, he charges.

Paws digging up the dry ground beneath my feet, I turn, luring him deeper into the woods. I could easily outrun him, it would be like child's play, but I let him get just close enough before pulling into the lead again. If I'm going to end him, I need witnesses. If they happen to be the werewolves from Iowa, then so be it.

The last thing I want is to defeat an alpha and take his place, but that's the furthest worry from me right now. I can't risk the chance of him or any of the other wolves making their way across the next border. This has to end, and now.

George gets close enough to snap at my hind legs and my anger gets the best of me. I haul myself around in time to get under him and kick him off, sending him into a pine tree. Needles rain down at the abrupt hit, and a loud gruff sound escapes him as he rolls to the side, shaking his head as he snarls.

The feelings are entirely mutual, and I turn it back at him as I bare my teeth. I was assured that these woods are free from humans, werewolves, or any other creatures that might take issue with our little war of sorts. So I don't hold back.

I lunge, taking him down on his back. He snaps and swipes but I'm quicker. I make contact with his snout, blood coating my claws. The equivalent of a scream comes bursting from his mouth and just as it wanes, something attacks me from behind.

We go rolling, scurrying to get our bearings as I process who it was that took me by surprise. The scent is like his father's but off. It must be Rodney's son, it has to be. He's lean, but not as great of a beast as I am. He might be younger and possibly quicker, but he isn't serving any other purpose than to fight because he was told to do so.

Does he even really know who I am? How I'm the family member who was shunned and hung out to dry like a dead carcass when I didn't fit into their mold of what a pack member should be?

I can only recall the small boy he was before I left. He was much younger than me, so we never really talked. There was nothing in common between us besides the pack we belonged to.

Rodney catches up, along with his presumed son, and together with George they surround me. Their growls strike the air, a cacophony of chaos as another joins them. They circle me, assessing as I dig my feet into the ground to get my bearings.

I hate depending on others at the moment, but it would sure help if I had some backup right now. Anything to take some of the heat off of me.

But I know the source I have to go after. I know that everyone but the alpha will aim to wound, leaving the final blow to come from him. And if I can just put an end to George, the rest will have no choice but to back off. They'll have to listen to me or to die themselves. I don't want to be their alpha, but I don't see any other way out of this to deter more unnecessary bloodshed.

One of the sons leaps at me from my side, light fur that's close to my coloring, nipping at my arm as I take off at George. He fends me off and I rebound, skirting around him and dodging my attacker on my heels. He's too close.

I have to turn, swiping at his chest as he makes contact with my shoulder. The same damn shoulder that I injured last fall. I can do nothing to hide the agony that overcomes me as he cuts through fur and skin, but I push on. Claws fighting left, right, then left again before someone else takes a cheap shot and attacks me from behind.

I howl, the pain taking over and rendering me useless for a moment with the intrusion. This injury feels deeper, and I can't help but suspect that they somehow dug through to my bone.

A chorus of howls and grunts comes from my left and I somehow manage to duck out of the way of another assailant as I witness Katrina's unmistakable blonde coat flash into view followed by three others.

It's the fuel I need. The help they said they would offer up when someone else is in trouble. This is the exact moment that I realize I'm not alone, and never will be again if I play my cards right.

Not-a-pack or not, and no matter how this fight turns out, I will be there for them, just as they were here for me. It's a sense of camaraderie that I have never known until now. Nobody *had* to come. My understanding is that all of this was done by volunteering, and it speaks volumes to their character.

A new surge of energy flows through me and I duck down onto all fours, racing forward and tumbling into one of my attackers before I take off in a sprint.

Katrina goes straight for Rodney and the others square off, letting out a series of strained cries as sharp nails scratch and teeth gnash. The trees and ground around us are being painted with red before my eyes as I zero in on George, who's trying to put distance between himself and the fight.

Fucking coward.

The fight is in full swing as I carry on, trying to ignore which wolves are gaining the upper hand. My focus is solely on George.

As if that realization sinks in, his eyes widen before he braces himself for impact. I go after his neck, jaws wide until someone hits my side and together, George and I take a tumble. We roll downhill and pick up speed. I try not to let it faze me, striking and swiping when presented the chance. I buck him off of me once we reach the bottom, sending him into a bulky tree trunk with a sickening crack.

I grasp onto the earth to come to a stop and get my bearings, recognizing the sound of one trying to capture their breath. The smell of his blood penetrates my nostrils as I shake my head to take a look at the scene.

George is struggling to shift back into his human form, his life force leaking from him and matting his fur as it runs off to soak the ground he lies upon. He wheezes, struggling to move, and I can't help but suspect that I did damage to his spine. His legs remain unmoving and my uncle is growing frantic, fighting to shift back but failing.

With a change in the wind, I barely catch a whiff of another guest and I turn, bracing myself. My body is far from ready for another round but I don't have much of a choice.

To my surprise, a young werewolf comes barreling down the hill but not toward me. He's headed straight for George with another from their pack hot on his heels and a wolf who I assume is Leo—the largest wolf I've ever seen. I shit you not, it's impressive. The brute is like a boulder, the force of a landslide and gaining quickly.

The kid guns right for my uncle, snapping his neck and taking the kill on his own and ending it all. He comes to a halt, huffing and puffing before lifting his head into the air and raising onto his back legs to stand tall.

A victorious and all-consuming howl spreads, silencing the ruckus that these unaccompanied woods have been victim to ever since we stepped out of our vehicles. Everything goes quiet as his voice draws to the end of his note.

I cast a glance at Leo. We keep ourselves upright, refusing to bow down to the victor. This isn't our pack, nor will he be our alpha.

Steps begin to descend upon us, rustling and crunching of leaves as the dead man before me permeates the air. I have no idea what this kid's intent is. He could order his pack to proceed in their attempts to end us, or he could call it off. Seeing how much went into this pursuit to end Katrina and me today, I don't think I have much hope in the latter.

One by one, werewolves straggle into the picture. Katrina first, followed by my nameless cousin. Edgar, with patches of gray within his fur, is limping along on all fours, followed by one who I assume to be Javi who's keeping him steady.

But that's it.

My Uncle Rodney is nowhere to be seen and I scent the air, but if the rest of my family is dead, I can't catch onto it yet.

Collectively, we all turn our attention to the one who slayed the alpha of my old pack. You would think I might be jealous that I didn't get to commit the act myself, but I'm not. I'm more concerned for this young wolf who had to take a life.

Was this his first? Has he killed before? I'm unsure of his age, but if I had to guess, he might already have me beat, younger than when I first took a life.

He stands triumphantly in front of George's body, but there's a slight quiver in his arm that he stills almost instantly. He lets out another howl, but it's only followed by the last of his company.

When they finish, they both lower, bringing along the change to revert back to their human forms. I take it as a sign that this feud is over and drop down myself, wincing as I take count of my wounds. My adrenaline is running out now that the main threat has been dealt with. They did some considerable damage to me, that's for sure, but I'm confident it's nothing I can't handle.

I barely register Katrina backing away and out of view, along with Edgar and Javi. But Leo stays with me, not opting to change forms. Probably wise, but I myself want to talk to the survivors to see what they expect to happen next.

As my shift completes, I turn my gaze on them again. The last one to have joined us is holding his ribs. A nasty coloring is rising to the surface.

We stand in silence for a while. Three stark-naked men in a forest far from our homes, and a werewolf about the size of the three of us combined looming nearby.

"You know what this means," I start, gesturing toward the dead.

He nods, keeping direct eye contact with me. His frame is smaller, closer to Katrina's to be exact. But I can see the potential in him. He's young, but he could be capable of so much. I can envision the strength he could come into, now that he's an alpha. There's a lot that falls on a pack leader's shoulders. You either step up to the plate for it, or you'll be trampled and snuffed out.

I can't help it. I have to ask the one question burning in my mind. Is he power hungry? Did he come along in the hopes of turning the tables in his favor, or was he acting on impulse? Even if it was a rash decision, we don't even know each other. We owe *nothing* to one another. "Why turn against your own alpha?"

The two before me exchange glances. Something unspoken passes between them before the one in front turns, signaling for the other to do the same. Their backs reveal scars and burns that sicken me. If I had to guess, they've been dealt shittier upbringings than my own. I was never burned, thank whatever holy entity there might be. Maybe, just maybe, they have seen more evil than I have.

"We hadn't planned on acting as soon as this but…" The new alpha exchanges another glance and when his companion nods for him to continue, he does. "When we saw the scars on your back, we saw the chance to end it."

"I have a friend," the one closer to me begins, staring at the ground. "He's part of another pack. Something so vastly different from our own, from what we were raised in. We knew that if we ever tried to leave for whatever reason, we would be hunted down just like you.

"This is our chance to change. This is our moment to try and become a better pack. One that doesn't attack and beat their own children. Kill when there's disagreements. Perhaps we can start off with a somewhat clean slate."

Well that was oddly…unexpected. I clear my throat to speak, but wince. It's like my body's been tossed and bounced about the forest like a pinball machine. "Don't suppose you two were blessed with knowing my bastard of a grandpa, Ernest."

I can't help but wonder how many generations the abuse goes back. I could practically be the father of this young new leader before me. And now he's in charge.

Both of them shake their heads in denial and while I am glad they never met his hands or the weapons he used, it wasn't enough. There were others to carry on the abhorrent abuse after his passing. These two are going to break the cycle and for once, I'm damn proud of these two unknowns.

"So with this clean slate," I begin, careful to choose my words. My gut is telling me that this is it, but I need some sort of clarification before we leave the confines of these woods. "Will you call off the hunt on my mate and me?"

"That depends." The alpha takes a few steps toward me. "Will you help us drag the dead weight back to our vehicles?"

I'm too chickenshit to admit that my injuries aren't necessarily going to help them, but I will push through the pain. They will want to bury their dead, even if it's by their own hands. Little does Mitch know, he has a few more bodies headed his way. I make a note to myself to check in with him once I'm back home and settled.

Home. I'm one step closer to returning to the one place I long to be, with the people who I've already chosen as my family.

"I would be more than happy to, as long as you two can answer a question for me."

They exchange looks again, confusion furrowing their brows, and I let out a soft chuckle, careful not to anger my wounds any further. "Please, help a guy out and tell me who you two are."

The young men laugh along with me and I swear Leo behind me, still in his wolf form, huffs along with us.

# 30

# Whole Again

## *Clara*

I jolt awake, clutching at my chest as my heart tries to kill me. I'm panting as my thoughts wrestle with the events of the past day to try and make sense of where I am and why I'm stricken with such panic.

As I fumble to the side in search of my phone, my surroundings only confuse me further. There's no nightstand and it isn't until I knock the remote on the floor that I realize I've fallen asleep in the living room.

Phone chiming, I search the darkness and roll myself from the couch and onto the floor. I must have knocked it off and the screen was face down. Turning it over, I see spots for a moment. It takes a few seconds to focus on the screen, straining my eyes as I make out a call and two missed texts from Seth.

Before I can even click on the voice message, my garage camera goes off. I open the app and see Seth's truck on the live camera feed. My socks slide on the carpet as I try to get my footing, launching myself headfirst, and I almost face-plant but catch myself.

Leaving my phone behind, I whip out of the living room and through the kitchen to struggle with the locks before racing out into the freezing early morning. My heart is racing faster than my feet will allow as I dart through the breezeway and when I round the corner, I run smack dab into Seth. I hold back a scream as he buckles over, groaning in pain.

"I'm sorry!" I say a bit too loud, then back down a bit as I try to hug him. "I'm so sorry!"

"Ah!" He hunches over and I take a step back. There are dark spots on his shirt and the pain evident on his face prevents me from trying to touch him again, no matter how relieved I am to see him. Seth and Joe have both put me through a lot in such a short span of time. I don't know how on earth I'm still functioning with the stress of it all.

"Come on, let's get you inside."

I shed my wet socks as soon as we enter, and Seth wastes no time dragging himself to our room. He kicks his shoes off, stifling grunts as he moves. Closing the bedroom door behind us, I flip on the light on his nightstand and we both flinch.

Seth's height has dropped due to the way he's holding himself. Dried blood is evident in more spots than I initially saw and it cues the waterworks before I can even process it. Just what in the hell has he been through?

"Oh, Seth." I cup a hand over my mouth, the ghastly sight of him almost too much. It might even be worse than last November when he duked it out with his cousins.

"I'm sorry, I should have gone home and showered first. I'm a wreck, I know."

I want to slug him. And kiss him. And yell at him. Fuck, there's a lot I want to do to him right now. But seeing him like this, a man who exudes such strength being rendered to this? It's heartbreaking, upsetting, and frightening.

"Shut up," I tell him, tears threatening my eyes. "This can't be a regular thing, Seth. These fights, these pestering family members and problems that won't go away. I can't keep doing this."

I know the moment I say that, it's a lie, but right now, it feels as close to the truth as I can get. I love this man. God, do I love him with every fiber of my being, but he can't keep putting me through this.

Seth's eyes are clenched shut as tears fall. The need to touch him is fierce. The desire to hold him close burns hot, but I know I can't do it without causing him any further pain.

"I have so much to tell you, Clara, I really do, but I've been driving all night to get to you and I'm really, *really* low on fumes here."

I nod, knowing from the mere look of him that he's exhausted beyond belief. "Do we need to go to the hospital? Do I need to call Larson? Tell me what you need."

He sways a bit and I jump as if I'll need to help steady him, but he leans awkwardly against the foot of our bed. When he opens his eyes into slits, he brings a hand up, knuckles sliding across my cheek until he can cup the side of my head. My breath catches and my eyes close on instinct, savoring his touch that I shouldn't crave so much. After our short time apart, it feels like an entire week had passed.

Seth tastes of caffeine as he takes my lips. The bitterness hits my taste buds but I don't care. Nor do I worry about the unpleasant smell that's now settling in my nose.

Our lips move languidly, my plight momentarily forgotten with this one moment in time. Seth is finally here, physically present and with me. The strength that settles in my gut grows stronger. It's not that I need a man to feel powerful, more that I want him to feel complete. That I desire his closeness in the hopes of becoming the best version of myself that I can be with him in my corner.

My friend, my confidant, my lover. My mate, in his terms. Seth is my other half in every sense of the word.

Seth sucks in a breath, breaking away from our reunion and bending over. It allows me to bear witness to the back of his shirt, which is almost entirely covered in a mixture of fresh and dried crimson.

"I'm calling Larson." I begin to leave but Seth still has enough strength in his debilitated state to snatch my arm, halting me.

He grimaces. "I know it doesn't look good, but I'm already healing, believe it or not."

I scoff, skepticism dripping from my voice. "You weren't exactly chasing rabbits in Nebraska. You're seriously hurt, Seth."

"I'll be fine. I just need a shower and possibly something to lay on the bed so I don't get blood on it. Do you still have any cruddy towels or blankets you're not particularly fond of?"

I nod. "Of course." The very blanket I'd meant for him to use the evening of the last full moon instantly comes to mind. I already washed and folded it; it's still sitting in the laundry room.

"And some scissors to cut my shirt off or something? There's no saving this."

I nod again, running as quietly as I can on the balls of my feet to retrieve said items. We still have a couple of hours before the kids start to stir and get ready for school so we have a bit of time on our side. While I'm out and about, I grab Seth's jar of pickles that Emmett has apparently been dipping into again, some water, and pills because anyone in their right mind could see just how much misery Seth is in.

By the time I make it back to the bedroom, my arms are full but I still close the door as silently as I can. Seth has already made his way to the bathroom and I hear the shower kick on.

Removing my sweater leaves me in my pants, a bra, and tank top. I don't want to chance getting anything on me that might stain. I'm rounding the corner to the bathroom, tossing my sweater into the hamper, when Seth's breath catches. He's trying to undress himself; the pain-stricken reaction to the movements has me bolting forward.

"Here, let me help." He's only made it as far as unbuttoning his jeans and they're only halfway down his rear. There's a gash on his calf and he holds back a sound of his discomfort in his throat. The blood is already clotted, but his clothes are sticking to his body, proving that I need to handle him with more delicacy than I initially thought I'd need.

I'm no nurse, but that wound alone looks like it needs stitches.

His pants fall to the ground in a thump, then I move up to his shirt. "Are you sure you want me to cut this off?"

Seth's eyes remain closed, and he only nods his confirmation. The scissors I secured from the office have rarely been used but obviously aren't meant for any kind of fabric cutting. Even so, I push through it, from the hem at the bottom and up his chest until I reach the neckline. Its stiffness proves difficult and every time Seth has to move to help me only brings him more pain. He turns, giving me his back, and I can't help but gawk at the sight before me.

Claw marks—deep, red, and angry—mar his back. I'm having trouble even finding the scars that I know were there before this trip. While I still don't know the entire story, it hits me hard. The severity of it is frightening.

With the amount of wetness still soaking the fabric, I throw his shirt into the tub before nabbing the rest of his clothes and depositing them in there too. I'll dispose of them later.

Seth hisses as he steps into the shower before spewing a barely audible string of choice words. Before I can talk myself out of it, I'm shedding the rest of my clothes so I can join him in the shower. His limited movements are going to prove difficult for him, and I grab a few washcloths and run them under the spray before squeezing some soap onto one.

"Clara." He's leaning against the shower wall, eyes and body tight. He'd better not pass out in here, or I *will* be making a phone call to Larson. "You don't have to do this."

"Shut up," I chide lightly as I wring the soapiness over his shoulder. He jerks, his wolf tattoo on his arm glaring at me when he can't. "I want to help."

Does he need to be on any kind of antibiotics to prevent infection? These injuries look serious. I'm afraid that the pain he's in will be too much, that he'll pass out from it, but I push through it, trying to gather my thoughts enough to try and come up with some sort of distraction.

"For better or for worse. Through sickness and in health." My throat works to swallow and I watch him carefully as my hands shake, knowing that this next move with the suds is going to hurt like a bitch. I squeeze it before continuing. Seth holds back his suffering, breathing harshly through gritted teeth. Seeing him in such agony brings fresh tears that fall before I can even blink. "You want to marry me someday, right? Guess we're getting a head start on those vows."

"Gah!" His voice grows as I quickly grab the other washcloth from my shoulder, letting it fill with as much water as it will hold before trying to lightly wash away the soap so it doesn't sit on his skin for too long. The spray is pattering my face, mingling with my tears as I try to push through the worst of it. After this, I should be able to scrub down all of the areas that are free of marks. His neck, his chest, his...

"Clara." I freeze on my name, gutted by how rushed and heavy it sounds on his tongue.

Joe deserves every inch of pain that he has. His stupidity, lack of care and brains could have cost him his life. His road to recovery isn't going to be a pleasant one, but he will have to deal with the consequences of his actions.

But Seth? He doesn't deserve this. He doesn't need the physical marks to remind him of a past that did so much damage. He's too good. He's protective and kind and considerate. He is doing everything he can to make sure that my family and I are safe, no matter the costs.

Both Seth and Larson have assured me that the threat looming over us has lifted. That Seth's old home is no longer an issue, and while I still don't know the logistics, I can't fully believe that's the case. At least not yet. Not while I'm still trying to navigate this life with Seth while trying to raise my kids.

"I..." Seth begins, but his chest rises and falls in heavy heaves. "I *will* marry you, Clara Rose. Be it a month or a year from now, I will make you mine and you will never want for anything else."

Crossing my arms uncomfortably over my chest, I still. Tying the knot with Seth and securing us together until the end is all I want. To believe that not even death can separate us. That one way or another, he will find me just as he did that first day out in the driveway.

With Seth, I envision a life together, raising Julie and Emmett with him by my side, and if Joe ever gets his act together, perhaps one day we can even somewhat get along for our children and future grandchildren's sake. Setting an example for my kids just as my parents did for me and my brother.

"Don't I have your mark to show that?" I tease as I break away from my daydreaming, casting my glance down at my arm. You can't even tell that anything happened. Not to me, anyway.

For the first time since he returned, a faint smile crosses his lips. "That will only show werewolves that you belong to someone. I want you to wear a ring to show the world that you're taken. I want to hold that hand and call you my wife for the rest of our lives."

His sweet words move me. I want to nuzzle into him, hug and kiss him until we're both breathless. But with his state of being, I don't act on it.

I work through another swallow, forcing my throat to work when I want to cry happy tears. "Let's just focus on you getting healed up first. Then, and only then, can we discuss our future."

A future that I am suddenly seeing more clearly with each ticking second. A tangible future that is just at my fingertips, begging to begin.

# 31

# Sunset and Chill

## *Clara*

S everal weeks later...

The table erupts in laughter, garnering attention from some of the other diners this evening. I'm trying to remember the last time I laughed this much. Felt good enough to let loose to the point that my cheeks are beginning to ache.

I may not have had the best of introductions to Seth's family, but his coworker Dante has been a presence in his life for quite some time now. Their friendship extends a little further than that of normal work acquaintances. And come to find out that over the years, they even got together occasionally on weekends just to hang out. That is until Dante met his wife, Susan, a glowing beauty with thick and bouncy hair who just so happens to be turning thirty today.

Therefore, the good food and drinks in sunny San Diego.

Seth recovered from his injuries in the weeks that followed his trip to Colorado. Even though he can heal quicker as a werewolf, he still went to the hospital and ended up getting some stitches after the whole ordeal. I was grateful that this Katrina and the other wolves hadn't obtained any serious wounds such as his. I keep nagging at Seth, asking when I can meet them and thank them for the part they played. Perhaps someday, I can.

I hope that Seth's uncles are burning in hell for an eternity, right alongside his father and grandfather. It seems their cruel treatment was a practice in more than one home, affecting so many children. The young man who just became the new pack leader being one of them. Knowing that Seth's trauma isn't limited to just him makes me sick.

Together, Seth and I forfeited the bets we made and told on ourselves. I came clean about wanting to spend a night with him out in the woods someday—er...some night—when he's in his werewolf form. I know we won't be roasting marshmallows or swapping scary stories, but I want to see what it's like for him. Some night when the weather isn't so humid it's trying to kill you or when winter is attempting to freeze you solid. When Julie and Emmett can either stay with their grandparents up north or at friends' houses.

On the other hand, Seth's intent had been bringing me here all along. To a conference held once a year by the company he works for. It's the one time he's guaranteed to see his friend and catch up in person.

The little sneak had even arranged everything. And I mean, *everything*. My job had already approved the time off, unbeknownst to me. The kids were taken care of and plane tickets had been bought. All I had to do was pack. Although, I didn't fully appreciate him keeping me in the dark about it, only telling me the Friday before we left on Sunday.

He'd even sprung for first-class seats on our flight, which I scolded him for, telling him that he could make better use of that money. But once I was in that seat next to only him, and not pressed up against some stranger, I hate to admit it, but it was worth it. Seth is ruining flying for me. I hate to think I might never be able to ride economy again. He's spoiling me, and while I don't want to confess it out loud, I like it.

"I mean, come on, man. I've never been so drunk that I took off my clothes and lost them." Dante's laugh is infectious and while I laugh along, I can't help but shoot a knowing look at Seth. I'm about ninety-eight percent sure that the night Dante's referring to was a full moon, and that's why Seth had to be rescued so he didn't get arrested or something.

Seth winks at me before raising his beer bottle to his friend. "And that's why I'm sticking with these tonight and not hard liquor."

"I'm just happy I have somebody to look forward to seeing now at these work things." Susan raises a perfectly manicured hand to my short nails and thicker fingers, gesturing for a cheer of our wine glasses.

I lift mine, meeting her gaze and smiling once more. "To the first of many."

With a little clink, we both drink, and with the warmth in my belly, I know I need to take a bite of something. This white wine is so delicious, it has to be trouble. Wonder if there's any way to find this stuff back home. I think my mom would fall for it too.

The guys keep veering off into work-related topics and while I'm afraid I keep talking about my kids too much, I can't help it. Susan is inquisitive, asking about them and my life, normal get-to-know-somebody type of stuff. She and Dante don't have any kids of their own—yet. I can't help but grin every time she nudges him, and at the looks they give one another. If I had to make an educated guess, they might already be trying. There's a gleam in their eyes, and while Dante might roll his dark eyes at times, it's not in annoyance. I think he wants kids just as much as she does. I can't help but be excited for this new friendship and the next chapter of their lives.

Seth squeezes my thigh under the table and I slip my hand over his. Neither of us looks at one another, fully engrossed in our squared-off conversations. His middle finger draws circles on my inner thigh and he'll stop for a few seconds, just to pick it back up again.

I know what he's doing. The alcohol, his touch, and the promise of what the night ahead of us brings is almost enough to make me end this meal early so we can disappear to our suite that overlooks the bay area. I spent all morning in a daze, watching the boats come and go, people-watching down below from the fourteenth floor.

Seth has to go to a session tomorrow morning because he's being recognized for a program that he made with his job. I guess whoever won gets some sort of prize and when I tried to hype the man up for his accomplishment, he just waved it off as if it were nothing. I wouldn't claim that I'm any sort of tech-savvy type of person, but to me, it feels like a big deal. Instead, he keeps telling me about how he wishes he could've made some improvements and tweaks before submitting it for consideration. I can appreciate his talents, even if I don't understand a single thing about the program when he tries to dumb it down for my understanding.

I didn't realize how dim the restaurant was until we walk hand in hand out and into the glorious sunset. A steady breeze is coming in from the bay, bringing with it the smells of food from nearby food joints, including the one we just exited.

We part ways with Dante and Susan, and I offer to come and find her tomorrow so we can go do some shopping together. After all, I want to find some souvenirs for Julie and Emmett. There's this one shop that engraves names on seashells but it doesn't open until noon tomorrow. I want that to be my first stop, and Susan wants to come along as well but warned me she wouldn't be getting up early if she could help it.

Seth and I begin to retreat in the direction of our hotel and once we're clear of nearby pedestrians from the little village of eats, treats, and unique shops, he spins me around. Giggling like a fool, a perhaps tipsy but happy one, I come crashing into his chest. Gazing up into his eyes, I hold steady to them. Even the butterflies in my stomach have had their fill of alcohol, but not to the point where I'm void of coherent thought and actions.

The love I have in my heart for this man is almost supernatural. Otherworldly in a way I'd never experienced before.

Seth's hand covers my wrist and he loops a thumb through the moon bracelet he gave me before planting a kiss on the top of my hand. "Come here."

I'm pulled toward the end of a short stone wall and into the sand. His linen slacks move with the wind as does my turquoise dress I plucked from another shop yesterday so I had something a little fancy for dinner tonight. It's strange showing my chest and arms when the past several months I've been covered and bundled up in the Midwest.

Slipping out of our sandals, we grab them with our free hands and I follow after him. The beautiful array of sunset colors is the perfect image to end the day with. Seth turns to me and lets go, taking a couple of steps back.

I turn sheepish, ever aware of people passing by and curious glances. My heart races, suddenly unsure if Seth is going to use this moment to propose. While we've begun discussing the possibility of marriage in theory, it still feels too early.

"What?" I laugh nervously. So help me, if he gets down on one knee, I don't know what I'll do. He still hasn't officially moved in. I haven't even been able to bring up the idea to the kids, who are still getting used to living with me full time. But that hasn't stopped Seth from turning the basement into a safe place that he can convert quickly from office to a soundproof sex dungeon of sorts. The man is on a mission with that task. "Seth."

He turns his charm on, retrieving something from his pocket, and my breath hitches. Sensing my inner turmoil, he flashes his phone to show me what's in his possession. I know he wants marriage and I want that too. Someday.

"You're absolutely breathtaking."

Air rushes back in at the relief as he holds out his phone to take a picture. I turn shy as I'm usually the one taking them myself but hardly ever in them. My camera roll is full of images of kids, food, and random shenanigans, but rarely ever me.

This is the precise moment that the mom guilt hits me hard. Here I am, prancing around San Diego with Seth while my kids are home going about their new normal routines. My mood drops as I have gnawing thoughts of how I shouldn't be here, that I'm abandoning my kids for this man who it feels like I've known forever but in reality, it's only been about eight months.

"Hey." Seth draws near, tipping my chin up. Somehow I feel even shorter in the sand up close. "Next time, we'll bring the kids."

I shake my head from his grasp, a bit stunned, but my shoulders sag. "How did you know?"

Seth shrugs. "You're a mother, beautiful. And a damn wonderful one at that. It's okay to miss them."

When he removes his hand from my chin, it's my turn to lead him away. The sand is harder to walk through than it looks, and feels funny as it tunnels through my toes. The salty blow of wind brushes my hair to the side, giving me the perfect view of Seth's profile. It's short-lived, however, because he looks right back at me.

For a moment, I'm dragged back to that Chinese restaurant in the next town over and our first date together. Even if I hadn't initially wanted to call it that. No longer do the longing and lustful stares of others bother me, because I know that I am his and he's mine. Nobody else matters and there will never be anyone else but him.

"I don't know how you ever managed to heal my broken heart, but you did." I'm not sure if I can ever truly confess just how much he means to me. How he turned my life around and gave me hope again. "And yet somehow, you made enough room to let yourself inside of it too."

Seth hums as he closes his eyes. When they reopen, those golden hues hold so much love and devotion that I get lost in the roller coaster ride of what our relationship has been so far. "Even so, I'm still not close enough. But you'll never go a day—"

"Without knowing how much I love you," I finish for him, my heart growing two damn sizes just to accommodate the heavy load of emotions coursing through me. The complexity and immense growth of our love is catapulting off the charts and into territory I'd never thought possible, especially for me.

About fifteen minutes later, we're riding the elevator to our floor and when we step out, the sun is barely a sliver on the horizon through the window at the end of the hallway. Seth unlocks our door with a key card and presses the button to lower the shades on the windows overlooking my favorite view of San Diego so far. Meanwhile, I meander toward the bed in the other room. The light from the entryway barely makes it in here, and there are twinkles of color outside in the distance from the obnoxiously large windows in here.

Seth comes up from behind and wraps his arms around my middle. My head leans back onto him, and I crane my neck to be met with his lips. He lets his hands roam over the cotton that covers me, sneaking one into the cup to grasp my breast while the other dips low. My behind grinds into him in response.

He groans a low and seductive sound as he grips me and grinds his fingers against my clit. While I like the friction, it's not enough. I know it won't be until he's there, burying himself until we become one.

"I'd like to try something." He leaves my lips and waits, signaling that he wants a verbal response. Perhaps it's a good thing I've never stated out loud to him that my body is his for the taking.

I don't meet him with a straight answer. "You're going to make it hard for me to keep quiet, aren't you?"

The wicked gleam in his eyes sends all sorts of signals to my core, and I'm buzzing. Alive with anticipation and want, even when I have no clue what's in store.

He unfastens the fabric behind my neck, and my dress falls and pools on the floor. Seth doesn't let me step out of it when I try to. He undresses the rest of me, and only then does he instruct me to sit on the bed. I do as he says, and he leaves me for the bathroom. I stare off after him for a moment, the chill of the air-conditioned room pricking at my skin now that I don't have a stitch of clothing on. But when I hear the rustling of clothes, excitement begins to strike my senses.

It all goes quiet before Seth finally emerges. His machine of a body still has the same effect on me that it did the first time I saw him in my darkened bedroom. He's stunning, mouthwatering, and even without a ring to prove it, I know he's mine. His dick is already solid and it's hard not to stare at any part of him, but his hands seem to be concealing something in each. One is suspiciously covered with a towel.

"What have you got there, little wolf?"

Seth halts about two feet away from the bed, and while I might be poking to make a bit of fun, there's a glimmer of something mischievous in those eyes of his.

"I think we've established I'm anything but little."

*Damn right.* I smirk, noting that he didn't completely write off that nickname.

His body leans over, towering really, and before I can steal another look at what he's got, his mouth finds mine. It's hot and needy and desperate. He's pressing me down into the mattress, his body following suit as my hands cup his face to keep it there. The way my body aches for him and the need he can fulfill is the only thing on my mind, that is until something buzzes to life and presses to my clit.

"Oh!" I break apart, trying to adjust myself to see what toy is being applied, but I can't make anything out. His name slips from my mouth as my hips try to meet the little accessory, eager for its vibrations. The way it nestles there so perfectly is spectacular.

I love that this man is never turned off by the use of toys. In fact, he embraces them. We don't have to use them all of the time but when we do, it unlocks another level of intimacy to explore. I moan, reflecting on every time they've led to satisfaction. He never treats them as competition, and damn do I benefit from it every time. It feels like us women have a plethora of options to choose from whereas men have sleeves and cock rings. We haven't even crossed into backdoor territory yet, but I know that will eventually come around the corner someday. With Seth, anything is possible.

I squirm against the toy and attempt to clutch at his sides to bring him closer, but he sits up. I'm not going to last long and all I can say is "Pillow."

Arms shooting up, I just barely grasp the corner of one before Seth grips my calves, tugging me down the bed until my rear end is at the edge. I stifle a yelp at the swift movement, heat coursing through my body.

To think there was a time when I cowered and attempted to cover my body in front of Seth. How embarrassed I was that when I lay down on my back, my breasts parted and fell away from each other. The curves and rolls on my body, that I used to be ashamed of, have only ever been worshiped and adored and cared for by him. He never makes me feel anything less than desirable and wanted.

Seth raises the mystery toy into view and I study it. He wants me to see it, the slender, black thing that has to be longer than the length of my hand. I'm then introduced to what else he snuck in here as he brings up a bottle of lube and pumps the liquid onto the shaft.

My heart kicks up a notch, like I'm off to the races. I don't think we really need lube, but who am I to deny how devastatingly hot it is that Seth is planning on inserting that toy himself?

He parts my flesh and eases the toy inside. It slides in without any resistance and when he turns it on, my back arches. I cup my own breasts, pressing them together when I don't know what else to do with my hands. I don't need to smother myself with a pillow. No, these vibrations I can handle. Until the buzzing curves up over my clit again.

Eyes shooting open, I bite my bottom lip as I look at Seth, who's appreciating his work. Everything is alive down there with melodious whirring that fills my ears. For such a small thing, it's rather loud even while half in and half out. His gaze flicks to mine, a needy hunger evident in his features.

Keeping one hand on me, he picks up the bottle of lube and pumps it twice onto his length. I'm jealous that I can't reach him as he tosses the bottle near my hips and begins to run his hand along the slickness. I'm jealous. Jealous that he gets to do that when I want to touch, squeeze, and stroke him while he uses this new toy on me.

Grabbing the towel at his side, he pats my bottom and I lift my hips in response. He slides the material under me and then uses his grasp on the toy to urge me back down. Then, he lines himself up at my entrance.

"Seth." I can't quite muster up the alarm that wants to make itself known as he presses the one end harder onto my clit. His wicked intent is more than obvious now as he nudges himself beside the bendable wand. That's why he needed the lube. Sneaky little—

"Oh..." I moan a little too loudly and reach for the pillow but Seth swipes my hand away, pressing into me more. The stretch isn't necessarily painful but damn, do I feel like he's really filling me up. I gasp, searching his eyes that bore into mine. The pleasure that envelops us is bone-deep.

Releasing the hold on myself, I reach for him, bringing his lips crashing down on my own as pressure builds and he swallows my vocal cry. Each kiss is wild and messy as he moves in and out. An orgasm is ready and waiting on the sidelines to make its grand entrance, and the whimpers that leave my throat are anything but quiet.

I break away, searching for the pillow, but find it nowhere. "Seth," I pant, knowing that these hotel walls are thin, "I can't..."

He rocks into me again, and the sight of him benefiting from the toy and our connection is almost enough to send me over the edge. Seth grows louder too, and there's nothing hotter than a man not hiding his enjoyment. I want to know that he's getting just as much out of this as I am. I want to hear him, but I don't want our surrounding neighbors to bear witness to it.

The build is too quick, taking charge on a path of its own, and I detonate. Seth's quick to clamp down on my mouth but it hardly does anything to stifle my cries as my body spasms around him. My hands are clawing as my body shakes, my core so tight on his cock and that toy that I swear the orgasm draws itself out longer.

It probably sounds like I'm dying from sex in here. I can't deny that there are worse ways I could go.

But Seth doesn't relent in his thrusts. He's still chasing after his finale, and as much as I try to fight him off, it's futile. My insides tremble and tears leak from the corners of my eyes, blurring my vision. Somehow, and I can't understand why, I can't tell him to stop. The word won't come out as I continue to take him.

The fullness, the unyielding buzz, and his vocal grunts drive me into another unannounced orgasm. It's so quick, barely giving me a chance to protest as warmth spreads down below, leaking out and running down my backside. I only hope that the towel is enough to help save the bed at this point.

A pillow is shoved between our faces and we both scream, yell, grunt, everything imaginable. While I struggle to process and listen to his own release over my own, he somehow removes the toy and only then do I finally feel relief from my body being fucked to the point of shattering.

I'm panting and hot-faced as Seth pulls the pillow away, revealing himself and a cocky grin. But when he takes notice of my tears, his mood softens. Using his thumb, he smooths away hair that's sticking to the side of my face before he begins to pepper me with light kisses. His lips drag as he moves, and I count each one as I come down from the soul-snatching height I fell from.

For once, we have no words. There's no need for them in the afterglow of what we've just done. Seth stays seated inside of me where he belongs, and I can't help but wonder how I ever got so lucky to have him in my life.

# 32

# Unexpected Visitor

## *Clara*

I'm barely conscious as Seth kisses me goodbye. There's a small strip of sunlight coming through the bottom of the window and shining onto the floor. He tucks the blanket around me at some point and I fall back asleep, basking in the memories of last night.

I don't know how much time passes, dozing on and off in sleepy bliss until my phone goes off. Tucking my hair behind my ear, I retrieve it and see a message from Julie, and it perks me right up. There are a few notifications along with a message reading "proof of life," and when I open it, there's a picture of her and Emmett posing with silly faces in front of my father who's nodding off on the couch. Judging by the light in the room, I assume it's from yesterday, and I giggle.

This vacation will be the longest I've ever spent away from my kids, and while I still go through guilt trips at least a dozen times a day, this helps. I know they'll be in school by now, the time zones messing with me a bit, but I send back a reply offering to do a video call with them later once they're home and settled. I know Julie more than likely won't get the message until after school is out, but at least it will be there waiting for her.

Taking my time getting ready, I apply a little bit of makeup and wear something comfortable for shopping around and hopefully, finding a shaded spot by the water to relax while Seth is away. This is the last day he plans on attending any sessions and it allows me some time to myself, or as I recall, to spend with a new friend, Susan. I'm rather excited to meet up with her, knowing that she has an understanding of our area and what all it has to offer. But I still have some time to kill before we get together. I gave her my number to reach out when she's ready.

I perch myself on the large windowsill overlooking the bay area and call my dad, deciding to check in. To thank him *again* for his part in this and catch up.

"Are you sunburned yet?" Dad doesn't sound anymore awake than I am right now.

"Nope, not yet," I answer as I play with the frilly sleeve of my pink blouse. "But it's beautiful here. The sea breeze, the palm trees, the little shops and all the food. I can see how easily one could forget sunscreen and just go with the flow."

"Enjoying yourself, huh?"

"I am, yeah." My mind flits to last night and I catch myself, clearing my throat to tear my thoughts away from such sinful things. "Thank you again, Dad."

"Oh, stop with the thanks. You know I'm happy to, since I'm retired anyway. Larson and I are going to head over to Benson Hills to grab a bite here soon."

"Good, that's great!" I say a little too enthusiastically. I'm genuinely glad that he's using his spare time to his advantage. And getting Larson out of the house too, for that matter.

The conversation doesn't last too long. He catches me up on how Emmett is trying to hide his homework and how Julie is outing him every time. The normal sibling bickering doesn't even stop for their grandpa. Our talk comes to an awkward pause, the first since we've been chatting, and just when I'm about to open my mouth to bring it to a close, he speaks up.

"This Seth really wants to take care of you, doesn't he?"

His question strikes me as odd, and I wiggle on my perch a bit, unsure of how to proceed. Not even the birds soaring past the building could sway me from wondering why he's asking this. Am I thinking too much about it?

"Yes," I draw out, hesitantly. "I guess you could say that the feeling is mutual?"

Mutual? God, what am I saying? And to my dad, even. I'm met with silence again and I sit forward. "Dad, is there something you want to share?"

Doubt creeps in. Fear that my dad doesn't approve of the romance and literal werewolf that came in and swept me off my feet. I know to the outside world, everything might be moving quickly, but with Seth, it all just seemed to fall into place.

"No, no," he backtracks, but it does nothing to soothe my worried thoughts. "He seems like a good guy, and Larson speaks highly of him too."

Great, so he's talking to his new bestie about Seth. Probably trying to gather more information by going around me. I wonder if this is all his doing or if my mother is trying to get my father to meddle for her when she can't be there.

"He's very protective of you, of your family."

I look down and into my lap. The fact that my dad has caught onto that somehow causes emotion to well up inside of me. He has no idea just how protective Seth is, the lengths he's gone to, to protect me and the kids. From werewolves and from my ex-husband. He's my knight in shining armor—well, except he's huge and can spout fur all over his body. Let's not forget the teeth and claws and—

"You know I only want what's best for you and your brother. Only you're not stationed overseas, so I'm sorry if your mom and I might seem a little overbearing but..."

"Dad?" I interrupt him. "It's okay, really. I think the world of Seth and I wouldn't have even let him meet the kids if it wasn't serious. I wouldn't even let him introduce himself until Julie and Emmett approved of meeting him. And I am so, so sorry that you and Mom found out about him the way you did." I cringe, briefly reflecting on an underwear-clad Seth trotting away, giving my parents and me a view of his backside. "But Seth is... He's everything and then some."

My dad sighs, a long and drawn out one that has me waiting on pins and needles for a reply of some sort. I don't care what it takes, but I'm sure that if they have any doubts, Seth can overcome them simply just by being himself. He will win them over, both of my parents.

I mean, what isn't to like? Seth is kind, considerate, loving and caring. The shoulder I needed to cry on, on multiple occasions. He's the type of support system I'd never had in any kind of relationship. He replaced Larson's deck and covered the costs of the materials himself. He paid off my damn mortgage, which is something I'm not going to be telling anyone anytime soon. And he has a steady job that he likes most of the time and the financial stability that comes along with it.

"I love him, Dad." I breathe in deep, taken aback for a moment that I just admitted that out loud, and to my father, of all people. He's not normally someone I would blurt or air out my feelings to unless I'm pissed off at something or someone, like my ex. I lowered the bar way down for Joe and my discussions of him.

"Well." He clears his throat again, and I can hear how uncomfortable he is on the other end. Probably readjusting his position on the couch too. "It's obvious he cares a great deal about you and the kids. They seem rather fond of him too. A lot of thought and planning went into this trip."

Boy, do I know it.

"As long as you're happy and he treats you alright, he's got my blessing then."

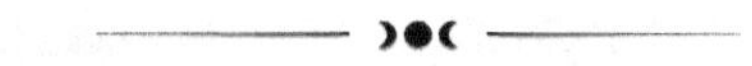

My mind keeps churning, thinking about how my dad chose to give Seth his blessing. It isn't a phrase I've ever heard him say before, furthering my suspicion that maybe Seth has something going on in the background unbeknownst to me. Such as a proposal.

Did Seth ask my dad for a blessing or something before this trip? It feels like too big of a coincidence, but I don't want to come right out and ask either. Just last night, I was panicking thinking that he was going to whip a ring box out of his pants and do it right there, but maybe he'd sensed that and backtracked. Maybe he knew I wasn't ready, at least not yet.

I should be flattered that Seth is so adamant. Persistent, even. Wanting to claim me in whatever way a human or werewolf would normally want for the person that makes them feel complete. Am I selfish for not accepting it yet?

A young child squeals with delight and I turn my head to find it. Not that far off is a little boy who couldn't be older than five, flying a kite with his parents. The wind is just strong enough to lift the frog kite to what probably seems like soaring heights to the kiddo. The father is crouched down to help him keep a hold of it, while the mother is a few feet away, happily snapping pictures of the glee on the little one's face.

I glance at my phone and see a message from Susan saying that she's running late and with that, I have about another hour to enjoy the spot I found.

The view of the bay from my seat is closer to the water, but just as captivating. The chair I'm in is so low I'm almost sitting on top of the sandy beach area. An umbrella provides shade for the time being, which helps when I need to look at my phone. But I don't even feel the need to use it because I'm so relaxed. Tilting my head back, I breathe in deeply, savoring how at peace I feel. The only thing that could make this better is if Seth were to join me at my side and Julie and Emmett were playing on the beach.

My grumbling tummy interrupts my silence, and I debate whether or not I should venture off down the trail to find some food. I can still enjoy the beautiful weather and water's edge as I go off on a hunt for something. Seth turned on a location thing on my phone just in case, and I can't help but wonder how often he's checking in on me, seeing where I'm at. I told him if he has that ability to keep tabs on me, I want it on him too. With a smirk, he did it without question.

I go to the app on my phone and check it for myself. Sure enough, his little picture still shows at the convention center a few blocks away. I can't help it, but I know how my face lights up, even just looking at his contact photo, his natural smile on full display in front of the Christmas tree, lights glowing behind.

"He really did mark you."

My name on her tongue causes arm hairs to raise instantly. I work hard to swallow, resentment building tenfold, providing me with ample courage before standing. I send a quick text to Seth before turning to meet her.

The woman who just won't stay gone.

# 33
# Mending Matters
## *Seth*

We're about to break for lunch, but Dante and I are already planning to make a run for it. We're trying to rub elbows as best as we can with others at the conference while we make our way toward the doors, and it's proving to be quite the feat.

Dante wants to find some food truck for lunch instead of sticking here and eating the hors d'oeuvres provided and I can't say that I blame him. Me, however? I just want to find my Rose and check in on her. I've been to enough of these things, seen and met enough people to last me a lifetime. If it wasn't for getting the opportunity to meet up with Dante, I probably wouldn't have even come this year. But the free trip and food on the company's dime was too good to pass up the opportunity to bring Clara out here, and I don't want her thinking that I've abandoned her.

My friend and I exchange annoyed looks as we finally exit the convention center and we both sigh with relief once we're out and in the open air.

"Are we getting too old for this?" Dante lets out a nervous laugh, glancing back at the doors.

"Yeah, I think we need to break up," I joke, and I'm met with a playful pat on my back. We both laugh, but now that we're finally skirting around the building, I use this as an opportunity to ask him about something that's been bugging me since last night. "Hey, you and Susan, are you two good?"

He rubs at the back of his neck, and while his body language shows that he might be uncomfortable, his face is telling me a different story. "More than."

I quirk a brow, then gesture for him to continue. But when he doesn't, I try to help him along. "Couldn't help but notice that Susan has a bit of um…" I try to pluck my words wisely. But there's no beating around it. Susan hasn't been just giving hints. She's been dropping bombs. "Baby fever?"

Dante barks out a nervous laugh. "Yeah, she's not very subtle, is she?"

"No," I agree, "she's not. Like, at all." I don't think she has a subtle bone in her body.

We approach a crosswalk and wait for the traffic to ease and stop before we continue on.

"We've been talking about it." His dark eyes bulge a bit, but there's a mischievous lift of his lips. "Practicing a bit."

"Gross, man." It's my turn to slug him back as I feign shock. But I can't help but feel happy for him. I had no idea they were even considering it. I know it isn't really any of my business, but I thought we were a bit closer than this. "I'm kidding. I'm happy for you guys."

"Thank you, but it's a bit overwhelming to think about."

I can't help but laugh again. Not at him, just at the position I'm currently in. "Try jumping into a relationship when she's got a freaking math whiz of a fourteen-year-old daughter who just got her learner's permit and an ornery gaming nine-year-old who wants to play football but doesn't want to get tackled."

Clara had been excited when Julie passed her exam on the first try, but terrified on the road with her for the first time that same day. And while Emmett might only be eligible for a noncontact version of the sport, Clara had turned whiter than a ghost.

Dante laughs. "Yeah, you really jumped in the deep end, didn't you?"

I nod. "Headfirst." But I would do it all over again. With Clara and her kids, my life has never felt fuller. Speaking of...

I retrieve my phone to check and see where my mate is at, and my brows instantly shoot together in concern.

**SOS**

"Hey, I'll catch you later." I barely lay a hand on his shoulder before darting out and through traffic before we've been given the signal for crossing. Behind me, Dante's words fade as I take off in a sprint. The sounds of my dress pants as I'm running are a minor annoyance as I whip out my phone to check her location, but I don't need to.

I catch her scent, and one other.

My blood boils, hot as hellfire, and I take off again. Determination drives me faster and faster until the combined scents hit me. They're together, and out in the open. That fact should been enough for me to dial it down. Clara has to be nearby, the breeze carrying her sweet smell straight to me like a messenger in the wind.

I slow, head on a swivel as I search left and right while I walk down the path that runs along the water. And then I lock in on her. On *them*.

Sitting side by side, Clara and my mother are looking at one another and speaking. Talking to each other calmly, as if Alice fucking Ries didn't just try to kill Clara last year. I'm storming off the concrete path and onto the beach, not bothering with my dress shoes as I hit the sand.

My mother takes notice of me first and Clara is quick to catch on. They both rise from their chairs and before I can get a word in, my Rose is pressing her palms into my chest to stop me.

"Seth, wait…"

"What are you doing here?" I try to step around her, but her hands try to find purchase on my sides in an attempt to keep me away. We might be out in public, but my mom has some damn nerve to be here.

"Seth!" Clara scolds me. "Seth, calm down."

"Calm down?" I repeat, scrambling to think of what possible reason she has to keep me from going after the woman that threatened the one person I'm meant for.

"Yes, calm yourself down." Clara's eyes are set on me, stern features ordering me to back off and for the life of me, I can't understand why. My gaze flits from her to my mother, then back again. She takes my hand and squeezes, urging me to come down, and it's taking everything in me to not cause a scene. "Just give her a chance. For me. Please."

Clara's pleading sounds more like an order, and I grit my teeth. What could be so important that my mother completely bypassed me and went straight to Clara? It's reminding me of the sneaky shit she pulled going to her place of employment. She's hiding something.

I'm not aware if my mother knows that I'm now involved with my old pack, even if it is only just through the sidelines. Their new leader, Ryan, who killed Uncle George, is a cousin I'd never even met from one of my aunts. He asked to stay in contact as more of a guidance type of thing, and he keeps my involvement a secret. He knows he's going to get pushback, especially from the older ones in the pack who are already set in their ways.

I was leery at first, but the more I talked with him and the other boy, Tony, the more comfortable I felt doing so. I'm hopeful that both boys—men, technically—will be able to put their troubled pasts behind them and move forward into a better future.

Not sure when I started to become an optimist. Well, an optimist about everything except my mother who is watching me with trepidation. Her eyes are round and as I examine her, I notice her thinning frame. She never had much to her to begin with, but she has lost a considerable amount of weight since I saw her at the funeral home. So much that her clothes are too big on her.

Removing Clara's hands on my chest, I keep one in my hold. She's hesitant, but she finally steps to my side. "Go ahead, Alice. Tell him what you told me."

Great. So now she's on a first-name basis, and from the sound of her words, on her side. Clara grips my hand tighter, as if she could try to fight off my rising annoyance. No, something stronger than that.

"I came to apologize."

Immediately, I scoff. "Little late for that."

The newly widowed woman before me drops her gaze before looking at Clara. But for what? What is she expecting her to do? My Rose nods for her to continue, stunning me for a moment. What does she know that I don't?

"I had quite the drive over here to figure out what I had to say and yet, none of it sounds right. None of it makes it alright, I know that." My mother speaks with shaken words.

*Damn, just spit it out so I can whisk Clara out and away from here.*

"Seth..." She crosses her arms, loose skin sagging that surprises me for some reason. "I know my methods aren't anything to be proud of, but I did have a purpose."

I roll my eyes. I can't believe I'm giving this woman my time. But why would Clara have sent that message if she didn't think she was in trouble?

"Adam was going to challenge his father to become Alpha. And nobody, I mean *nobody* wanted him as our leader. Him or any of his brothers. They were each a piece of work. Wreckless boys that never grew up and didn't have any business having power. George knew it was coming and greedy as he was, he was trying to figure out a way to kill his son before he could ever make a play for his role."

Sounds like something he would do. It was my uncle's authority above all and everyone else. His rule, or none at all. There was little doubt on my part that he would kill his own son to retain his position.

"When the pack found you, alive and well, I threw your name in there. Hoping, no, *praying* that you would come back to save us. I knew you wouldn't bend to their rules, that you wouldn't conform."

The curveball that hits me steals my breath away. She wanted me to come back to become the new alpha of a pack that wanted nothing to do with me? This has to be a joke.

"You were the one that got away. That got out and stayed hidden. You drove George into madness. I mean, how dare someone leave the pack without them putting you in the ground to make it happen?"

"That doesn't make any sense. You wanted me to come home to marry Penelope and raise her children."

"Well I couldn't exactly tell you to come back and kill the alpha and the one that intended to take his place, now could I?" she says vehemently. "Your father had struck a deal with George to bring you back into the fold after Penelope's husband's transgressions came to light. Penelope was refusing to allow any other pack member to take Warren's place by her side. Why couldn't it have been you? You two were happy once."

I shake my head, disgust thick on my tongue. "And what about Clara? Hm?" I step toward her, my mate tugging at my arm in an attempt to pull me back but she merely slides along in the sand as I move. "You sent Adam and Bradley after her. To *kill* her."

"You hadn't marked her, Seth." My mother's volume grows as her posture stiffens. "How was I supposed to know that you were serious about her? That it wasn't just an infatuation with a human?"

As if that makes things any better. "Would it have been enough? Would my mark on her have given her any kind of protection against you or the pack?"

She pales. My mother drops her gaze away from me and from Clara. Am I naive to think that it would have been enough? Apparently so.

"You haven't been a part of my life for so long, you don't even know me anymore. If Clara had died"—I pinch the bridge of my nose, dreading to even entertain the thought—"I would have killed every living person who'd had a hand in it."

Clara steps in closer, gripping my arm gently to let me know that she's still here, keeping me grounded.

"I see that now," my mother adds. "I'm glad to see that Penelope wasn't lying when she gave her report on her visit."

It's on the tip of my tongue to ask what would have happened next. What their next play would have been had my dad not passed away and I made the trip down to Colorado.

"Clara and her family are my life now. If anyone or anything threatens to put that in jeopardy, I won't think twice. I will end whoever tries to lay a finger on any of them. If anyone so much as comes near them I'll—"

"I know." She holds up a hand, and I snap my mouth shut. She shifts her stance, an unease settling as she looks around us. I don't know if she's looking for someone, surveying the area, or just calculating her next move. "The pack is in new hands now, since George's passing."

I stay stone-faced, not letting her get a hint of any kind that I know more than I probably should. They're not my pack anymore; it shouldn't concern me.

"Even though Tony was a witness, most of the pack doesn't believe that Ryan was the one to kill the alpha. He's young, soft-spoken, reserved. A bit of a late bloomer, like you were."

"I was also a witness. As was another wolf who doesn't want to get involved any further," I state.

My mother nods, but studies me. There's a micro-expression, so small it's hard to detect, but she's trying to gain knowledge. Trying to catch me slipping up on something. Which won't happen, considering I didn't land the final blow on Uncle George. I might have set him up, practically given Ryan the opportunity on a silver platter, but he was the one to take the shot.

"Yes, I heard about your new...pack."

I'm so used to responding that I'm not with a pack, but refrain from clarifying. She doesn't need to know specifics. It's good for her to think that I belong to something else back home. Let her believe that I have fully integrated into another pack. It'll be another level of protection, should I ever need it again.

"Is that all?" I inquire, ready for her to leave so I can whisk Clara away.

She blinks, staring up at me and poised to say something, but stops. If she's expecting some kind of forgiveness for her absence, for her actions and ability to be the worst mother ever, she couldn't be more wrong. With wounds like mine? I'm not sure if they'll ever truly heal.

"With news of you joining another pack and the damage from the fallout in Nebraska, Ryan has called off the hunt on you."

I already knew that, of course. But it's not quite enough. "And what about you?" I take a deep breath as my nostrils flare. "Will you stop calling and showing up unexpectedly? Today, for example."

"Seth, I..." Her eyes scan the sand, searching for something before they turn glassy. "I have nothing to be proud of. I can't change the past and I can't excuse my actions and I know it's not worth much, but I *am* sorry. Since your father passed..."

She hiccups, swiping away at tears that fall, and there's this small crack inside of me that fissures and spreads. I might not make any public acclamations about Mike and Alice Ries being my parents, but she has lost her mate. The one connection that werewolves are supposed to hold sacred above all else, and he's gone.

She is alone now. Is it really that far of a stretch to think that in this time, she's been able to reflect on all of the wrongs now that my abuser is finally six feet under?

It's a bit disturbing, but the thought comes rushing through unannounced. What if my mother was complacent because of their mate bond? It doesn't excuse her from what happened, but what if she was merely blinded by their connection? By the rabid toxicity of the pack I grew up in? Could my mother really be capable of this kind of change now that my dad is out of the picture?

A sob escapes her and Clara leaves my side. The beautiful, wondrous, and caring mate of mine is stepping beside the woman and comforting her. The woman who tried to have her killed.

How could Clara...forgive her?

My mother buries her head onto Clara's shoulder, muttering over and over, "I'm sorry. I'm so, so sorry."

Deep down, I know that my mother isn't putting on a show. This isn't like her. She didn't even cry when her own parents passed away, and besides seeing her mourning at the funeral home, this is the most emotion I've ever witnessed.

Clara looks up at me, crestfallen. I'm too stunned to speak, frozen in place as I look at the combined forces of my past, present, and future colliding right in front of me.

# 34

# Home Sweet Home

## *Clara*

The rest of our trip felt...off.

Seth's mother really has a knack for showing up at the weirdest times, and while I am grateful she wasn't trying to kill me this go-around, it seemed to put Seth in a weird place.

I knew his past had been painful, with grudges that he will probably take to his grave, but this? His mother profusely apologizing and bawling her eyes out under the sunny California weather? God, I was even moved to tears and I've spent most of my time with Seth hating the woman too.

While I'd been alarmed at her visit initially, there was something about her that propelled me to stay and not run off. No longer was she the strange woman at the dental office with a weird curiosity that was too obvious not to notice. But there was something about the way she seemed to be holding herself together, pleading to talk to me before Seth, and her willingness and openness to do so. There was something in my gut that wanted to hear her out.

I couldn't pretend to understand why she'd stood by when Seth's father hurt him. Why she would let harm come to her one and only child, I'll never be able to comprehend. There was a lot I didn't understand, and while I should've turned my back on her, I didn't.

My body was on high alert when she first arrived, but the longer we sat together, the more my nerves receded. I can recall the shake in her voice, the tremble in her fingers, and how she was unable to look me in the eye for most of it. Her apologies started with me first and foremost, before she even got to talk about her son.

By the time Seth showed up, I was even talking about my home life with her, trying to turn the conversation around before I started to cry. There was something so raw and painful in her voice, as she confessed to what kind of mother she had been, that tugged at my heartstrings. Alice knew that her son would likely never talk to her again after this visit, and she was fully prepared to accept that.

And I believe her.

She has no one. As an only child herself, her parents and mate are now gone. I guess when you have someone ripped away from you, it gives you time to really think through your life choices. I don't think Seth knows, but she even admitted that she's been going to therapy since Mike received his diagnosis. Alice appears to be making some progress with her sessions and the decisions of her past, confronting topics and memories that led her to this moment—seeking Seth and me out one last time to say what she needed to before trying to find a way to move on.

Alice is lost and trying to figure out who she is for the first time in her life. She married Mike at seventeen and has never been on her own. This is all new territory for her.

Come to find out, she hadn't made the drive from Colorado on her own. Ryan, the new pack leader who doesn't look that much older than Julie, had accompanied her. He's so young. Not a shadow of facial hair, but defined muscles that I could see filled out his shirt even from the wide berth he'd given us and our chat.

If I hadn't caught on to a nod from Seth in his direction as Alice took her leave, I might not have even noticed him. Ryan blended in pretty well amongst the people around us.

Our time with Seth's mother keeps replaying in my head throughout the flight and drive home. At every chance I have, I lay my head on Seth's shoulder or hold his hand. He doesn't question what music I play on my phone and stops for food without any hesitation. It isn't until we're about ten minutes from Alton that I finally break the awkward silence. Seth is physically here, but mentally, somewhere else entirely.

"You know you can talk to me," I offer gently, trying not to put too much pressure on him. He's still as a statue at the wheel, one hand on it while leaning back on the headrest.

"I know, Clara." He sighs, readjusting himself in the seat and placing both hands on the wheel now, eyes fixed forward. I turn my gaze outward too. Spring isn't quite here yet, but things are looking a little less dead with the promise of new life on the horizon. I'm already missing the warmth that California had to offer. "I'm just...processing."

I nod, glancing down at my moon bracelet. "You'll stay over tonight, right? You're not going to run off and shift or something, are you?"

When Seth's anger gets the better of him, he does that. But this, this silence that he's reduced to, is rattling me. He doesn't normally stay this quiet, this hushed for so long.

"Afraid my side of the bed is going to get cold?" There's a hint of playfulness in his tone and I'm a bit surprised by how much that lifts my troubled thoughts.

"You're not answering the question," I volley back.

It takes a moment, but he finally breaks. "I'll be over after the kids go to bed."

"Will you stay for dinner?"

"Your worry for me isn't necessary." He takes my hand and brings it to his lips for a peck when I glare at him. "But I'll savor it like everything else that you give me."

"I can't help it." I shrug. "You're a part of me now. There's no letting you go."

"Not that I would ever let that happen anyway."

"Of course not, you're very stubborn." I wrinkle my nose at him. We grin at each other as he holds my hand between us on the center console of his truck. "I know I've told you like a hundred times, but thank you for this week. San Diego was beautiful. Dante and Susan are awesome. The entire trip was relaxing and fun and—"

"The first of many," Seth assures me. He's even suggested that we make a trip to Texas sometime to visit his friends. And I can't think of a reason not to. "And like I've said before, you never have to thank me. I want to spoil and pamper you, dote on you until you're sick of me."

I laugh. "You're going to set the bar impossibly high for Julie and Emmett. No one is going to compare to you and live up to your standards."

"Well why would we want them settling for anything less?" Seth makes a good point. If there's even the slightest chance that my kids could have an ounce of the happiness I've found with Seth someday, even if it's a failed marriage later and well into their thirties, I'd want them to take that shot.

I'm glad Seth showed up that day in my driveway. Or the following, when I was looking up YouTube videos on how to work the damn riding lawn mower and he invited me out to dinner. He quickly became my best friend, confidant, fierce protector, and partner. And I wouldn't have it any other way.

Before long, we're taking our exit and entering Alton. The small town is quite active with the after-school buses and their routes. The excitement that rushes me as I take notice of the kids' bus heading out and away from our house brings an insurmountable joy to my face.

As we turn onto my dead-end road, I see my dad's vehicle and Larson's truck, and before we even park, Julie and Emmett are bolting from the house. I highly doubt they had time to even sit down after arriving home.

"Go get 'em, beautiful." Seth flashes a smile and as soon as the truck comes to a stop, I leap out and embrace the both of them. We squeeze each other in an awkward, three-person hold, and we're all smiling and laughing and greeting each other as if it's been months when it's barely been a week.

They're both quick to greet Seth with friendly hellos as he exits his truck and begins to collect my purse and suitcase from behind his seat. The kids are ushering me down the sidewalk and into the house as I wave to the men in the driveway. I'm more than ready for the kids to talk my ear off and get back to everyday life.

But someday, Seth will be bringing his bag in too. There will come a time when we won't have to pretend to part ways just for him to sneak back in later. And I look forward to when that day will come.

# 35

# In Full Bloom

## *Clara*

One year later...and then some.

I've no sooner dropped my purse on the counter than Julie and Emmett come skidding to a stop in the kitchen. Their eyes are bright and wide, something shining within them. I don't even get a chance to take my shoes off before they're rushing up to me.

"Come with us," Emmett gushes as he pulls me toward the back door. Julie is behind us, following as we exit the house.

"What's going on?" I ask, completely oblivious as to what could be so urgent that the kids are escorting me from the house before I even get a chance to get settled. I'm tired, worn out, and need to find Seth. Not calling him on my lunch today was a break from our routine once again, and I'm positively buzzing with the need to get him alone. I'm too happy, stunned, and honestly, beside myself. This is the second time this week I've missed our lunch check-in and I can finally tell him. Can finally reveal what I had suspected but needed proof of before spilling the beans.

"Here." Julie skirts around us, bringing a blindfold into view, and I study her for a moment.

"Um...excuse me, but why are you trying to blindfold your mother?" I look between the two of them and they are absolutely about to break with their excitement. Very, very suspicious. Or "sus" as Emmett would put it.

"A surprise, obviously." Julie rolls her eyes before placing the black satin blindfold on my head. She tugs it into place, her fingers gentle against my cheeks, and when she's absolutely certain I can't make anything out, they both take my hands and lead me away from the house.

I know we're going into the woods, leaving the flat grass of our backyard behind and entering the tree line. The terrain change is enough to tell me that, and they're careful with me, giggling and guiding me through the trees. I can't help but smile in return. I don't know what the meaning of this is, but they're not fighting and in this together so I decide to let them have their fun.

The walk is fairly short and we eventually come to a stop. They grow quiet, almost too hushed as they instruct me to wait in the spot they've chosen, and they both walk off and away from me but not too far. I cross my arms, impatiently awaiting further orders when everything goes still. My heartbeat is another matter, though. Their sneaky tactics and lack of information are spurring eager anticipation.

"Okay," Julie exhales.

Emmett follows after her. "You can take it off now."

I take a deep breath, still smiling after this whole charade, and when I remove the mask I'm temporarily stunned by the amount of white roses decorating our surroundings. There are so many, creating an arch of sorts and then some. An abundance of them frame Seth, flanked by Emmet and Julie at his sides. All three are grinning from ear to ear, but my daughter has her hands clasped in front of her chest.

"What is all this? How long did it take you to...to..." My words get lost somewhere between the three most important people in my life when I meet Seth's golden hues.

"Believe me, I had a good reason for pulling them out of school a bit early to help with this. I thought it fitting that they be here too." Seth takes a step forward, and my breath catches. "This was a group effort."

This is it. I know deep down in my bones that this is the moment he's been so anxiously waiting for. The reason he hasn't been teasing me about marriage for a while now. He was gearing up for this.

Seth has already moved in, getting rid of his rental and integrating into our lives so seamlessly that it felt natural. Helping shuffle the kids to and from friends' houses and events. Gaming it up with Emmett and teaching him football while trying to grasp an understanding of Julie's math—though in turn, she just ended up trying to teach him. He then made it a point to learn all of her chants for cheerleading, just to prove that he could conquer something she participated in.

Seth dresses up in school colors for most of the kids' activities and has begun jogging with Julie in the mornings. When he has nothing going on, he even goes so far as to help her get her driving hours in. It appears that she prefers Seth in the passenger seat over myself, and honestly, I am okay with that.

Emmett and Seth are thick as thieves as well, hiding snacks and candy from me at one moment, to—shockingly—Seth getting Emmett involved with yard work. Who would've thought that Emmett would actually take some kind of pride in it? Especially once he found out you could make money from it. Mowing, raking leaves, shoveling, and so on.

I can't help but notice how the kids look up to Seth. Which makes my news all the sweeter, but it will have to wait.

Seth kneels down before me, taking my left hand in his, and my eyes fill with tears before he can even get a single word out.

This feels right. It's finally time, and with obvious approval and involvement from my kids, it takes everything in me not to hurl myself onto him and accept before he's even said a damn thing.

But I wait. Impatiently wait, and my heart beats faster as Seth pulls out a dark maroon box from his back pocket.

"Clara Rose," he begins as tears roll down my cheeks, "life with you, Emmett, and Julie has been a life I never could have dreamed up myself. You all have accepted me and everything I am. Put up with my random growl of a snore when I'm sleeping."

The kids snicker playfully behind him. Seth has been the butt of many jokes. He doesn't always grumble like that in his sleep, but they've had the pleasure of hearing it firsthand. I don't think any of us will ever let him forget it either.

"Bro, it's so weird." Emmett laughs as he gives his glasses a shove.

I roll my eyes. His use of the words "bro" and "bruh" always gets on my nerves, but I give him a pass for right now.

Seth stares up at me with nothing but love. A feeling that is shared so mutually that the word doesn't even do it justice. There has to be something stronger than love. That four-letter word just doesn't cover it.

"I want to spend the rest of my life laughing and crying with you. Learning and teaching with Julie and Emmett. Growing and aging until we're old, gray, and embarrassing the kids with so many 'back in our day' stories that they tell us to stop and go back to the seventies."

Julie sighs, but it's playful, feigning indifference which is something she does quite often now.

I'm not sure why they always refer to the seventies. It's a good two decades before either Seth or I were born.

"I keep telling them, we're not *that* old," I finally speak up, defending our ages. Even though when Seth has his way with me sometimes, it feels like my body is older than what it really is. But boy, are Seth and I just getting started on this wild ride of life together or what. He really has no idea what he's getting himself into now.

"The puzzle that is my life was never complete until I came here—until I found you. I know our journey has been anything but smooth, but there's no one else who understands me like you. Who loves like you do. That unconditional and pure love that knows no bounds and has no restrictions."

Seth fumbles for a moment as he attempts to open the box one-handed, earning another grin from me as I can detect what his nerves are doing to him. Showing his vulnerability and expanding my heart to the point that it might burst.

Nestled inside is a silver ring with a round-cut diamond raised from the rest. The setting has smaller diamonds in sets of three on each side of the center one, glistening in what little rays from the sun break through the trees. It's not too much, nothing flashy or gaudy, but utterly perfect in every way.

"Clara, with the blessing of your parents, Julie and Emmett, will you marry me?"

Fresh tears trail faster down in the wake of the previous ones as I look to my kids who are silently cheering us on from behind. Julie nods enthusiastically and Emmett looks like he's about to make a break and charge us.

Returning my attention to Seth, I give him the biggest, most heartfelt smile I can as I reply with the answer that everyone knows I will give. "Yes."

The kids can't wait long enough for Seth to slip the ring on my finger, and the relief that floods me when it actually fits my finger is almost too much. I hadn't expected it to, but it just goes to show how much thought went into this. The flowers, the approvals, the ring, damn. Everything coming together like this is too much.

Little does Seth know, there's more.

As soon as he rises, we're bombarded. Squeals of excitement and exclamations about their involvement in planning are running from their lips faster than I can keep up. This had been in the works for a little while. Julie and Emmett were questioned about a month ago, but didn't know when it would happen exactly. The fact that they'd all been in cahoots, and keeping this from me, only speaks to the connection they all share now. The fact that they all approved and participated brings even more emotion to the surface.

We make plans to celebrate for dinner after we haul all of the flowers back home, but first, I ask the kids to give us a little privacy. When I'm met with a little resistance, I just tell them that I want to kiss Seth really badly right now and that does the trick. They're okay with modest displays of affection but they draw the line at kissing. Emmett will even pretend gag if we so much as engage in more than a quick smooch.

Once Seth senses that they're out of earshot, he finally loosens up a bit. "You've had me a bit worried this week." He scratches at the back of his head as I look up from my ring. "Been kind of quiet."

I shake my head, pretending that it's nothing. "Two calls, Seth. I've missed two calls."

"That's two too many." He laughs nervously. I get the feeling that he knows something is up. Those damn werewolf abilities are too good. It's a miracle I've been able to keep hush-hush about it this long.

"You really don't know?" I tease lightly. Nerves of my own at how he's going to handle the news are lighting fast, zapping through me.

"You smell different, but you haven't changed soaps or shampoos or anything."

I nod, knowing that he's always called my scent sweet like vanilla. But not quite like my iced coffee, more like freshly baked treats. "Like…"

My prompt works and he leans forward, smelling my neck and breathing deeply. When he stands again, his eyes are closed, as if he's trying to place it. "Vanilla and spring, perhaps? It's something floral maybe, but…"

"Uh, hello? We're surrounded by flowers," I joke. But when his bright eyes find mine, I know he's serious, and I can't hold out any longer. "I'm pregnant, Seth."

I hold my breath, waiting. Looking at him with a newfound curiosity. This is something that he never thought he would have. He was told that he never could have any biological children of his own. Against all odds, our obsessive need to screw and lose ourselves in one another has led to something neither of us were expecting.

And I think he's in shock. Can werewolves go into shock?

"Seth." I step closer, placing my hand on the side of his face. I let my thumb brush against his facial hair, trying to coax him into saying something, to snap out of it. "I peed on about five different tests at work on Monday, and I had an appointment today with my doctor. They took a positive test after tubal ligation pretty seriously and worked me into their schedule. Somehow, you've gone and knocked me up."

Still nothing. Silence. This is getting weird.

I think I broke him.

I take his hand in mine and place his palm to my not-so-soft-for-long belly, and look up at him again. "There's a baby in here. Your baby." I then correct myself, "*Our* baby."

Only then do I detect a small quiver of his lips before he blinks away, finally breaking from his frozen state. Then he's kneeling before me once more, staring at my belly as he takes hold of it in both hands.

"You're sure?" His voice cracks. "You're really sure?"

His tone grasps my throat in a constricting manner, bringing on a fresh set of tears. Seth had his dream of having children of his own ripped away so long ago that he eventually made peace with it. And now? Now that dream is finally a reality.

"Yes." I place a hand over his. "It's about the size of a pomegranate seed and very alien-like right now, but yes. I hope you're ready for more sleepless nights, spit-up, and diapers and wipes galore."

Seth's disbelief finally vanishes as he leans into my stomach. A hushed sob escapes him, totally catching me off guard. The sound is so powerful that I can't help but cry along with him.

Admittedly, I was scared shitless when that first pregnancy test turned out positive. Fearing for my body and how it would handle it. That something would go wrong with the pregnancy since I'd had my tubes tied, but after a vaginal ultrasound, they confirmed that everything was normal. I hate that stupid wand thing they had to use, though. It was uncomfortable, and the crap ton of pictures they had to take to ensure that everything was alright made me feel all weird, and now I want a shower. But that can wait a little longer.

I can't deny that everything feels different now. The support I have with Seth, and the care he takes with me and the kids, already sets him miles apart from when I was with Joe. There isn't a doubt in my mind that this pregnancy will be different because of who I have by my side.

It's strange to think about how the family dynamic is going to drastically change. Things just got settled with Seth moving in and now with an upcoming wedding on the horizon and a baby on the way?

"Thank you," Seth whispers low, so quiet that I almost don't catch it over a wind that arose between the trees. The scent of the flowers dominates my sense of smell as I stroke the back of his head. "You've given me so much."

Brushing away my tears even though it won't do much good, I kneel down. I let him keep his hands on my stomach, coming to a rest on the grass. "I didn't do it by myself, you know."

"I love you so much," Seth chokes out, tears wetting his beard as he looks at me with so much affection that I can't help but cry too. Happy tears that show no signs of slowing.

"I love you too. So, so much."

We rest our foreheads against one another's, basking in the news that neither of us ever perceived as possible and yet somehow, makes our future together even sweeter.

# 36

# Epilogue: Thriving Roots

## *Seth*

Beautiful chaos.

That's what I see when I look around the house. Dishes that need washed and others that need put away. Laundry that's folded but needs taken upstairs, sitting on the bottom step of the stairwell, and a mysterious pair of shorts that look like they belong to the now middle child of the home.

Julie's homework is sprawled out on the table and Emmett's backpack is thrown haphazardly onto a chair, some of its contents spilling out. Ava's toys take the cake, though. Now that she's wandering about, I swear she can't walk into a room without taking one with her and finding a new place for it. I think it's a game for her now.

All of it is a reminder of how full my life is. How busy and crazy and wonderfully messy it is. But I know that the sight will stress Clara out, so I get started. I worked through my lunch today and clocked out early, knowing that I could help sort through and manage some of the clutter before she makes it home.

There's an in-home daycare just down the street that Ava has been going to four times a week so she has other kids to play with. Julie and

Emmett have taken it upon themselves to pick her up when they get home from school. It helps that the daycare owner used to teach at their school, so they're all familiar with one another.

A scream of pure delight perks my ears up, and I nab a couple of toys on the floor as I make my way to the living room window. Julie and Ava are running away from Emmett, who has the hose and is spraying them with different settings to get reactions out of them. Julie is fast to swoop little Ava into her arms and turn her back, shielding her little sister from the blast.

They're all drenched, even Emmett who's in control.

Ope. Yep, that's why.

Emmett turns the nozzle upward, letting water rain down on himself, turning himself soggy in the process. They're all a wet and barefoot mess and it's the damn best feeling to see them all get along, playing and creating fun of their own.

Julie was ecstatic to gain a little sister. Her brother, not so much. More than once, Emmett has complained about how the girls are taking over the house, but yet he seems to be the sibling most taken with Ava. He's constantly trying to make her laugh, which always makes him do so in return. If he isn't the source of Ava's glee, he's a bit sour about it.

We've finally reached a point in our lives where Joe is becoming less and less of a problem but more of a necessary annoyance, in my opinion anyway. After his accident, that's when Clara's lawyer really did some digging. I wasn't exactly proud to be right, but the money problems were greater than I'd initially thought. At some point he'd even purchased a boat, for some reason.

And there was more.

Joe had already been on a tightrope at work. Multiple complaints had been reported and when the lawyer started inquiring, the dam broke. His temper had been getting the best of him. He was let go from his job at the events center shortly after being put on leave from the accident. I guess all it took was for Joe to be out of the picture before more staff members began to come forward.

Not even his parents, who were helping him through his recovery, could dig him out of his hole. The house was foreclosed on, truck and such repossessed, and only then did he finally, *willingly* let Clara take full custody. He barely had a leg to stand on at that point, literally.

Chassidy had hightailed it shortly after the accident. Guess the injuries he'd sustained were too much for her to handle. Going off of her social media, she's now living it up in the Ozarks with another man who has some mansion. Still posing for the camera and glorifying her life, but with someone else. I've never heard the kids ask about her absence once.

To both Clara's and my surprise, Emmett and Julie have adjusted remarkably well to life here, with the both of us. They've accepted me and I've integrated into the house and family without protest.

I even went as far as taking a couple of online math courses from a nearby community college so I could try to keep up with a flourishing Julie. She's on track to start some college courses in high school, even. I know she's going to tackle it like her brother's growing interest in football.

Clara is less than excited about this fascination and adventure for Emmett, but it does get him away from all the electronic devices around. The kid even made the switch to contacts because of the sport, but he still opts for his glasses whenever he's home and lounging around.

Then there is Ava. Our very own miracle baby. A dream that miraculously came true when neither Clara or I had expected it. Her hair inherited a mix between Clara's and my coloring, eyes not quite as bright as mine. I couldn't have imagined anything more perfect even if I'd tried.

I went to every doctor's appointment, asked so many questions that I know the staff was growing tired of me, and waited on Clara hand and foot. Massaging her calves and feet when they grew too sore and weary, ran into a larger town when she was craving buffalo wings from one place and a vanilla shake from another. It was also to my benefit, because whenever Clara was happy, so was our baby. Little Ava would get so active when she was met with spicy and sweet, and Clara would have to fight me off with her pregnancy pillow. She didn't think I was serious about my offer of using my body instead of the giant pillow, and I would slowly move her onto me once she passed out. But that plan would get thwarted with all of the bathroom trips she'd have to take in the night.

But damn, if feeling our baby kicking wasn't enough to bring tears to my eyes and make my knees buckle. Knowing that we'd somehow managed to create life when neither of us thought it possible was the sweetest dream coming true.

My arms are nearly full after picking up the living room as I meander through the dining room and stop short. On the wall that used to house only Julie's and Emmett's school pictures, are strategically placed clusters of photos. So many memories on display that I swear it grips my heart in an emotional overload.

It was through Clara and her family that I finally found acceptance. I finally stopped running state to state and found a home. I am needed and wanted and appreciated. I don't know how my life could be any fuller.

The biggest picture of them all is from our wedding. I spoiled Clara with white roses and all three kids were able to be present for the big day. Julie holds Ava, standing next to Emmett in front of Clara and me. Joyce and Charles are also by their daughter's side, and nothing brings people together like a wedding or funeral, spurring the return of a brother who I finally had the opportunity to meet. He's due to retire from the military within the next year and is planning on settling down in Iowa somewhere. If Clara has any kind of pull, it will be in or near our little town of Alton.

Hell, Larson even made it onto the wall. Or should I say, the Honorary Uncle Larson. All the kids have taken a liking to him and his presence around here. Pair that with my father-in-law's unwavering buddy status with him, and he's now a constant at all the major holidays. Although on occasion, I still call him dipshit, even if only inside the confines of my own head.

But perhaps in the biggest plot twist of my life, my mother is at my side in the large portrait.

Some time passed after her visit and the revelation she brought along in California, but I was the one to contact her for once. It was something that I'd occasionally brought up with Clara, and if it hadn't been for her support, I don't know if I would've ever had the balls to call her up. We know we still have a lot of healing to do, but we're finding a way to move forward and stay in each other's lives. Now that my dad is out of the way, it's like she's an entirely different woman. Getting to know my own mother in my late thirties is a strange yet interesting turn of events.

Clara was well into her third trimester before I even told Alice about our baby. That call was full of apologies and tears, and that was just on her end of the line. We'd already been rebuilding our relationship on new grounds. Ever since that news had broken, she's been the epitome of a beloved and doting grandma. It's a title she wears with great pride.

And the thing that really gagged me was when she traveled to Iowa—with mine and Clara's approval first—for Ava's arrival into the world. While most people made a beeline to see my Rose and child, my mother didn't. She clasped a hand over her mouth as tears fell, and—albeit hesitant at first—she wound up throwing her arms around me, hugging me with a strength I hadn't thought that she possessed. With the affection I'd never had growing up.

Goddamn, I'm getting so choked up at the mere memory and all of the photos before me that I barely register Clara coming in the kitchen door. I mutter a silent scolding to myself for not getting things tidied up before she stepped foot in here.

Her mixed scent floods into the house as she kicks off her shoes and sets her purse down on the counter. She's a bit pale, and I can't help but wonder if she's even aware of her state yet.

"Sorry, I got distracted while"—I glance down at my arms before returning my attention to her—"picking up."

I set my stash of things on the table and saunter over to her, wrapping my arms around her and kissing her head. My eyes drift closed for a moment as I argue with myself over whether I should say something or not. If she doesn't know yet, she will soon. Is it my place to say something?

"It's fine. It's not like I asked you to or anything," she mumbles into my chest.

A small laugh escapes me. "You don't have to. I know how much this stresses you out. I meant to have it looking somewhat cleaned up before you got here."

Clara backs out of my hold and shrugs, exhaustion pulling at her features. It looks like she's endured an all-nighter. She rubs at her face before she catches onto a squeal from Ava outside. That girl has a serious set of lungs on her. She already tries to participate in Julie's cheers even though she can't quite form full sentences yet.

"Looks like they're having fun." She cracks a smile but it doesn't make it all the way to her eyes. That cues me in on just how miserable she's feeling. Any other day she might be rushing to get outside and join in on the fun, and I would happily tag along, hot on her heels.

I lead her into the living room so she can see the grassy, muddy, and wet mess that's being created, and her smile deepens.

That's it, I can't take it anymore. Her smell and demeanor are like alarm bells ringing inside my head.

"Hey, are you feeling okay?" I brush her cheek and she leans into my touch.

"Hm? Yeah." She shakes her head when my hand falls. "Just tired."

*Just tired.* I grin to myself. If she's trying to fool me, it's not going to work.

"Are you sure there's nothing else?" I goad her, but she still gives nothing away. There's nothing but confusion.

"What else would there be?" Her innocence in the matter is as maddening as it is sweet. Has she really no idea? If I were a patient man, I would let her arrive at this information herself. But patience wasn't always my strong suit.

"Clara..." I tuck her hair behind her ear. It's longer than when we first met, but she's been contemplating cutting it off again. And don't get me started on the time she opted for full-on bangs. I was told to never let her do that again. "Your period is late."

Eyes narrowed into slits, she tilts her chin up a tad. "Not that late."

I grin, studying her face. "It's been seven weeks since your last one."

Her jaw drops, shock registering before skepticism. "It has not," she begins, then fumbles through her words. "It can't be. I just... There's no... You don't know my schedule. It changes. Sometimes."

Her face is reddening, color creeping into her fair skin. I've got her, and I know I do.

"Clara," I say as calmly as I can. "I know the moon phases like the back of my hand and every curve of your body. I think I can keep up with your menstrual cycle."

And just like that, her eyes widen, the color rushing out of her face just as fast as it appeared. "It's... It's really been that long?"

I nod, brushing my thumb across her cheek as she comes to the realization that she's pregnant. I lean my forehead down toward hers, savoring this moment, knowing that this will be our last child. It's something that we've at least talked about the possibility of. If it happened, then it was meant to be. And if it did, we would graciously accept that child before I have a vasectomy. It's the least I can do since she's doing the hard work of growing and carrying life inside of her. The minimum for her granting me these little treasures and the fatherhood I'd always wanted.

And when Clara said the vasectomy wouldn't be enough by itself, I told her it was her decision if she wanted to try a tubal again or some other procedure. I'm leaving that entirely up to her. We've beaten many odds with the arrival of our Ava already.

With Clara, Julie, Emmett, Ava, and this new little tyke currently forming, I am one proud man. Is this what it feels like to have it all?

Placing a hand on her stomach, I look down into her brown eyes. "Want to know what I smell this time?"

"No." Clara's eyes become glassy as she shakes her head. "At least, not yet."

I pretend to lock my lips with an imaginary key and throw it over my shoulders. She giggles, swiping away at falling tears. Tears that I've learned are happy ones. She often jokes about how motherhood has made her soft over the years and emotional at times she thinks she shouldn't be, but I do all I can to reassure her that what she's feeling is valid. There's no need to apologize for feeling something. From happy to sad, and everything in between, I will be here for it all.

I wrap her in my arms, and she squeezes me back while we bask in our happy news. I don't think I'll ever be able to thank her enough for all that she's given me and continues to give. The unconditional love and companionship that I'd never thought possible for myself. A future that I am ecstatic beyond belief to take each new day and night in stride.

"I love you." We speak at the same time, then laugh at one another for being on the same train of thought. Clara is my person, my mate, and my everything.

I breathe in deep, savoring her vanilla scent mixed with notes of the woods I'm all too familiar with, and a hint of mint. It'll be a struggle to keep the news of our little one under wraps, especially from my stunning and beautiful Rose. But if that's what she wishes, then so be it.

Just as I always tell Clara—that she'll never go a day without knowing my love for her—the same applies to our children. To Julie, Emmett, Ava, and the soon-to-be newest and last addition to our family. I have everything I'd ever dared to dream of a long time ago...and so much more.

# Also by Krystal Kae

**Tethered To You Series**
Watching Me
Altering Me
Revealing Me
Unleashing Me

**The Rose Duet**
Chasing Petals
Howling Blooms

If you enjoyed this book, a quick rating or review on Goodreads, Amazon, or wherever you got your copy would mean the world to me. Your support helps others discover the book— thank you!

# Acknowledgements

The Rose Duet holds a special place in my heart. Being a child of divorce isn't easy. Being a mom, a parent of any kind, is hard work even while it can be rewarding. We're our own worst critics to the jobs we're doing both at home and anywhere else we find ourselves. It's so easy to focus on the negatives and drown in them. And you know what? It's ok to cry, to vent, to want to lean on someone when times are tough because sometimes, life sucks.

That being said...

Josh—my high school sweetheart, my rock, the left hand to my right—thank you for everything you do for me, our family, and what you continue to do. There truly are good guys out there (except guys like Joe, don't be a Joe, people), who are capable of being your biggest cheerleader, the shoulder to cry on, the one who will come to your defense even when you're not looking, and love you unconditionally.

Oh yeah, and thank you for the cover, the formatting, the uploading of files, the help with social media posts, etc. Seriously, you do A LOT for me. You know it, I know it, and I try to make sure everyone else knows it.

Rebecca at Rebecca Joy Editing, I applaud your awesomeness and all that you do to whip my stories into shape. These books would look vastly different (and painfully so) without your magic touch. I can never say thank you enough.

Book Vault and HEA Book Boutique, it's always an honor to be on your shelves. Thank you for the chance you take on indie authors like me and for the sense of belonging in your stores. Indie bookshops do it best.

To the readers, no matter how you found me, I am so incredibly grateful that you chose to take a chance on me. Whether you're new to my work or have been with me since the beginning, thank you for your time and energy spent within the pages I've filled. I sincerely appreciate each and every one of you.

Romance isn't dead. It does exist and sometimes not always in the way we see depicted in books and showing in movies. Maybe it's the hopeless romantic in me, but personally, I'm always looking for that happily ever after. I don't feel complete unless it's there, and I hope that my first shot at it didn't disappoint.

Thank you for reading The Rose Duet.

# About the Author

Krystal Kae lives in the corn-filled Midwest with her husband, children, and pets. Her love of reading and writing started back in high school, but it was over a decade later when she decided to put her overactive imagination to work again and began filling blank pages.

Fascinated by all things paranormal, fantasy, and romantic-you can find these topics the center of her writing universe. When she's not working her full-time office job or buried in a story, she loves to create memories with loved ones, travel, and take long walks in cemeteries.

Get the latest updates at **KrystalKae.com** and follow
@krystalkaewrites

www.ingramcontent.com/pod-product-compliance
Lightning Source LLC
Chambersburg PA
CBHW020332180726
47991CB00020B/1428